VAULT

PUBLISHER DAMIAN A. WASSEL

EDITOR-IN-CHIEF ADRIAN F. WASSEL

ART DIRECTOR NATHAN C. GOODEN

EVP BRANDING/DESIGN TIM DANIEL

MANAGING EDITOR TAY TAYLOR

DIRECTOR OF PR & RETAILER RELATIONS DAVID DISSANAYAKE

OPERATIONS MANAGER IAN BALDESSARI

PRINCIPAL DAMIAN A. WASSEL, SR.

SPECIAL BOOK DESIGN BY JAYDEN WASSEL

SERA & THE ROYAL STARS VOLUME ONE. JANUARY, 2020.

Colurus
URSA MINOR
DRACO

JON TSUEI
WRITER

AUDREY MOK
ARTIST

RAÚL ANGULO
COLORIST

JIM CAMPBELL
LETTERER

KARINA PLAJA
ASSISTANT COLORIST

VAULT COMICS
PRESENTS

SERA AND THE ROYAL STARS

LYRA
HERCULES
DRACO
Colurus
Polus Eclipt Borealis
URSA MINOR

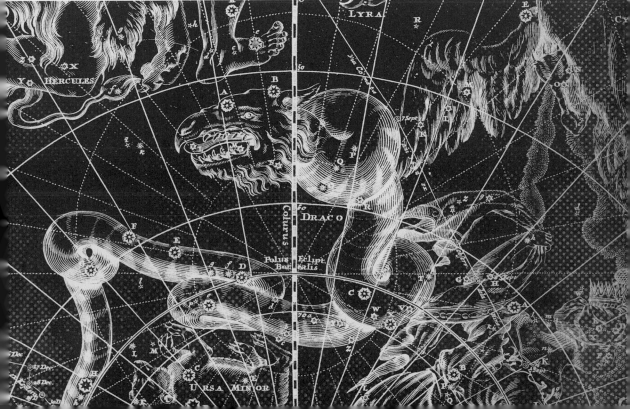

ONE

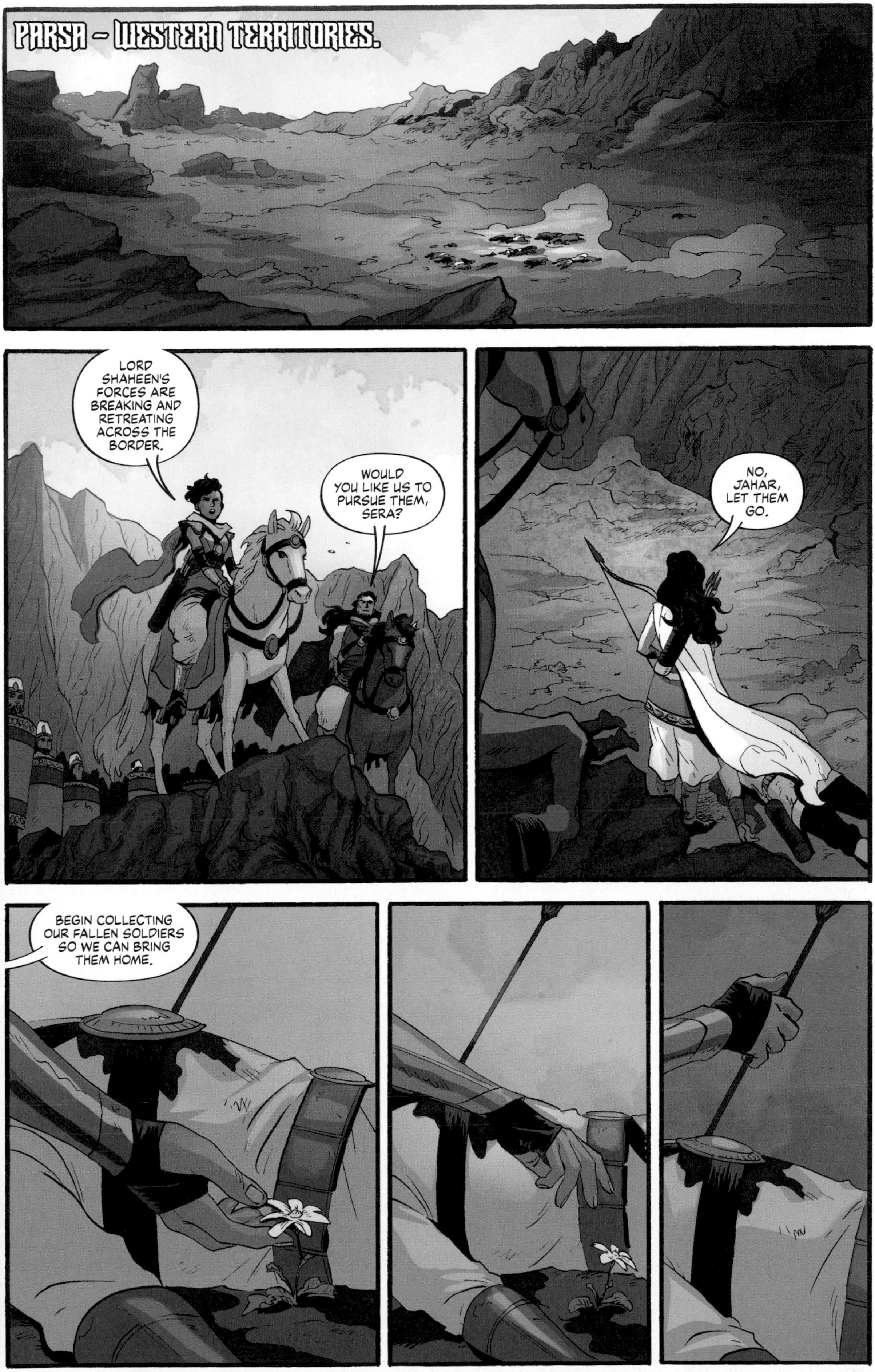
PARSA – WESTERN TERRITORIES.
LORD SHAHEEN'S FORCES ARE BREAKING AND RETREATING ACROSS THE BORDER.
WOULD YOU LIKE US TO PURSUE THEM, SERA?
NO, JAHAR, LET THEM GO.
BEGIN COLLECTING OUR FALLEN SOLDIERS SO WE CAN BRING THEM HOME.

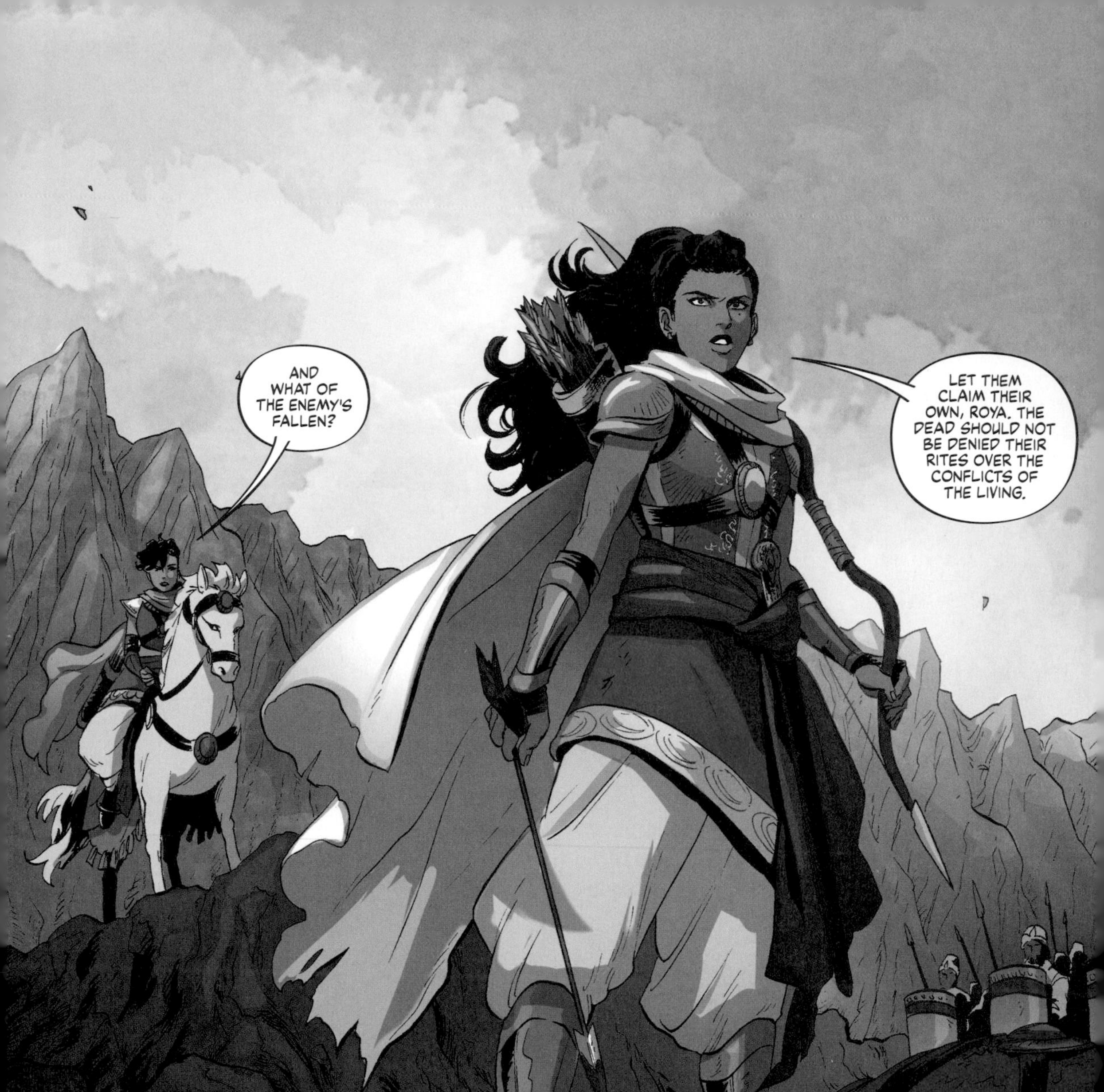
AND WHAT OF THE ENEMY'S FALLEN?
LET THEM CLAIM THEIR OWN, ROYA. THE DEAD SHOULD NOT BE DENIED THEIR RITES OVER THE CONFLICTS OF THE LIVING.

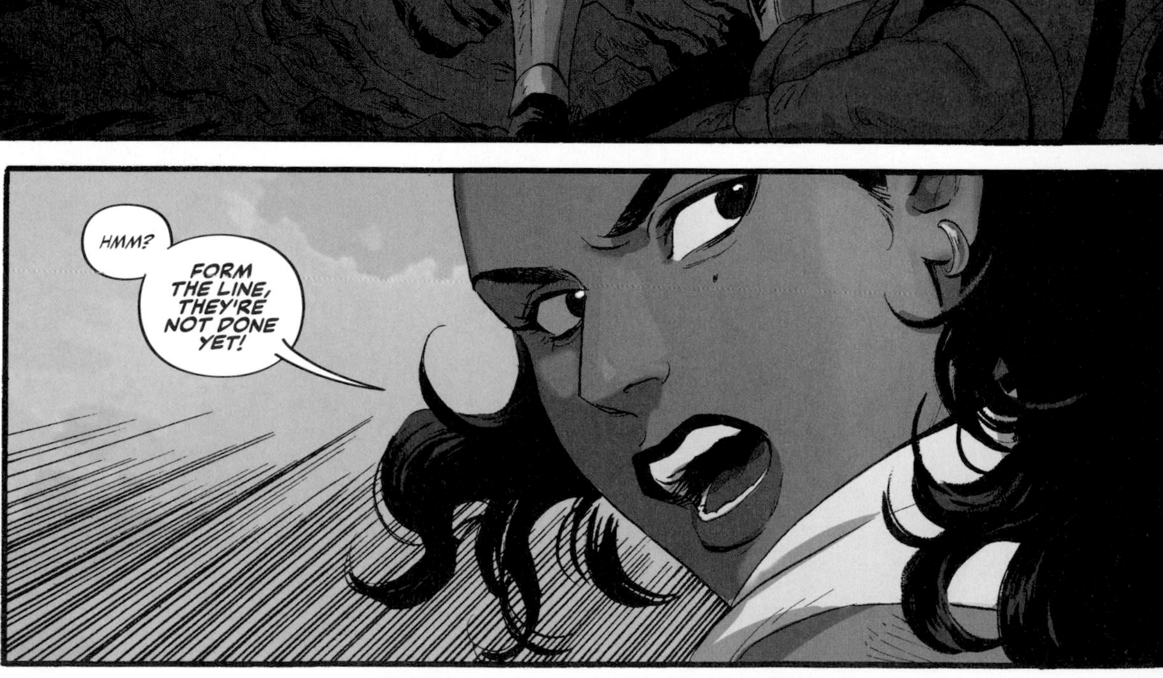
HMM?
FORM THE LINE, THEY'RE NOT DONE YET!

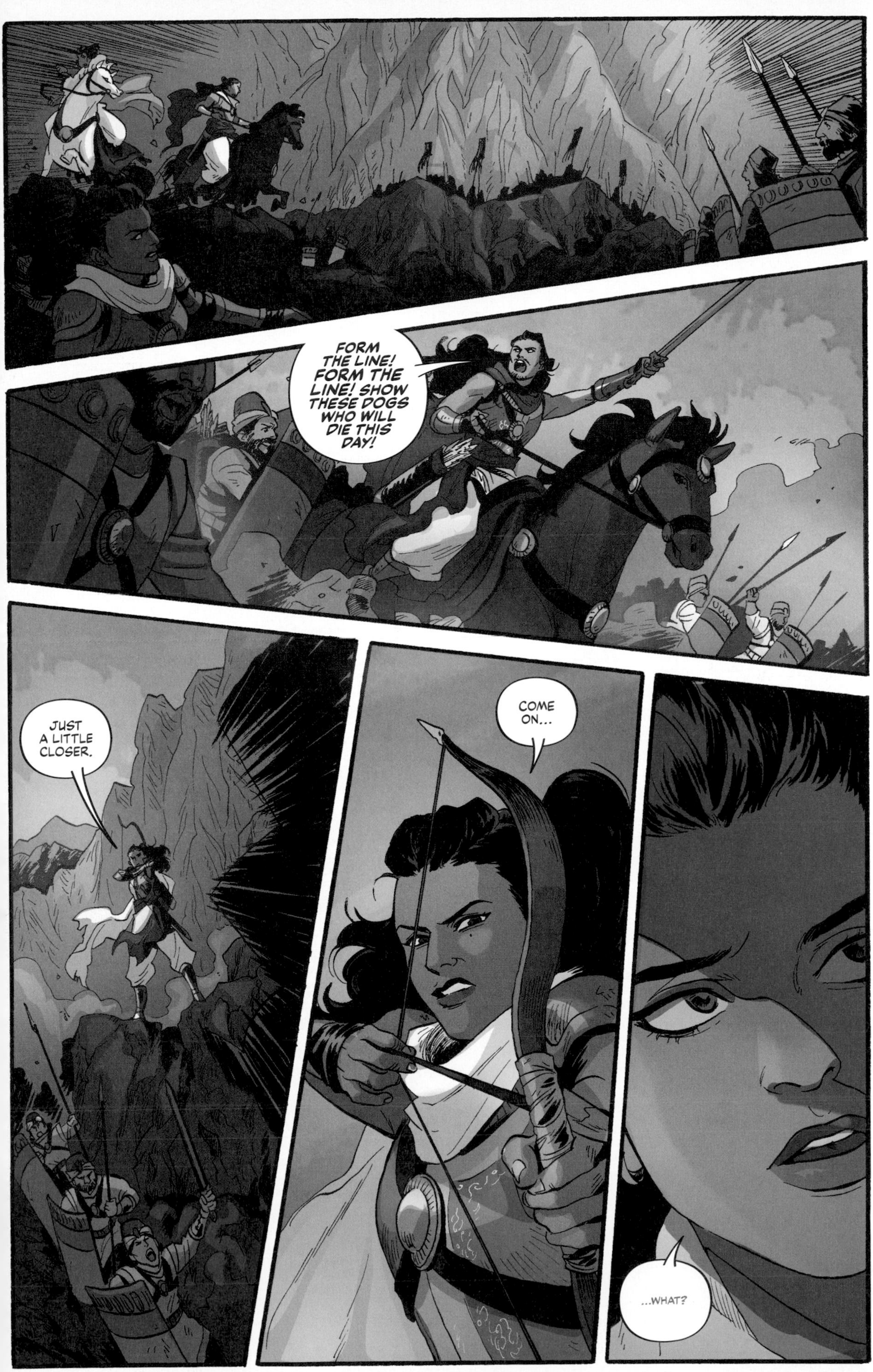
FORM THE LINE! FORM THE LINE! SHOW THESE DOGS WHO WILL DIE THIS DAY!
JUST A LITTLE CLOSER.
COME ON...
...WHAT?

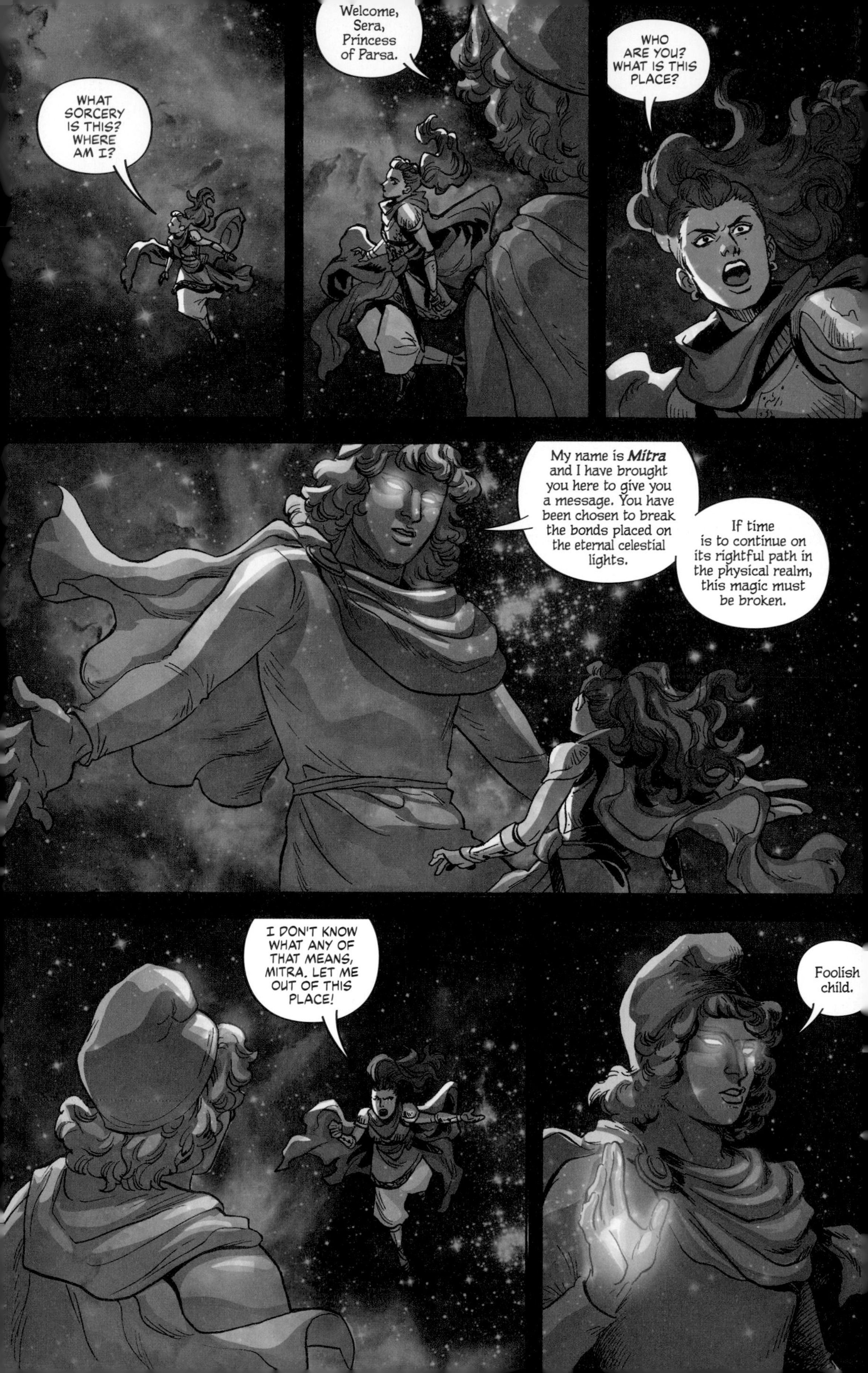
WHAT SORCERY IS THIS? WHERE AM I?
Welcome, Sera, Princess of Parsa.
WHO ARE YOU? WHAT IS THIS PLACE?
My name is *Mitra* and I have brought you here to give you a message. You have been chosen to break the bonds placed on the eternal celestial lights.
If time is to continue on its rightful path in the physical realm, this magic must be broken.
I DON'T KNOW WHAT ANY OF THAT MEANS, MITRA. LET ME OUT OF THIS PLACE!
Foolish child.

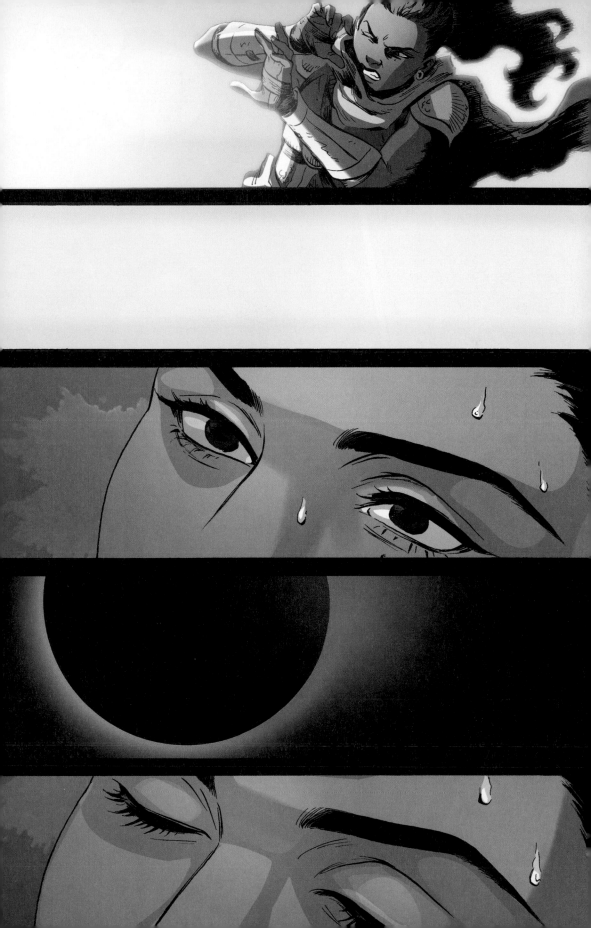

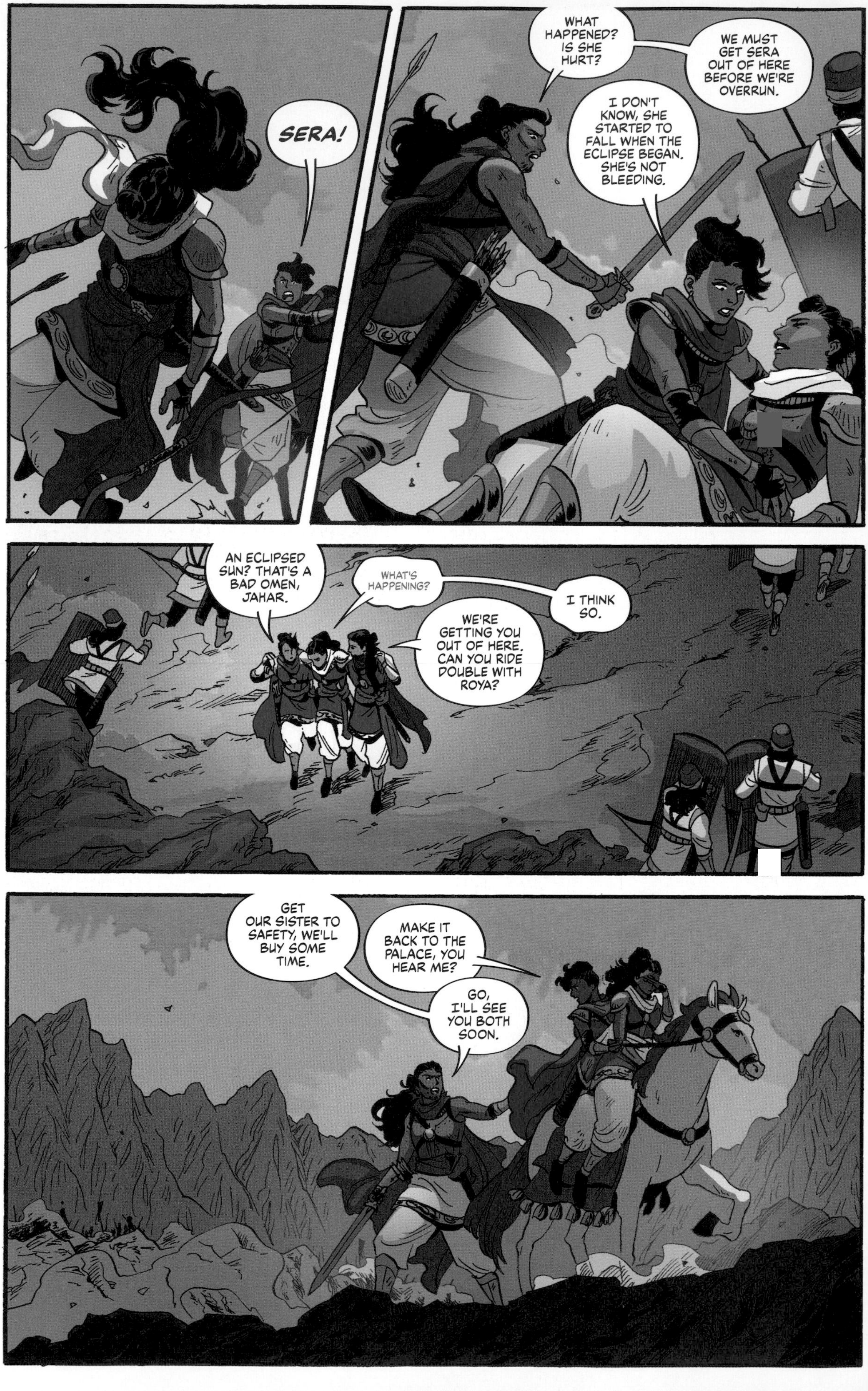
SERA!
WHAT HAPPENED? IS SHE HURT?
I DON'T KNOW, SHE STARTED TO FALL WHEN THE ECLIPSE BEGAN. SHE'S NOT BLEEDING.
WE MUST GET SERA OUT OF HERE BEFORE WE'RE OVERRUN.
AN ECLIPSED SUN? THAT'S A BAD OMEN, JAHAR.
WHAT'S HAPPENING?
WE'RE GETTING YOU OUT OF HERE. CAN YOU RIDE DOUBLE WITH ROYA?
I THINK SO.
GET OUR SISTER TO SAFETY, WE'LL BUY SOME TIME.
MAKE IT BACK TO THE PALACE, YOU HEAR ME?
GO, I'LL SEE YOU BOTH SOON.

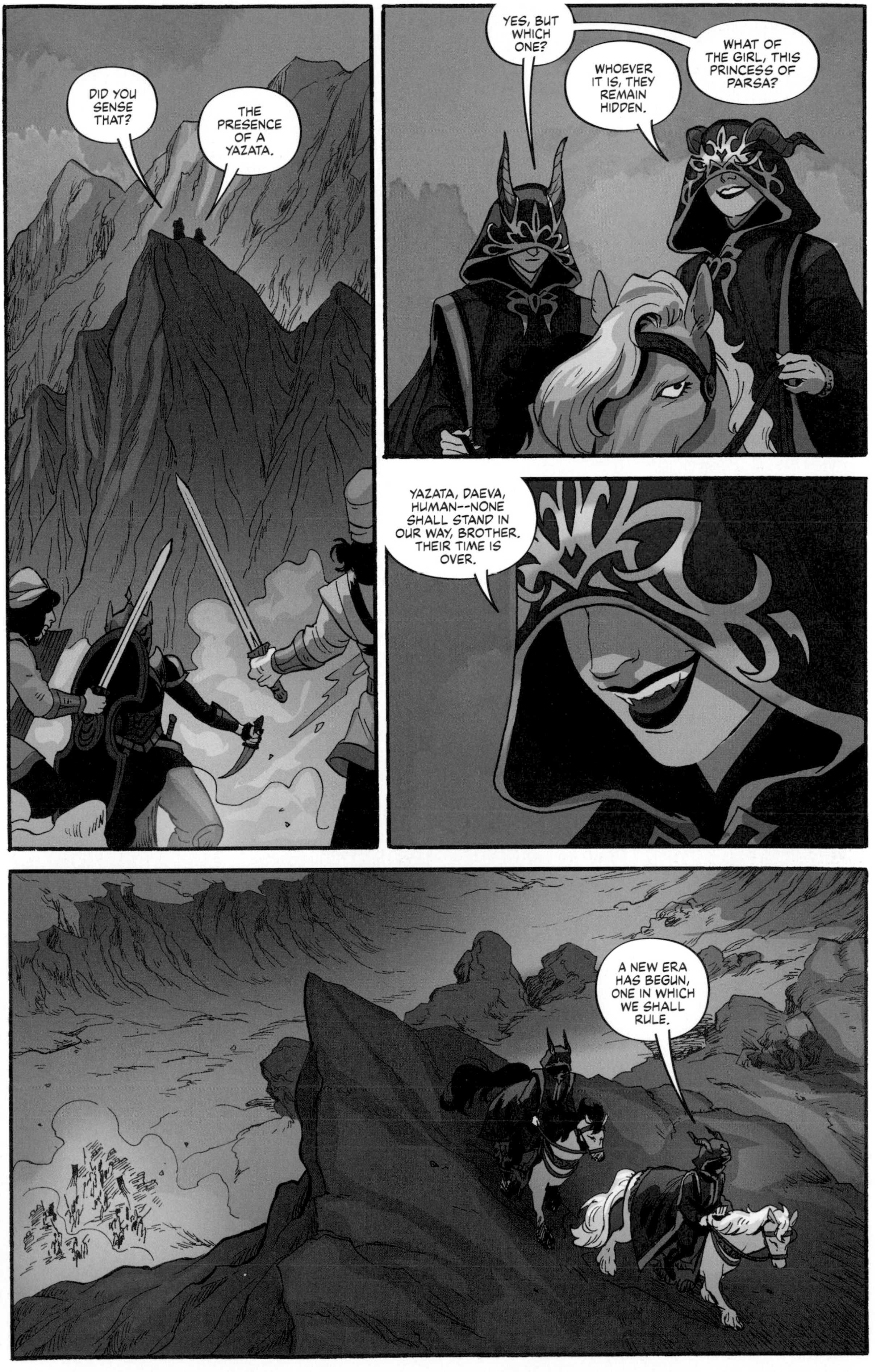
DID YOU SENSE THAT?
THE PRESENCE OF A YAZATA.
YES, BUT WHICH ONE?
WHAT OF THE GIRL, THIS PRINCESS OF PARSA?
WHOEVER IT IS, THEY REMAIN HIDDEN.
YAZATA, DAEVA, HUMAN--NONE SHALL STAND IN OUR WAY, BROTHER. THEIR TIME IS OVER.
A NEW ERA HAS BEGUN, ONE IN WHICH WE SHALL RULE.

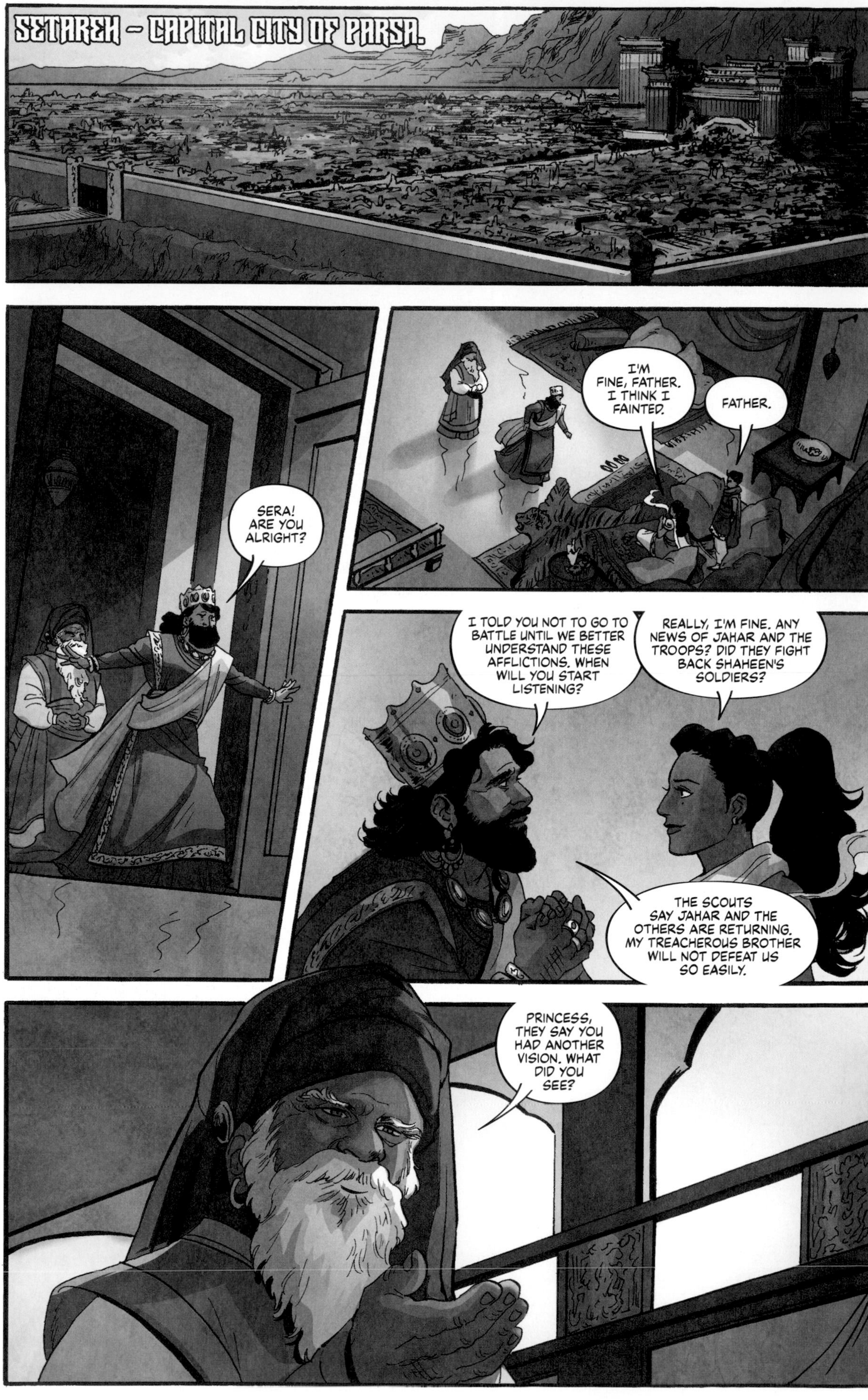
SETAREH – CAPITAL CITY OF PARSA.
SERA! ARE YOU ALRIGHT?
I'M FINE, FATHER. I THINK I FAINTED.
FATHER.
I TOLD YOU NOT TO GO TO BATTLE UNTIL WE BETTER UNDERSTAND THESE AFFLICTIONS. WHEN WILL YOU START LISTENING?
REALLY, I'M FINE. ANY NEWS OF JAHAR AND THE TROOPS? DID THEY FIGHT BACK SHAHEEN'S SOLDIERS?
THE SCOUTS SAY JAHAR AND THE OTHERS ARE RETURNING. MY TREACHEROUS BROTHER WILL NOT DEFEAT US SO EASILY.
PRINCESS, THEY SAY YOU HAD ANOTHER VISION. WHAT DID YOU SEE?

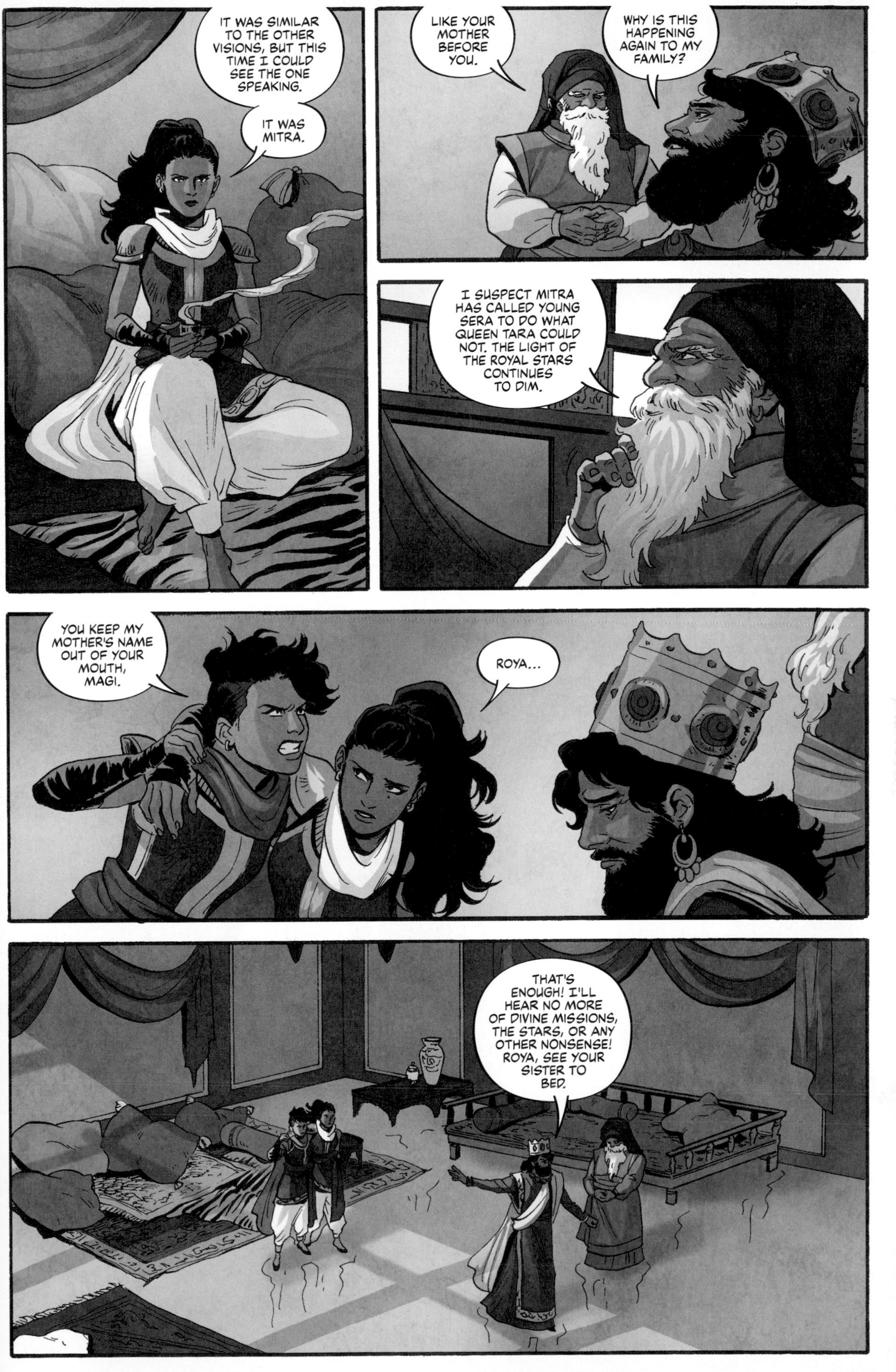
IT WAS SIMILAR TO THE OTHER VISIONS, BUT THIS TIME I COULD SEE THE ONE SPEAKING.
IT WAS MITRA.
LIKE YOUR MOTHER BEFORE YOU.
WHY IS THIS HAPPENING AGAIN TO MY FAMILY?
I SUSPECT MITRA HAS CALLED YOUNG SERA TO DO WHAT QUEEN TARA COULD NOT. THE LIGHT OF THE ROYAL STARS CONTINUES TO DIM.
YOU KEEP MY MOTHER'S NAME OUT OF YOUR MOUTH, MAGI.
ROYA...
THAT'S ENOUGH! I'LL HEAR NO MORE OF DIVINE MISSIONS, THE STARS, OR ANY OTHER NONSENSE! ROYA, SEE YOUR SISTER TO BED.

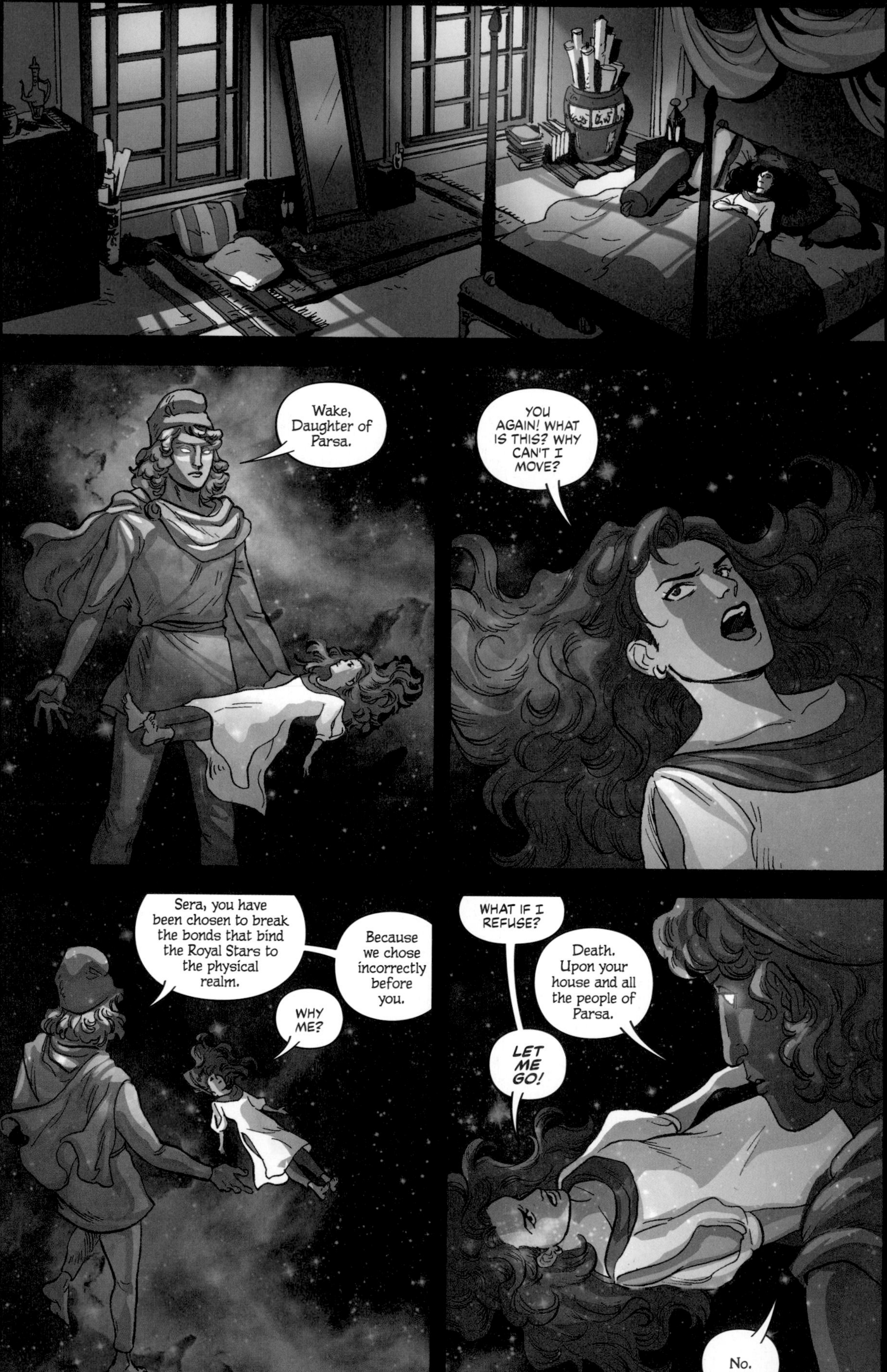
Wake, Daughter of Parsa.
YOU AGAIN! WHAT IS THIS? WHY CAN'T I MOVE?
Sera, you have been chosen to break the bonds that bind the Royal Stars to the physical realm.
WHY ME?
Because we chose incorrectly before you.
WHAT IF I REFUSE?
Death. Upon your house and all the people of Parsa.
LET ME GO!
No.

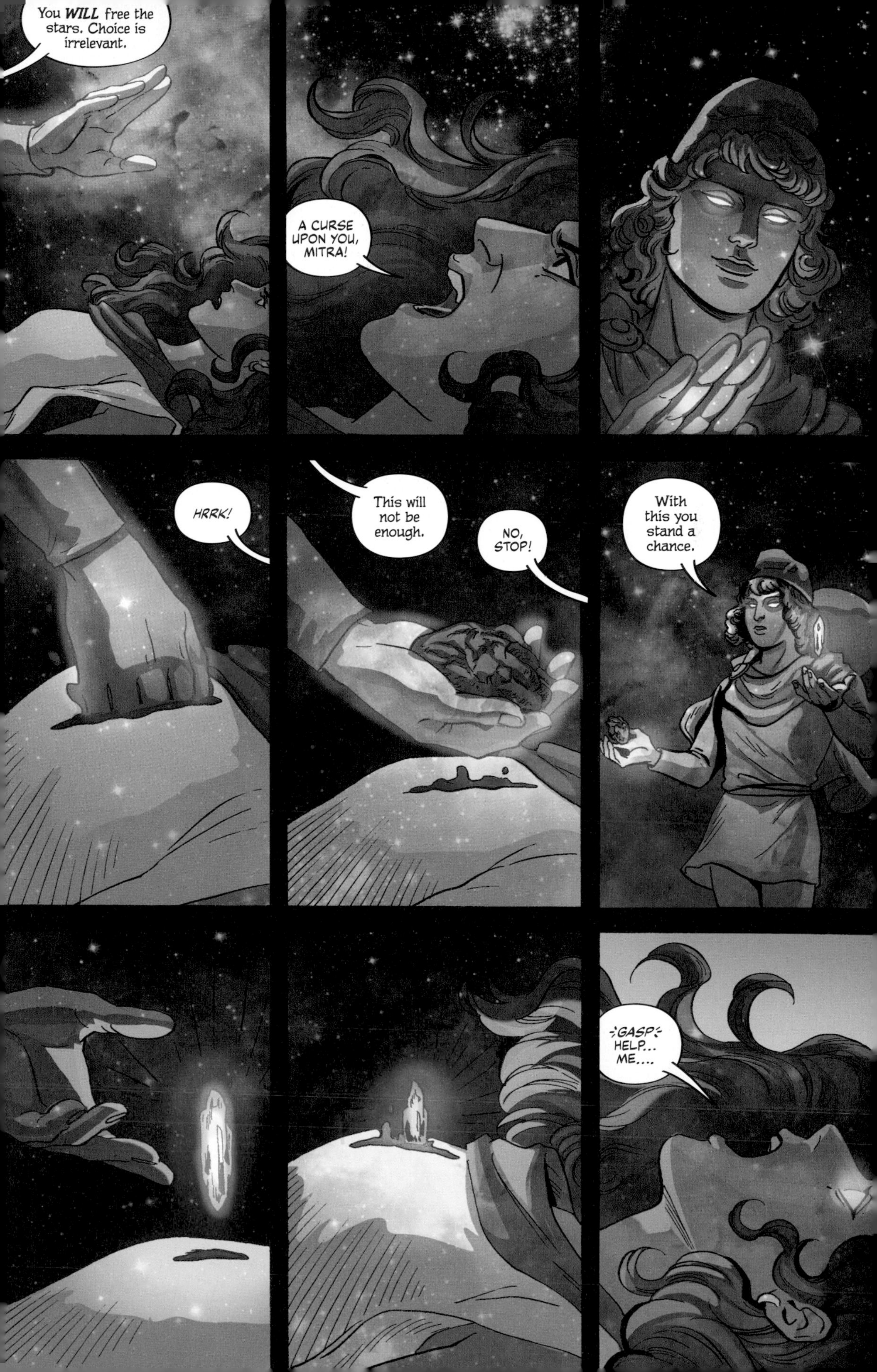
You **WILL** free the stars. Choice is irrelevant.
A CURSE UPON YOU, MITRA!
HRRK!
This will not be enough.
NO, STOP!
With this you stand a chance.
GASP HELP... ME....

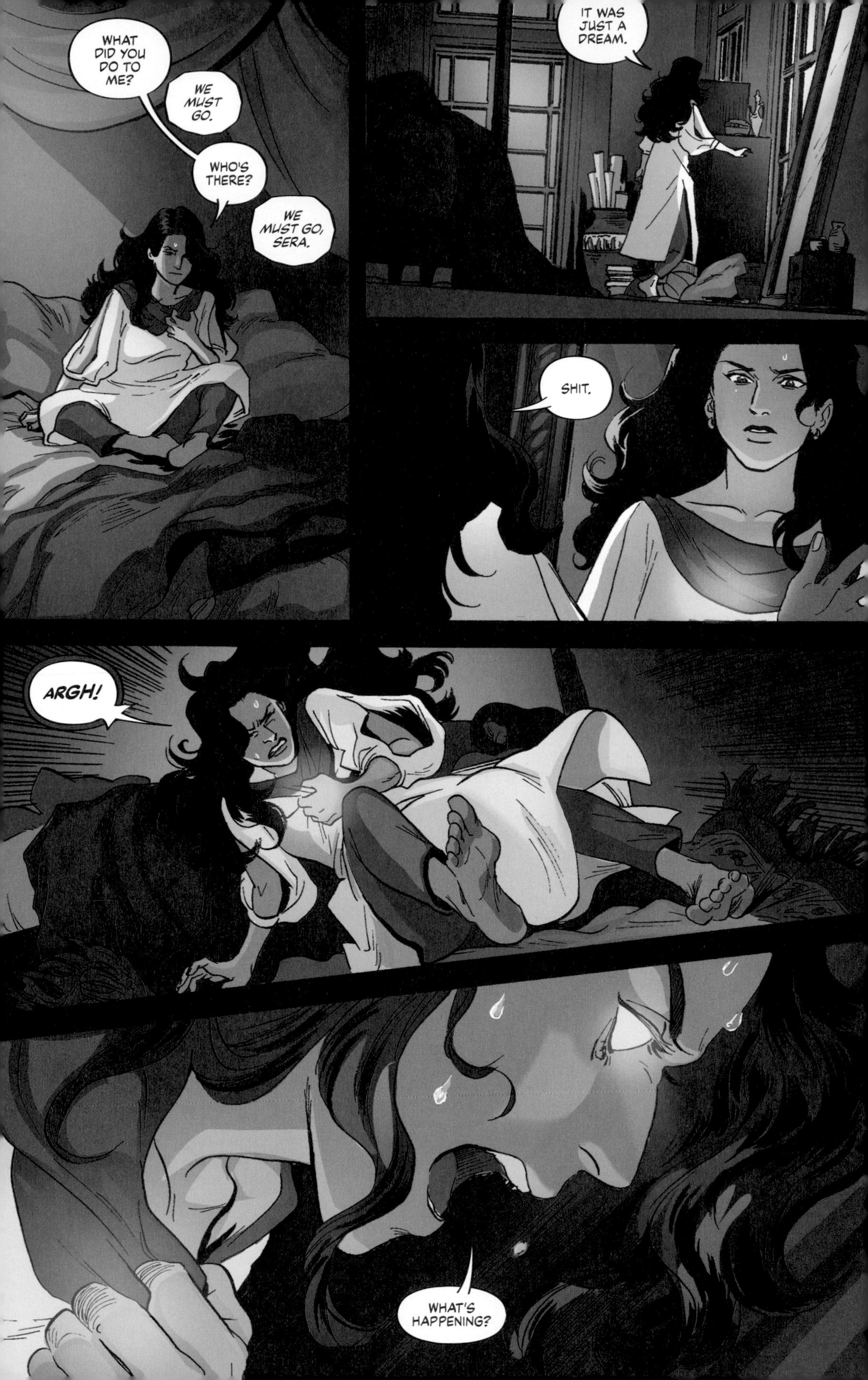
WHAT DID YOU DO TO ME?
WE MUST GO.
WHO'S THERE?
WE MUST GO, SERA.
IT WAS JUST A DREAM.
SHIT.
ARGH!
WHAT'S HAPPENING?

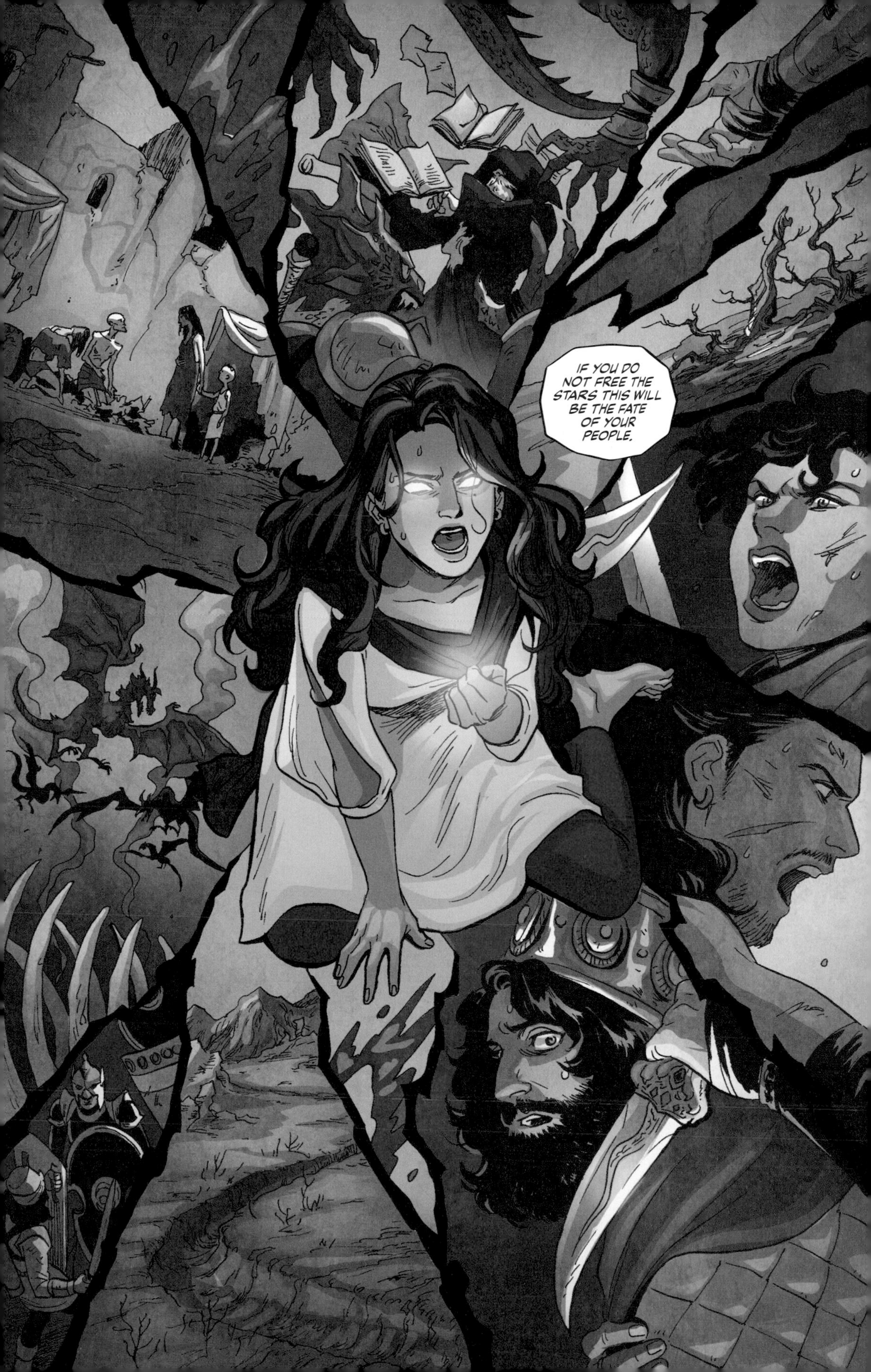
IF YOU DO NOT FREE THE STARS THIS WILL BE THE FATE OF YOUR PEOPLE.

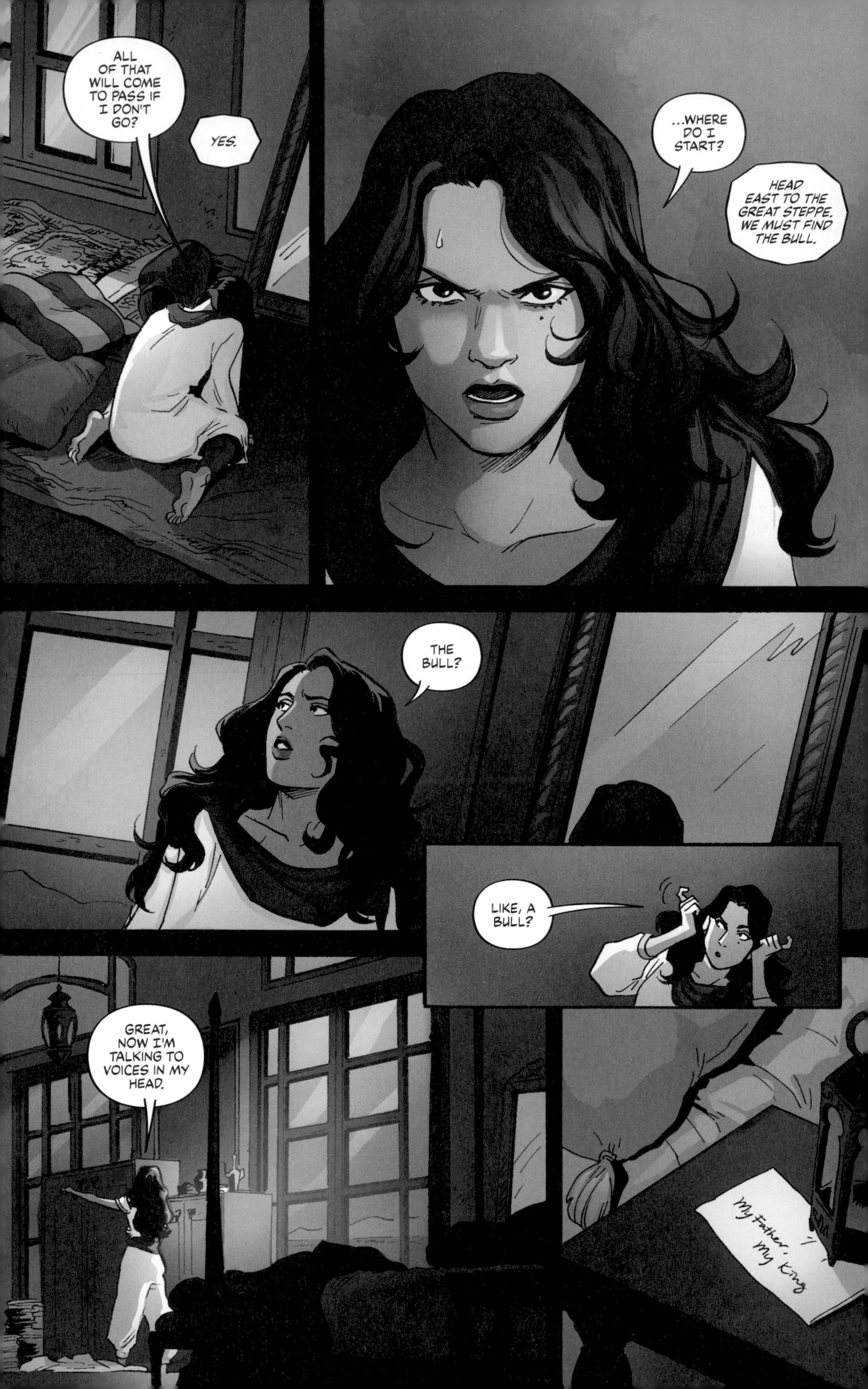
ALL OF THAT WILL COME TO PASS IF I DON'T GO?
YES.
...WHERE DO I START?
HEAD EAST TO THE GREAT STEPPE. WE MUST FIND THE BULL.
THE BULL?
LIKE, A BULL?
GREAT, NOW I'M TALKING TO VOICES IN MY HEAD.
My Father, my King

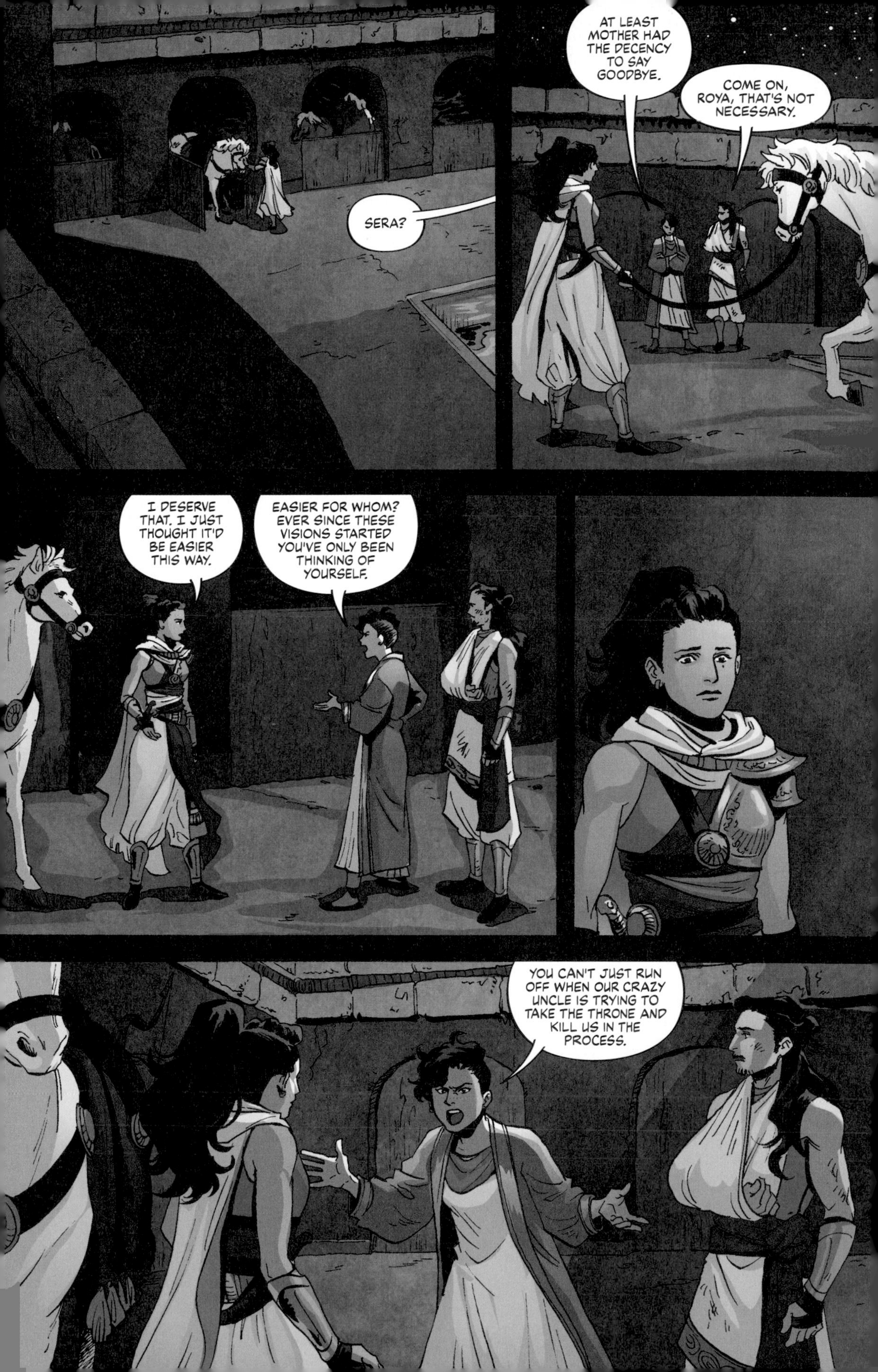
SERA?
AT LEAST MOTHER HAD THE DECENCY TO SAY GOODBYE.
COME ON, ROYA, THAT'S NOT NECESSARY.
I DESERVE THAT. I JUST THOUGHT IT'D BE EASIER THIS WAY.
EASIER FOR WHOM? EVER SINCE THESE VISIONS STARTED YOU'VE ONLY BEEN THINKING OF YOURSELF.
YOU CAN'T JUST RUN OFF WHEN OUR CRAZY UNCLE IS TRYING TO TAKE THE THRONE AND KILL US IN THE PROCESS.

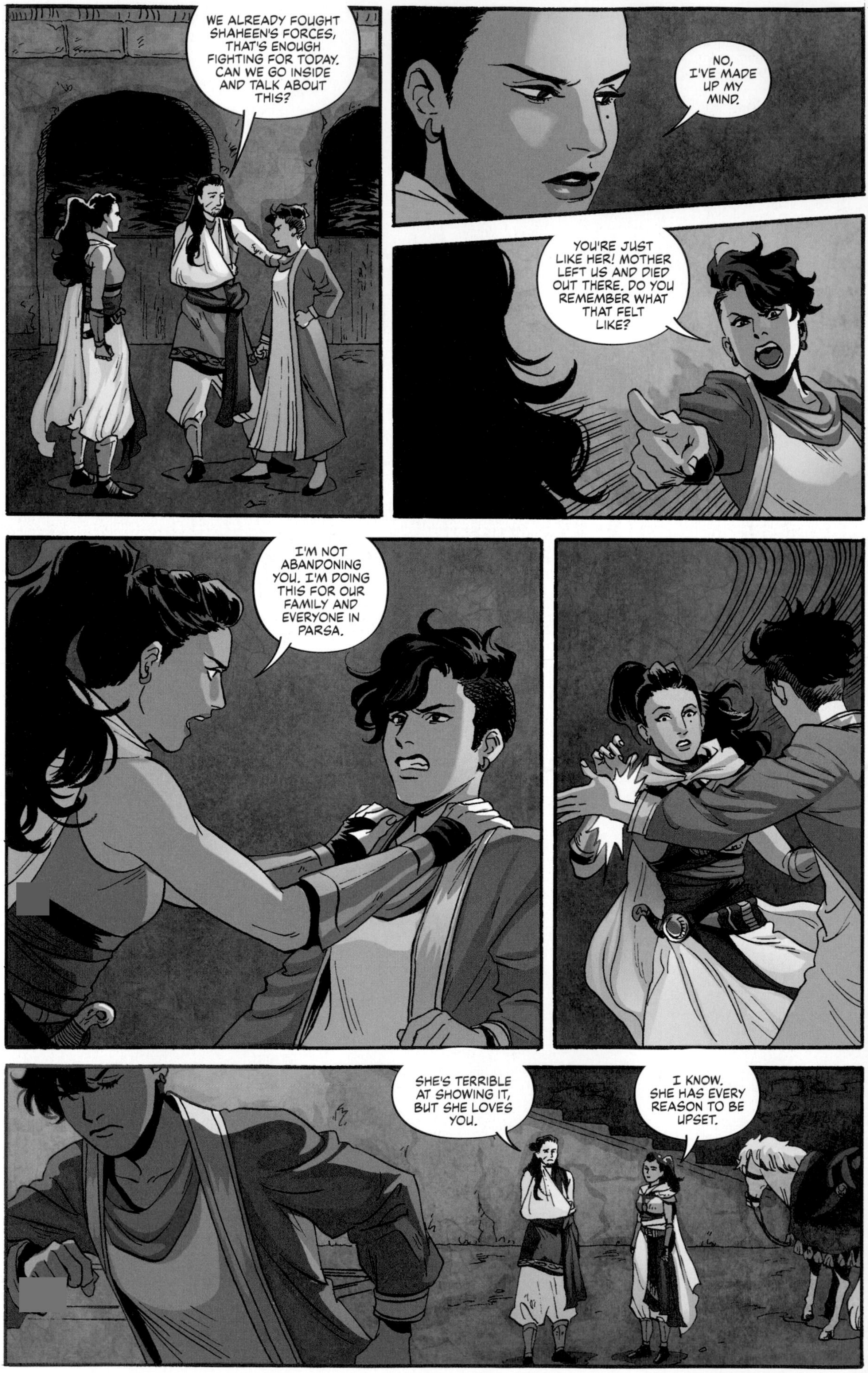
WE ALREADY FOUGHT SHAHEEN'S FORCES, THAT'S ENOUGH FIGHTING FOR TODAY. CAN WE GO INSIDE AND TALK ABOUT THIS?
NO, I'VE MADE UP MY MIND.
YOU'RE JUST LIKE HER! MOTHER LEFT US AND DIED OUT THERE. DO YOU REMEMBER WHAT THAT FELT LIKE?
I'M NOT ABANDONING YOU. I'M DOING THIS FOR OUR FAMILY AND EVERYONE IN PARSA.
SHE'S TERRIBLE AT SHOWING IT, BUT SHE LOVES YOU.
I KNOW. SHE HAS EVERY REASON TO BE UPSET.

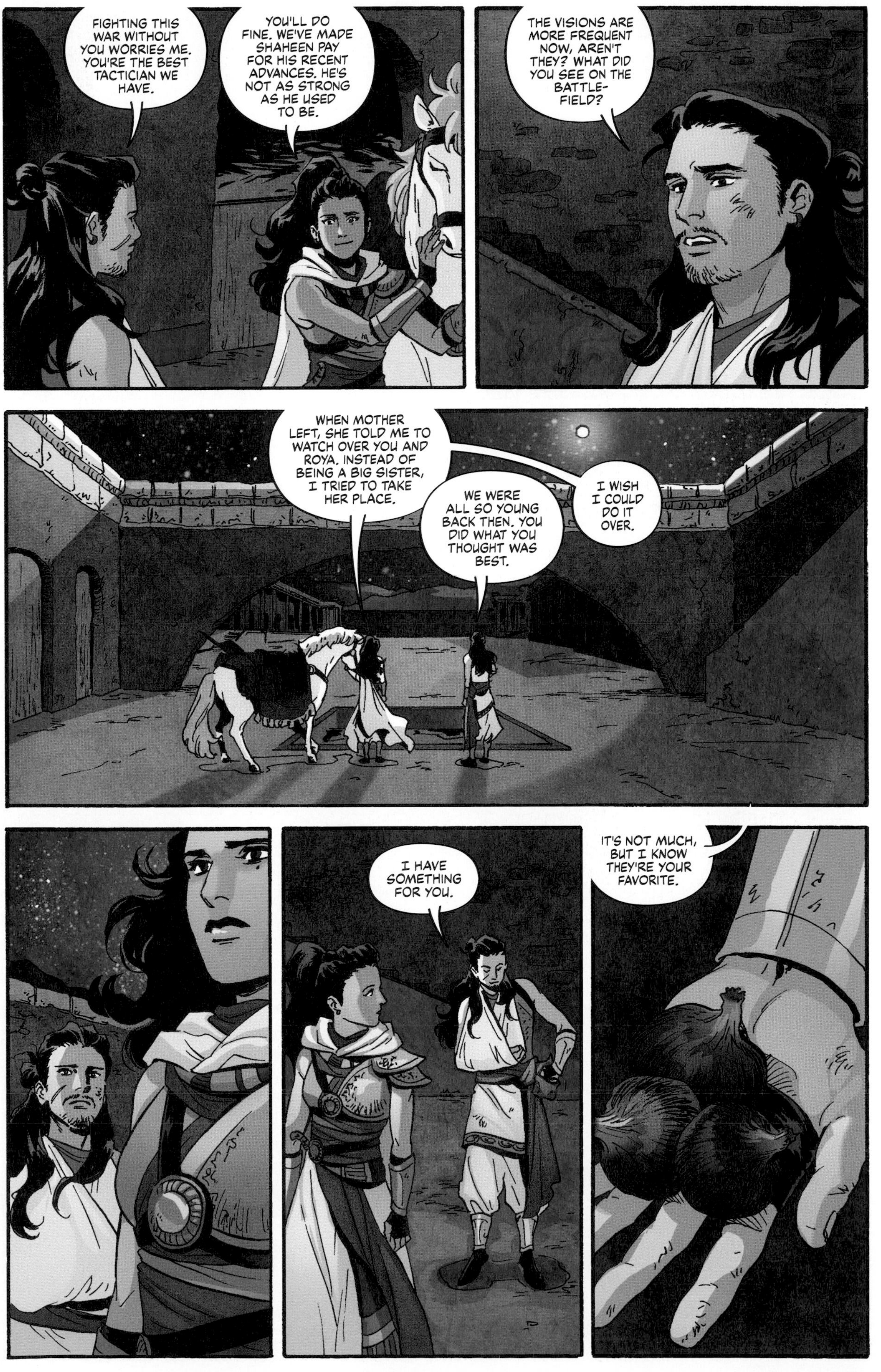
FIGHTING THIS WAR WITHOUT YOU WORRIES ME. YOU'RE THE BEST TACTICIAN WE HAVE.
YOU'LL DO FINE. WE'VE MADE SHAHEEN PAY FOR HIS RECENT ADVANCES. HE'S NOT AS STRONG AS HE USED TO BE.
THE VISIONS ARE MORE FREQUENT NOW, AREN'T THEY? WHAT DID YOU SEE ON THE BATTLE-FIELD?
WHEN MOTHER LEFT, SHE TOLD ME TO WATCH OVER YOU AND ROYA. INSTEAD OF BEING A BIG SISTER, I TRIED TO TAKE HER PLACE.
I WISH I COULD DO IT OVER.
WE WERE ALL SO YOUNG BACK THEN. YOU DID WHAT YOU THOUGHT WAS BEST.
I HAVE SOMETHING FOR YOU.
IT'S NOT MUCH, BUT I KNOW THEY'RE YOUR FAVORITE.

HOW DID YOU FIND THESE? IT'S BEEN MONTHS SINCE I'VE SEEN ANY FIG TREES ALIVE.

I MASTERFULLY NAVIGATED THE PARCHED LANDSCAPE AND FOUND THE LAST LIVING FIG TREE.

YOU GOT LUCKY.

I GOT LUCKY.

TAKE CARE OF ROYA AND FATHER.

DON'T WORRY ABOUT US, JUST MAKE SURE YOU COME BACK SAFELY.

I WILL.

FOR THE GLORY OF PARSA.

FOR THE GLORY OF PARSA.

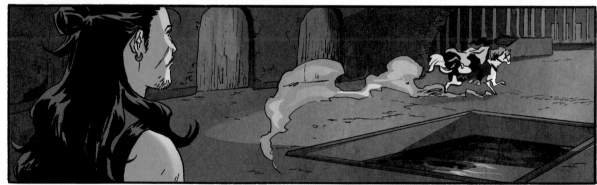

MY EARLIEST MEMORIES OF FAMILY ALL REVOLVE AROUND WAR.

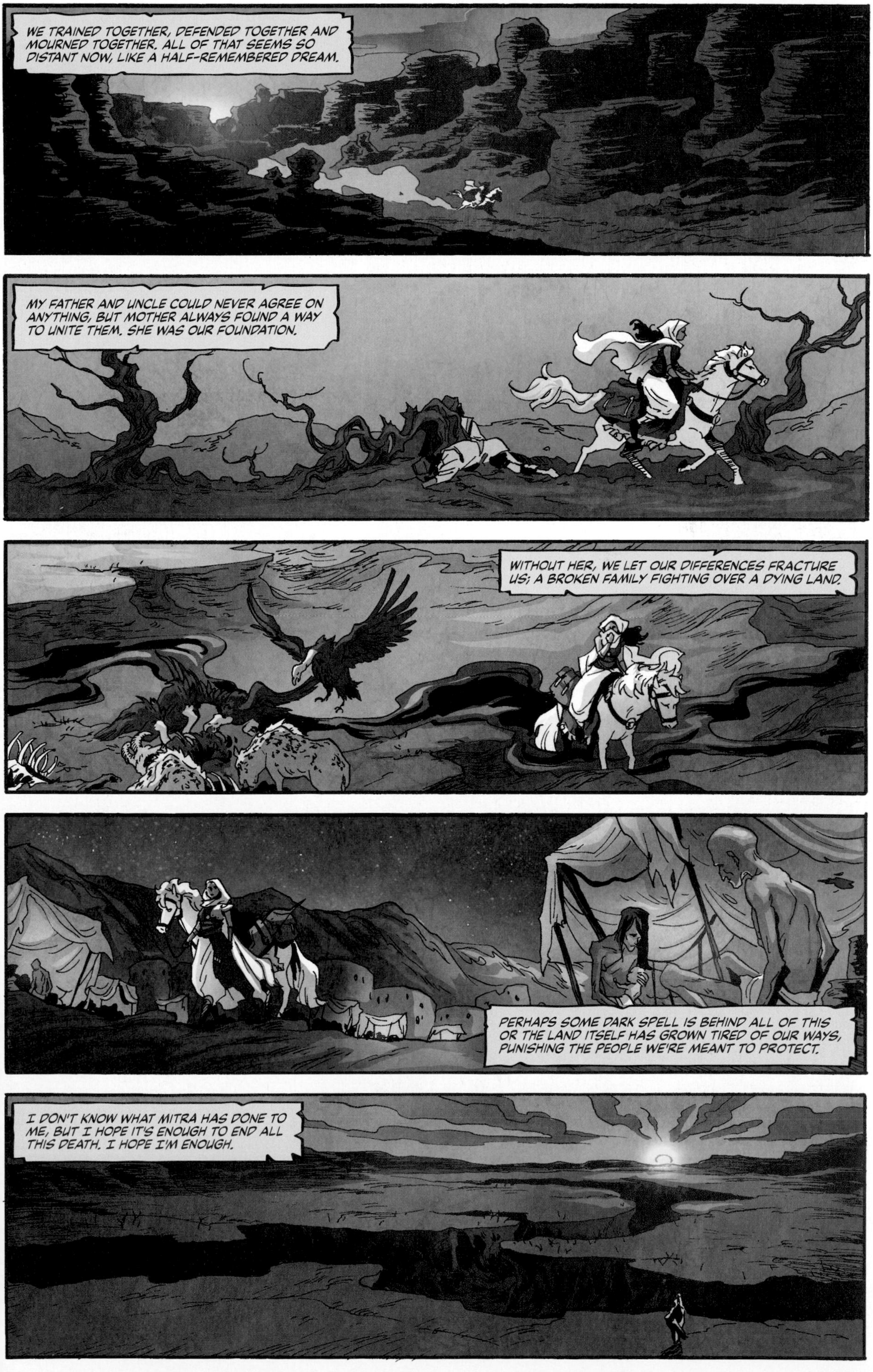
WE TRAINED TOGETHER, DEFENDED TOGETHER AND MOURNED TOGETHER. ALL OF THAT SEEMS SO DISTANT NOW, LIKE A HALF-REMEMBERED DREAM.
MY FATHER AND UNCLE COULD NEVER AGREE ON ANYTHING, BUT MOTHER ALWAYS FOUND A WAY TO UNITE THEM. SHE WAS OUR FOUNDATION.
WITHOUT HER, WE LET OUR DIFFERENCES FRACTURE US; A BROKEN FAMILY FIGHTING OVER A DYING LAND.
PERHAPS SOME DARK SPELL IS BEHIND ALL OF THIS OR THE LAND ITSELF HAS GROWN TIRED OF OUR WAYS, PUNISHING THE PEOPLE WE'RE MEANT TO PROTECT.
I DON'T KNOW WHAT MITRA HAS DONE TO ME, BUT I HOPE IT'S ENOUGH TO END ALL THIS DEATH. I HOPE I'M ENOUGH.

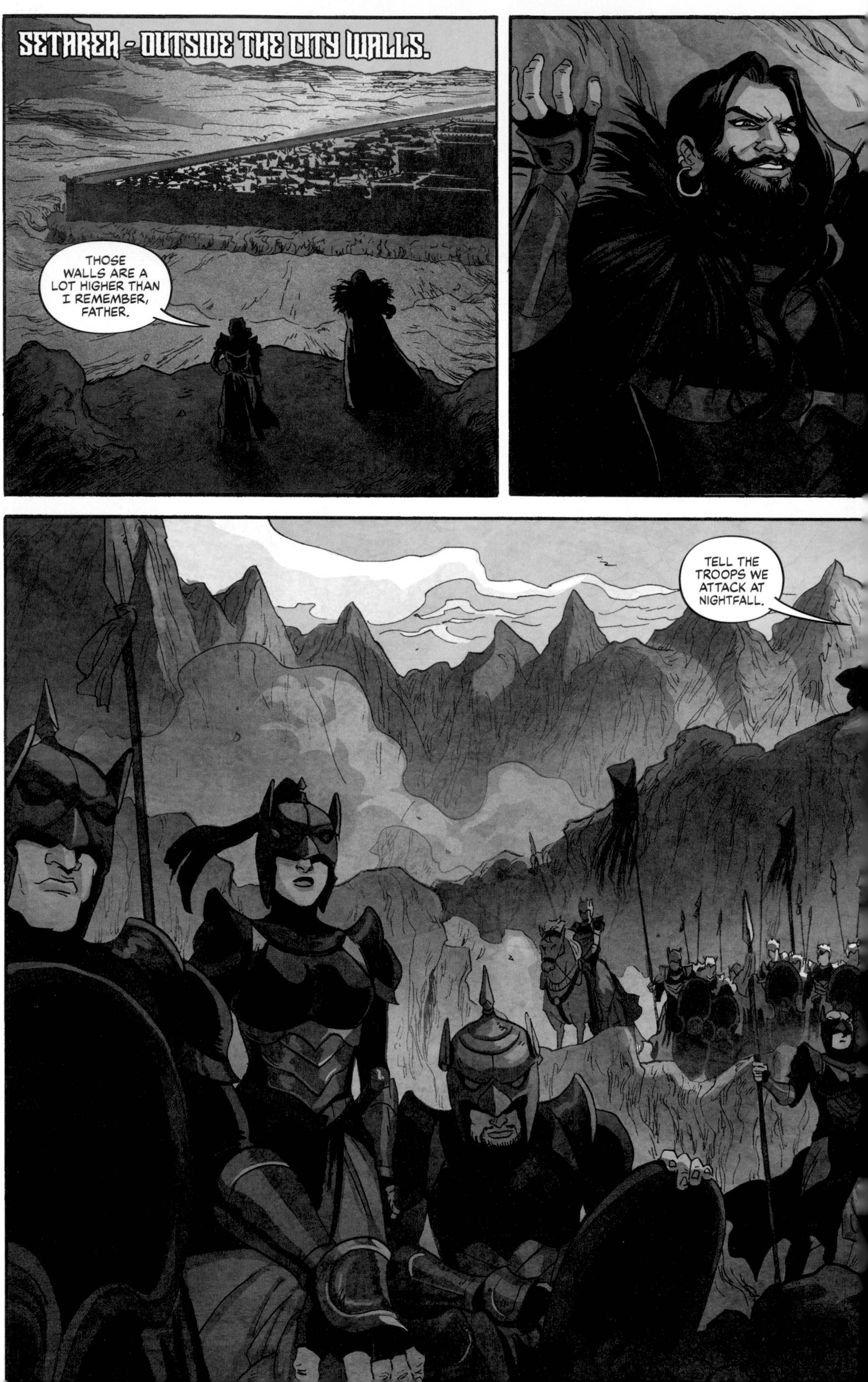
SETAREH - OUTSIDE THE CITY WALLS.
THOSE WALLS ARE A LOT HIGHER THAN I REMEMBER, FATHER.
TELL THE TROOPS WE ATTACK AT NIGHTFALL.

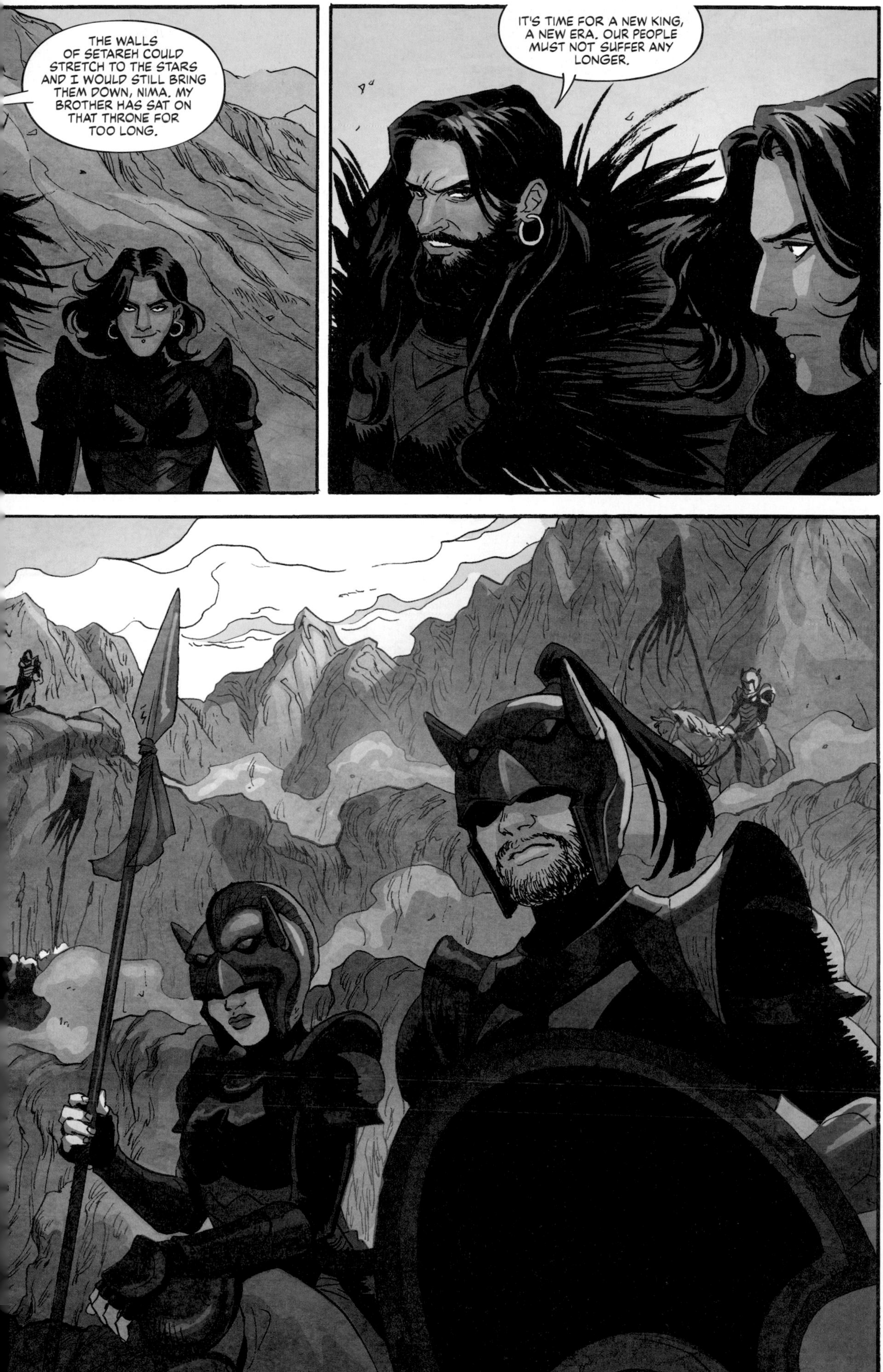
THE WALLS OF SETAREH COULD STRETCH TO THE STARS AND I WOULD STILL BRING THEM DOWN, NIMA. MY BROTHER HAS SAT ON THAT THRONE FOR TOO LONG.
IT'S TIME FOR A NEW KING, A NEW ERA. OUR PEOPLE MUST NOT SUFFER ANY LONGER.

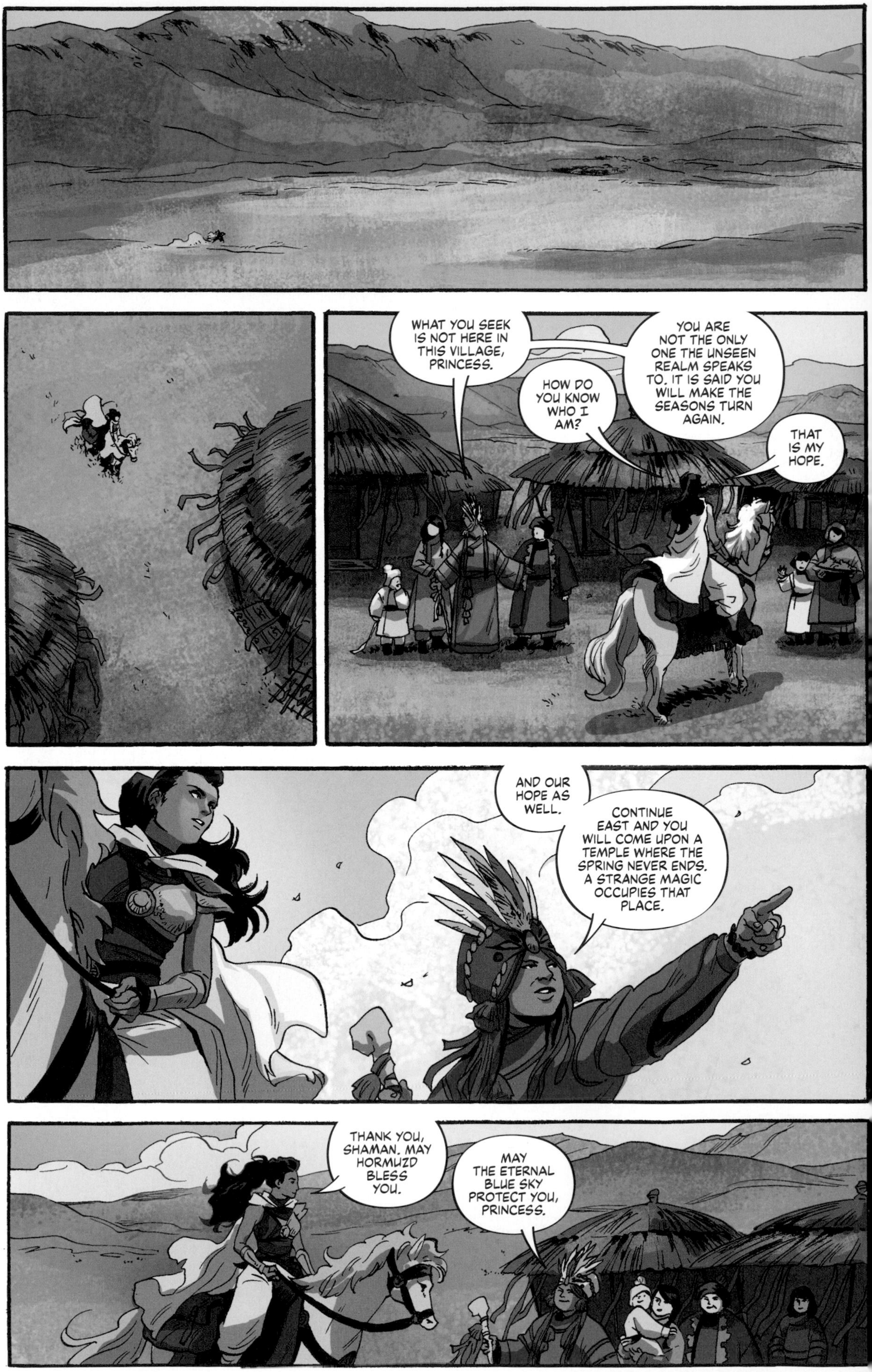
WHAT YOU SEEK IS NOT HERE IN THIS VILLAGE, PRINCESS.
HOW DO YOU KNOW WHO I AM?
YOU ARE NOT THE ONLY ONE THE UNSEEN REALM SPEAKS TO. IT IS SAID YOU WILL MAKE THE SEASONS TURN AGAIN.
THAT IS MY HOPE.
AND OUR HOPE AS WELL.
CONTINUE EAST AND YOU WILL COME UPON A TEMPLE WHERE THE SPRING NEVER ENDS. A STRANGE MAGIC OCCUPIES THAT PLACE.
THANK YOU, SHAMAN. MAY HORMUZD BLESS YOU.
MAY THE ETERNAL BLUE SKY PROTECT YOU, PRINCESS.

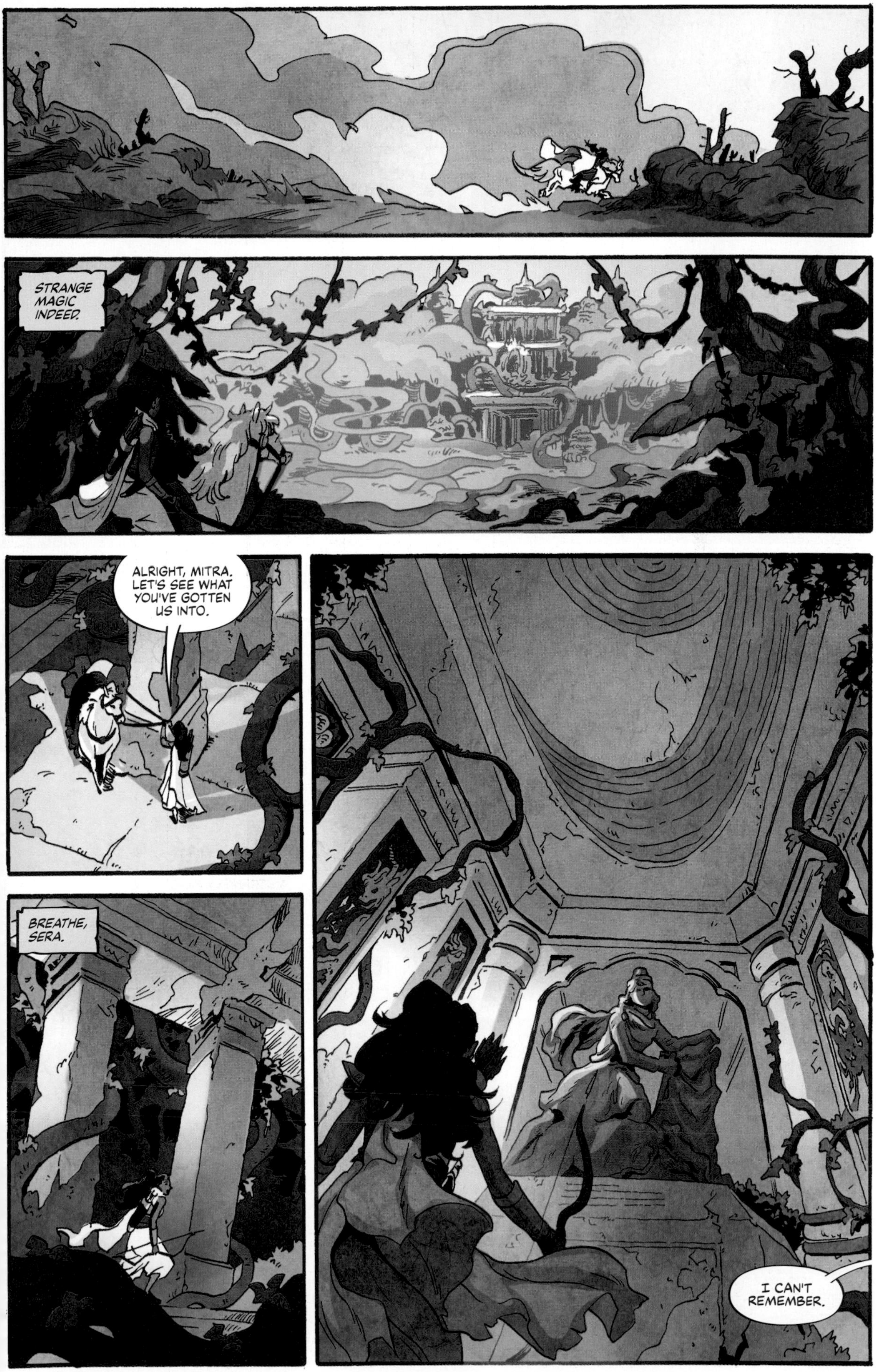
STRANGE MAGIC INDEED.
ALRIGHT, MITRA. LET'S SEE WHAT YOU'VE GOTTEN US INTO.
BREATHE, SERA.
I CAN'T REMEMBER.

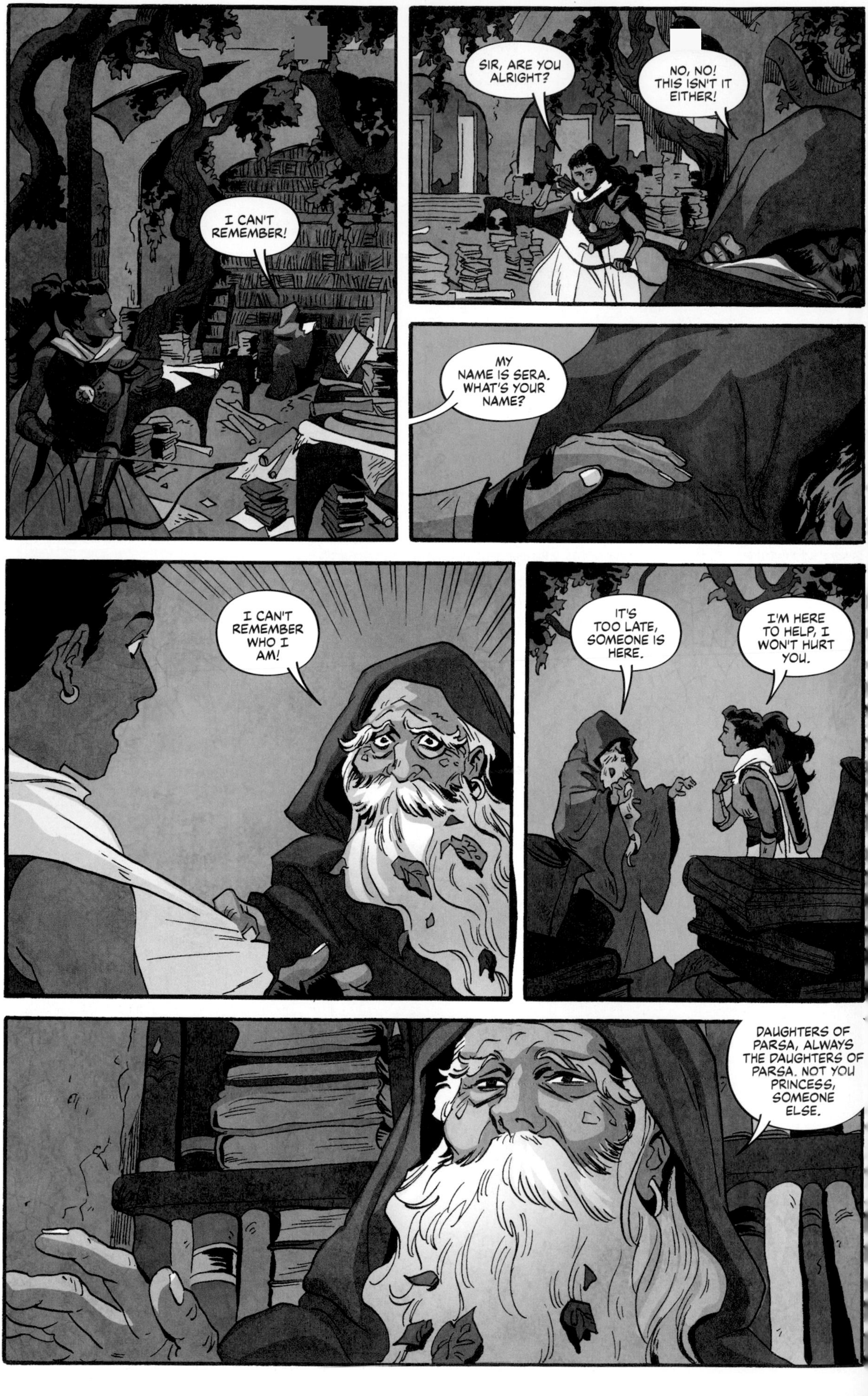
I CAN'T REMEMBER!
SIR, ARE YOU ALRIGHT?
NO, NO! THIS ISN'T IT EITHER!
MY NAME IS SERA. WHAT'S YOUR NAME?
I CAN'T REMEMBER WHO I AM!
IT'S TOO LATE, SOMEONE IS HERE.
I'M HERE TO HELP, I WON'T HURT YOU.
DAUGHTERS OF PARSA, ALWAYS THE DAUGHTERS OF PARSA. NOT YOU PRINCESS, SOMEONE ELSE.

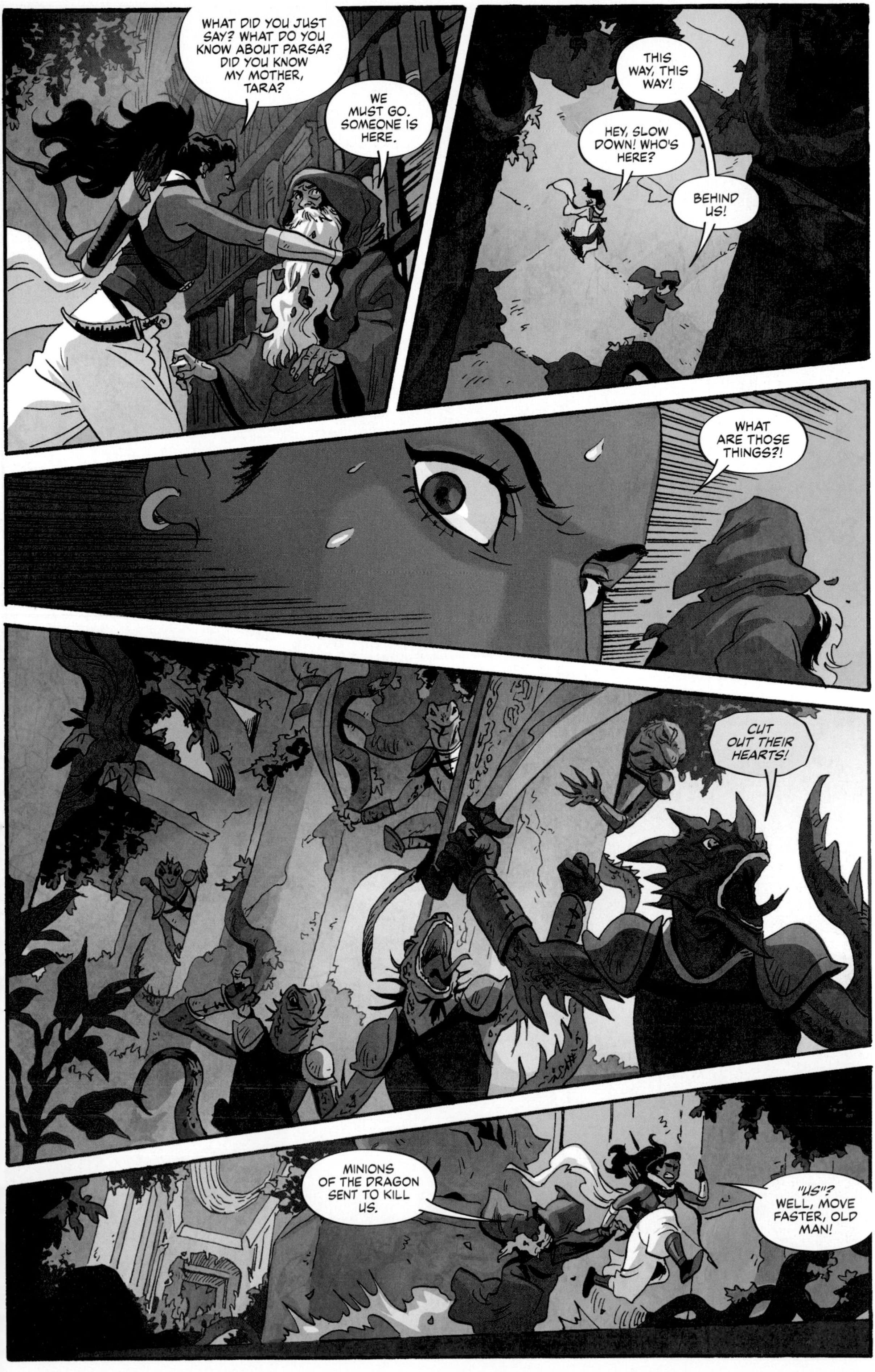
WHAT DID YOU JUST SAY? WHAT DO YOU KNOW ABOUT PARSA? DID YOU KNOW MY MOTHER, TARA?
WE MUST GO. SOMEONE IS HERE.
THIS WAY, THIS WAY!
HEY, SLOW DOWN! WHO'S HERE?
BEHIND US!
WHAT ARE THOSE THINGS?!
CUT OUT THEIR HEARTS!
MINIONS OF THE DRAGON SENT TO KILL US.
"US"? WELL, MOVE FASTER, OLD MAN!

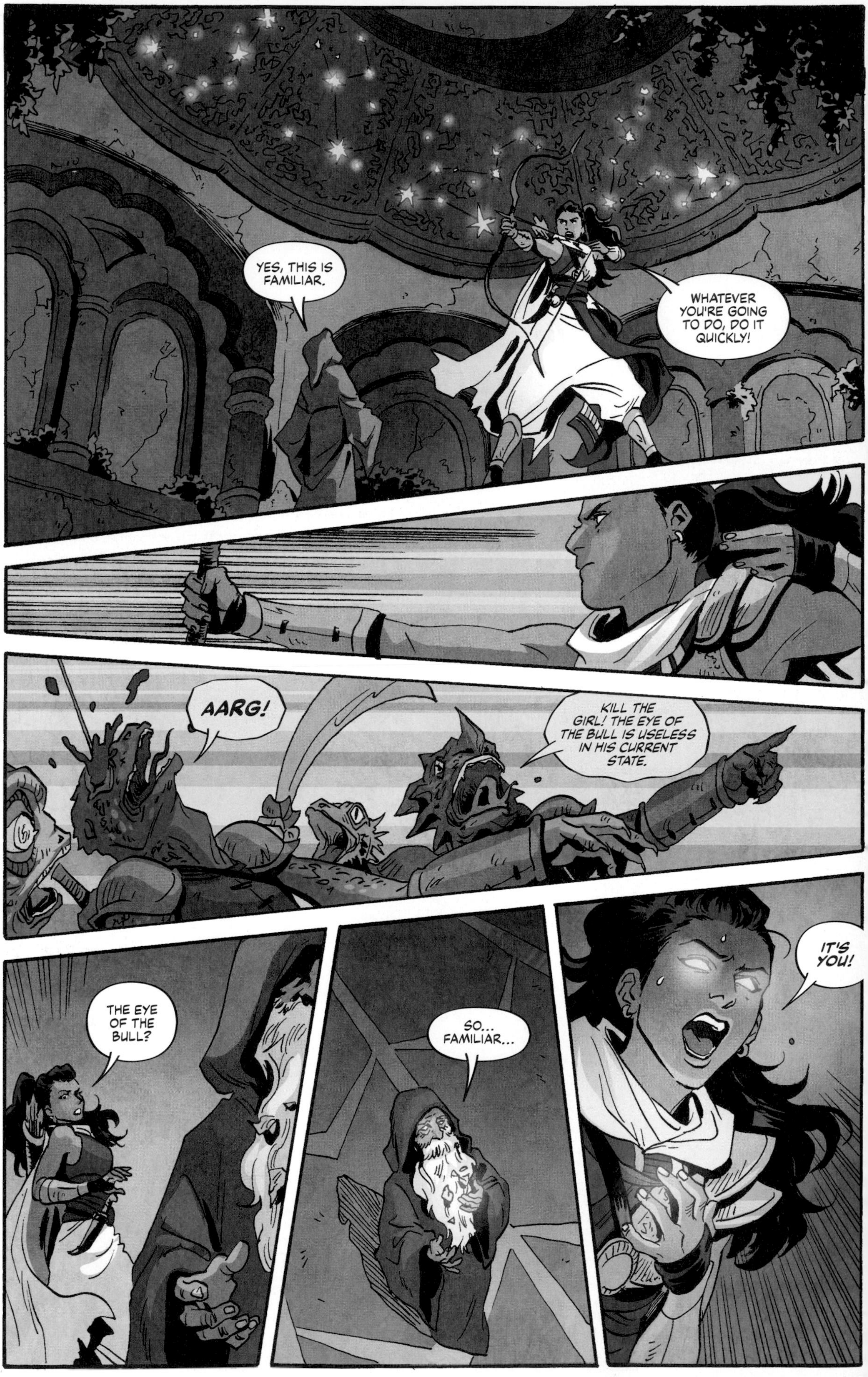

YES, THIS IS FAMILIAR.
WHATEVER YOU'RE GOING TO DO, DO IT QUICKLY!
AARG!
KILL THE GIRL! THE EYE OF THE BULL IS USELESS IN HIS CURRENT STATE.
THE EYE OF THE BULL?
SO... FAMILIAR...
IT'S YOU!

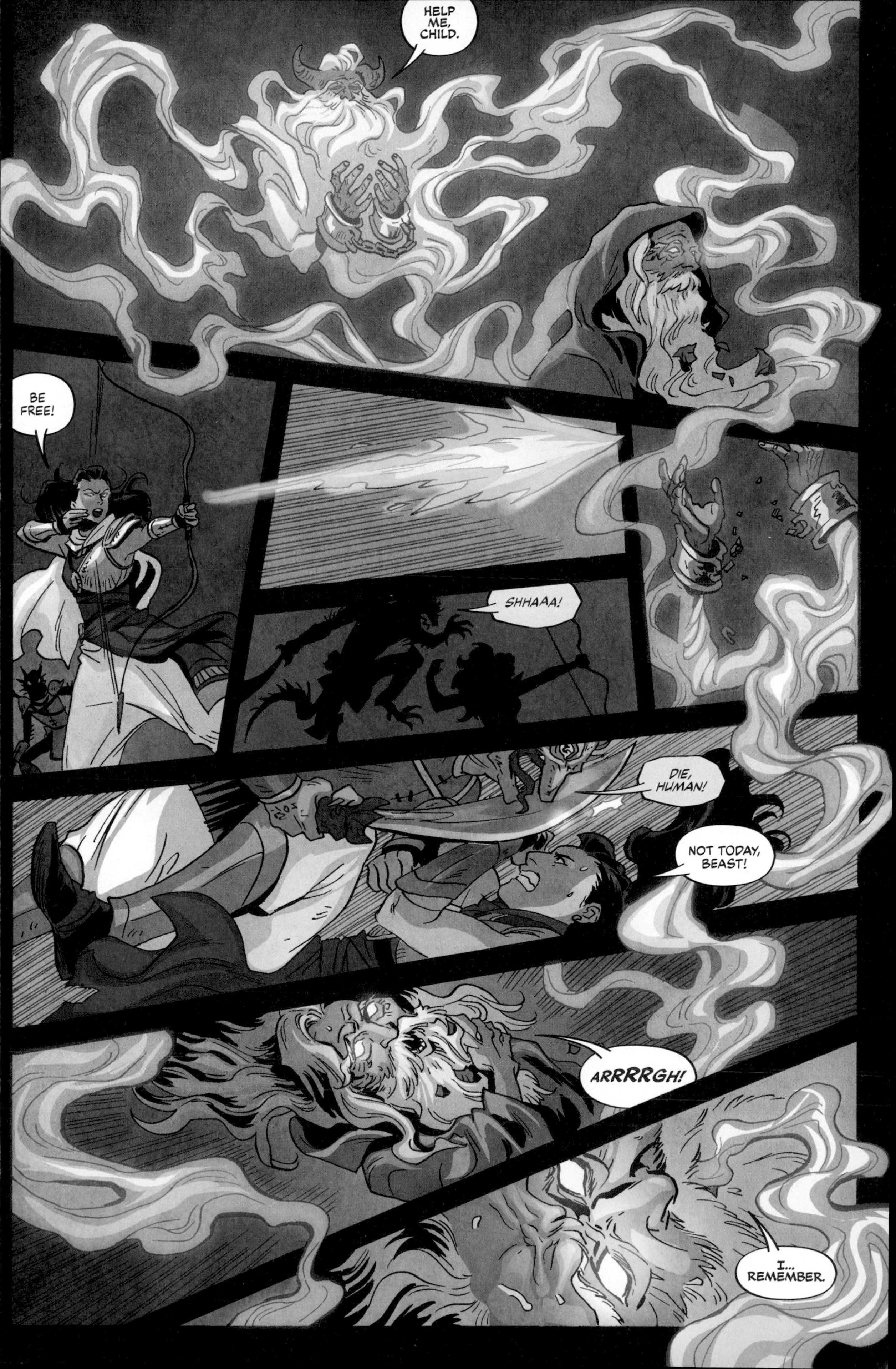
HELP ME, CHILD.
BE FREE!
SHHAAA!
DIE, HUMAN!
NOT TODAY, BEAST!
ARRRRGH!
I... REMEMBER.

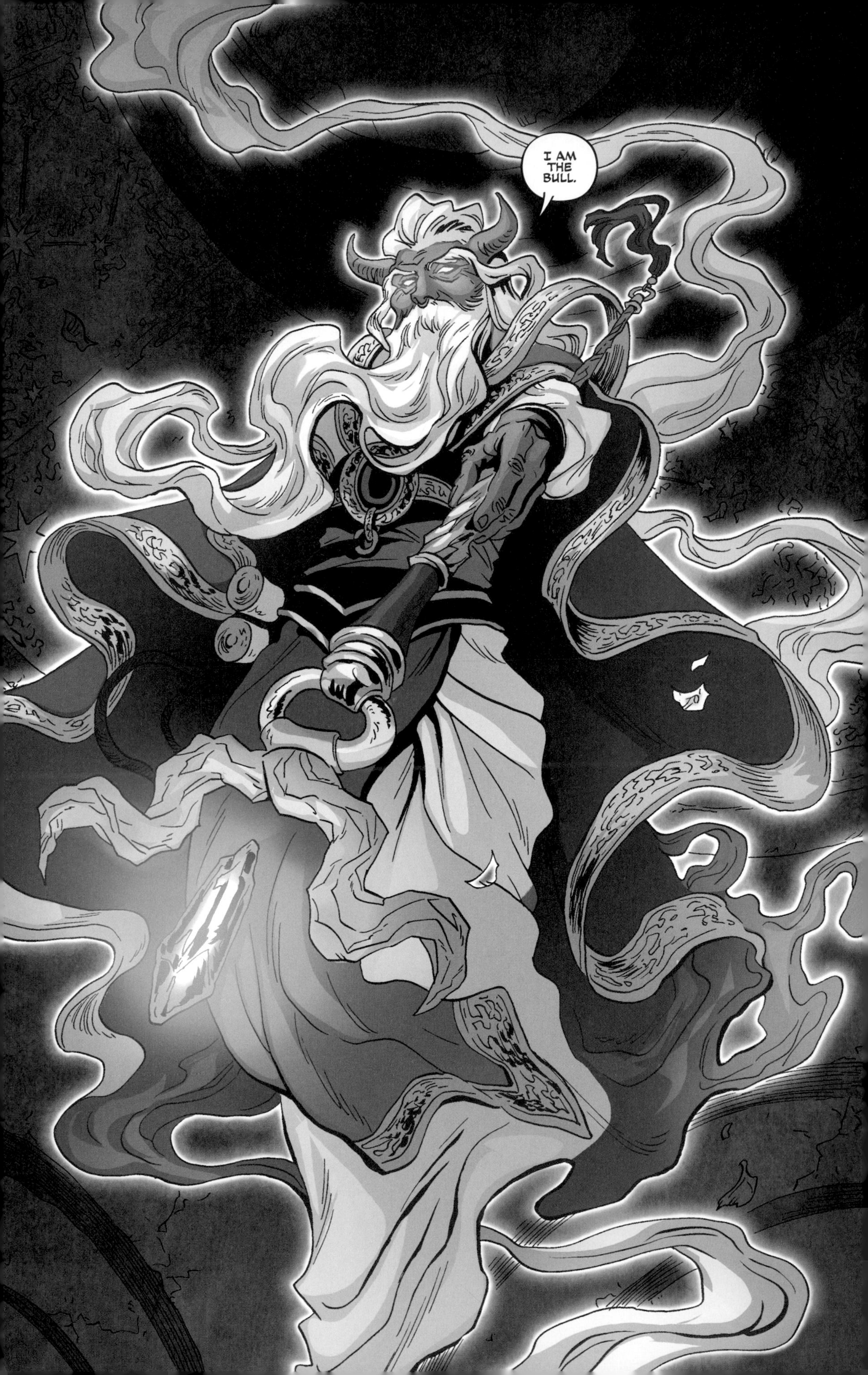
I AM THE BULL.

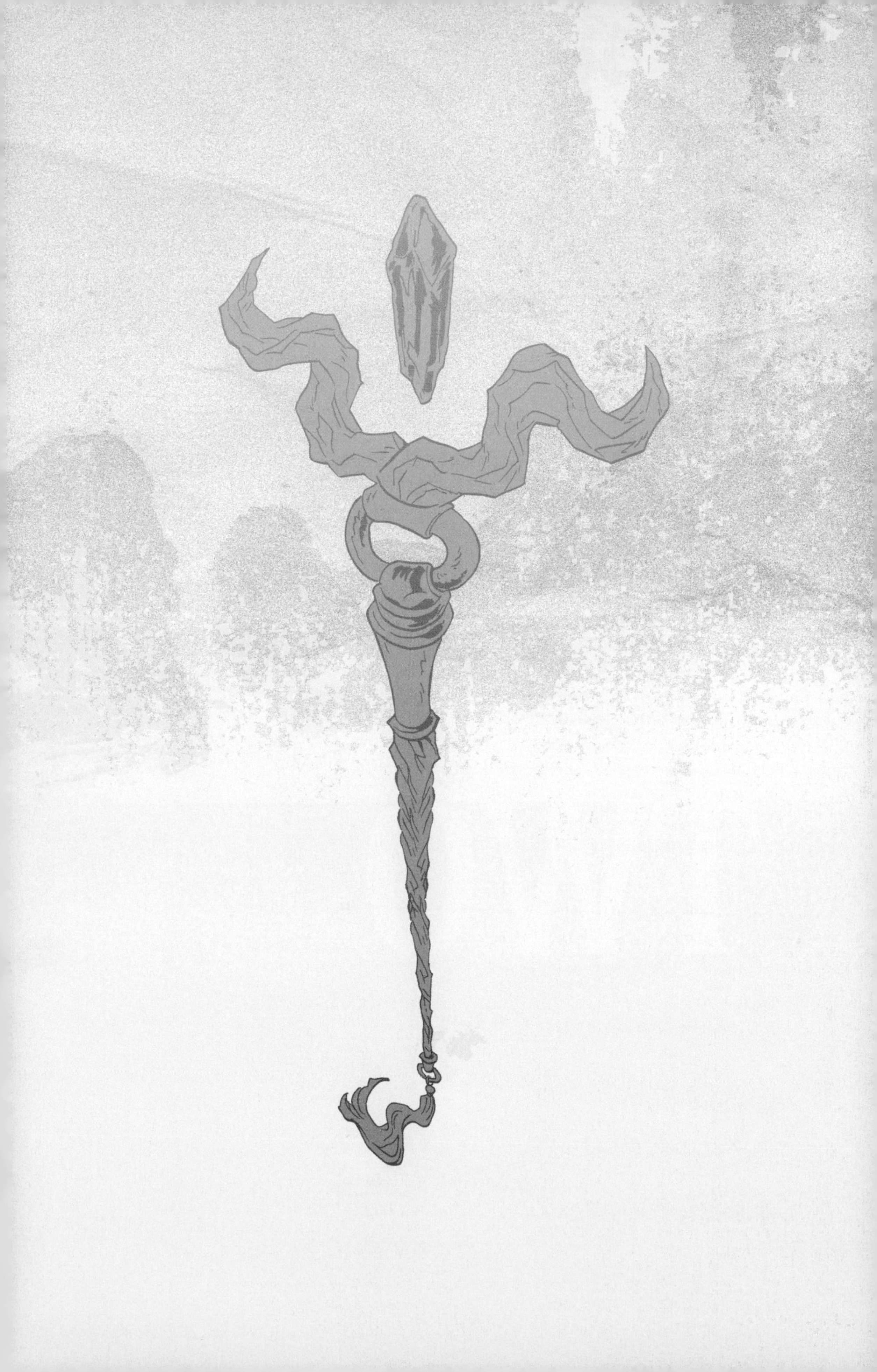

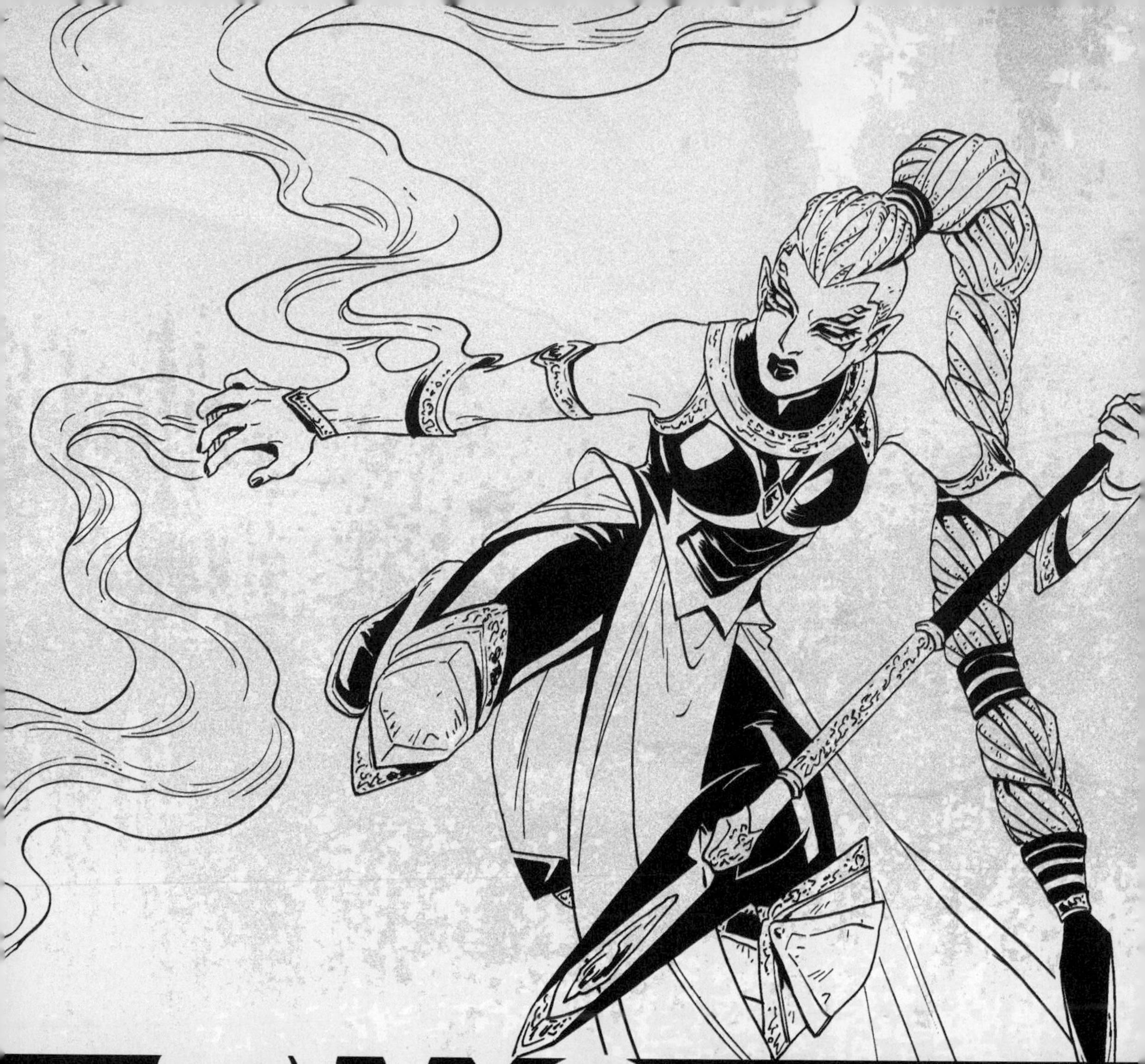

TWO

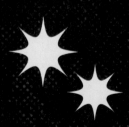

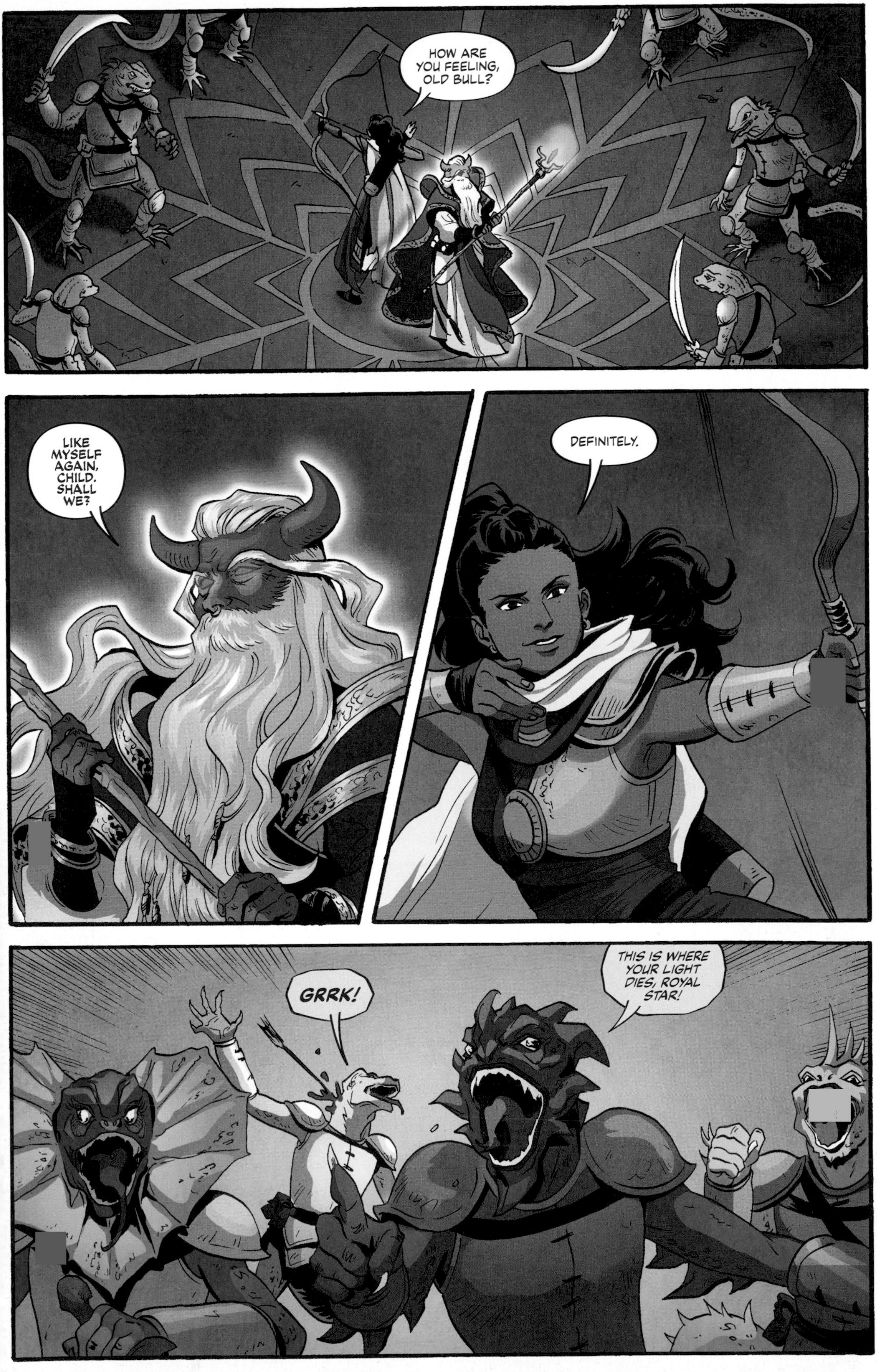
HOW ARE YOU FEELING, OLD BULL?
LIKE MYSELF AGAIN, CHILD. SHALL WE?
DEFINITELY.
GRRK!
THIS IS WHERE YOUR LIGHT DIES, ROYAL STAR!

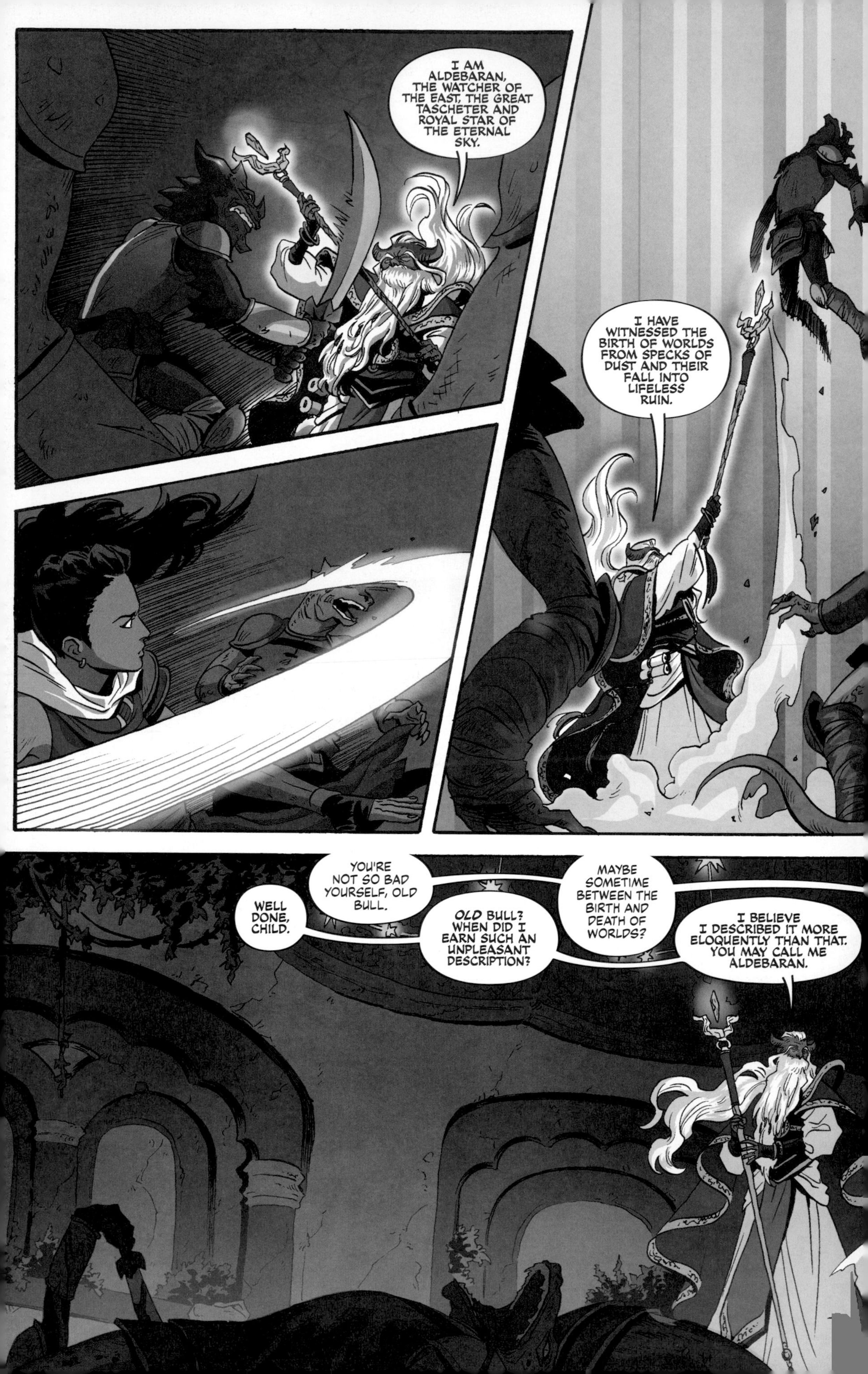
I AM ALDEBARAN, THE WATCHER OF THE EAST, THE GREAT TASCHETER AND ROYAL STAR OF THE ETERNAL SKY.
I HAVE WITNESSED THE BIRTH OF WORLDS FROM SPECKS OF DUST AND THEIR FALL INTO LIFELESS RUIN.
WELL DONE, CHILD.
YOU'RE NOT SO BAD YOURSELF, OLD BULL.
OLD BULL? WHEN DID I EARN SUCH AN UNPLEASANT DESCRIPTION?
MAYBE SOMETIME BETWEEN THE BIRTH AND DEATH OF WORLDS?
I BELIEVE I DESCRIBED IT MORE ELOQUENTLY THAN THAT. YOU MAY CALL ME ALDEBARAN.

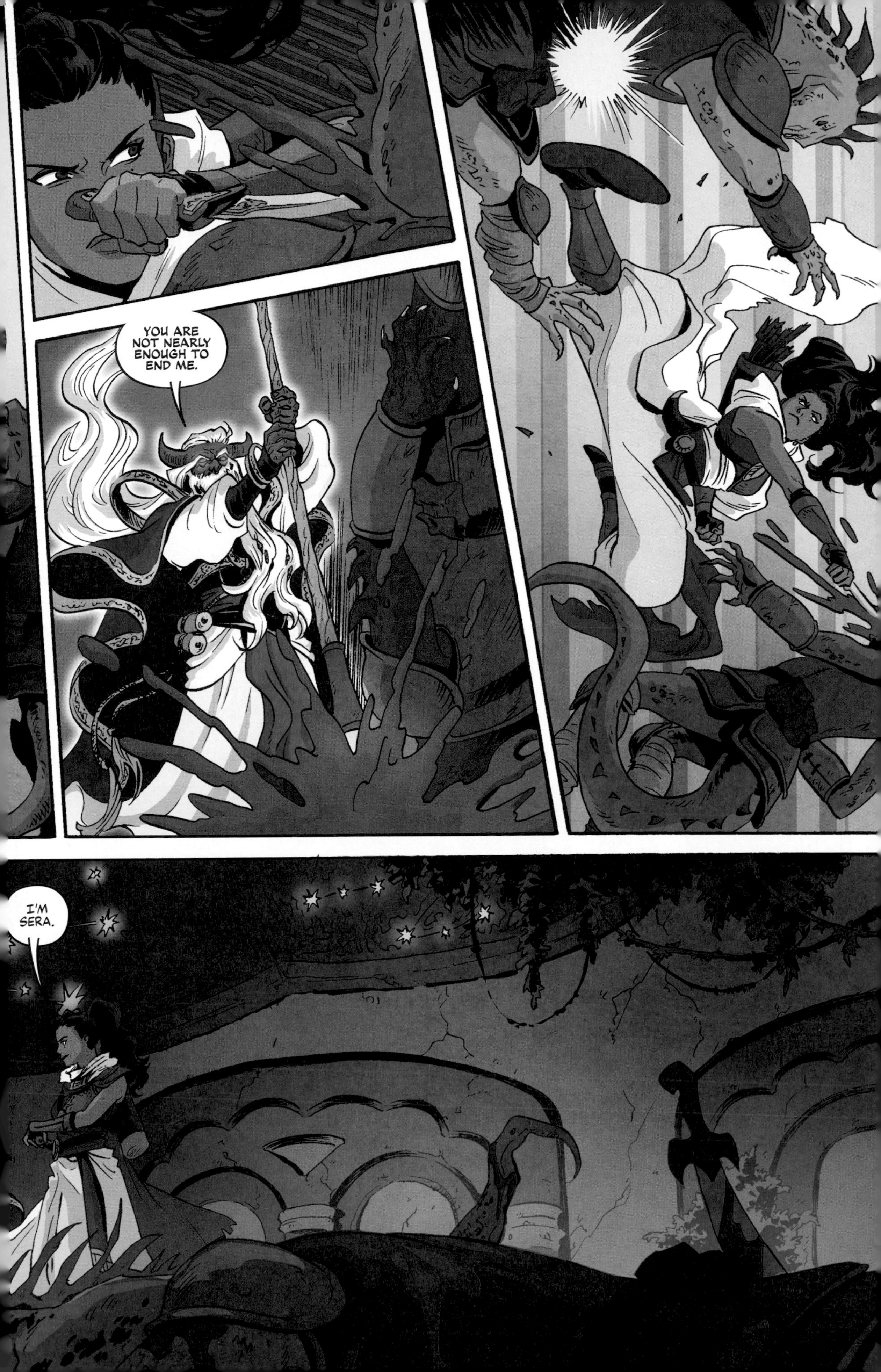
YOU ARE NOT NEARLY ENOUGH TO END ME.
I'M SERA.

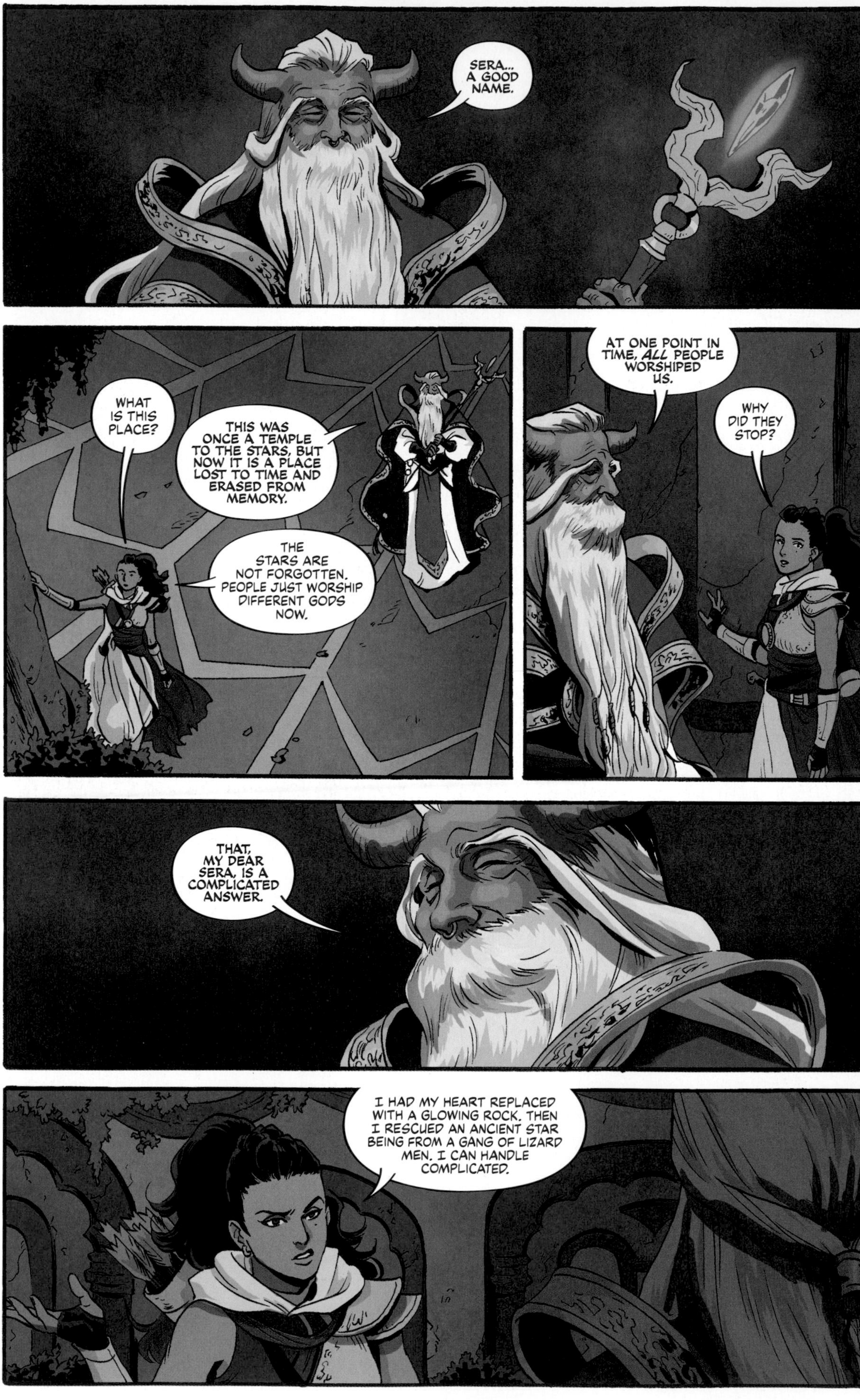
SERA... A GOOD NAME.
WHAT IS THIS PLACE?
THIS WAS ONCE A TEMPLE TO THE STARS, BUT NOW IT IS A PLACE LOST TO TIME AND ERASED FROM MEMORY.
THE STARS ARE NOT FORGOTTEN. PEOPLE JUST WORSHIP DIFFERENT GODS NOW.
AT ONE POINT IN TIME, ALL PEOPLE WORSHIPED US.
WHY DID THEY STOP?
THAT, MY DEAR SERA, IS A COMPLICATED ANSWER.
I HAD MY HEART REPLACED WITH A GLOWING ROCK. THEN I RESCUED AN ANCIENT STAR BEING FROM A GANG OF LIZARD MEN. I CAN HANDLE COMPLICATED.

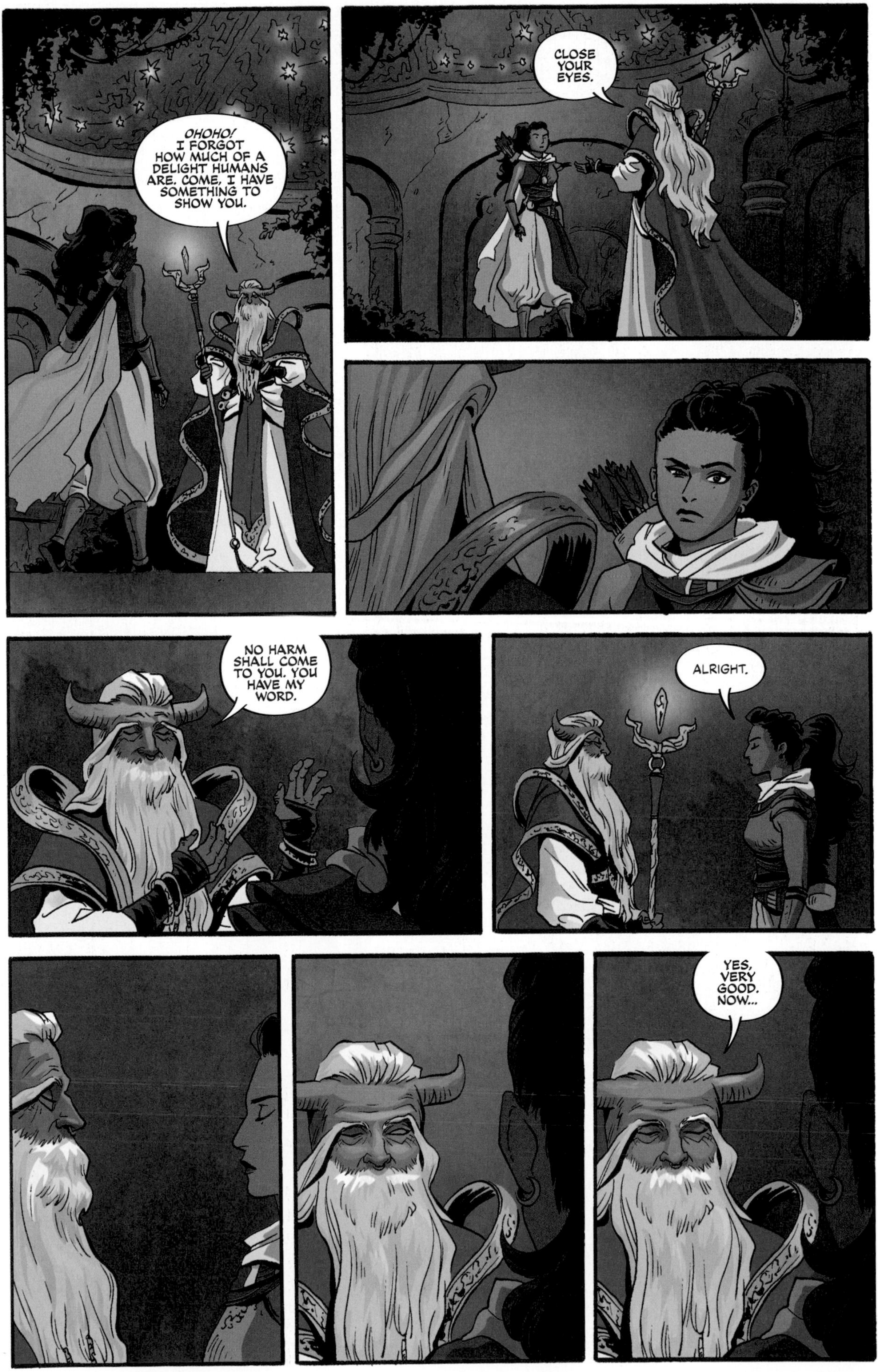
OHOHO! I FORGOT HOW MUCH OF A DELIGHT HUMANS ARE. COME, I HAVE SOMETHING TO SHOW YOU.
CLOSE YOUR EYES.
NO HARM SHALL COME TO YOU. YOU HAVE MY WORD.
ALRIGHT.
YES, VERY GOOD. NOW...

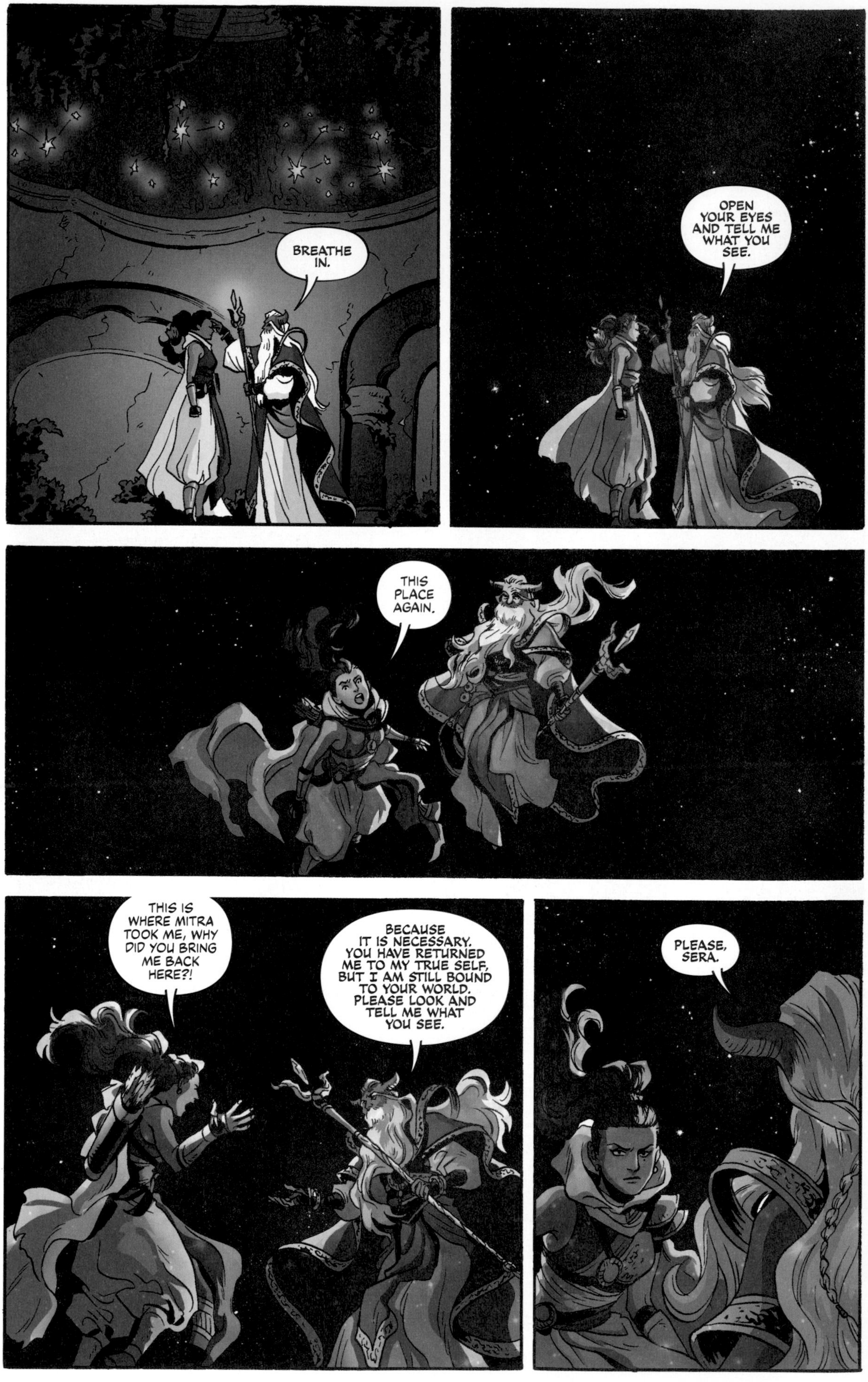
BREATHE IN.
OPEN YOUR EYES AND TELL ME WHAT YOU SEE.
THIS PLACE AGAIN.
THIS IS WHERE MITRA TOOK ME, WHY DID YOU BRING ME BACK HERE?!
BECAUSE IT IS NECESSARY. YOU HAVE RETURNED ME TO MY TRUE SELF, BUT I AM STILL BOUND TO YOUR WORLD. PLEASE LOOK AND TELL ME WHAT YOU SEE.
PLEASE, SERA.

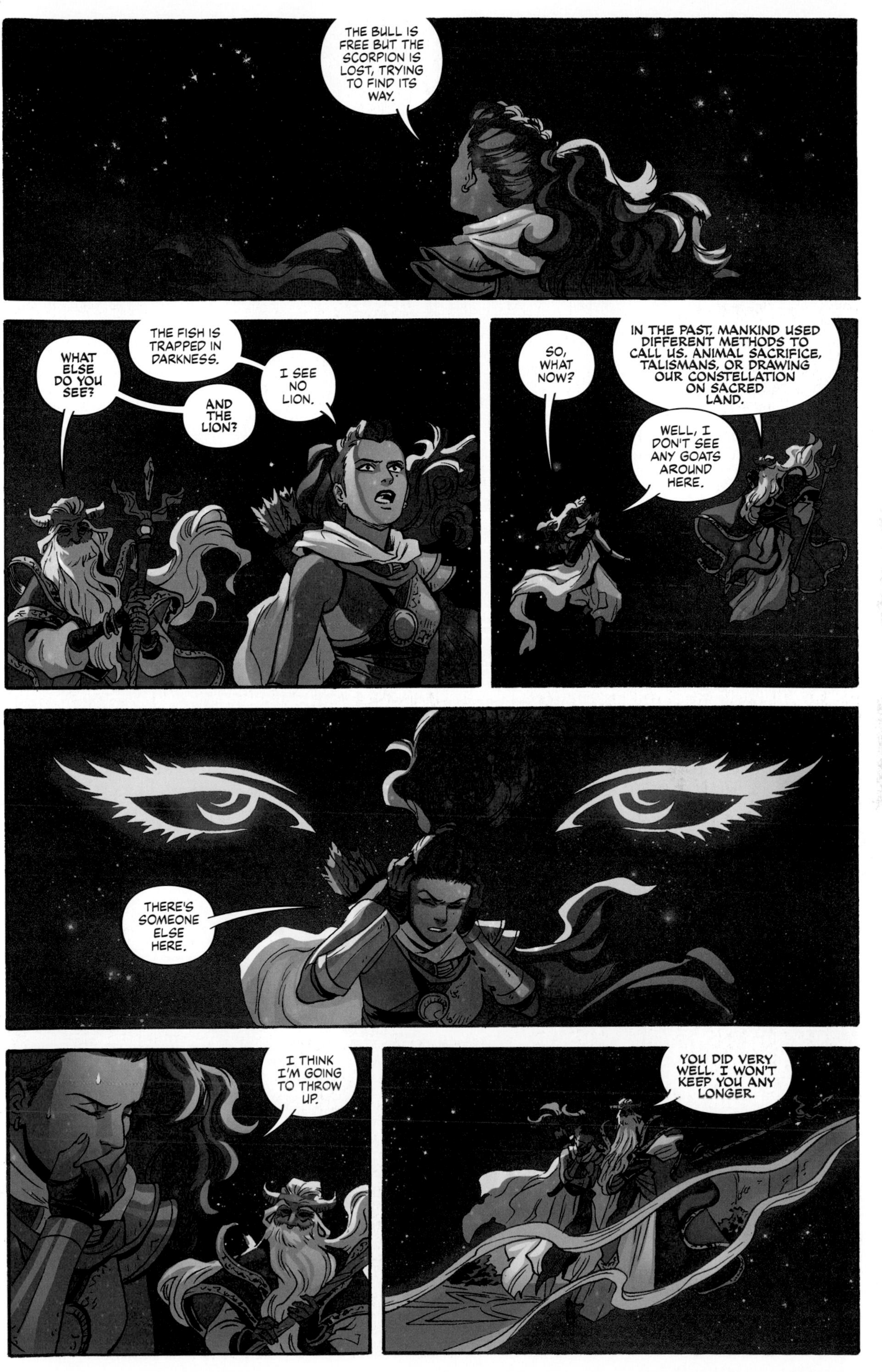
THE BULL IS FREE BUT THE SCORPION IS LOST, TRYING TO FIND ITS WAY.
WHAT ELSE DO YOU SEE?
THE FISH IS TRAPPED IN DARKNESS.
AND THE LION?
I SEE NO LION.
SO, WHAT NOW?
IN THE PAST, MANKIND USED DIFFERENT METHODS TO CALL US. ANIMAL SACRIFICE, TALISMANS, OR DRAWING OUR CONSTELLATION ON SACRED LAND.
WELL, I DON'T SEE ANY GOATS AROUND HERE.
THERE'S SOMEONE ELSE HERE.
I THINK I'M GOING TO THROW UP.
YOU DID VERY WELL. I WON'T KEEP YOU ANY LONGER.

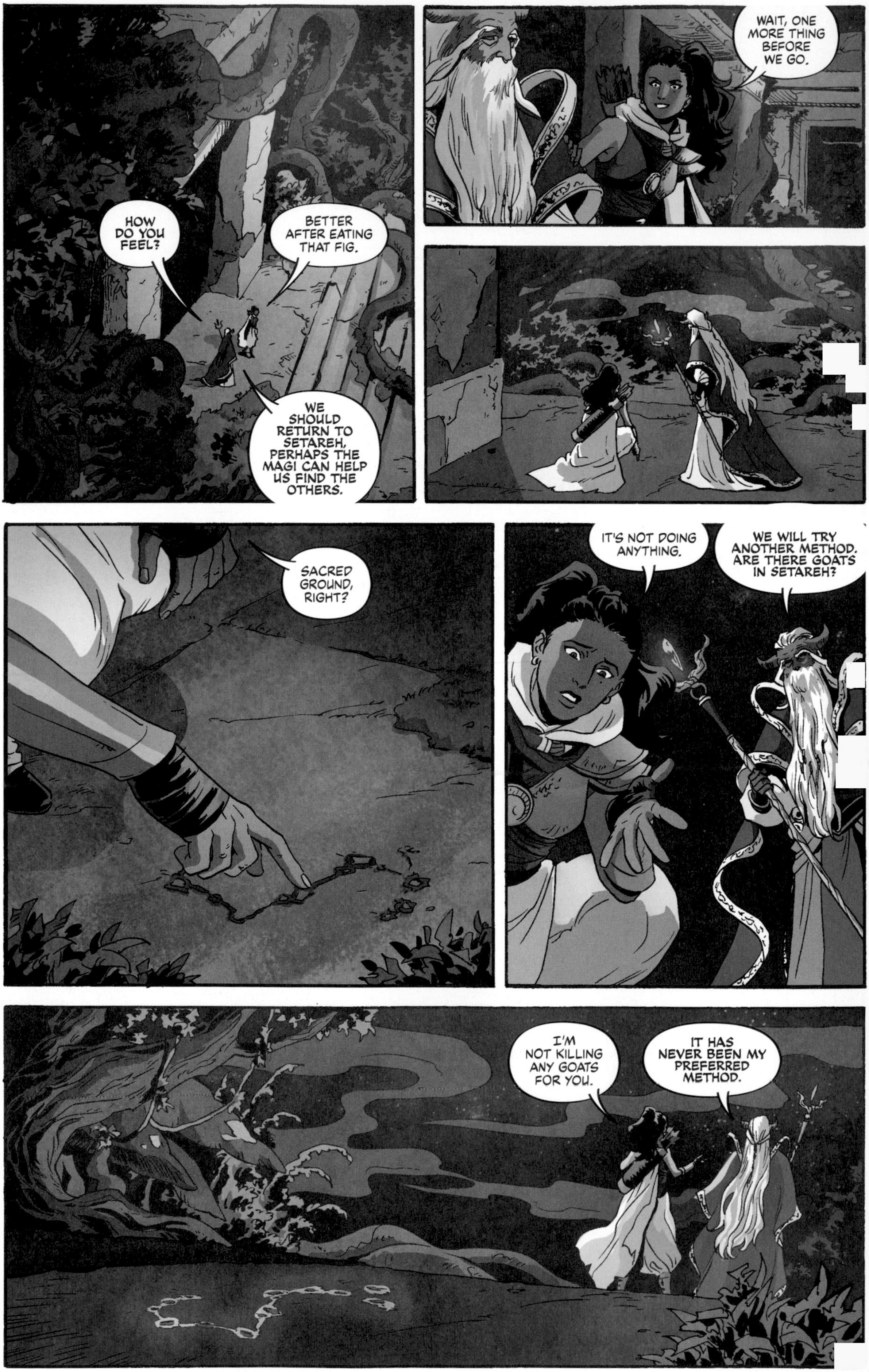
HOW DO YOU FEEL?
BETTER AFTER EATING THAT FIG.
WE SHOULD RETURN TO SETAREH, PERHAPS THE MAGI CAN HELP US FIND THE OTHERS.
WAIT, ONE MORE THING BEFORE WE GO.
SACRED GROUND, RIGHT?
IT'S NOT DOING ANYTHING.
WE WILL TRY ANOTHER METHOD. ARE THERE GOATS IN SETAREH?
I'M NOT KILLING ANY GOATS FOR YOU.
IT HAS NEVER BEEN MY PREFERRED METHOD.

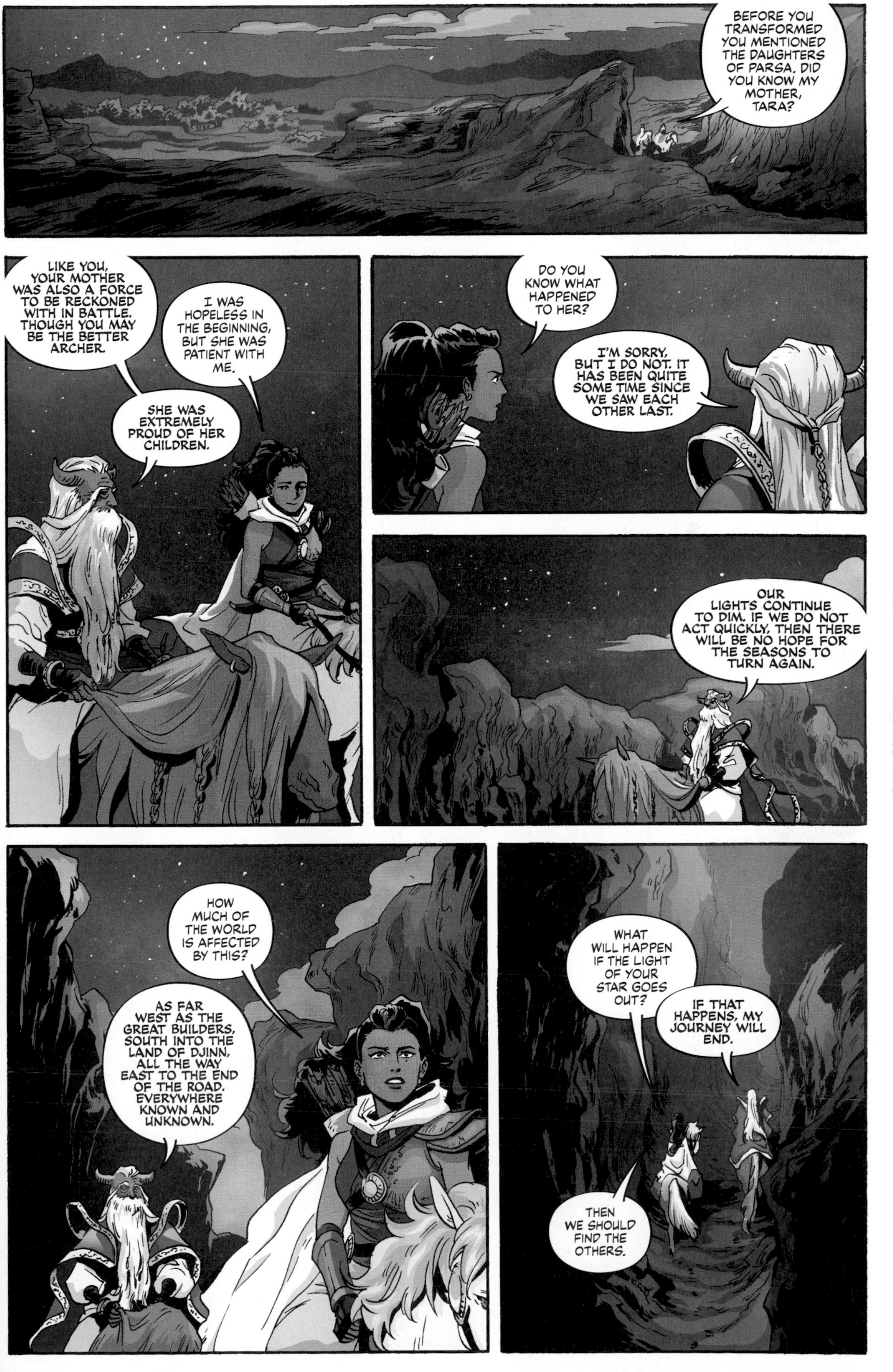
BEFORE YOU TRANSFORMED YOU MENTIONED THE DAUGHTERS OF PARSA. DID YOU KNOW MY MOTHER, TARA?
LIKE YOU, YOUR MOTHER WAS ALSO A FORCE TO BE RECKONED WITH IN BATTLE. THOUGH YOU MAY BE THE BETTER ARCHER.
I WAS HOPELESS IN THE BEGINNING, BUT SHE WAS PATIENT WITH ME.
SHE WAS EXTREMELY PROUD OF HER CHILDREN.
DO YOU KNOW WHAT HAPPENED TO HER?
I'M SORRY, BUT I DO NOT. IT HAS BEEN QUITE SOME TIME SINCE WE SAW EACH OTHER LAST.
OUR LIGHTS CONTINUE TO DIM. IF WE DO NOT ACT QUICKLY, THEN THERE WILL BE NO HOPE FOR THE SEASONS TO TURN AGAIN.
HOW MUCH OF THE WORLD IS AFFECTED BY THIS?
AS FAR WEST AS THE GREAT BUILDERS, SOUTH INTO THE LAND OF DJINN, ALL THE WAY EAST TO THE END OF THE ROAD. EVERYWHERE KNOWN AND UNKNOWN.
WHAT WILL HAPPEN IF THE LIGHT OF YOUR STAR GOES OUT?
IF THAT HAPPENS, MY JOURNEY WILL END.
THEN WE SHOULD FIND THE OTHERS.

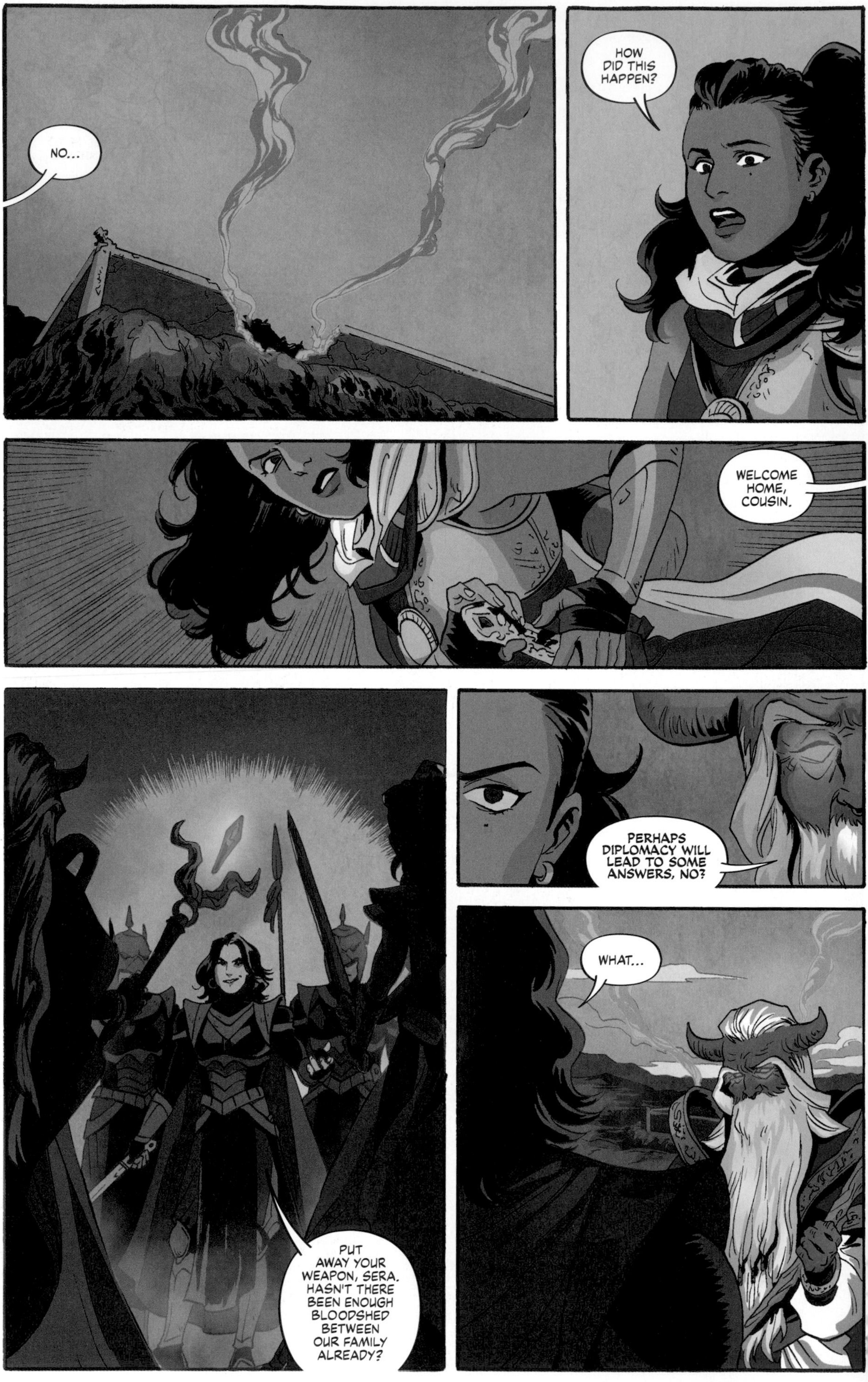
NO...
HOW DID THIS HAPPEN?
WELCOME HOME, COUSIN.
PUT AWAY YOUR WEAPON, SERA. HASN'T THERE BEEN ENOUGH BLOODSHED BETWEEN OUR FAMILY ALREADY?
PERHAPS DIPLOMACY WILL LEAD TO SOME ANSWERS, NO?
WHAT...

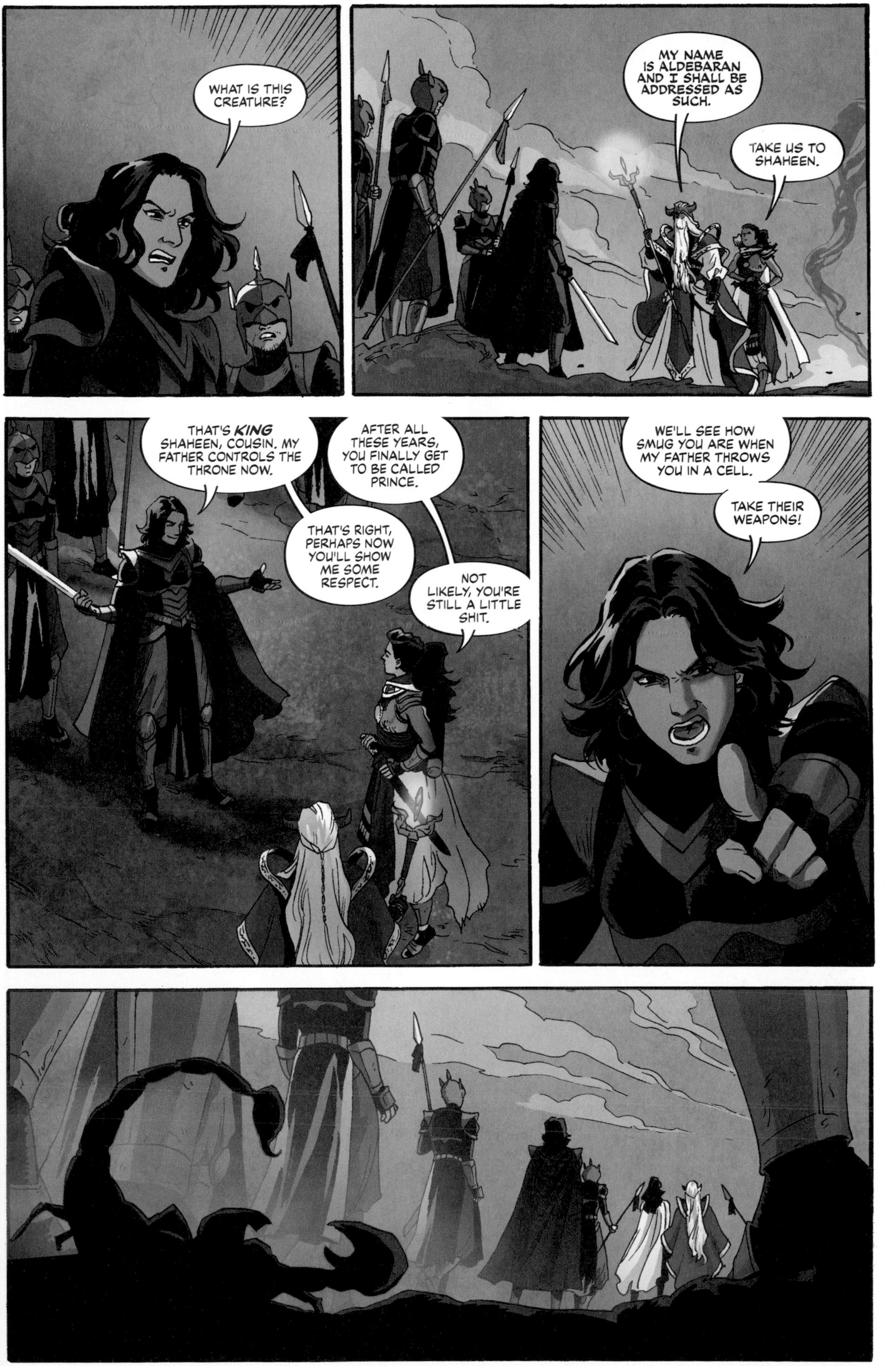

WHAT IS THIS CREATURE?
MY NAME IS ALDEBARAN AND I SHALL BE ADDRESSED AS SUCH.
TAKE US TO SHAHEEN.
THAT'S *KING* SHAHEEN, COUSIN. MY FATHER CONTROLS THE THRONE NOW.
AFTER ALL THESE YEARS, YOU FINALLY GET TO BE CALLED PRINCE.
THAT'S RIGHT, PERHAPS NOW YOU'LL SHOW ME SOME RESPECT.
NOT LIKELY, YOU'RE STILL A LITTLE SHIT.
WE'LL SEE HOW SMUG YOU ARE WHEN MY FATHER THROWS YOU IN A CELL.
TAKE THEIR WEAPONS!

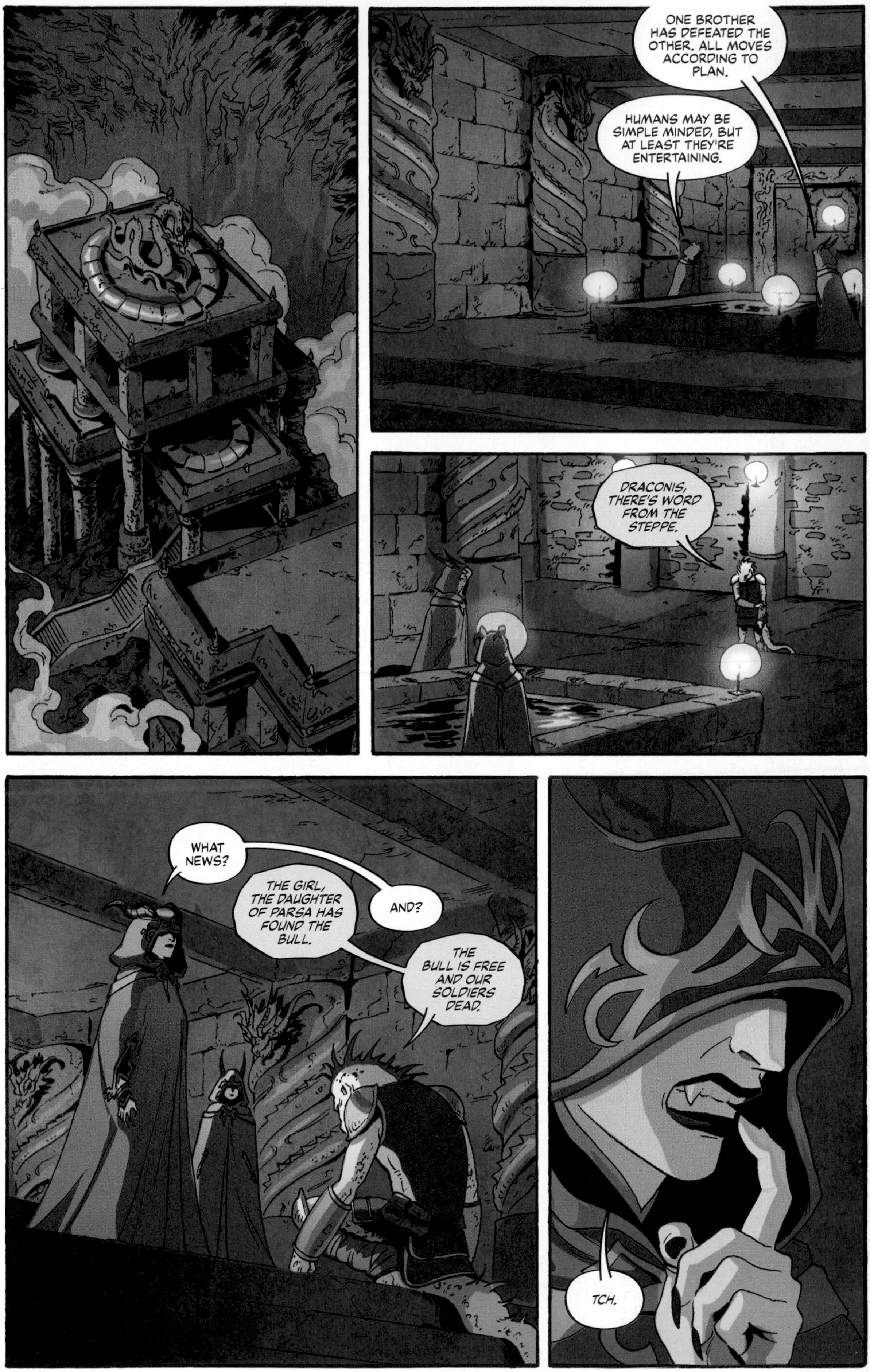
ONE BROTHER HAS DEFEATED THE OTHER. ALL MOVES ACCORDING TO PLAN.
HUMANS MAY BE SIMPLE MINDED, BUT AT LEAST THEY'RE ENTERTAINING.
DRACONIS, THERE'S WORD FROM THE STEPPE.
WHAT NEWS?
THE GIRL, THE DAUGHTER OF PARSA HAS FOUND THE BULL.
AND?
THE BULL IS FREE AND OUR SOLDIERS DEAD.
TCH.

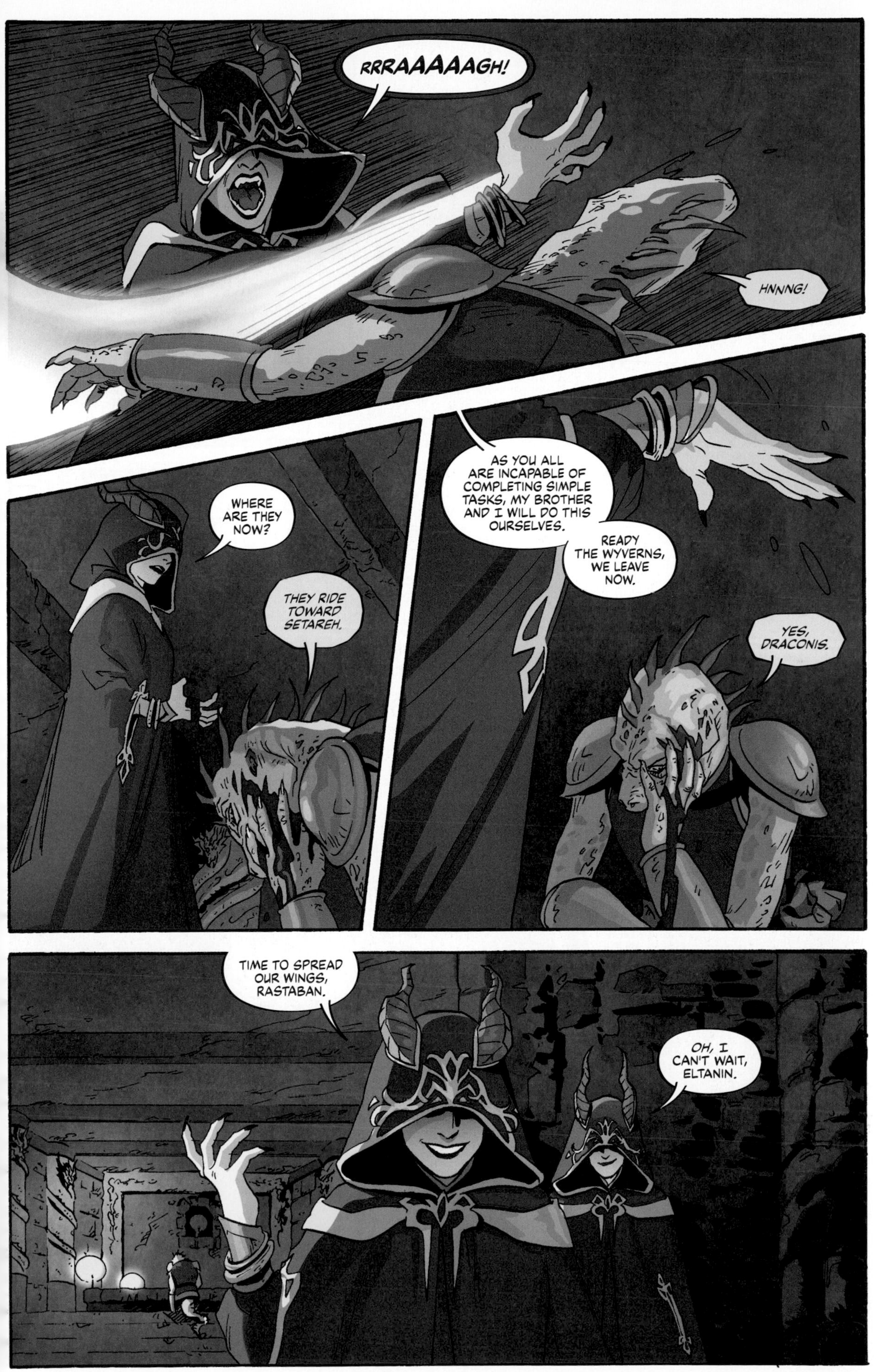
RRRAAAAAAGH!
HNNNG!
WHERE ARE THEY NOW?
THEY RIDE TOWARD SETAREH.
AS YOU ALL ARE INCAPABLE OF COMPLETING SIMPLE TASKS, MY BROTHER AND I WILL DO THIS OURSELVES.
READY THE WYVERNS, WE LEAVE NOW.
YES, DRACONIS.
TIME TO SPREAD OUR WINGS, RASTABAN.
OH, I CAN'T WAIT, ELTANIN.

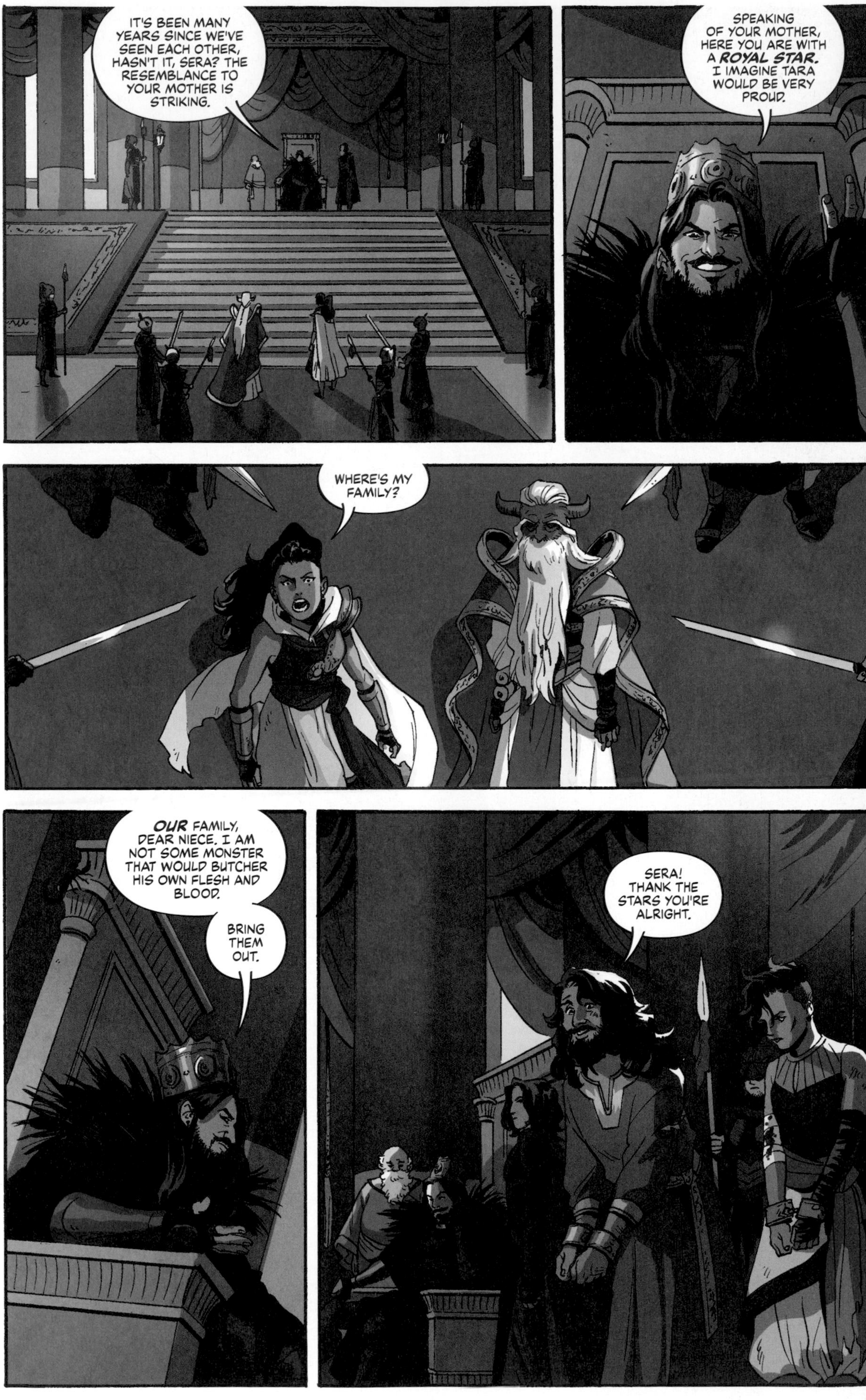
IT'S BEEN MANY YEARS SINCE WE'VE SEEN EACH OTHER, HASN'T IT, SERA? THE RESEMBLANCE TO YOUR MOTHER IS STRIKING.
SPEAKING OF YOUR MOTHER, HERE YOU ARE WITH A ROYAL STAR. I IMAGINE TARA WOULD BE VERY PROUD.
WHERE'S MY FAMILY?
OUR FAMILY, DEAR NIECE. I AM NOT SOME MONSTER THAT WOULD BUTCHER HIS OWN FLESH AND BLOOD.
BRING THEM OUT.
SERA! THANK THE STARS YOU'RE ALRIGHT.

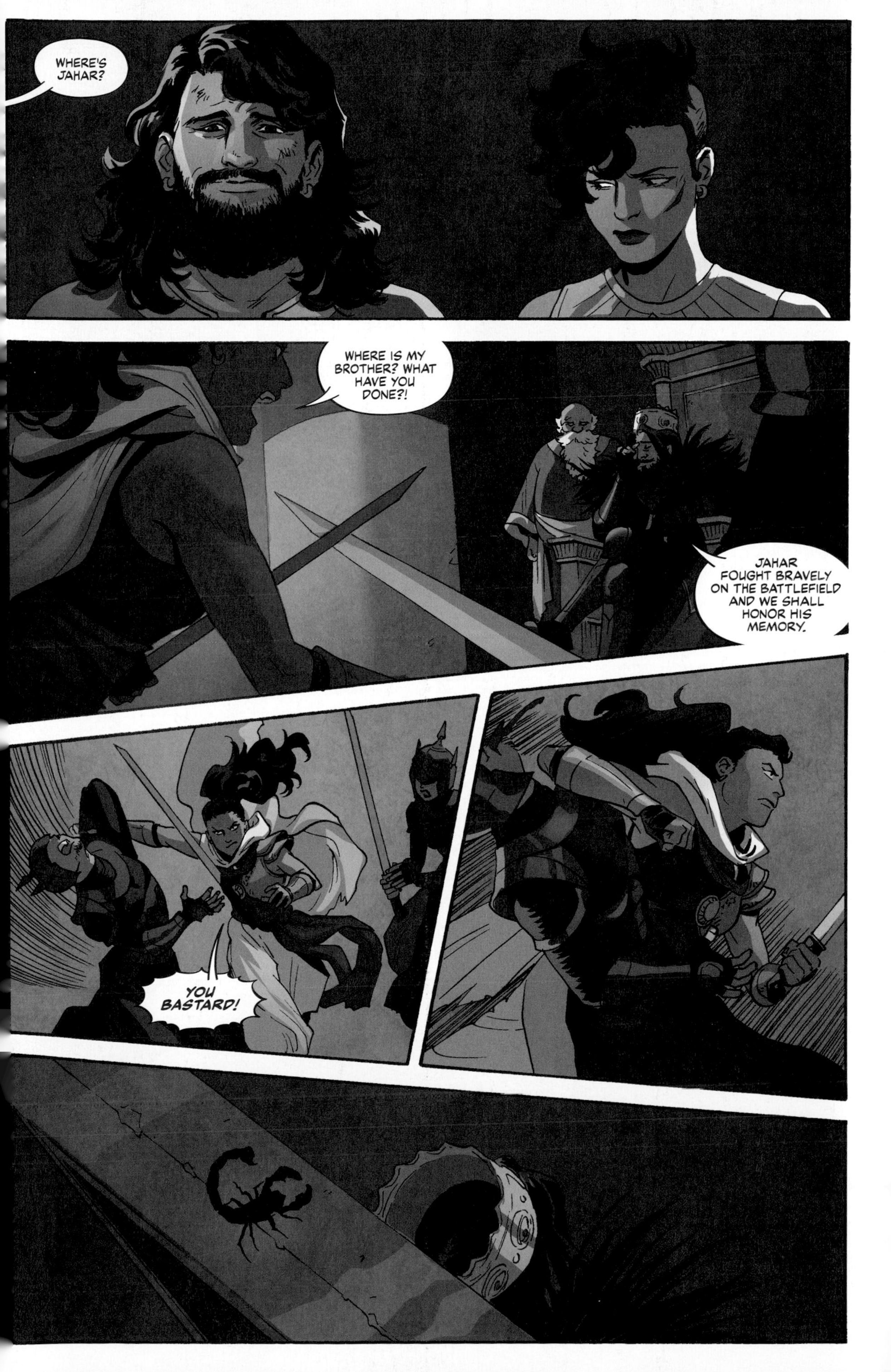
WHERE'S JAHAR?
WHERE IS MY BROTHER? WHAT HAVE YOU DONE?!
JAHAR FOUGHT BRAVELY ON THE BATTLEFIELD AND WE SHALL HONOR HIS MEMORY.
YOU BASTARD!

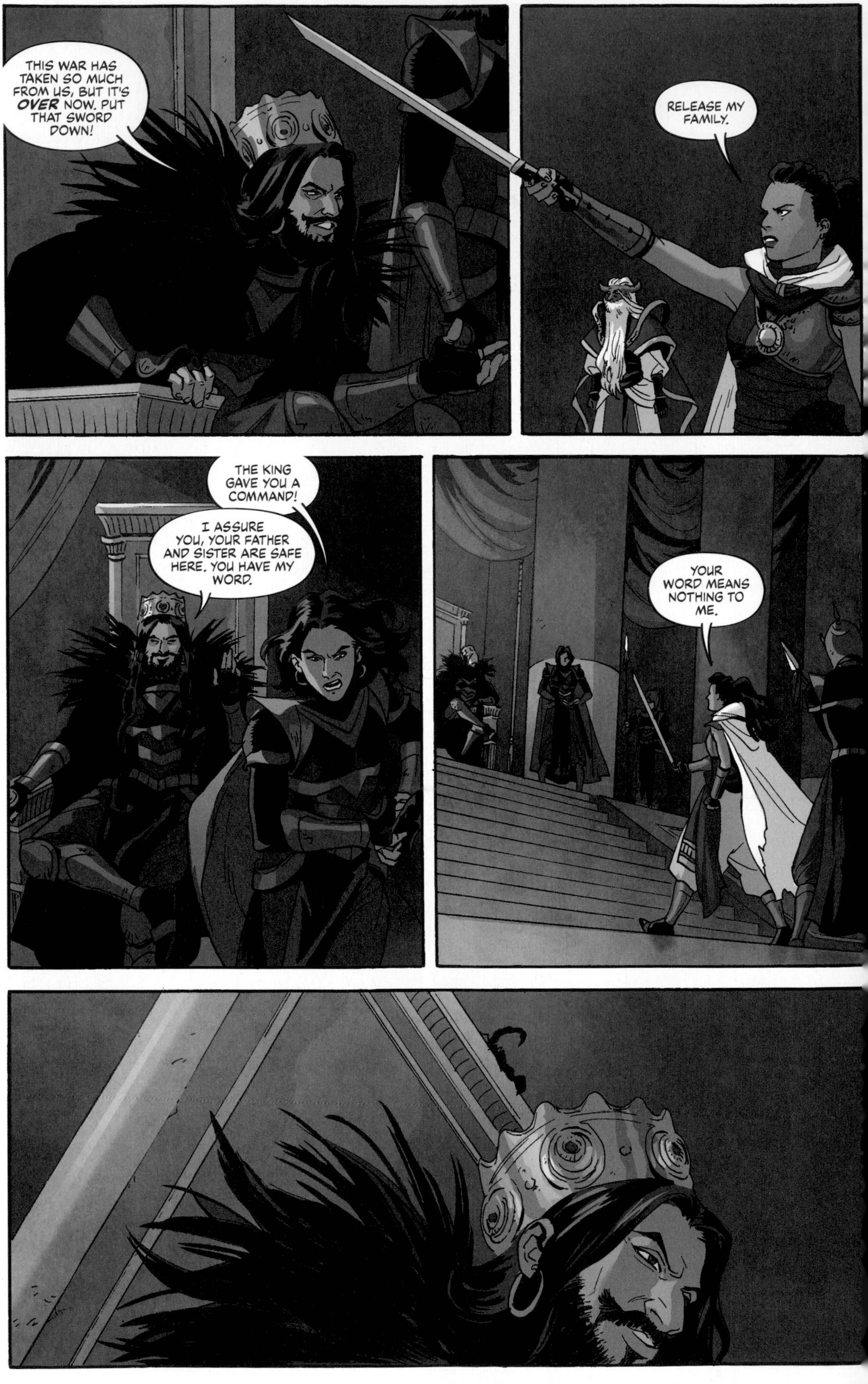
THIS WAR HAS TAKEN SO MUCH FROM US, BUT IT'S **OVER** NOW. PUT THAT SWORD DOWN!
RELEASE MY FAMILY.
THE KING GAVE YOU A COMMAND!
I ASSURE YOU, YOUR FATHER AND SISTER ARE SAFE HERE. YOU HAVE MY WORD.
YOUR WORD MEANS NOTHING TO ME.

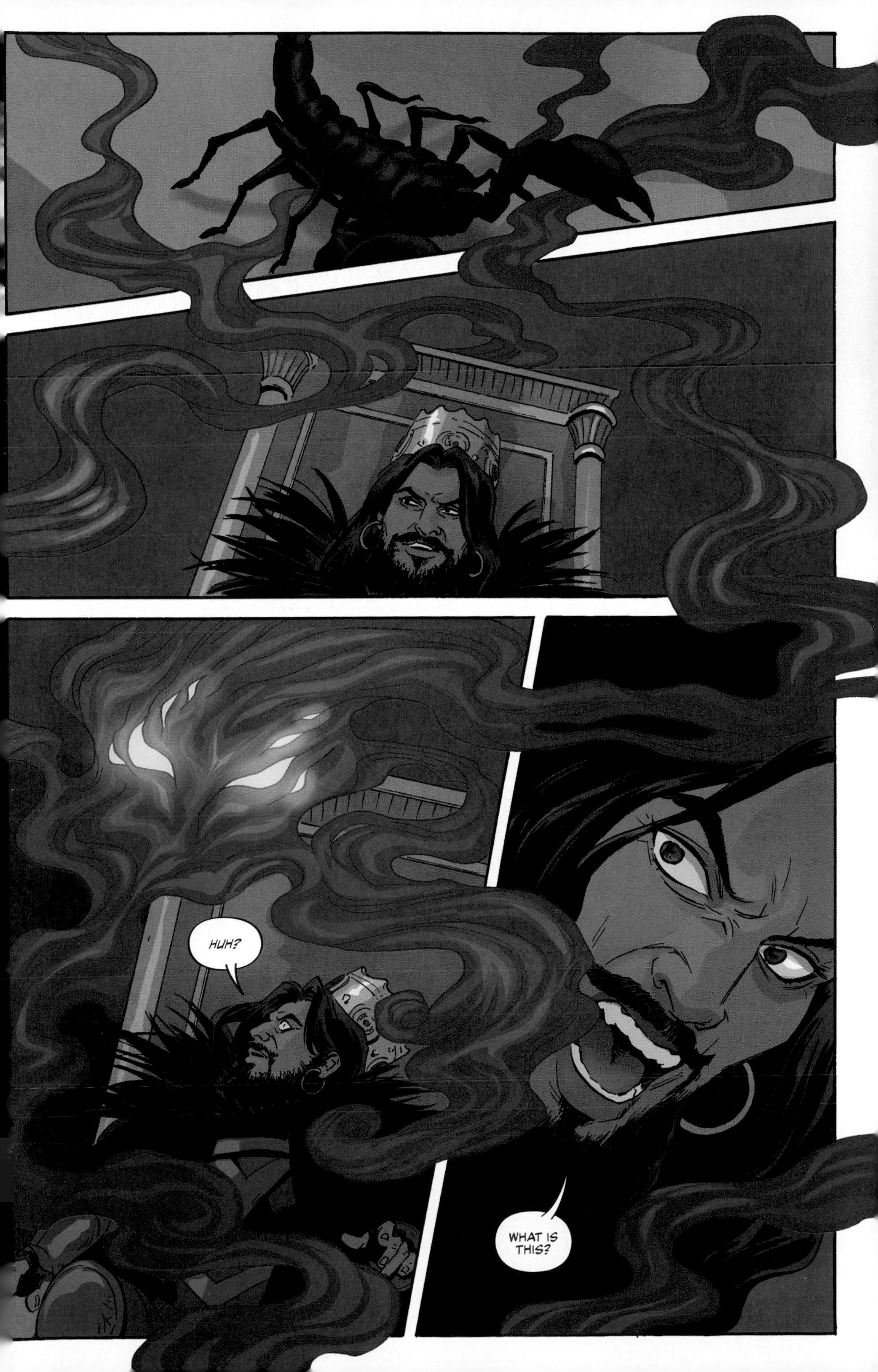
HUH?
WHAT IS THIS?

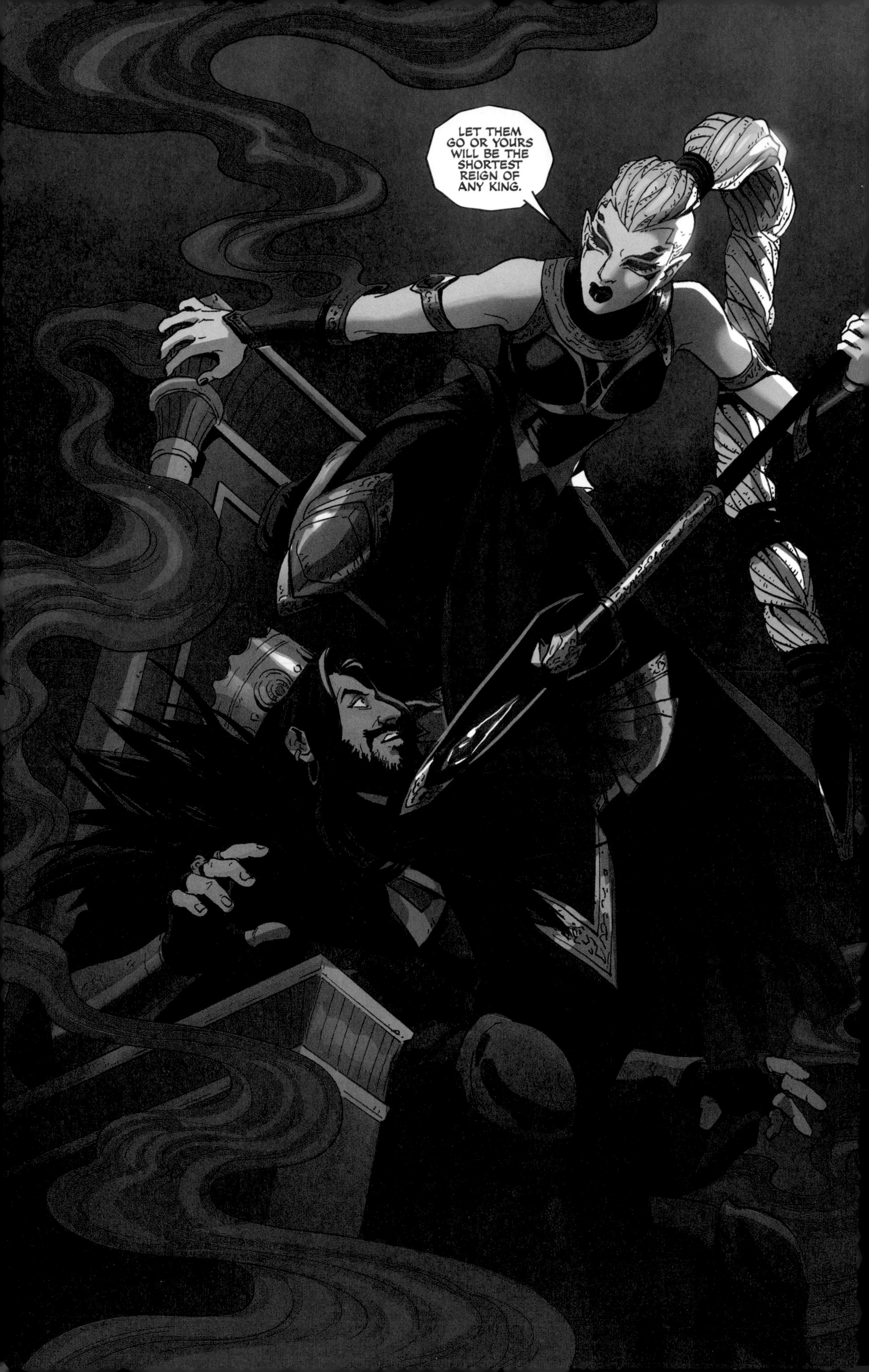
LET THEM GO OR YOURS WILL BE THE SHORTEST REIGN OF ANY KING.

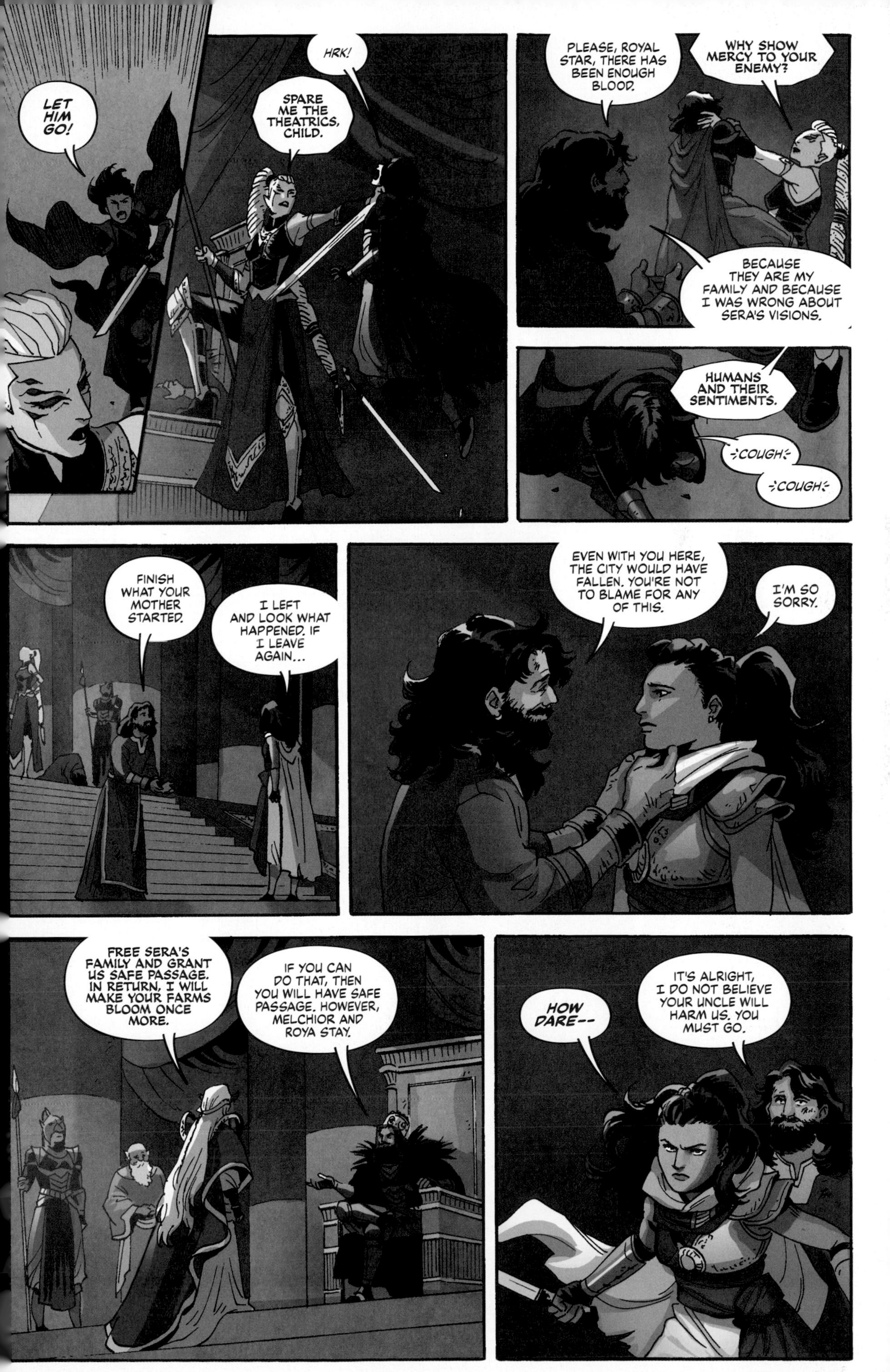
LET HIM GO!
HRK!
SPARE ME THE THEATRICS, CHILD.
PLEASE, ROYAL STAR, THERE HAS BEEN ENOUGH BLOOD.
WHY SHOW MERCY TO YOUR ENEMY?
BECAUSE THEY ARE MY FAMILY AND BECAUSE I WAS WRONG ABOUT SERA'S VISIONS.
HUMANS AND THEIR SENTIMENTS.
COUGH
COUGH
FINISH WHAT YOUR MOTHER STARTED.
I LEFT AND LOOK WHAT HAPPENED. IF I LEAVE AGAIN...
EVEN WITH YOU HERE, THE CITY WOULD HAVE FALLEN. YOU'RE NOT TO BLAME FOR ANY OF THIS.
I'M SO SORRY.
FREE SERA'S FAMILY AND GRANT US SAFE PASSAGE. IN RETURN, I WILL MAKE YOUR FARMS BLOOM ONCE MORE.
IF YOU CAN DO THAT, THEN YOU WILL HAVE SAFE PASSAGE. HOWEVER, MELCHIOR AND ROYA STAY.
HOW DARE--
IT'S ALRIGHT, I DO NOT BELIEVE YOUR UNCLE WILL HARM US. YOU MUST GO.

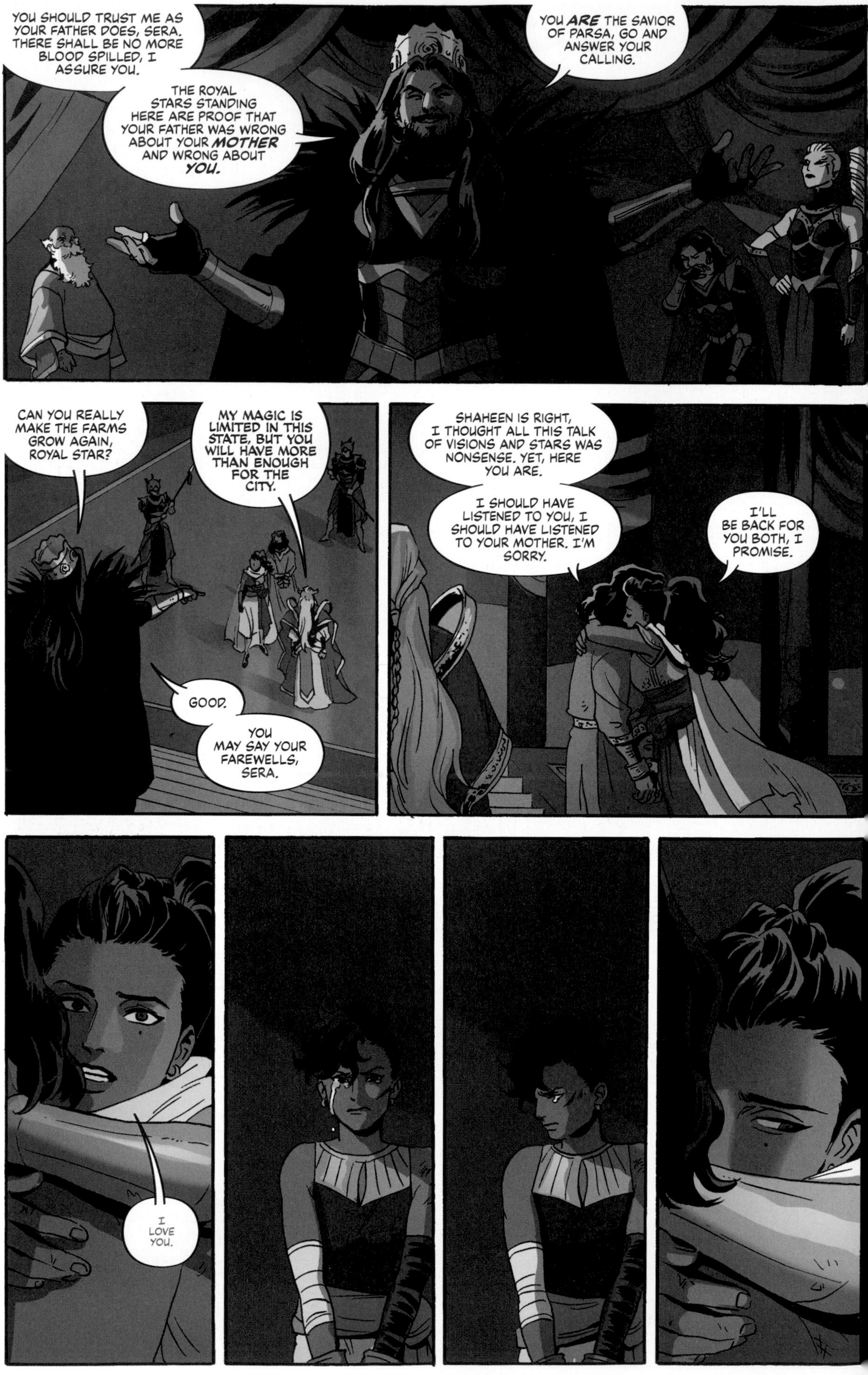
YOU SHOULD TRUST ME AS YOUR FATHER DOES, SERA. THERE SHALL BE NO MORE BLOOD SPILLED, I ASSURE YOU.
THE ROYAL STARS STANDING HERE ARE PROOF THAT YOUR FATHER WAS WRONG ABOUT YOUR MOTHER AND WRONG ABOUT YOU.
YOU ARE THE SAVIOR OF PARSA, GO AND ANSWER YOUR CALLING.
CAN YOU REALLY MAKE THE FARMS GROW AGAIN, ROYAL STAR?
MY MAGIC IS LIMITED IN THIS STATE, BUT YOU WILL HAVE MORE THAN ENOUGH FOR THE CITY.
GOOD.
YOU MAY SAY YOUR FAREWELLS, SERA.
SHAHEEN IS RIGHT, I THOUGHT ALL THIS TALK OF VISIONS AND STARS WAS NONSENSE. YET, HERE YOU ARE.
I SHOULD HAVE LISTENED TO YOU, I SHOULD HAVE LISTENED TO YOUR MOTHER. I'M SORRY.
I'LL BE BACK FOR YOU BOTH, I PROMISE.
I LOVE YOU.

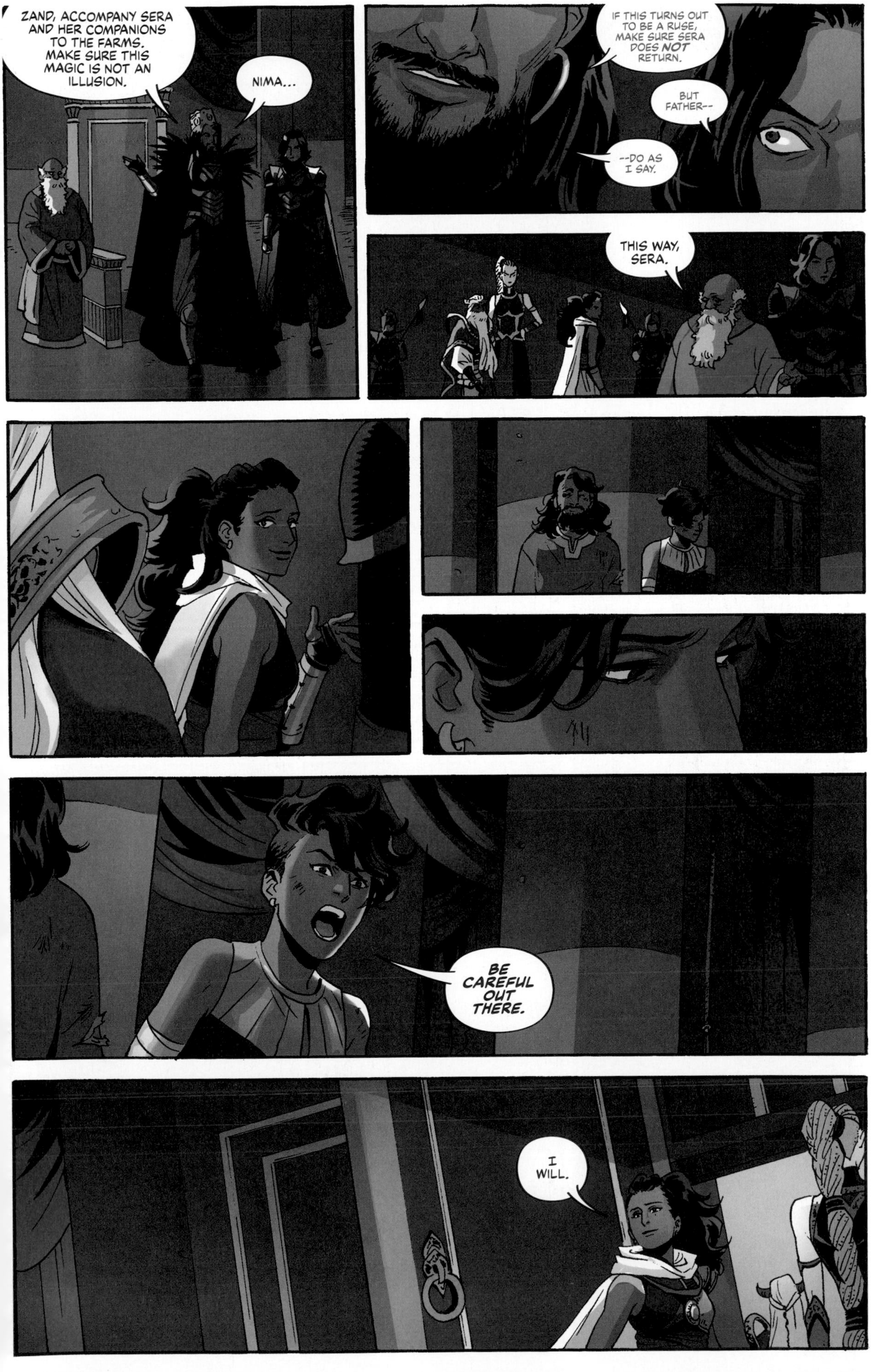
ZAND, ACCOMPANY SERA AND HER COMPANIONS TO THE FARMS. MAKE SURE THIS MAGIC IS NOT AN ILLUSION.
NIMA...
IF THIS TURNS OUT TO BE A RUSE, MAKE SURE SERA DOES NOT RETURN.
BUT FATHER--
--DO AS I SAY.
THIS WAY, SERA.
BE CAREFUL OUT THERE.
I WILL.

WE'RE HERE.

DO YOU HAVE THE STRENGTH TO PULL THIS OFF, ALDEBARAN?

IF YOUNG SERA ASSISTS, THEN YES, ANTARES.

ME?

PICTURE IN YOUR MIND THE SPROUTING OF A SEEDLING THROUGH THE SOIL AND HOLD THAT IMAGE.

AND THEN WHAT?

CONCENTRATE ON THE ONE IMAGE, ALLOW ALL OTHER THOUGHTS TO FALL AWAY.

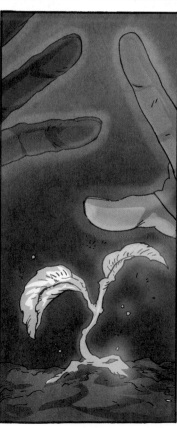

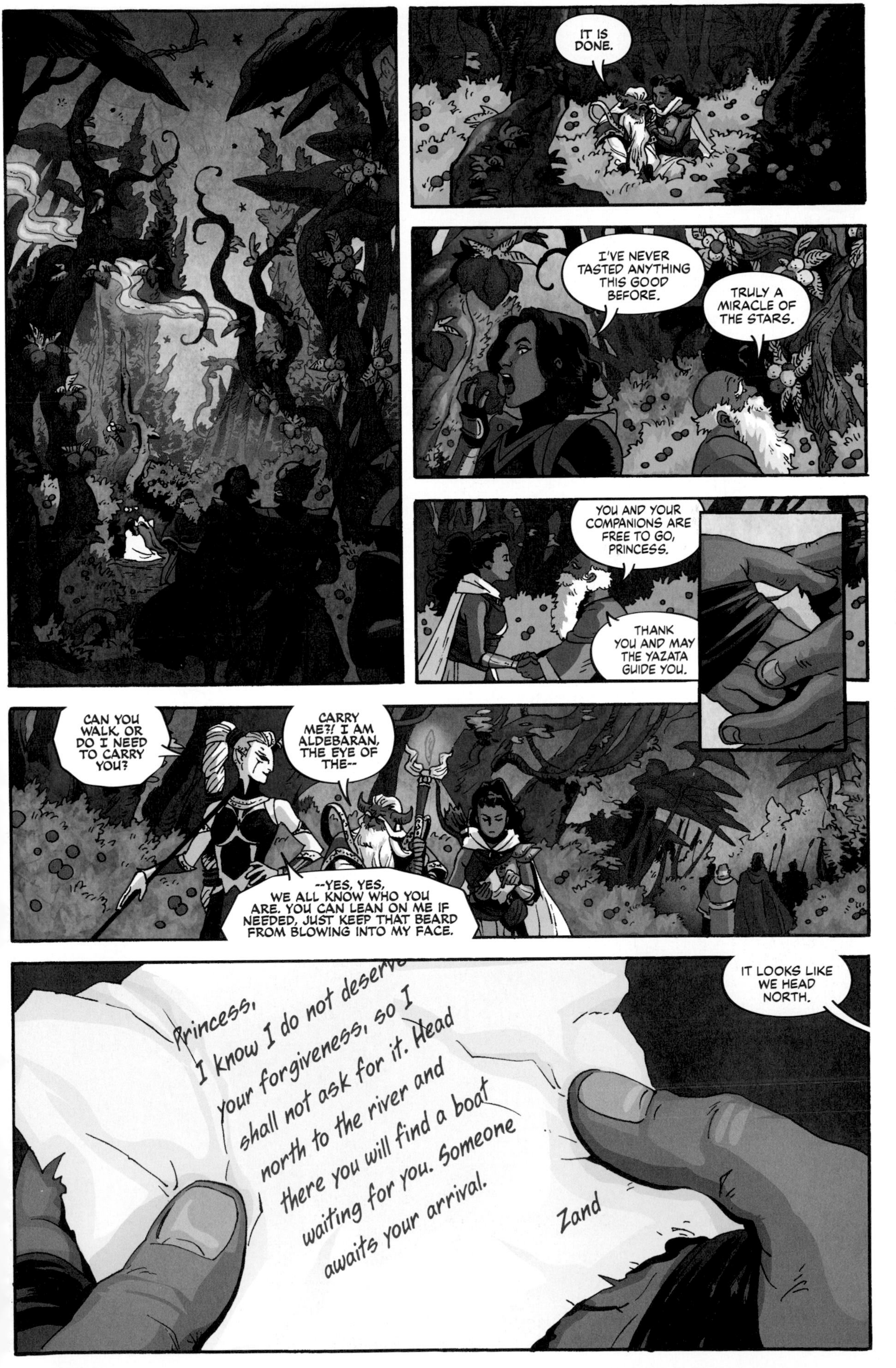
IT IS DONE.
I'VE NEVER TASTED ANYTHING THIS GOOD BEFORE.
TRULY A MIRACLE OF THE STARS.
YOU AND YOUR COMPANIONS ARE FREE TO GO, PRINCESS.
THANK YOU AND MAY THE YAZATA GUIDE YOU.
CAN YOU WALK, OR DO I NEED TO CARRY YOU?
CARRY ME?! I AM ALDEBARAN, THE EYE OF THE--
--YES, YES, WE ALL KNOW WHO YOU ARE. YOU CAN LEAN ON ME IF NEEDED, JUST KEEP THAT BEARD FROM BLOWING INTO MY FACE.
Princess,
I know I do not deserve your forgiveness, so I shall not ask for it. Head north to the river and there you will find a boat waiting for you. Someone awaits your arrival.
Zand
IT LOOKS LIKE WE HEAD NORTH.

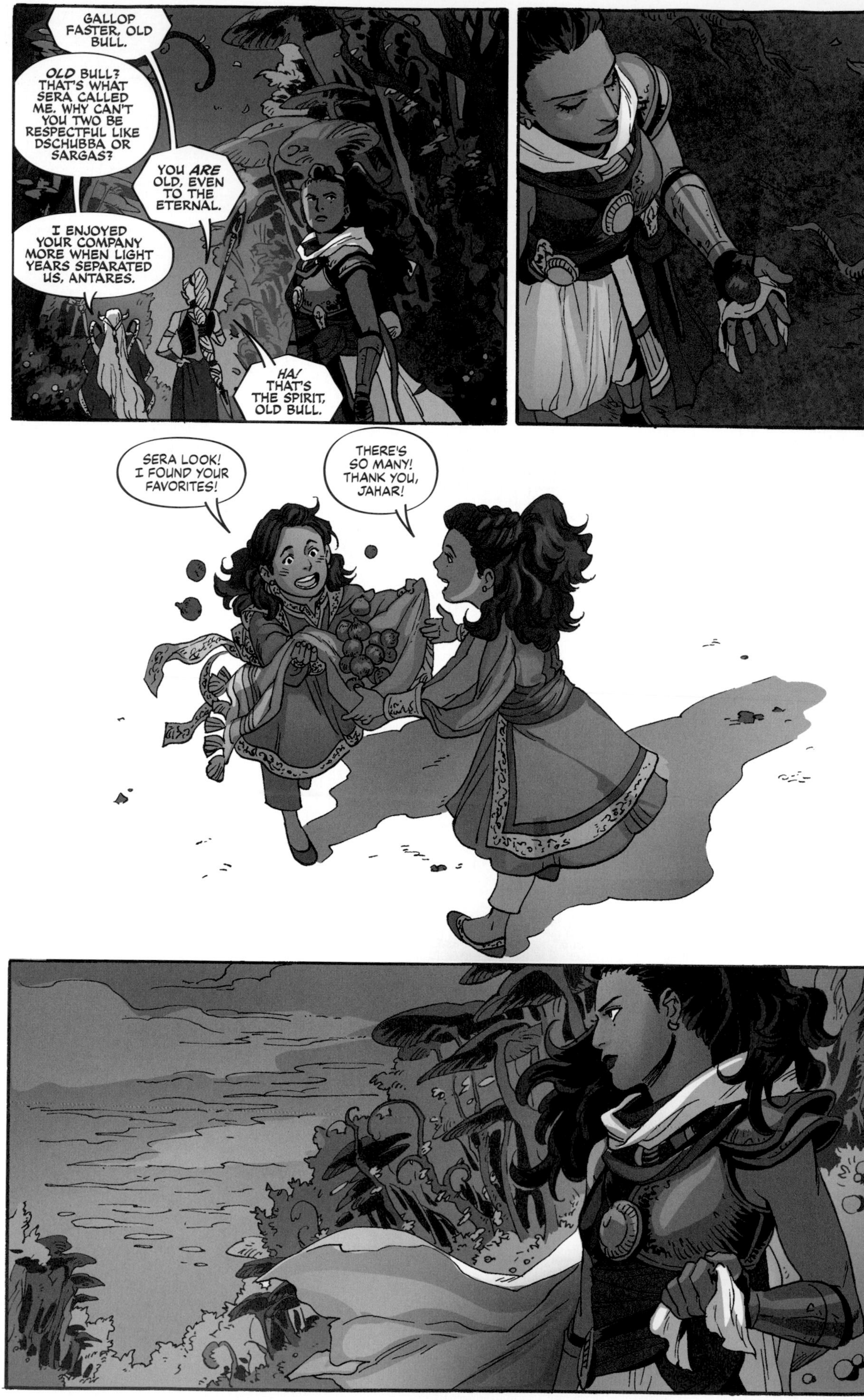
GALLOP FASTER, OLD BULL.
OLD BULL? THAT'S WHAT SERA CALLED ME. WHY CAN'T YOU TWO BE RESPECTFUL LIKE DSCHUBBA OR SARGAS?
YOU ARE OLD, EVEN TO THE ETERNAL.
I ENJOYED YOUR COMPANY MORE WHEN LIGHT YEARS SEPARATED US, ANTARES.
HA! THAT'S THE SPIRIT, OLD BULL.
SERA LOOK! I FOUND YOUR FAVORITES!
THERE'S SO MANY! THANK YOU, JAHAR!

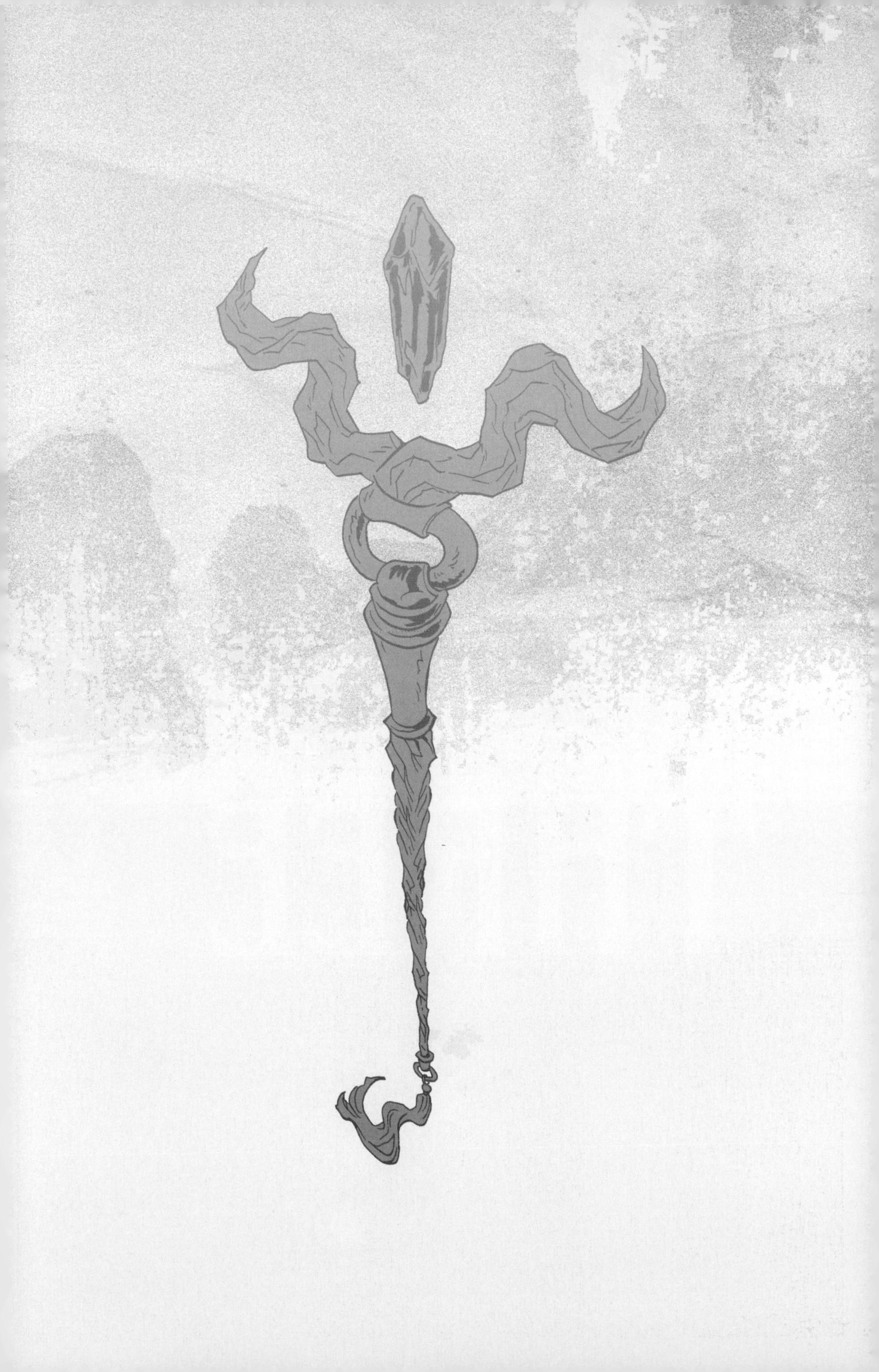

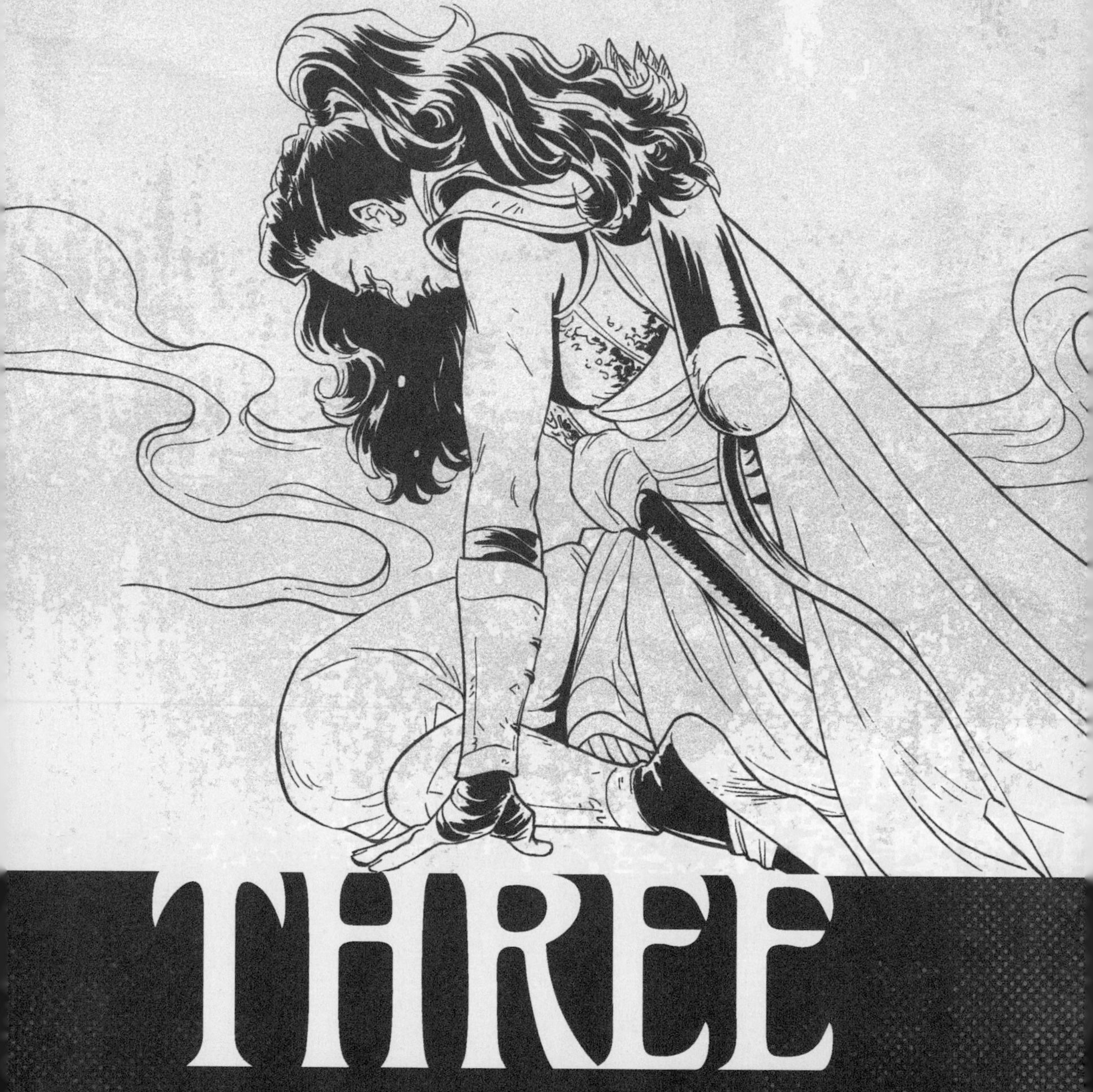

THREE

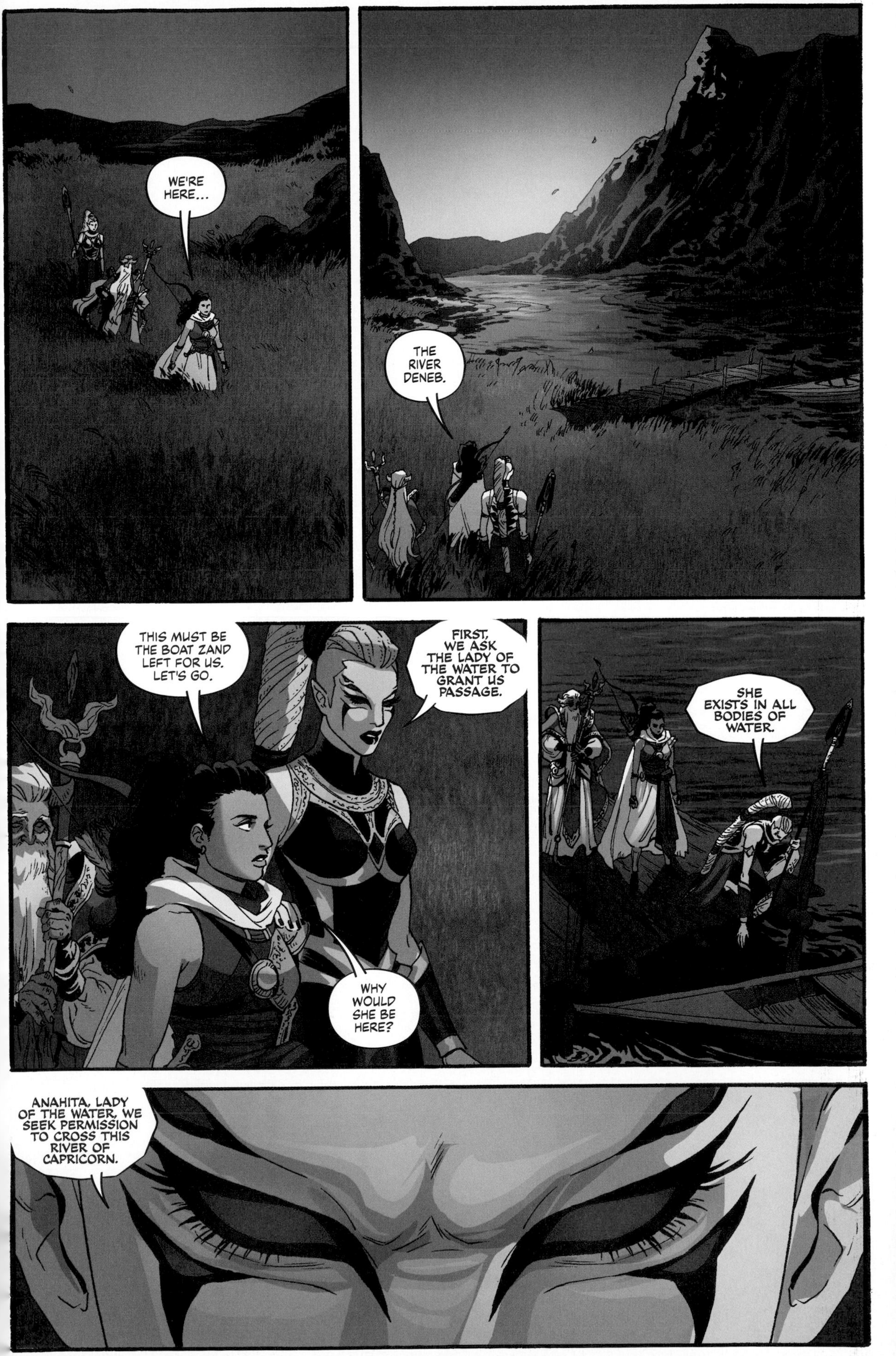
WE'RE HERE...
THE RIVER DENEB.
THIS MUST BE THE BOAT ZAND LEFT FOR US. LET'S GO.
FIRST, WE ASK THE LADY OF THE WATER TO GRANT US PASSAGE.
WHY WOULD SHE BE HERE?
SHE EXISTS IN ALL BODIES OF WATER.
ANAHITA, LADY OF THE WATER, WE SEEK PERMISSION TO CROSS THIS RIVER OF CAPRICORN.

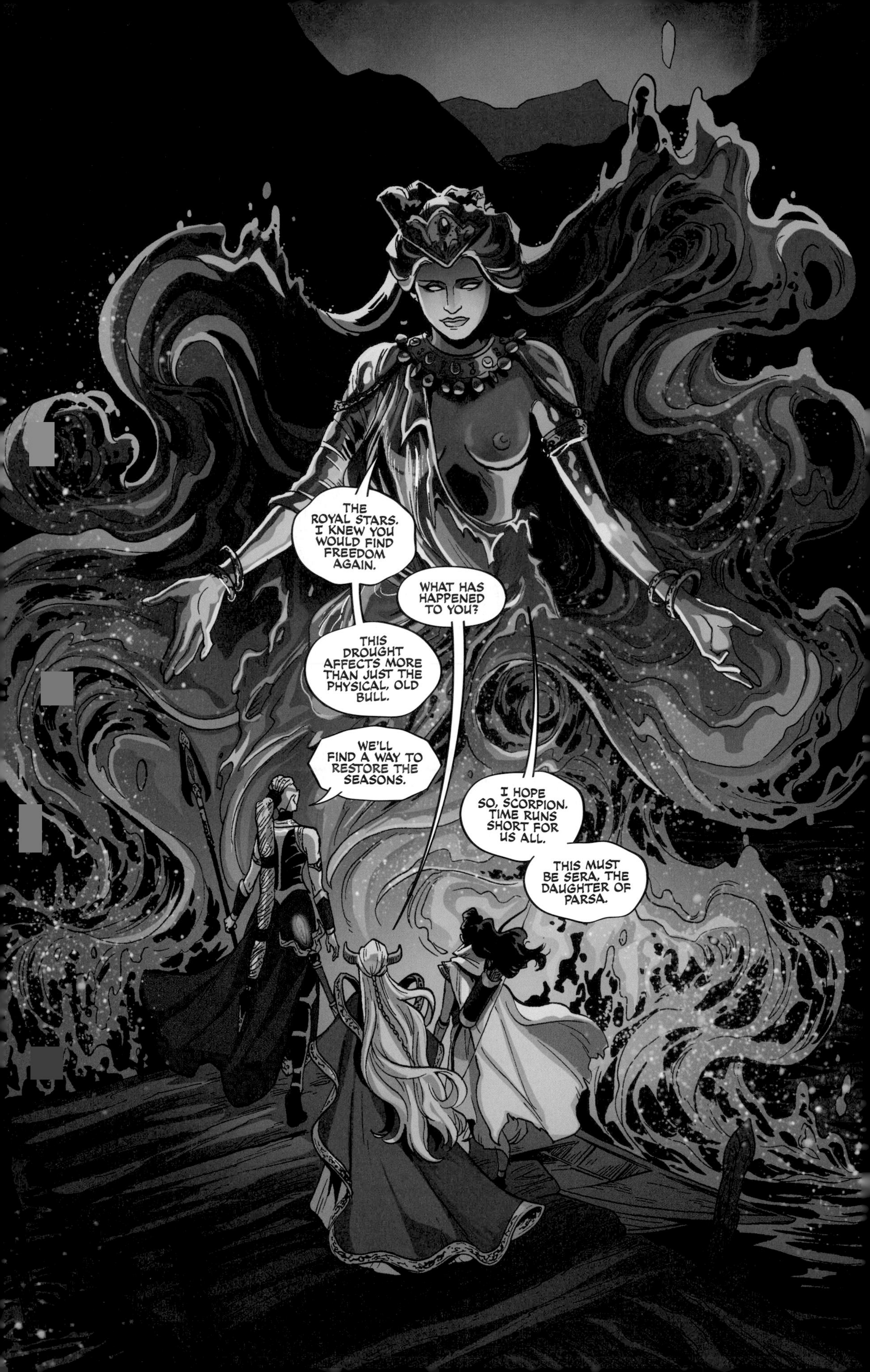
THE ROYAL STARS. I KNEW YOU WOULD FIND FREEDOM AGAIN.
WHAT HAS HAPPENED TO YOU?
THIS DROUGHT AFFECTS MORE THAN JUST THE PHYSICAL, OLD BULL.
WE'LL FIND A WAY TO RESTORE THE SEASONS.
I HOPE SO, SCORPION. TIME RUNS SHORT FOR US ALL.
THIS MUST BE SERA, THE DAUGHTER OF PARSA.

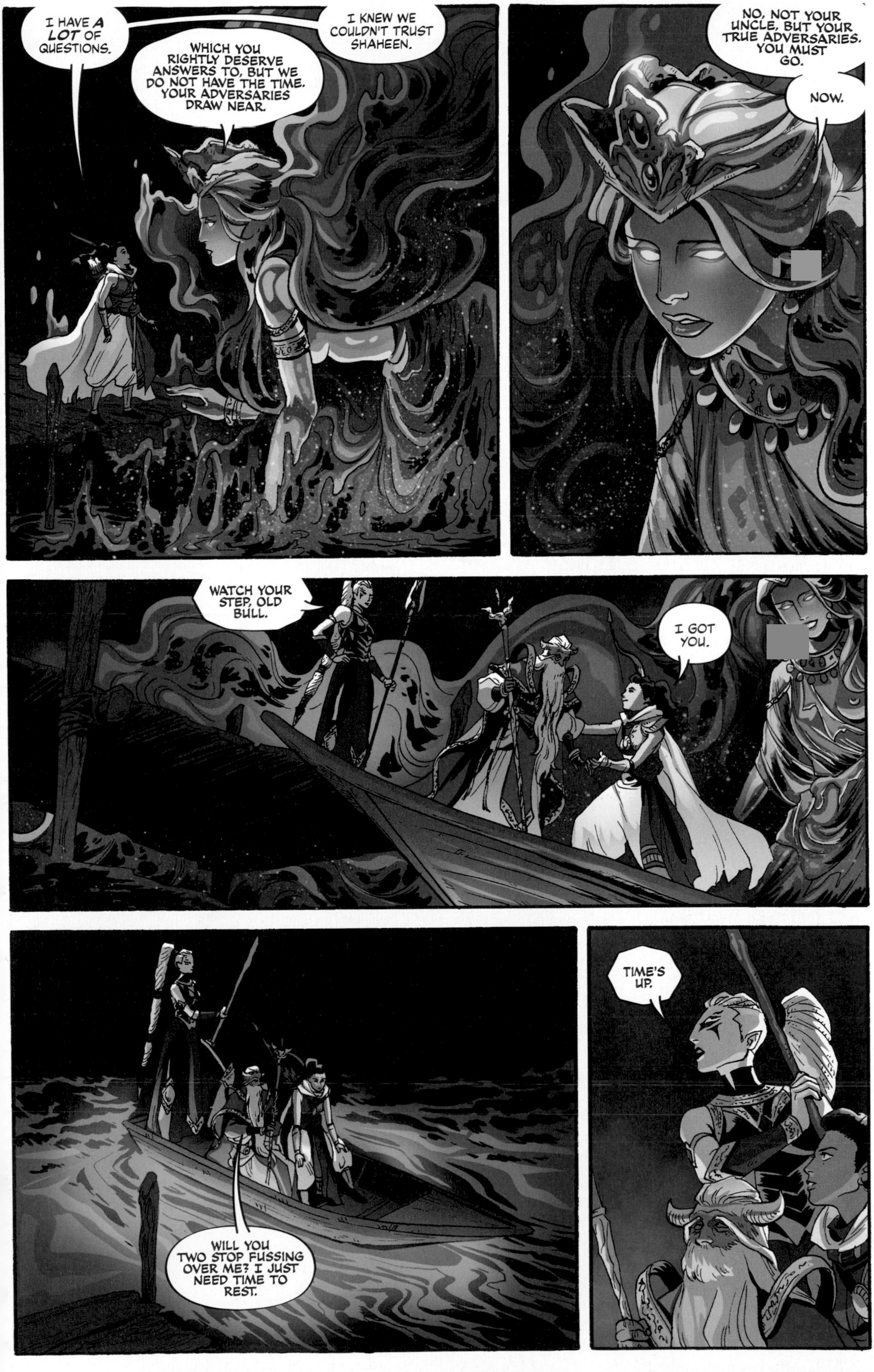
I HAVE A LOT OF QUESTIONS.
I KNEW WE COULDN'T TRUST SHAHEEN.
WHICH YOU RIGHTLY DESERVE ANSWERS TO, BUT WE DO NOT HAVE THE TIME. YOUR ADVERSARIES DRAW NEAR.
NO, NOT YOUR UNCLE, BUT YOUR TRUE ADVERSARIES. YOU MUST GO.
NOW.
WATCH YOUR STEP, OLD BULL.
I GOT YOU.
WILL YOU TWO STOP FUSSING OVER ME? I JUST NEED TIME TO REST.
TIME'S UP.

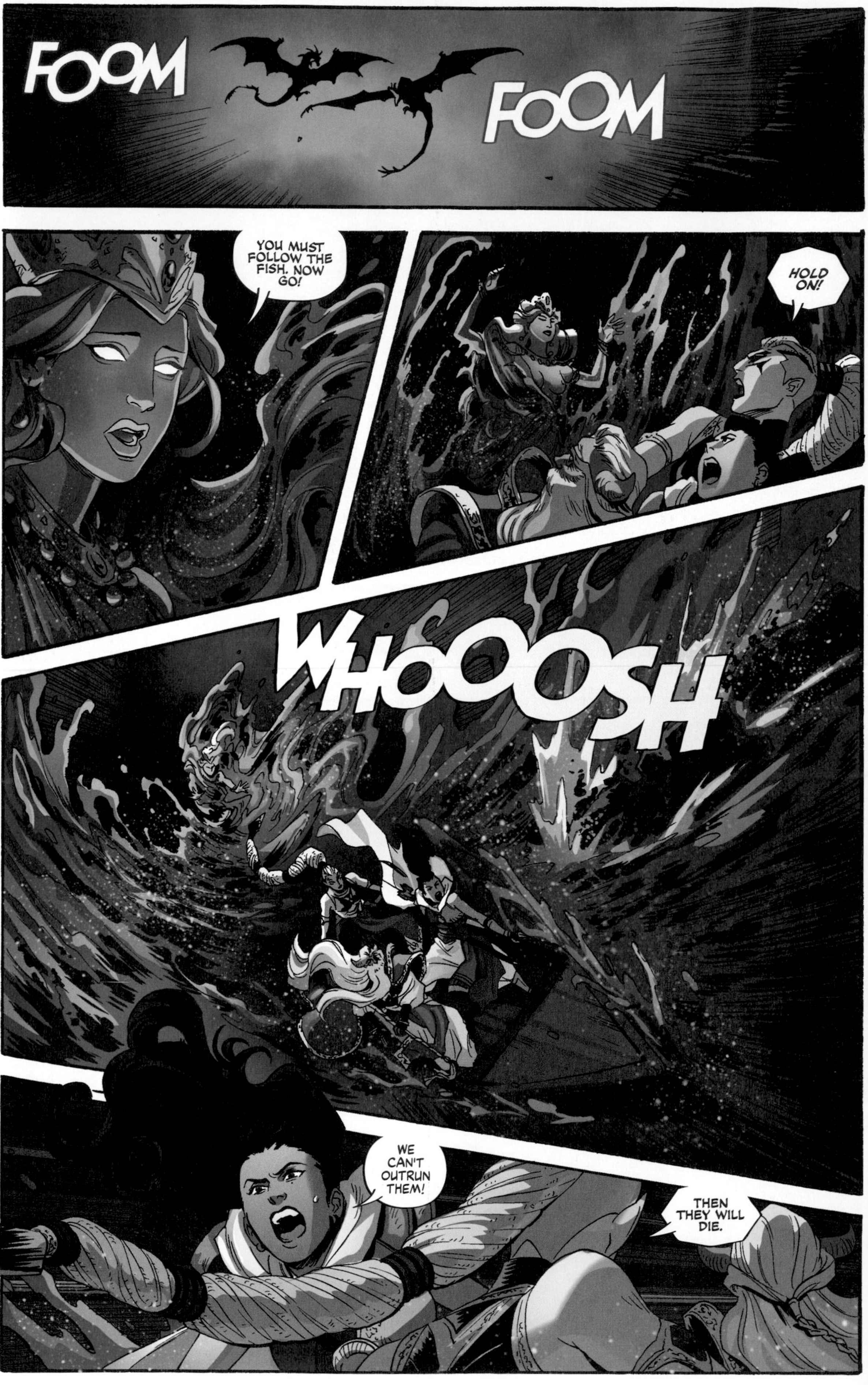
FOOM
FOOM
YOU MUST FOLLOW THE FISH. NOW GO!
HOLD ON!
WHOOOOSH
WE CAN'T OUTRUN THEM!
THEN THEY WILL DIE.

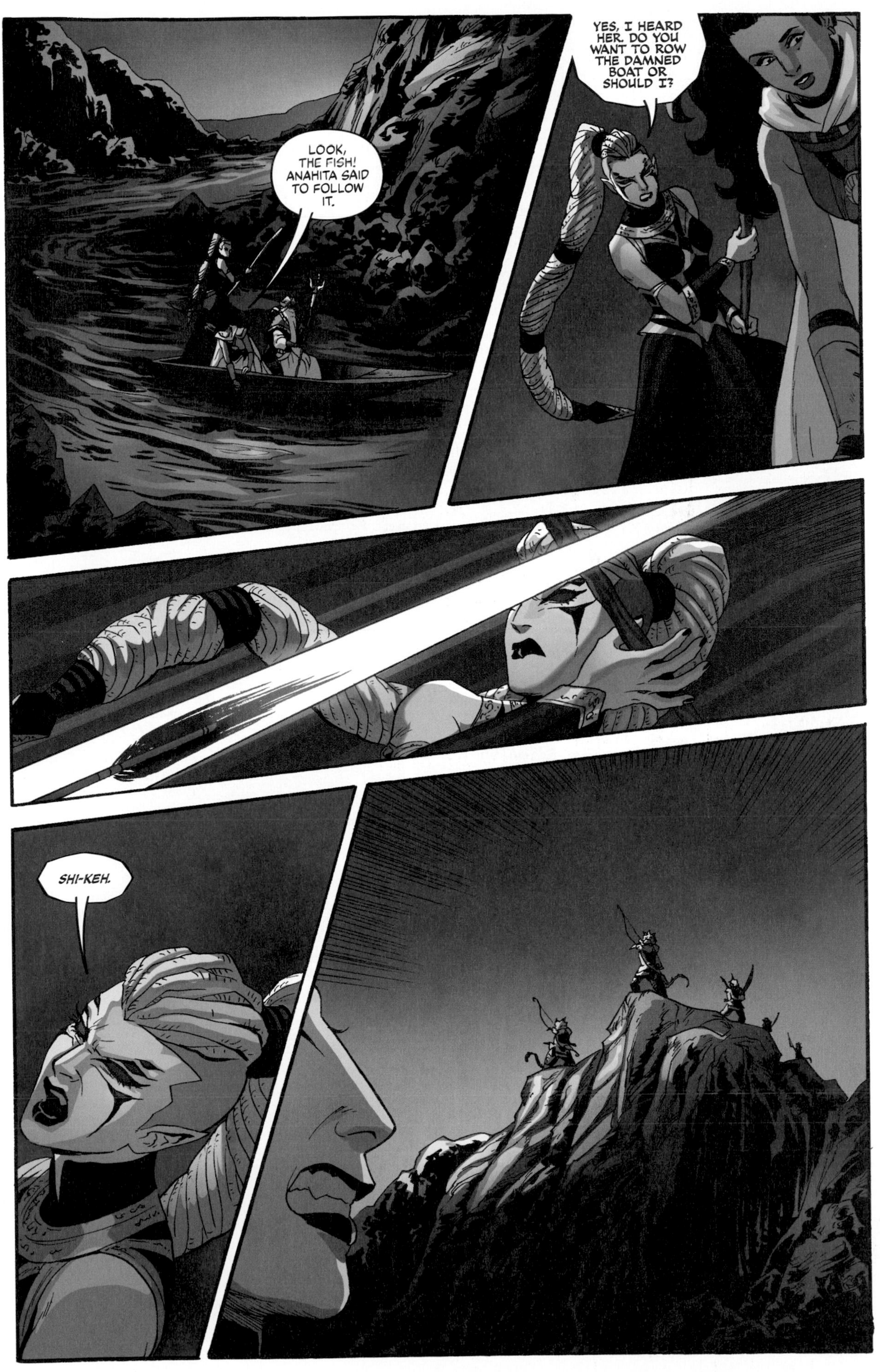
LOOK, THE FISH! ANAHITA SAID TO FOLLOW IT.
YES, I HEARD HER. DO YOU WANT TO ROW THE DAMNED BOAT OR SHOULD I?
SHI-KEH.

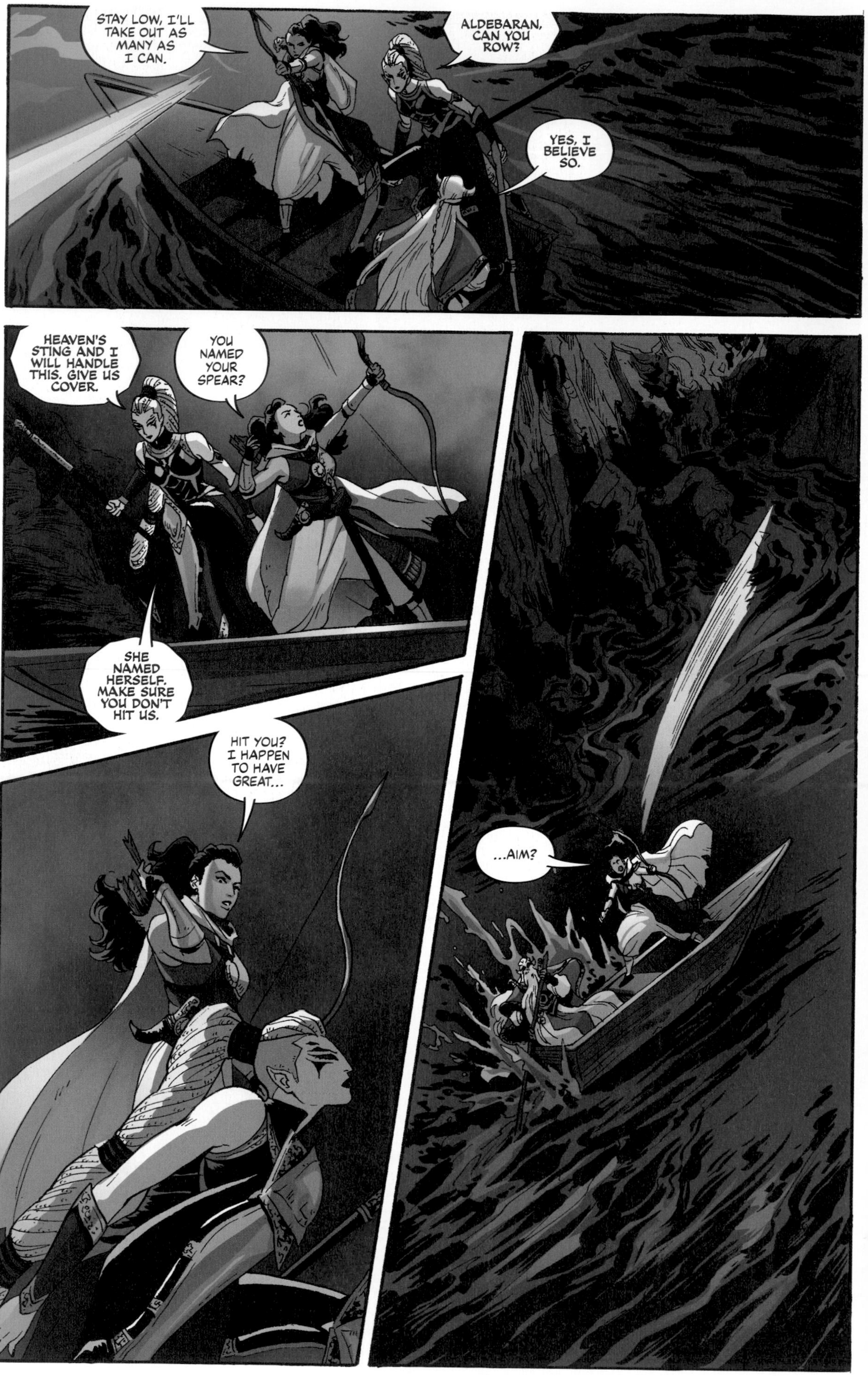
STAY LOW, I'LL TAKE OUT AS MANY AS I CAN.
ALDEBARAN, CAN YOU ROW?
YES, I BELIEVE SO.
HEAVEN'S STING AND I WILL HANDLE THIS. GIVE US COVER.
YOU NAMED YOUR SPEAR?
SHE NAMED HERSELF. MAKE SURE YOU DON'T HIT US.
HIT YOU? I HAPPEN TO HAVE GREAT...
...AIM?

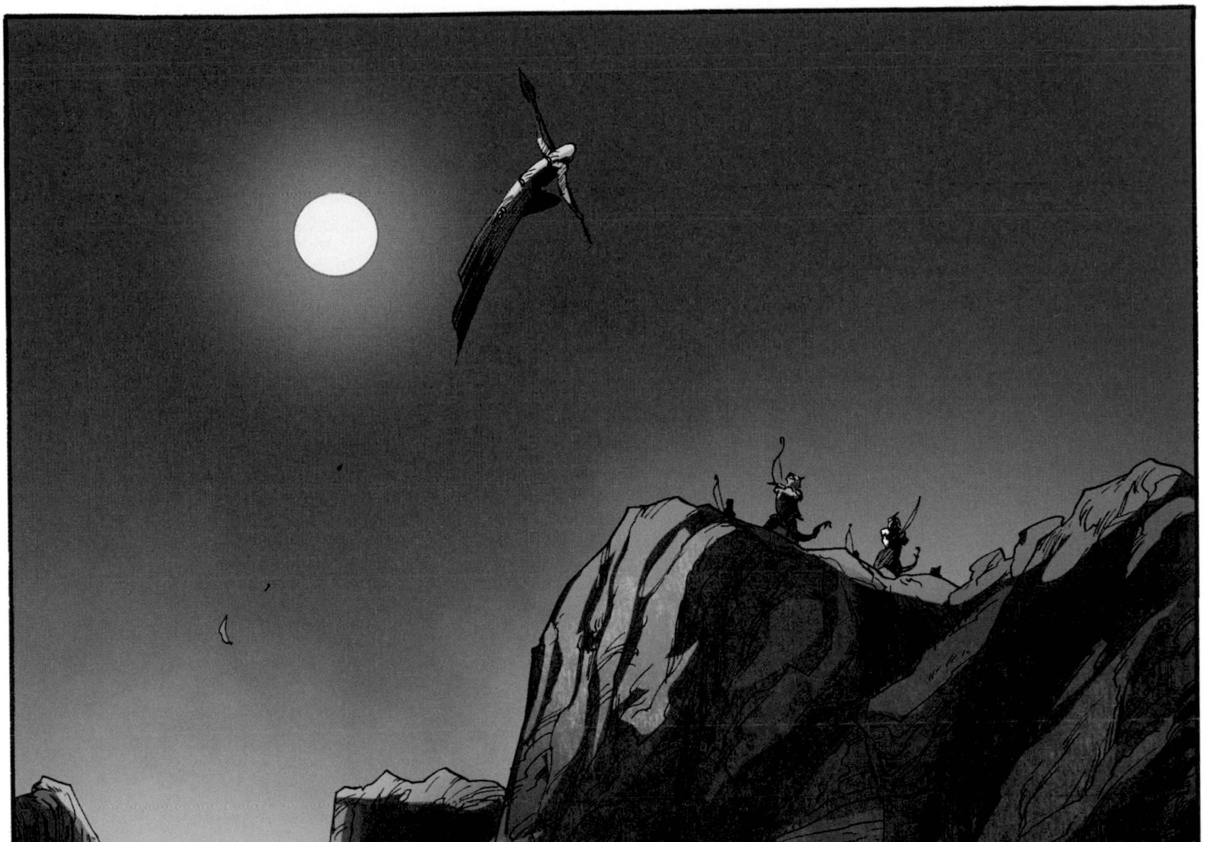
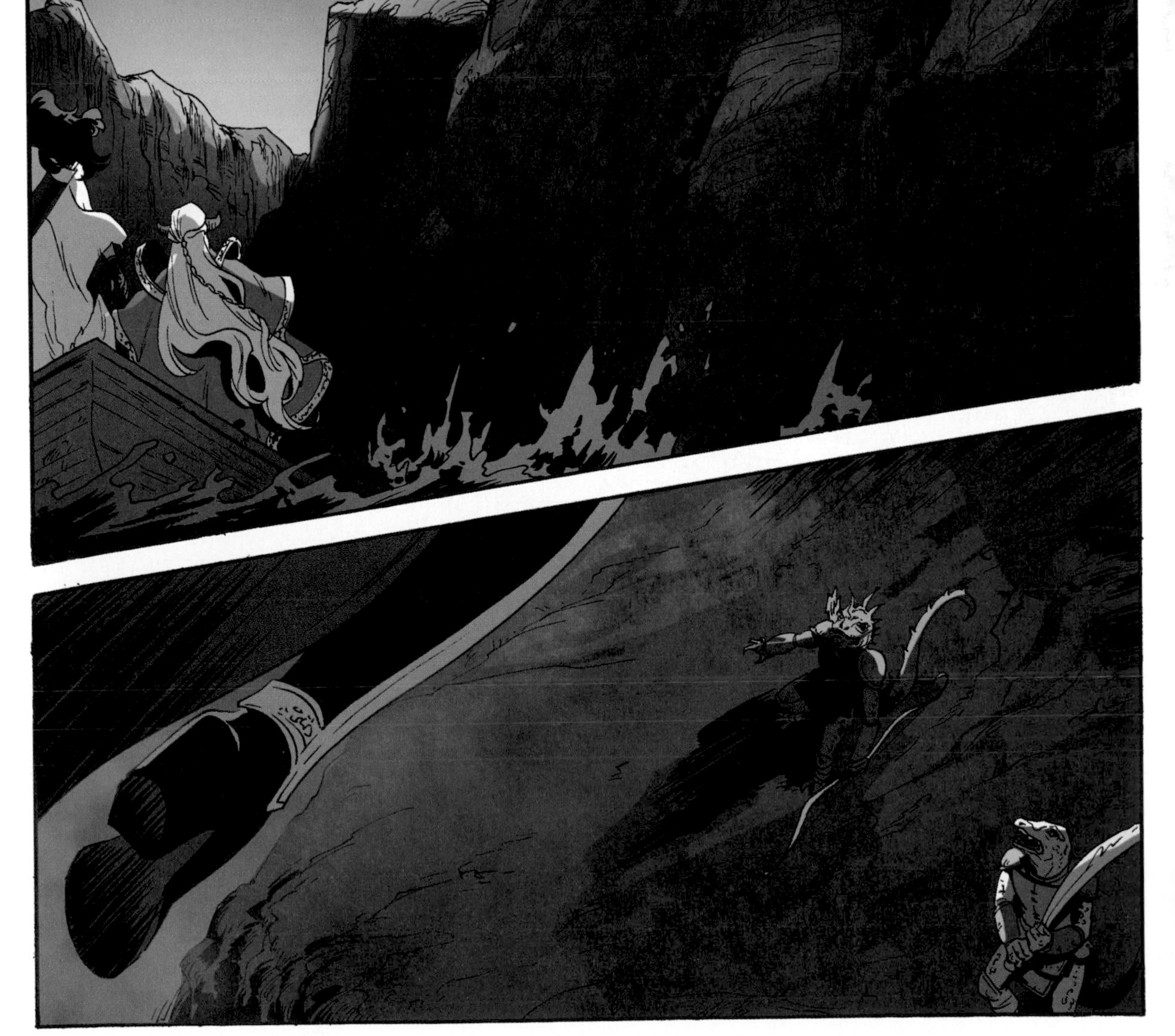

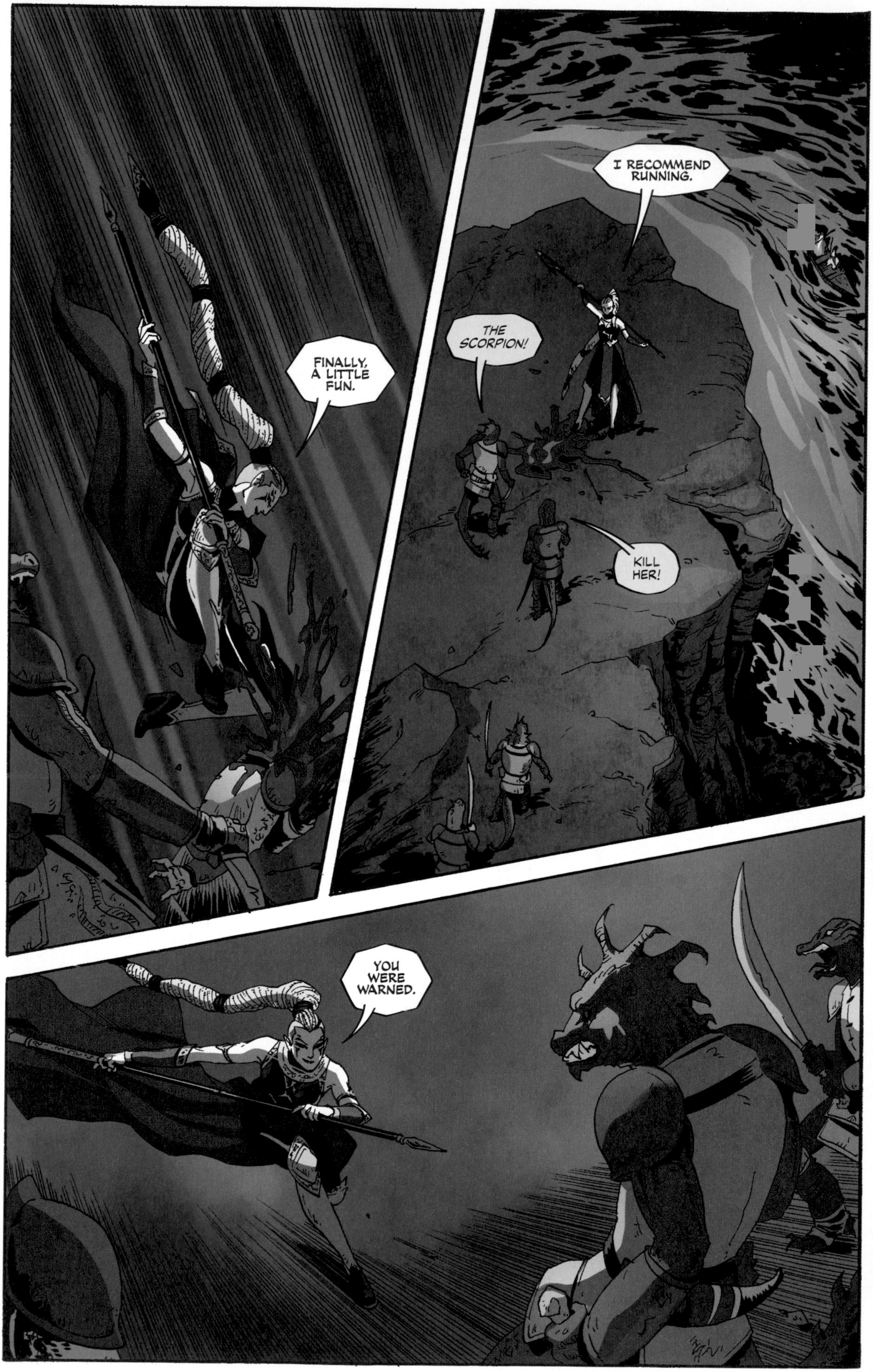
FINALLY, A LITTLE FUN.
I RECOMMEND RUNNING.
THE SCORPION!
KILL HER!
YOU WERE WARNED.

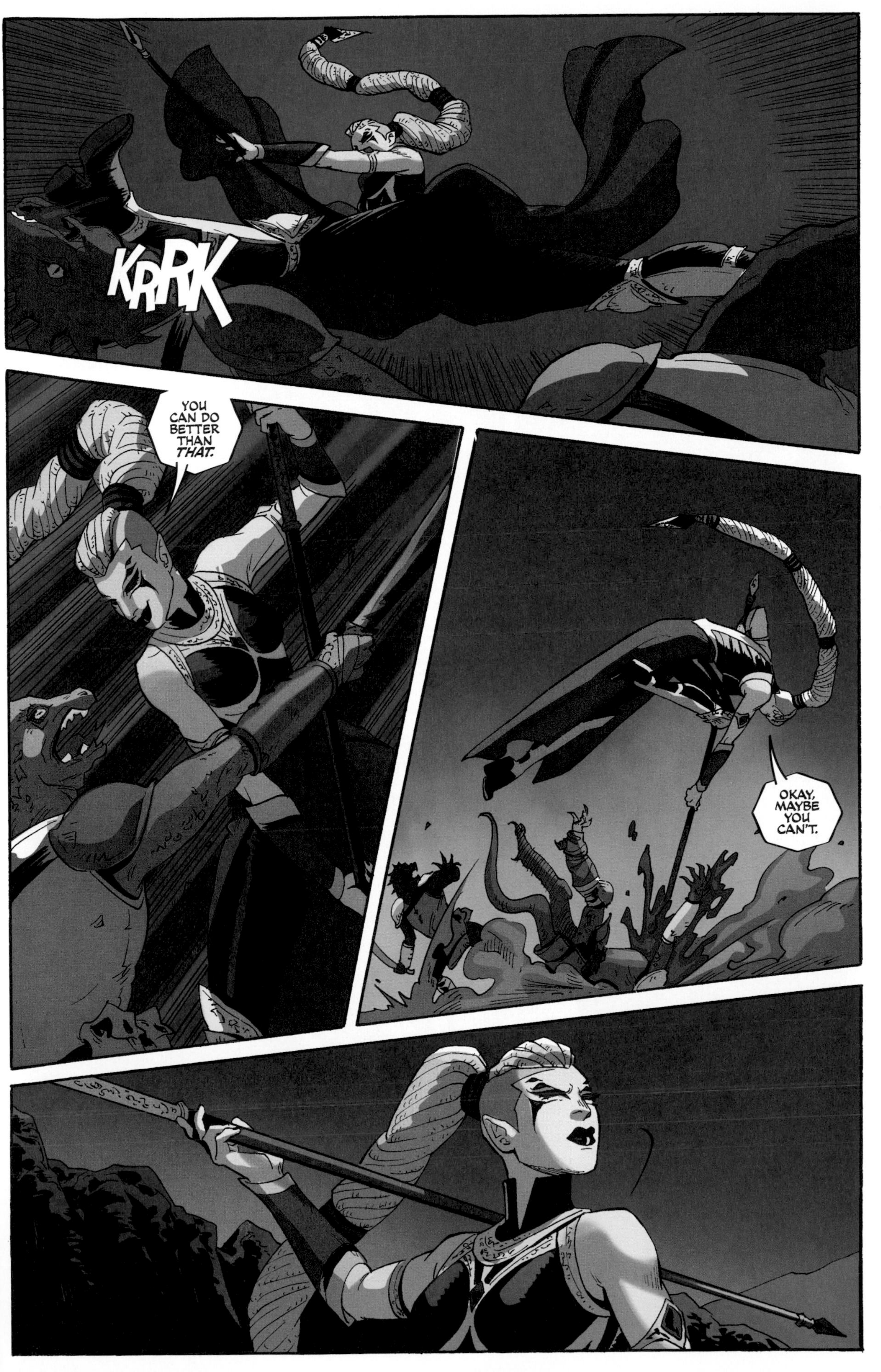
KRRK
YOU CAN DO BETTER THAN *THAT.*
OKAY, MAYBE YOU CAN'T.

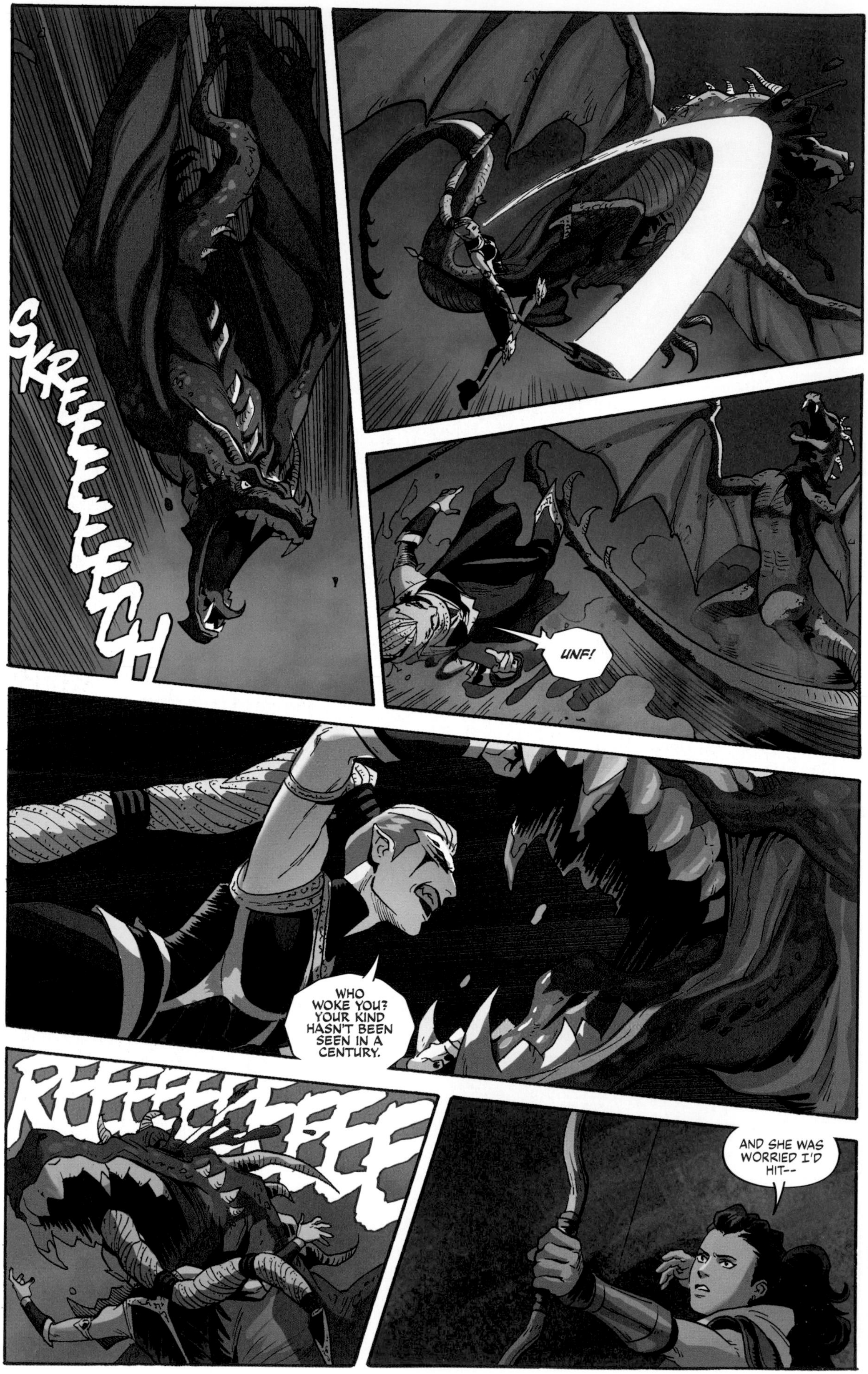
SKREEEEEEECH
UNF!
WHO WOKE YOU? YOUR KIND HASN'T BEEN SEEN IN A CENTURY.
REEEEEEEEEE
AND SHE WAS WORRIED I'D HIT--

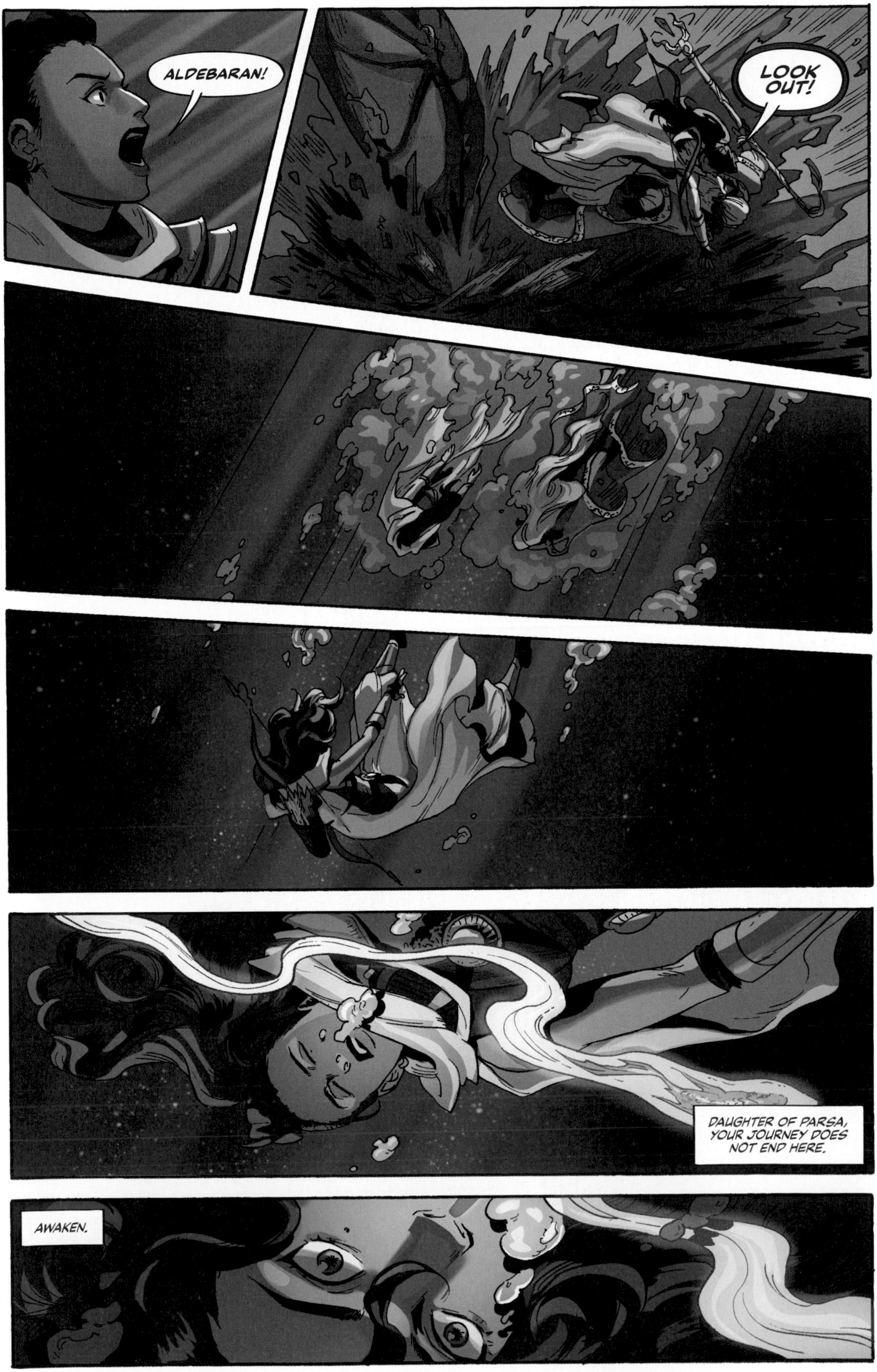
ALDEBARAN!
LOOK OUT!
DAUGHTER OF PARSA, YOUR JOURNEY DOES NOT END HERE.
AWAKEN.

I DON'T KNOW WHO COMMANDS THE WYVERNS TO FLY AGAIN.

BUT I WILL CUT DOWN EVERY ONE OF YOU THAT COMES AFTER US.

NO...

FOOM
FOOM

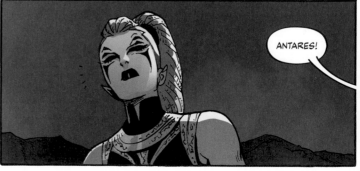

ANTARES!

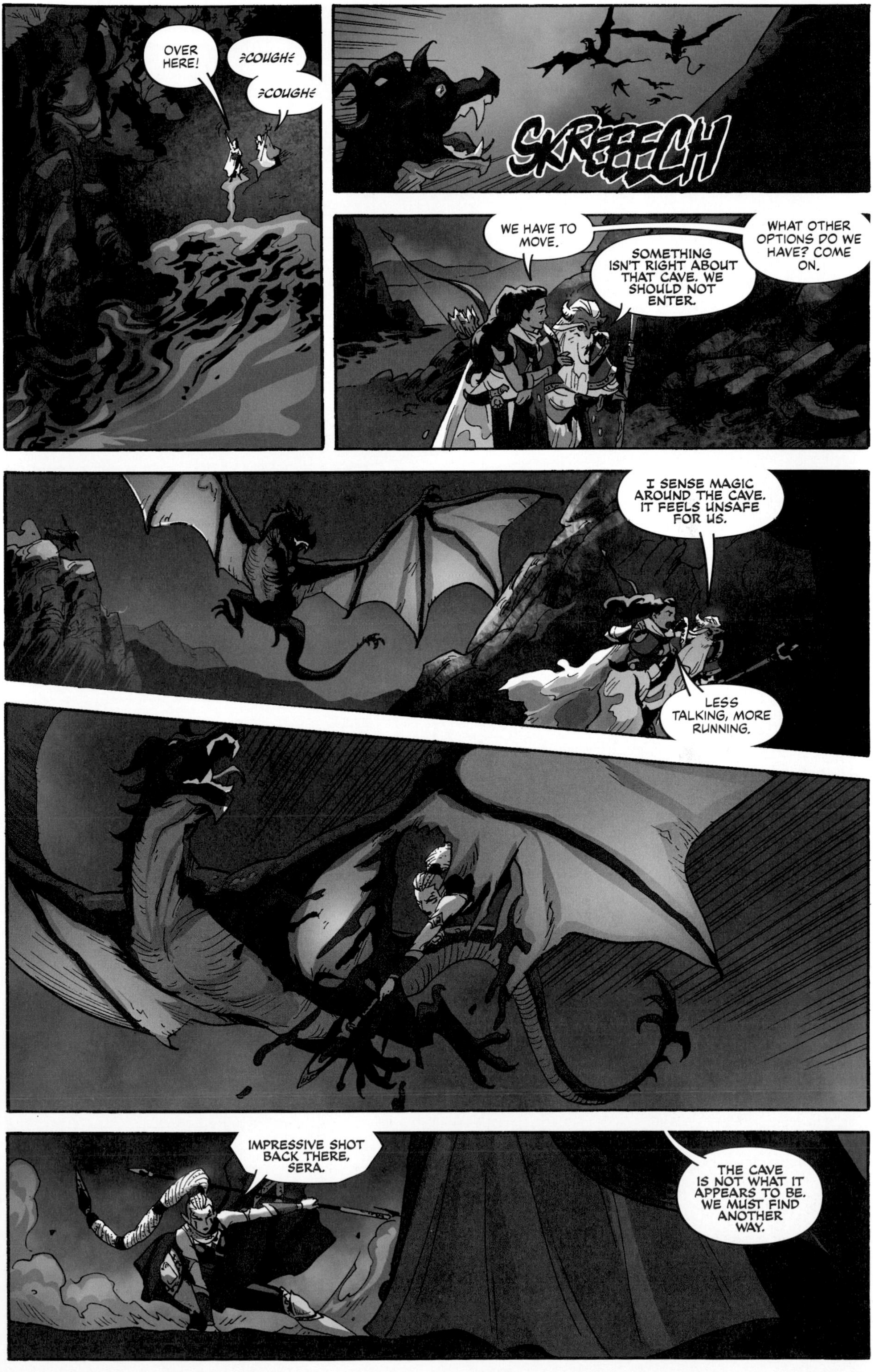
OVER HERE!
COUGH
COUGH
SKREEECH
WE HAVE TO MOVE.
SOMETHING ISN'T RIGHT ABOUT THAT CAVE. WE SHOULD NOT ENTER.
WHAT OTHER OPTIONS DO WE HAVE? COME ON.
I SENSE MAGIC AROUND THE CAVE. IT FEELS UNSAFE FOR US.
LESS TALKING, MORE RUNNING.
IMPRESSIVE SHOT BACK THERE, SERA.
THE CAVE IS NOT WHAT IT APPEARS TO BE. WE MUST FIND ANOTHER WAY.

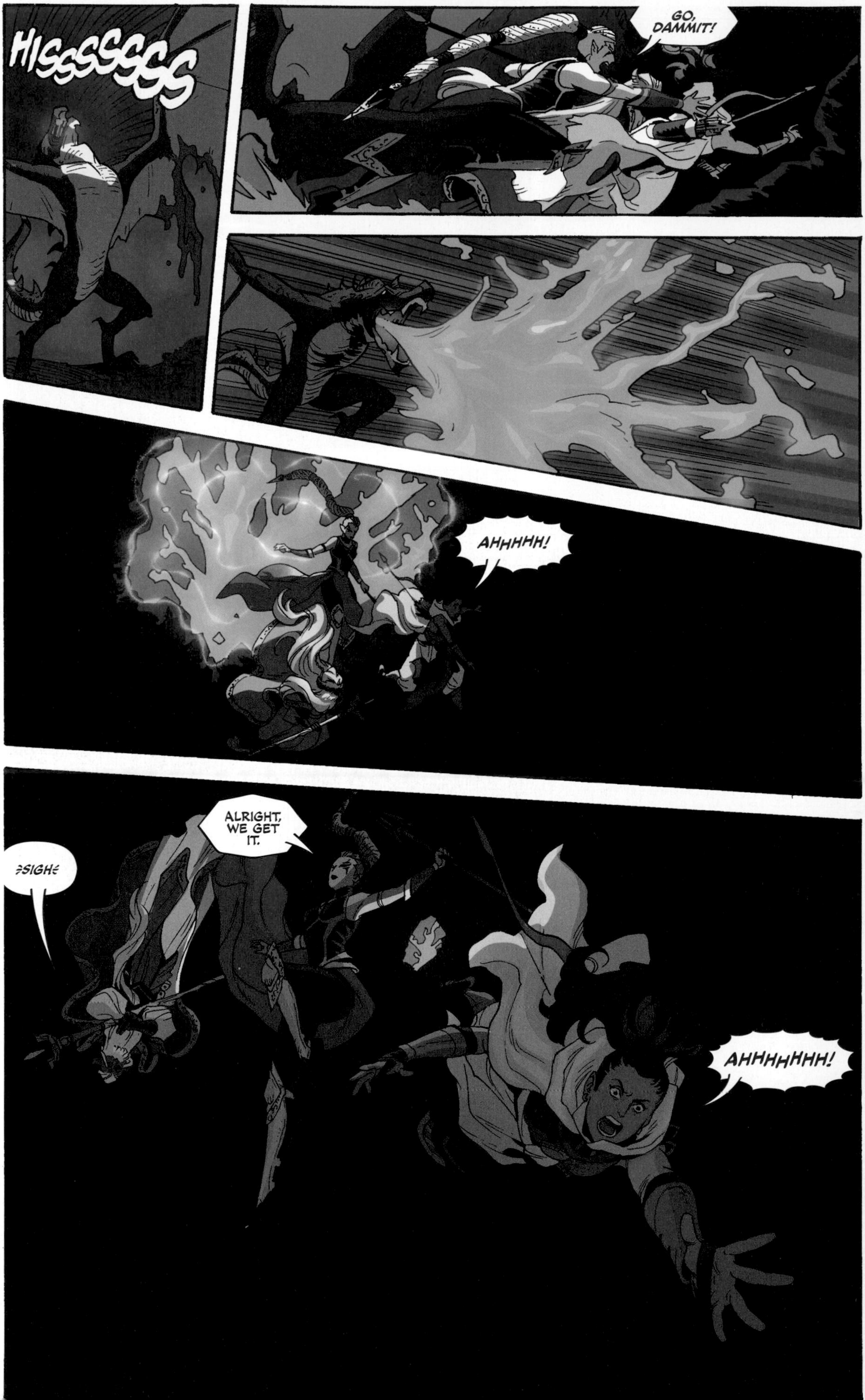
HISSSSSSS
GO, DAMMIT!
AHHHHH!
ALRIGHT, WE GET IT.
SIGH
AHHHHHHH!

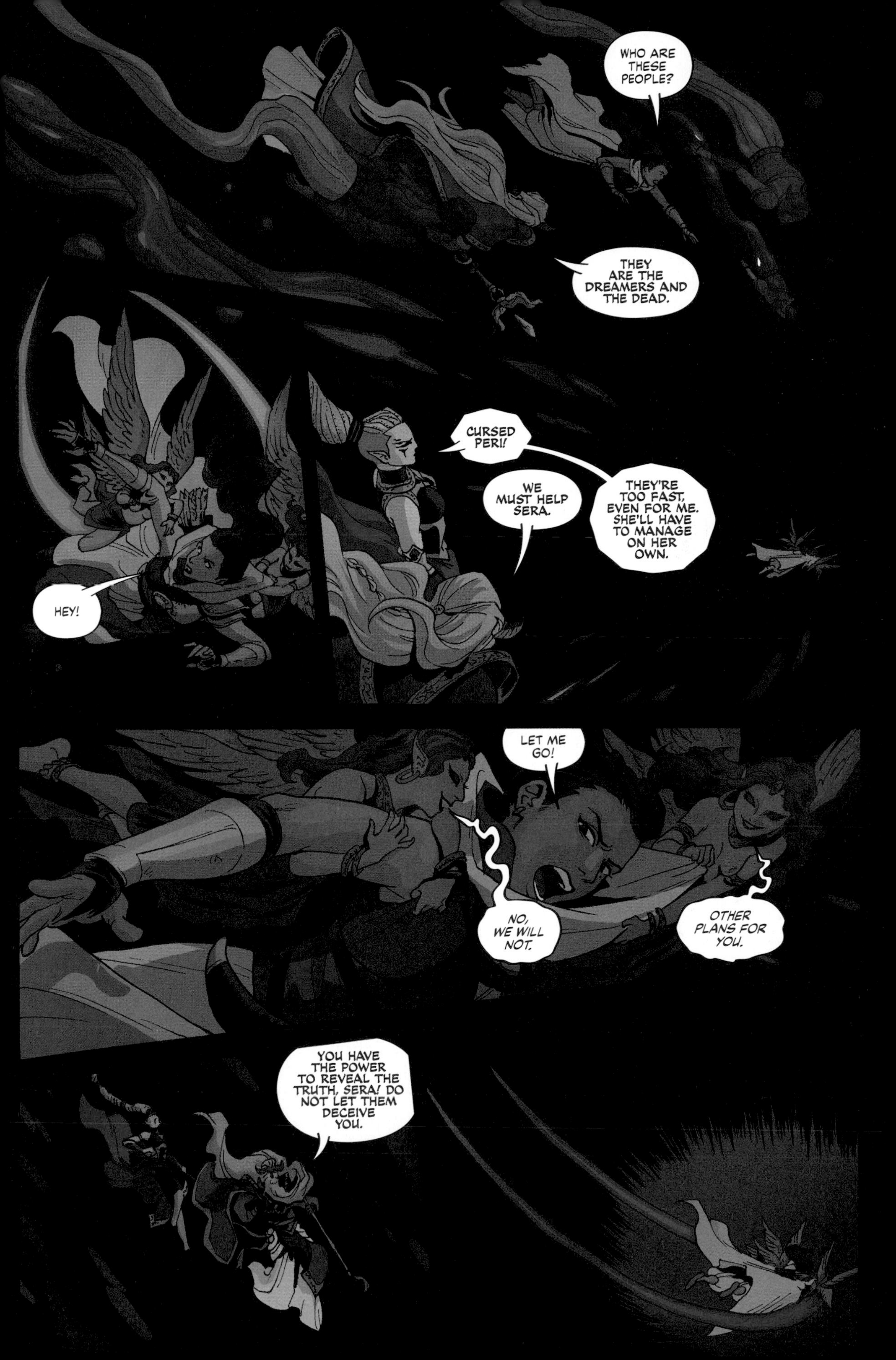
WHO ARE THESE PEOPLE?
THEY ARE THE DREAMERS AND THE DEAD.
CURSED PERI!
THEY'RE TOO FAST, EVEN FOR ME. SHE'LL HAVE TO MANAGE ON HER OWN.
WE MUST HELP SERA.
HEY!
LET ME GO!
NO, WE WILL NOT.
OTHER PLANS FOR YOU.
YOU HAVE THE POWER TO REVEAL THE TRUTH, SERA! DO NOT LET THEM DECEIVE YOU.

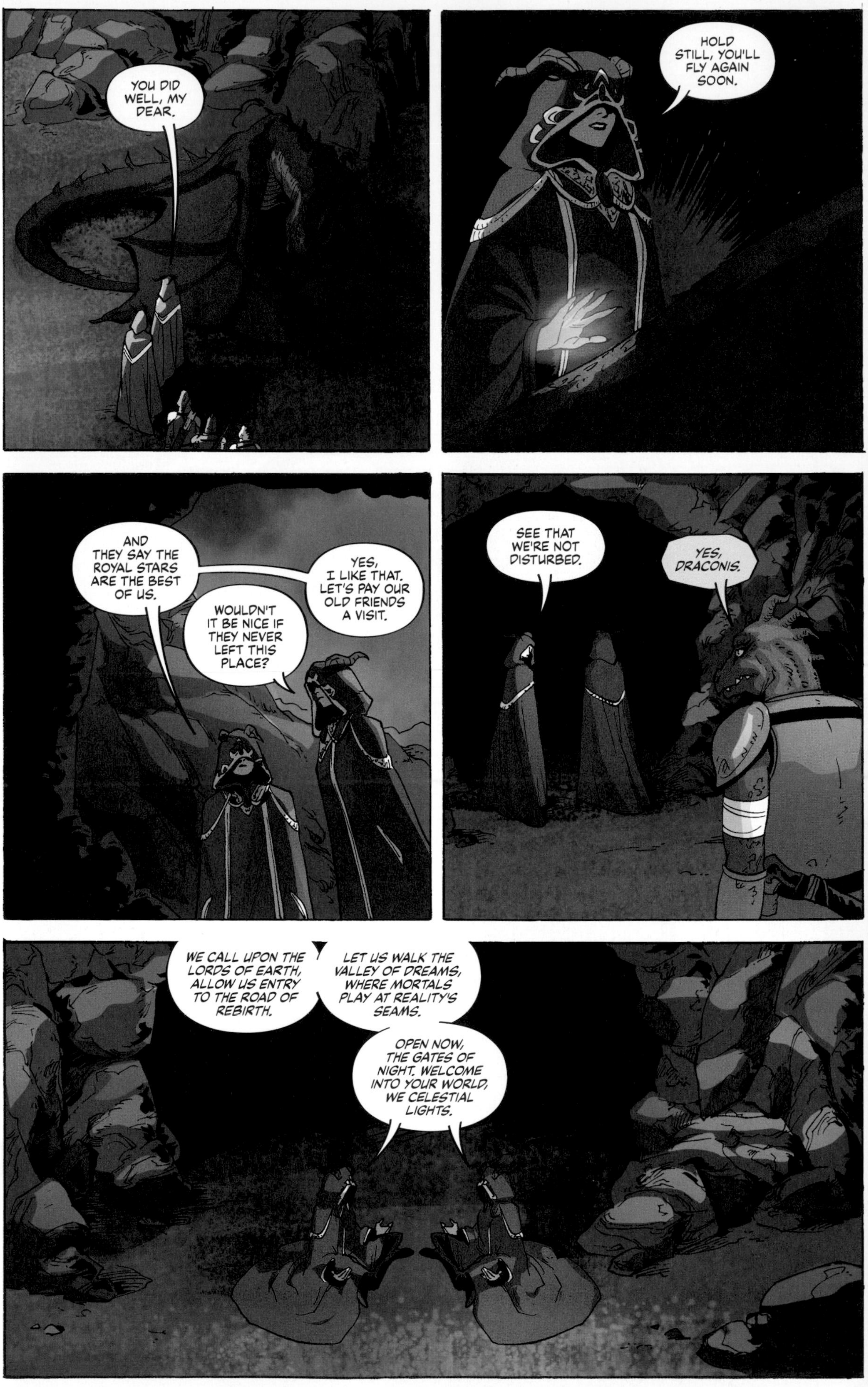
YOU DID WELL, MY DEAR.
HOLD STILL, YOU'LL FLY AGAIN SOON.
AND THEY SAY THE ROYAL STARS ARE THE BEST OF US.
WOULDN'T IT BE NICE IF THEY NEVER LEFT THIS PLACE?
YES, I LIKE THAT. LET'S PAY OUR OLD FRIENDS A VISIT.
SEE THAT WE'RE NOT DISTURBED.
YES, DRACONIS.
WE CALL UPON THE LORDS OF EARTH, ALLOW US ENTRY TO THE ROAD OF REBIRTH.
LET US WALK THE VALLEY OF DREAMS, WHERE MORTALS PLAY AT REALITY'S SEAMS.
OPEN NOW, THE GATES OF NIGHT. WELCOME INTO YOUR WORLD, WE CELESTIAL LIGHTS.

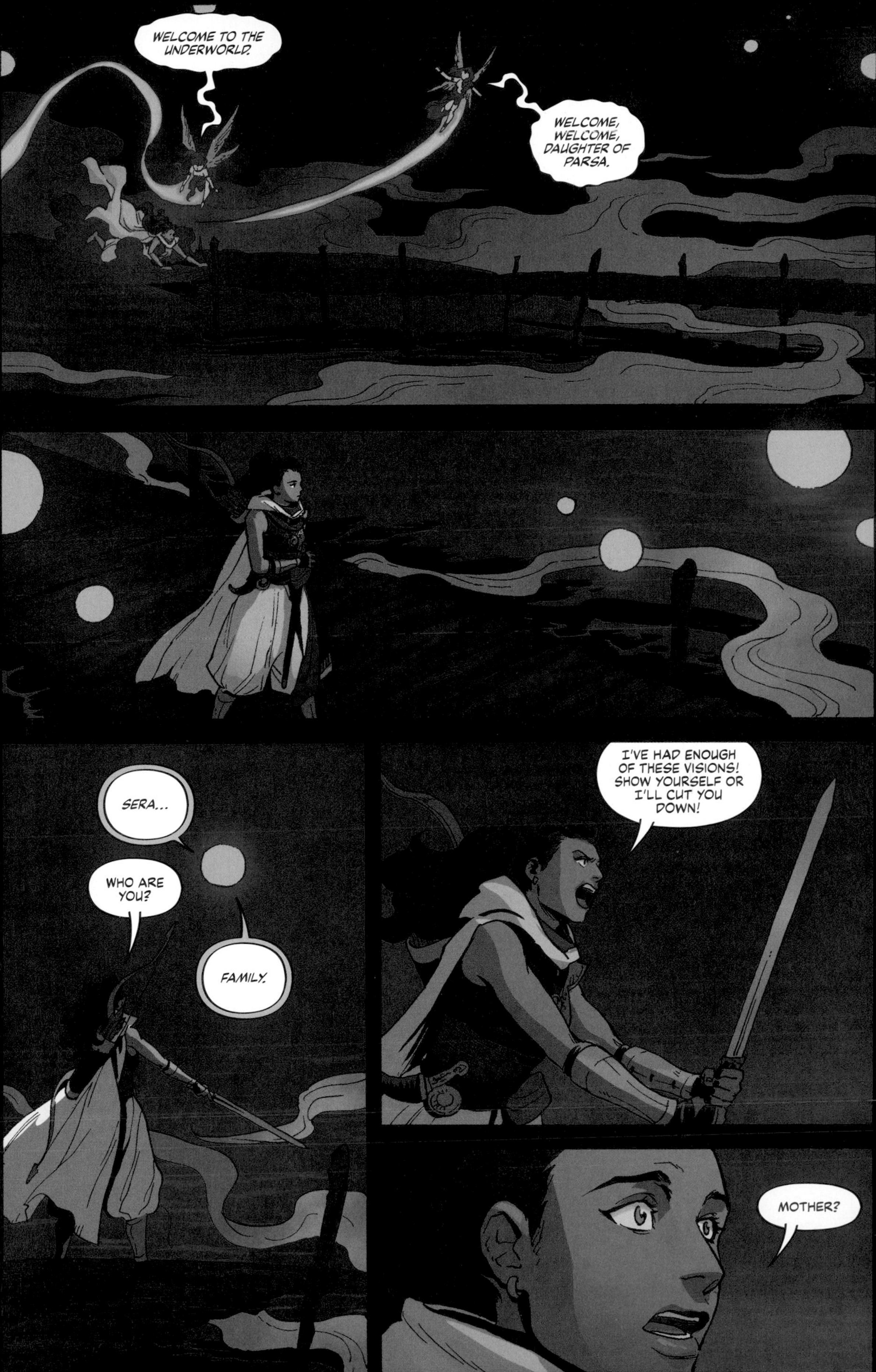
WELCOME TO THE UNDERWORLD.
WELCOME, WELCOME, DAUGHTER OF PARSA.
SERA...
WHO ARE YOU?
FAMILY.
I'VE HAD ENOUGH OF THESE VISIONS! SHOW YOURSELF OR I'LL CUT YOU DOWN!
MOTHER?

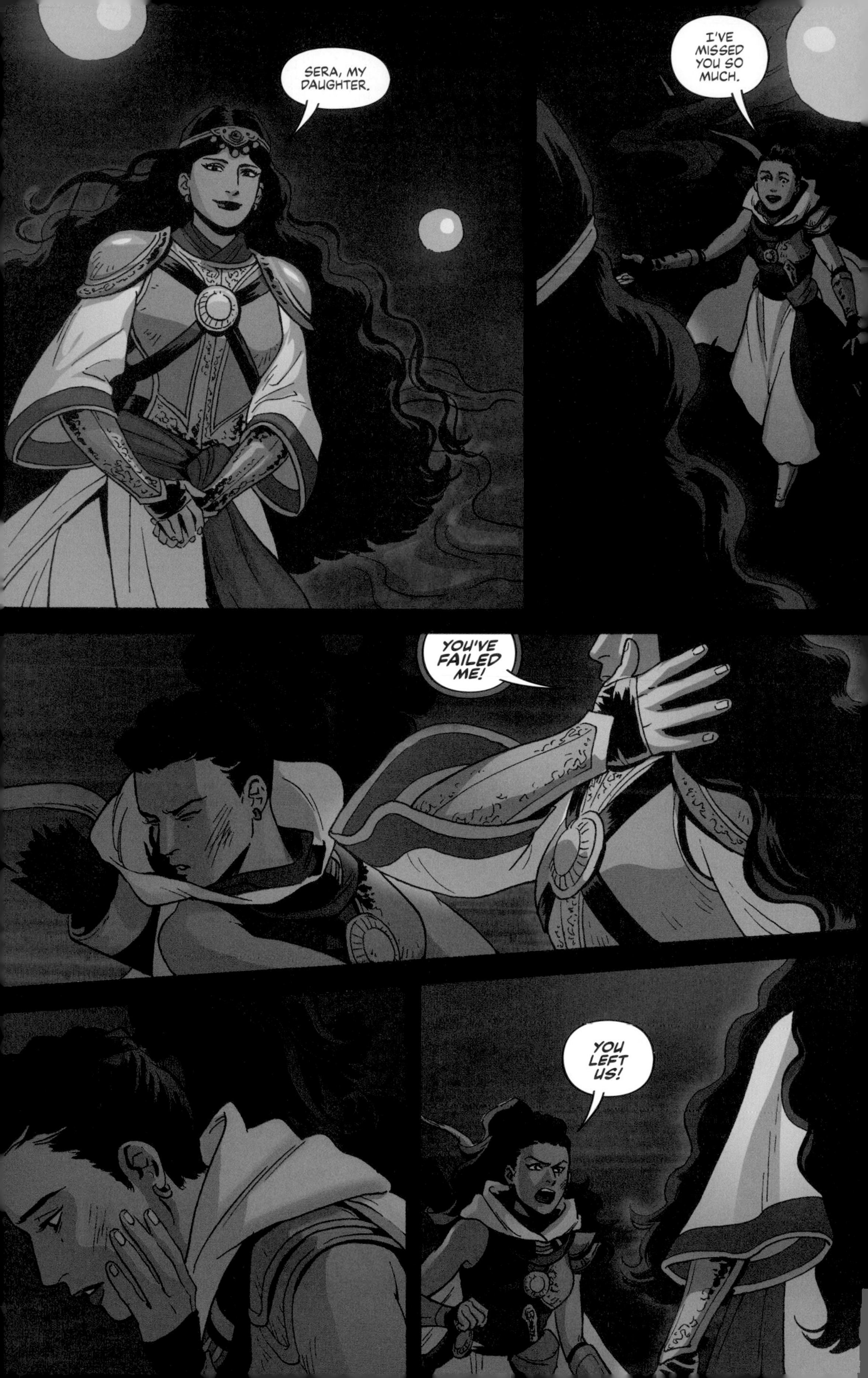
SERA, MY DAUGHTER.
I'VE MISSED YOU SO MUCH.
YOU'VE FAILED ME!
YOU LEFT US!

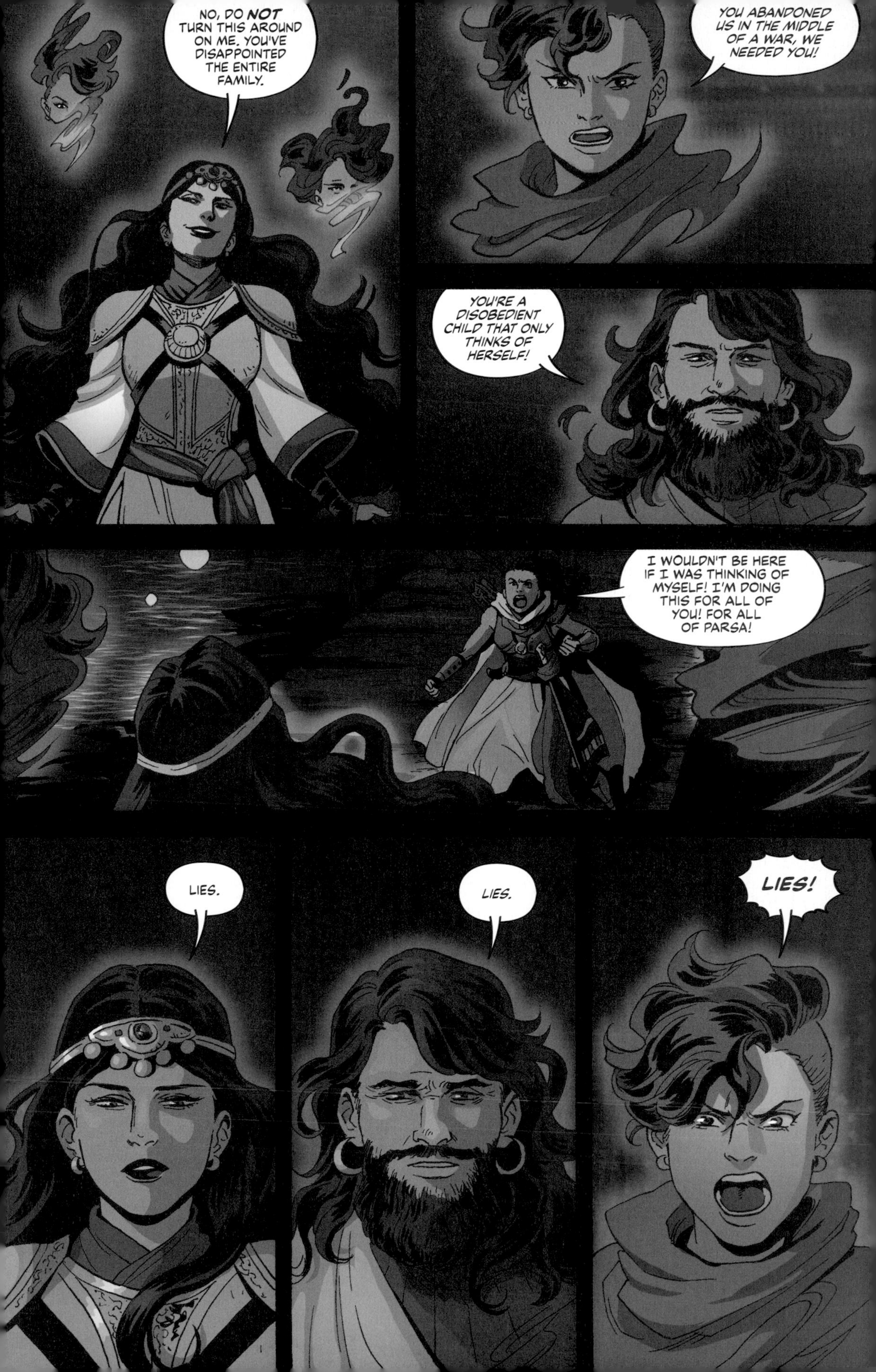

NO, DO **NOT** TURN THIS AROUND ON ME. YOU'VE DISAPPOINTED THE ENTIRE FAMILY.
YOU ABANDONED US IN THE MIDDLE OF A WAR, WE NEEDED YOU!
YOU'RE A DISOBEDIENT CHILD THAT ONLY THINKS OF HERSELF!
I WOULDN'T BE HERE IF I WAS THINKING OF MYSELF! I'M DOING THIS FOR ALL OF YOU! FOR ALL OF PARSA!
LIES.
LIES.
LIES!

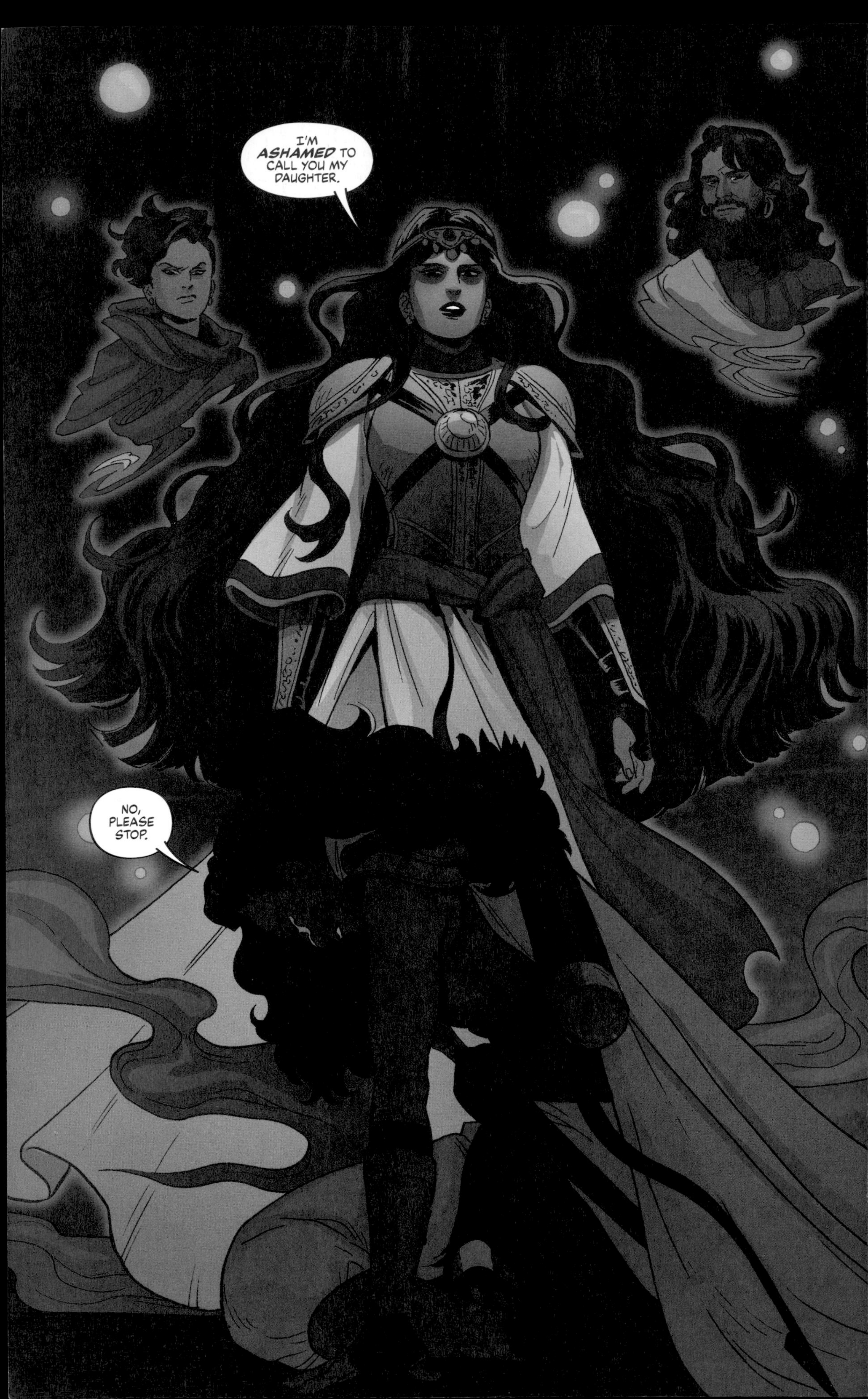
I'M *ASHAMED* TO CALL YOU MY DAUGHTER.
NO, PLEASE STOP.

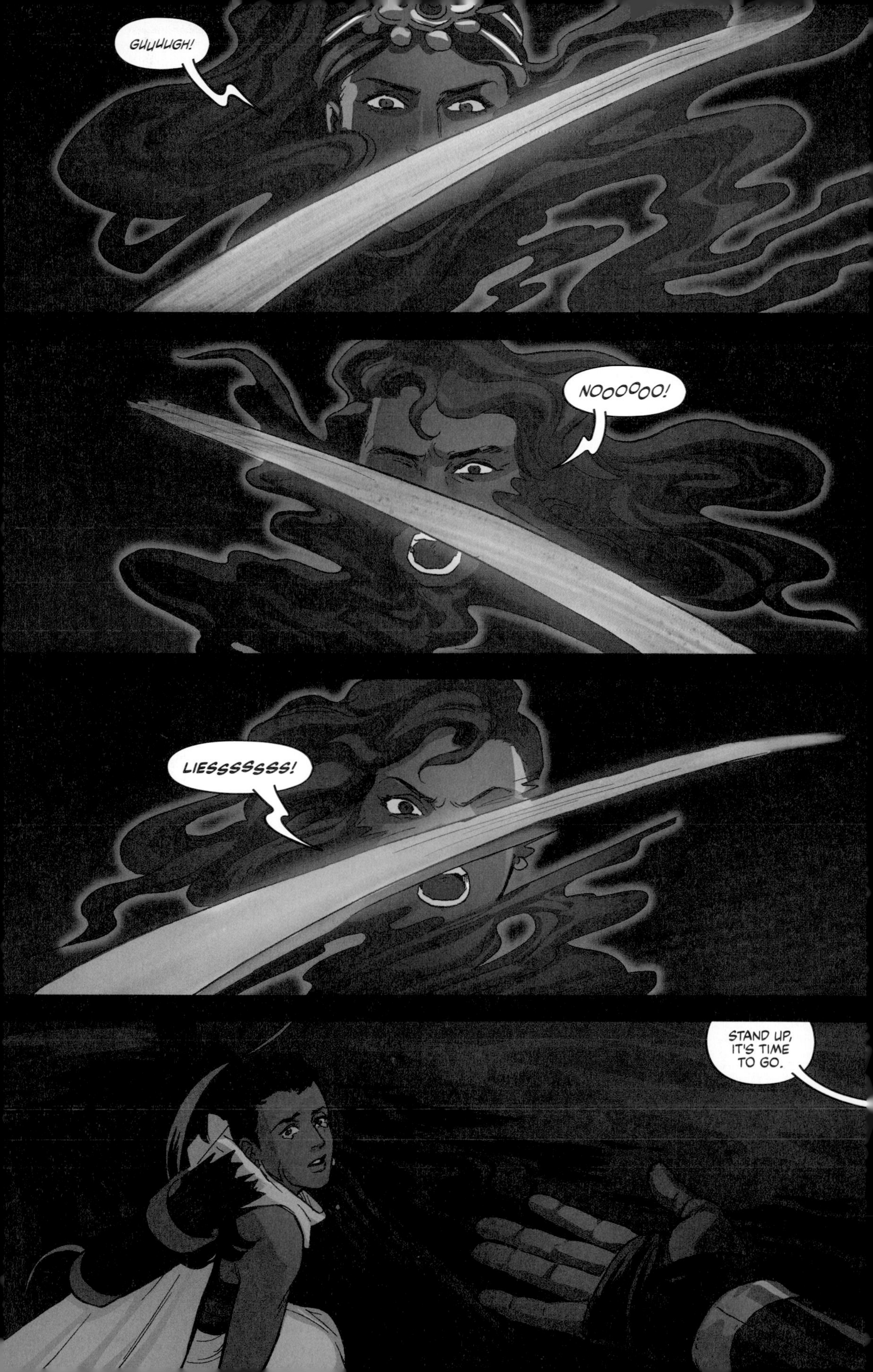
GUUUUGH!
NOOOOOO!
LIESSSSSSS!
STAND UP, IT'S TIME TO GO.

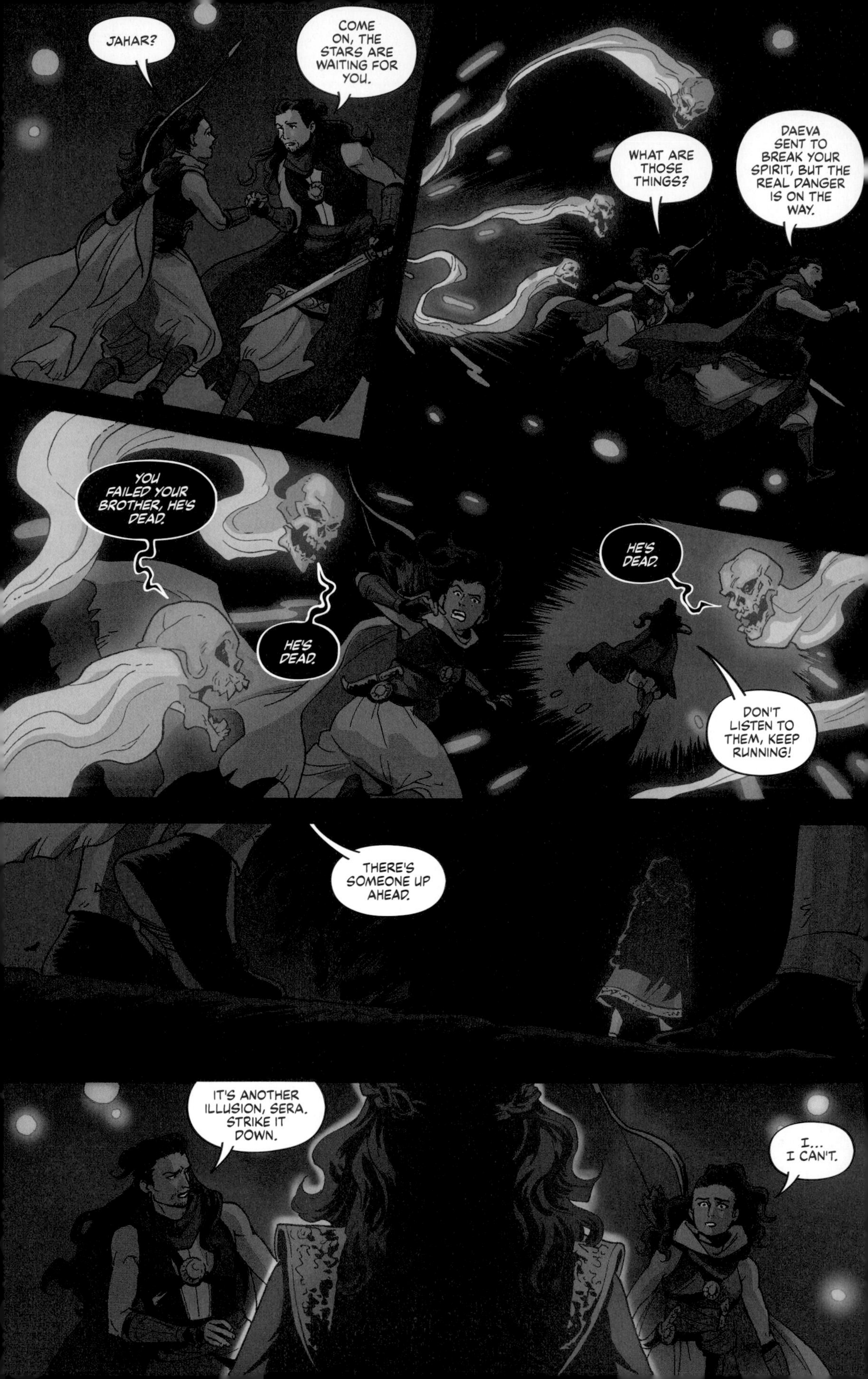
JAHAR?
COME ON, THE STARS ARE WAITING FOR YOU.
WHAT ARE THOSE THINGS?
DAEVA SENT TO BREAK YOUR SPIRIT, BUT THE REAL DANGER IS ON THE WAY.
YOU FAILED YOUR BROTHER, HE'S DEAD.
HE'S DEAD.
HE'S DEAD.
DON'T LISTEN TO THEM, KEEP RUNNING!
THERE'S SOMEONE UP AHEAD.
IT'S ANOTHER ILLUSION, SERA. STRIKE IT DOWN.
I... I CAN'T.

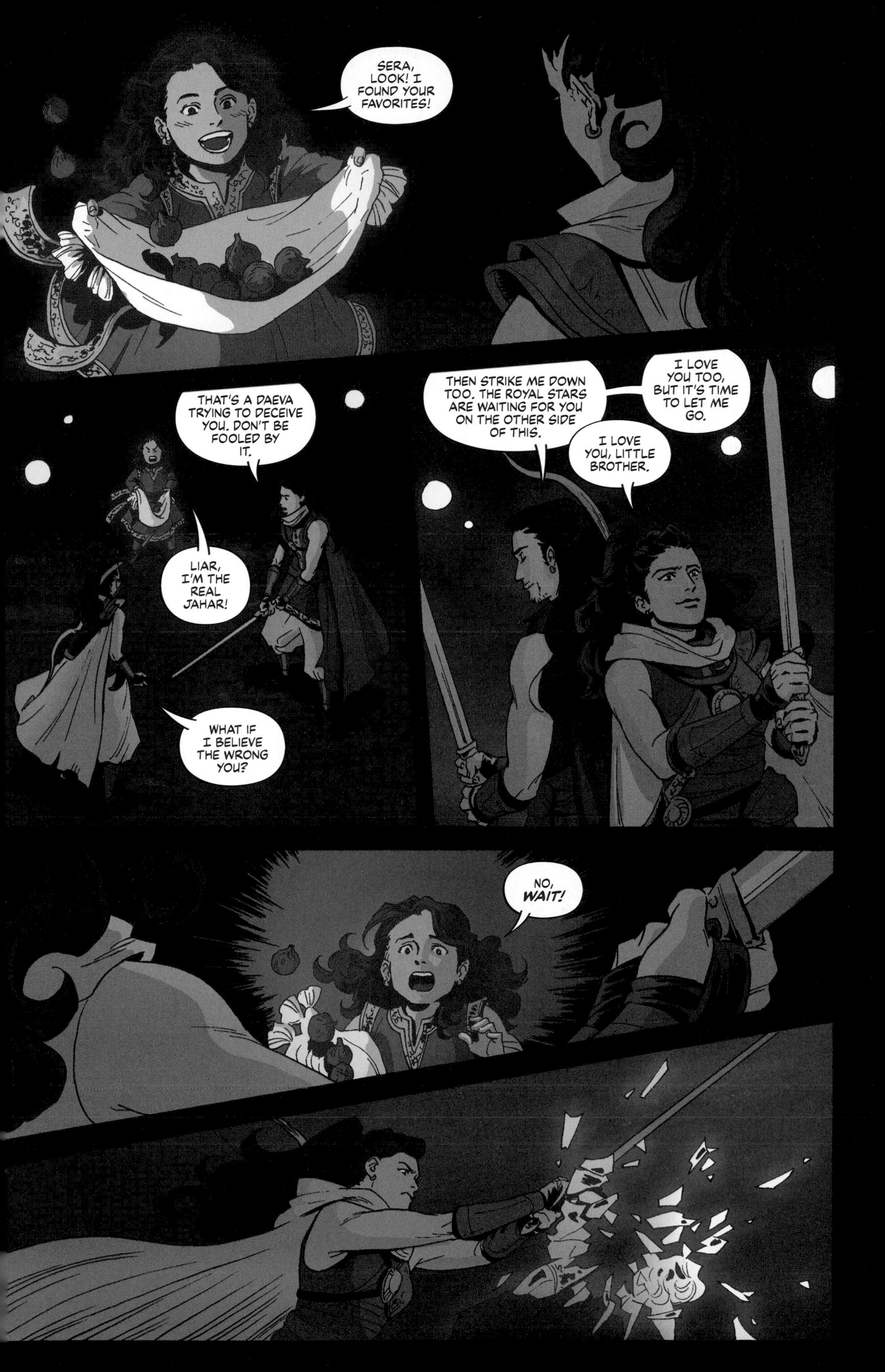
SERA, LOOK! I FOUND YOUR FAVORITES!
THAT'S A DAEVA TRYING TO DECEIVE YOU. DON'T BE FOOLED BY IT.
LIAR, I'M THE REAL JAHAR!
WHAT IF I BELIEVE THE WRONG YOU?
THEN STRIKE ME DOWN TOO. THE ROYAL STARS ARE WAITING FOR YOU ON THE OTHER SIDE OF THIS.
I LOVE YOU TOO, BUT IT'S TIME TO LET ME GO.
I LOVE YOU, LITTLE BROTHER.
NO, *WAIT!*

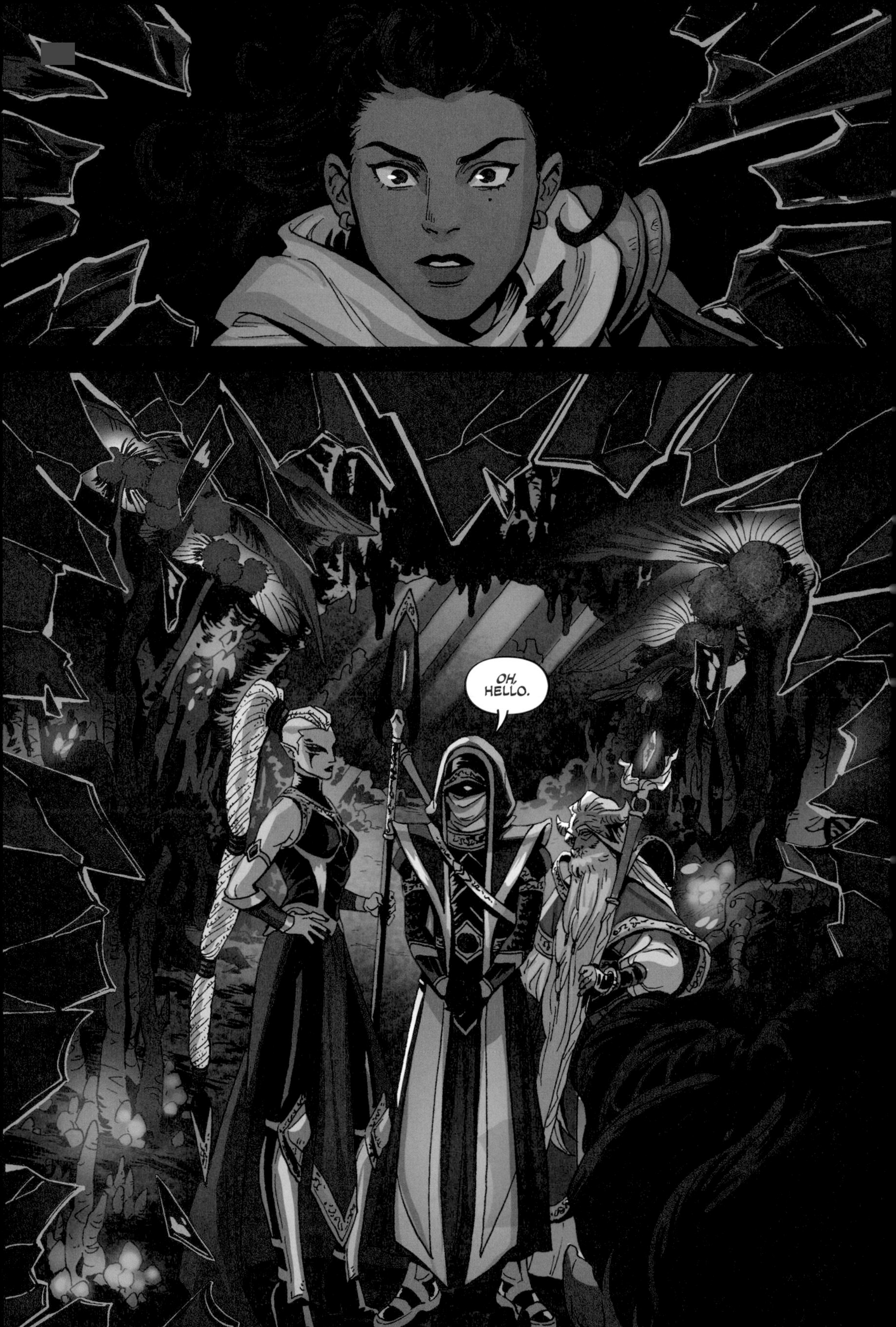
OH, HELLO.

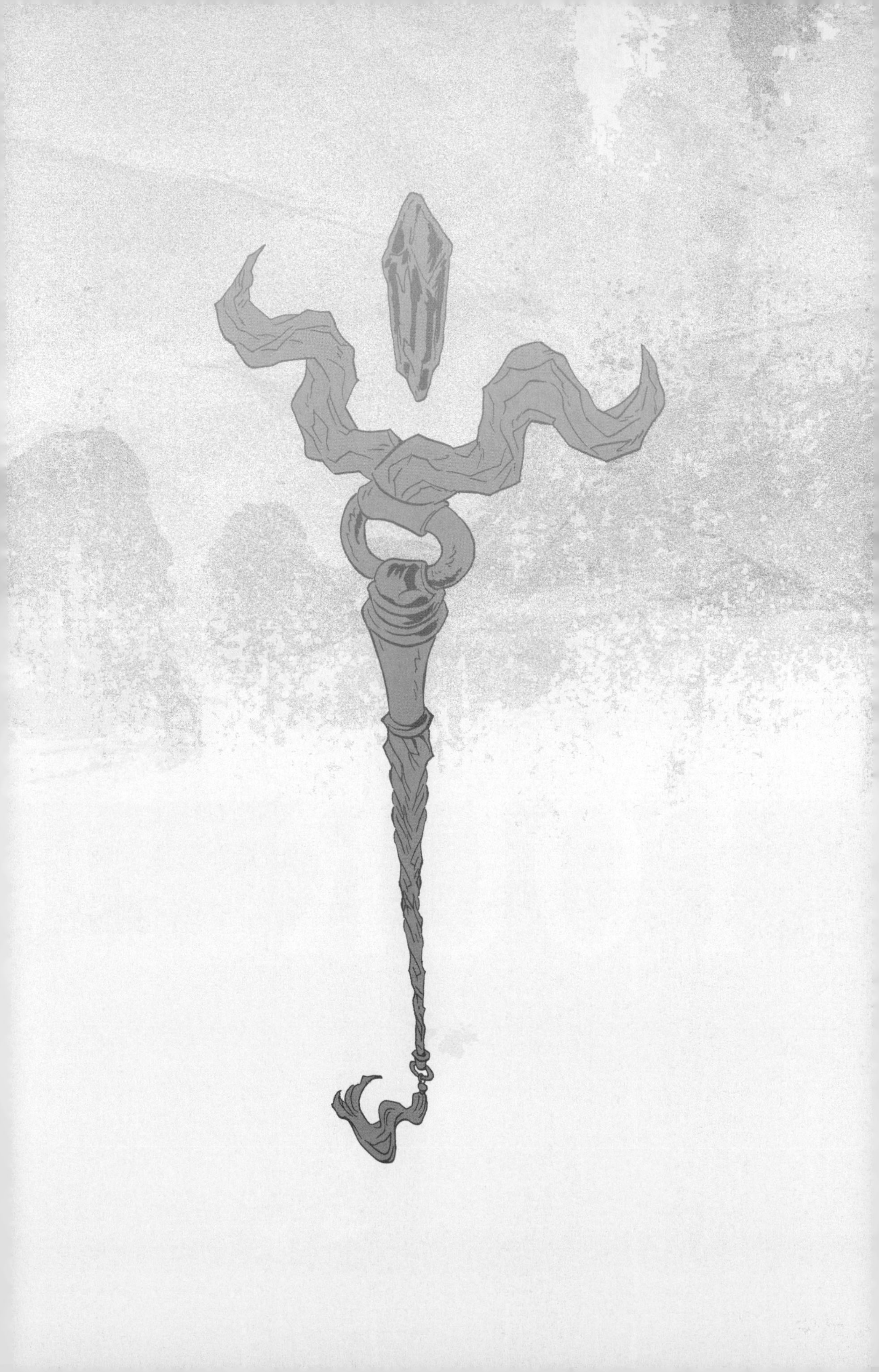

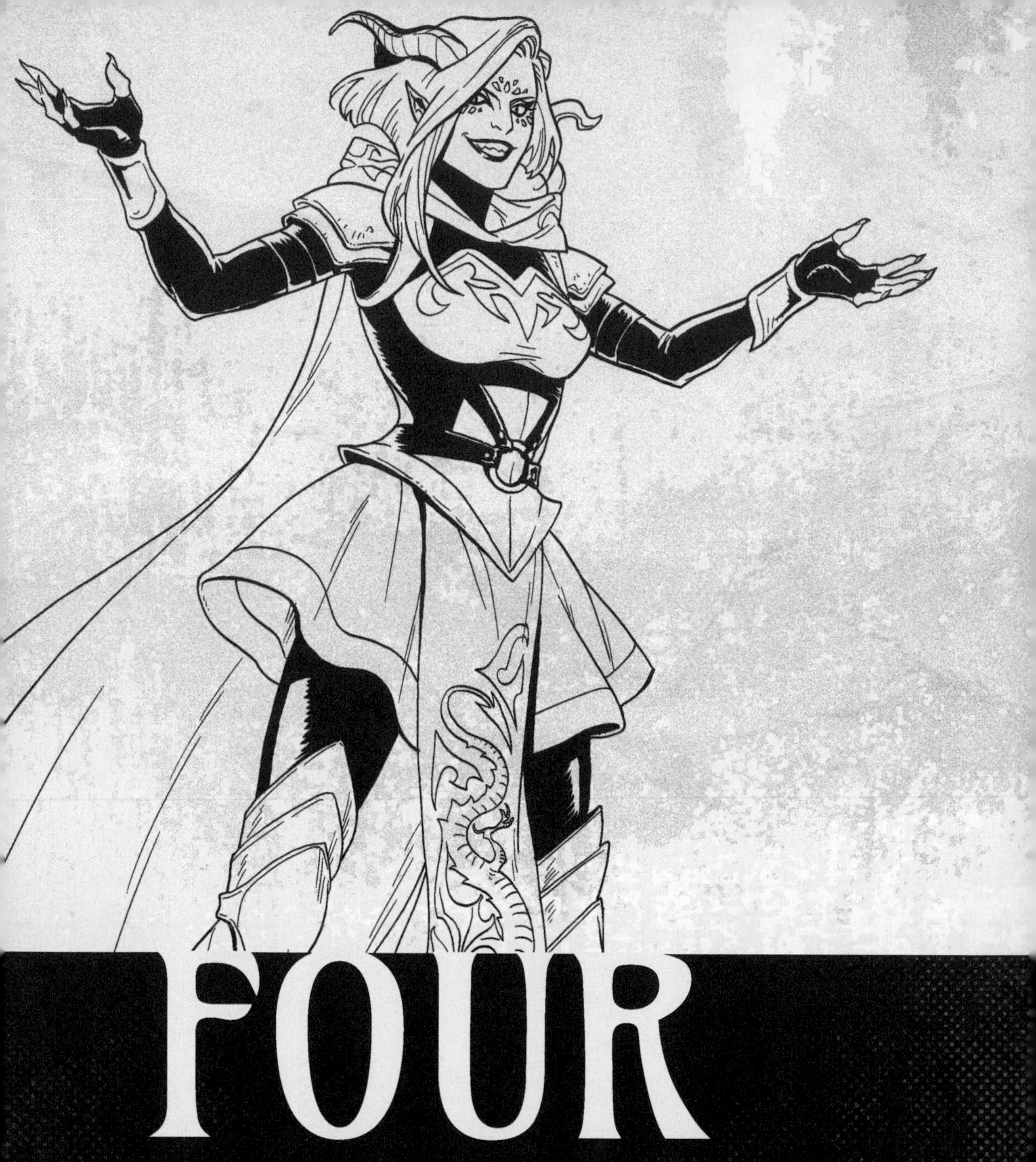

FOUR

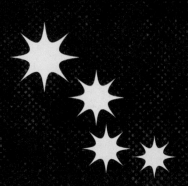

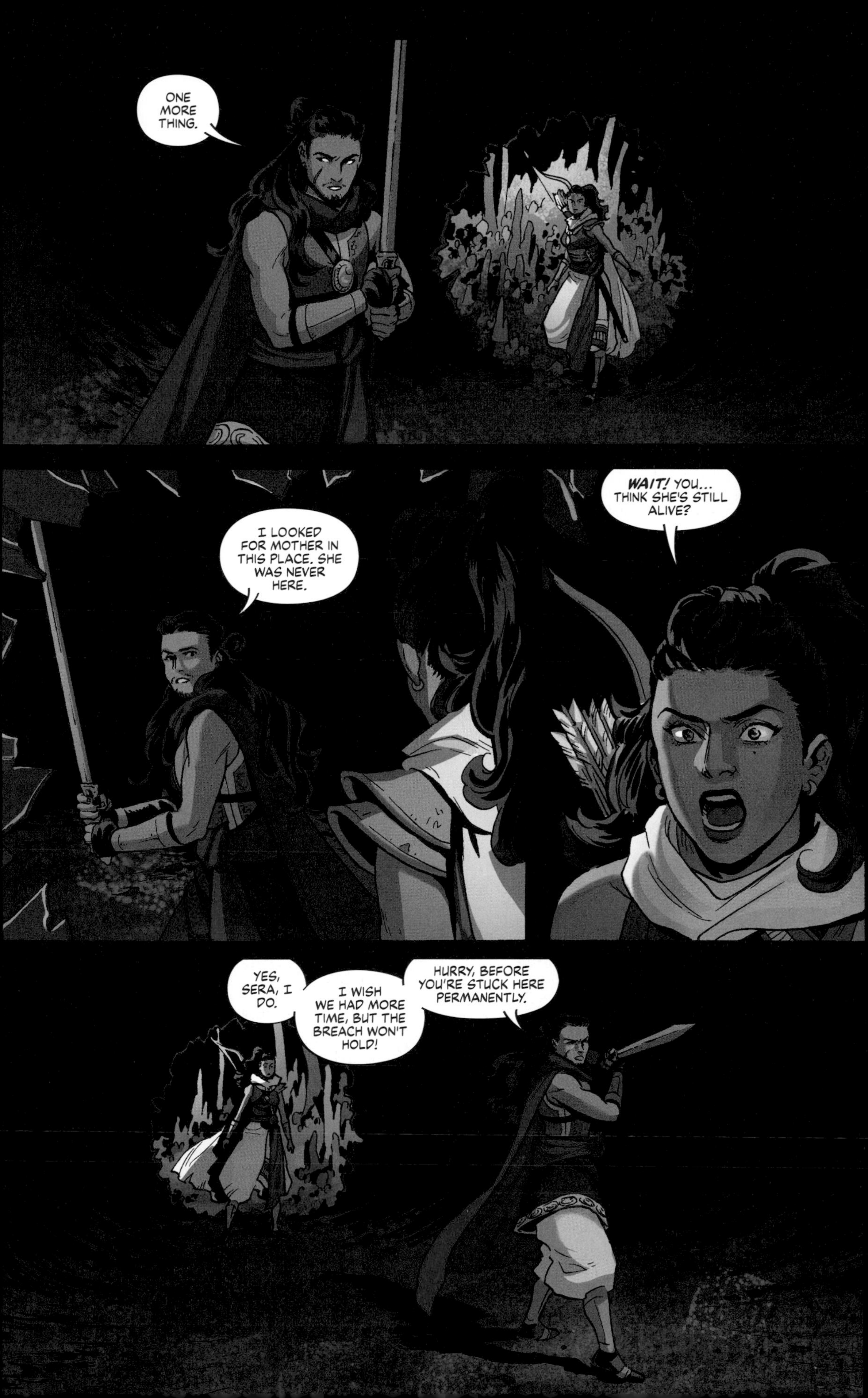
ONE MORE THING.
I LOOKED FOR MOTHER IN THIS PLACE. SHE WAS NEVER HERE.
WAIT! YOU... THINK SHE'S STILL ALIVE?
YES, SERA, I DO.
I WISH WE HAD MORE TIME, BUT THE BREACH WON'T HOLD!
HURRY, BEFORE YOU'RE STUCK HERE PERMANENTLY.

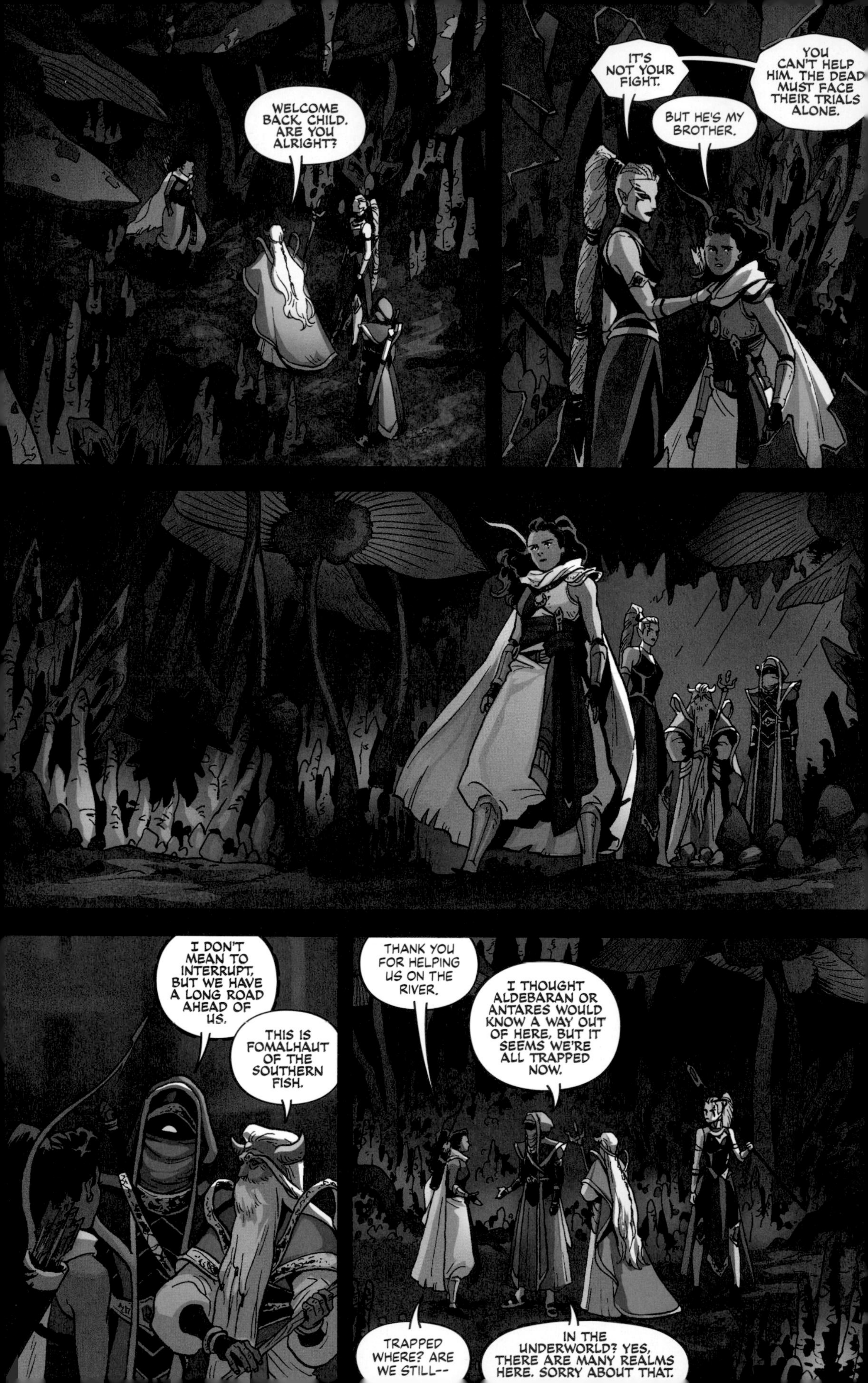
WELCOME BACK, CHILD. ARE YOU ALRIGHT?
IT'S NOT YOUR FIGHT.
YOU CAN'T HELP HIM. THE DEAD MUST FACE THEIR TRIALS ALONE.
BUT HE'S MY BROTHER.
I DON'T MEAN TO INTERRUPT, BUT WE HAVE A LONG ROAD AHEAD OF US.
THIS IS FOMALHAUT OF THE SOUTHERN FISH.
THANK YOU FOR HELPING US ON THE RIVER.
I THOUGHT ALDEBARAN OR ANTARES WOULD KNOW A WAY OUT OF HERE, BUT IT SEEMS WE'RE ALL TRAPPED NOW.
TRAPPED WHERE? ARE WE STILL--
IN THE UNDERWORLD? YES, THERE ARE MANY REALMS HERE. SORRY ABOUT THAT.

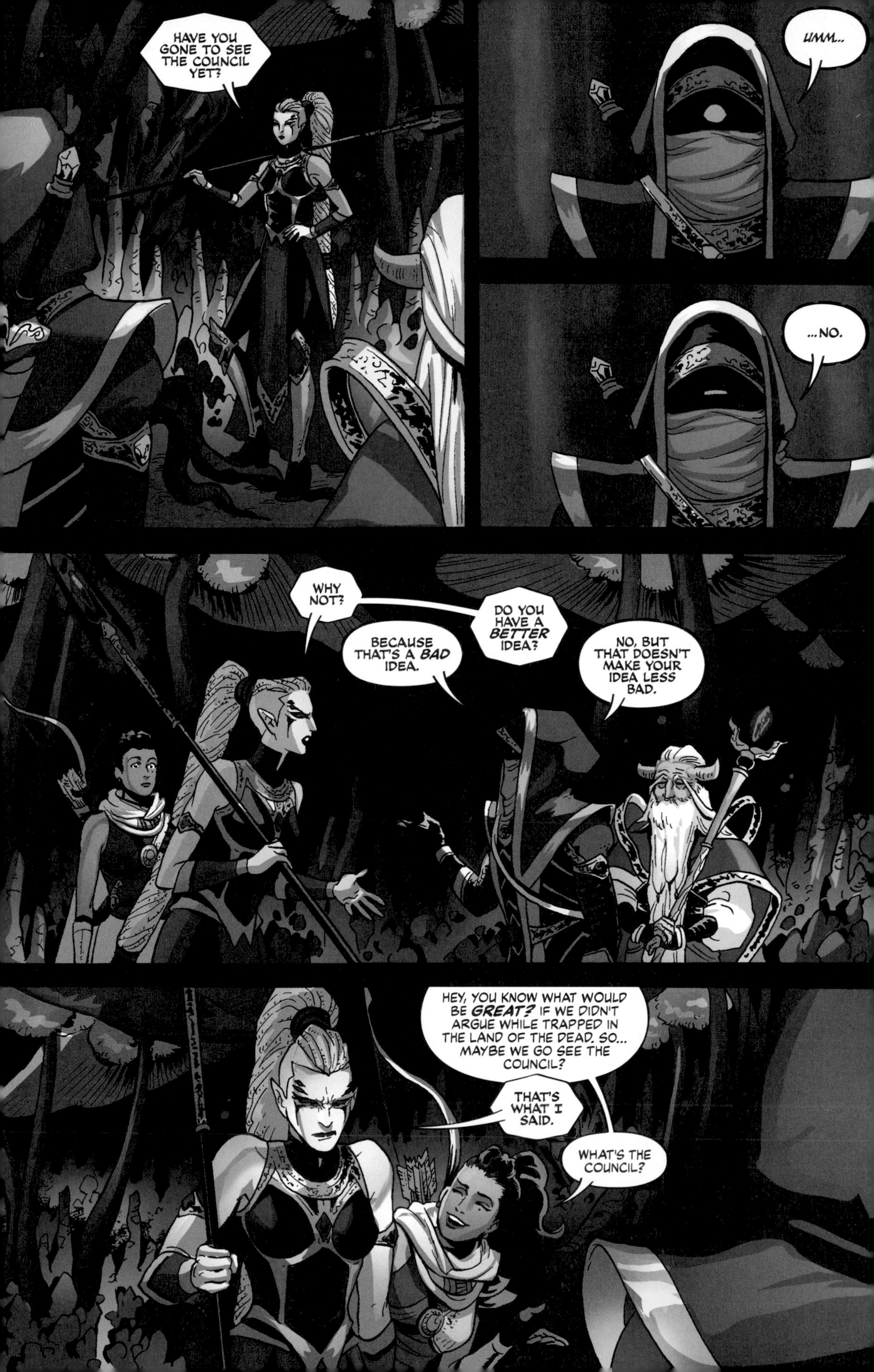
HAVE YOU GONE TO SEE THE COUNCIL YET?
UMM...
...NO.
WHY NOT?
BECAUSE THAT'S A BAD IDEA.
DO YOU HAVE A BETTER IDEA?
NO, BUT THAT DOESN'T MAKE YOUR IDEA LESS BAD.
HEY, YOU KNOW WHAT WOULD BE GREAT? IF WE DIDN'T ARGUE WHILE TRAPPED IN THE LAND OF THE DEAD. SO... MAYBE WE GO SEE THE COUNCIL?
THAT'S WHAT I SAID.
WHAT'S THE COUNCIL?

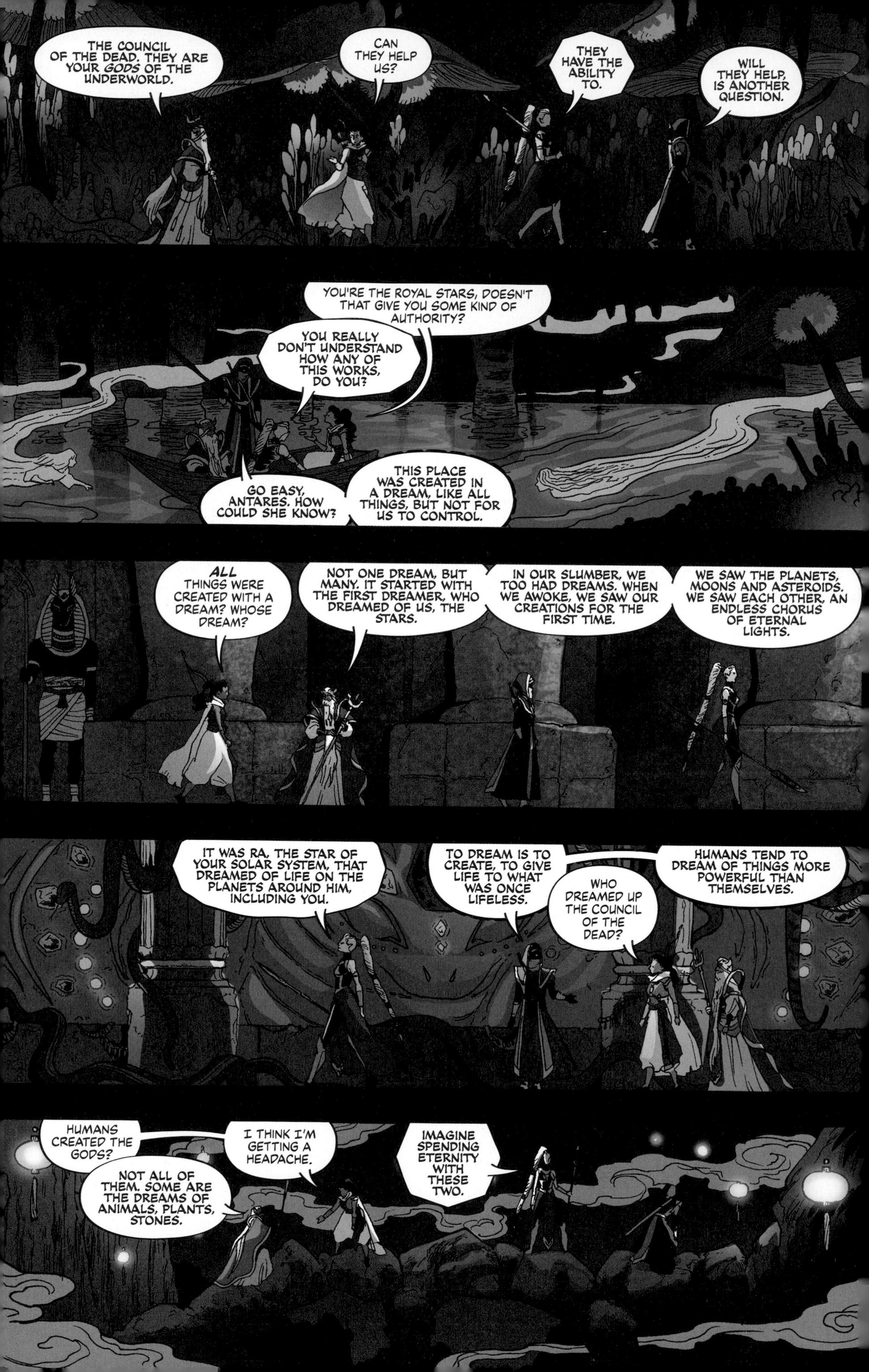
THE COUNCIL OF THE DEAD. THEY ARE YOUR GODS OF THE UNDERWORLD.
CAN THEY HELP US?
THEY HAVE THE ABILITY TO.
WILL THEY HELP, IS ANOTHER QUESTION.
YOU'RE THE ROYAL STARS, DOESN'T THAT GIVE YOU SOME KIND OF AUTHORITY?
YOU REALLY DON'T UNDERSTAND HOW ANY OF THIS WORKS, DO YOU?
GO EASY, ANTARES. HOW COULD SHE KNOW?
THIS PLACE WAS CREATED IN A DREAM, LIKE ALL THINGS, BUT NOT FOR US TO CONTROL.
ALL THINGS WERE CREATED WITH A DREAM? WHOSE DREAM?
NOT ONE DREAM, BUT MANY. IT STARTED WITH THE FIRST DREAMER, WHO DREAMED OF US, THE STARS.
IN OUR SLUMBER, WE TOO HAD DREAMS. WHEN WE AWOKE, WE SAW OUR CREATIONS FOR THE FIRST TIME.
WE SAW THE PLANETS, MOONS AND ASTEROIDS. WE SAW EACH OTHER, AN ENDLESS CHORUS OF ETERNAL LIGHTS.
IT WAS RA, THE STAR OF YOUR SOLAR SYSTEM, THAT DREAMED OF LIFE ON THE PLANETS AROUND HIM, INCLUDING YOU.
TO DREAM IS TO CREATE, TO GIVE LIFE TO WHAT WAS ONCE LIFELESS.
HUMANS TEND TO DREAM OF THINGS MORE POWERFUL THAN THEMSELVES.
WHO DREAMED UP THE COUNCIL OF THE DEAD?
HUMANS CREATED THE GODS?
NOT ALL OF THEM. SOME ARE THE DREAMS OF ANIMALS, PLANTS, STONES.
I THINK I'M GETTING A HEADACHE.
IMAGINE SPENDING ETERNITY WITH THESE TWO.

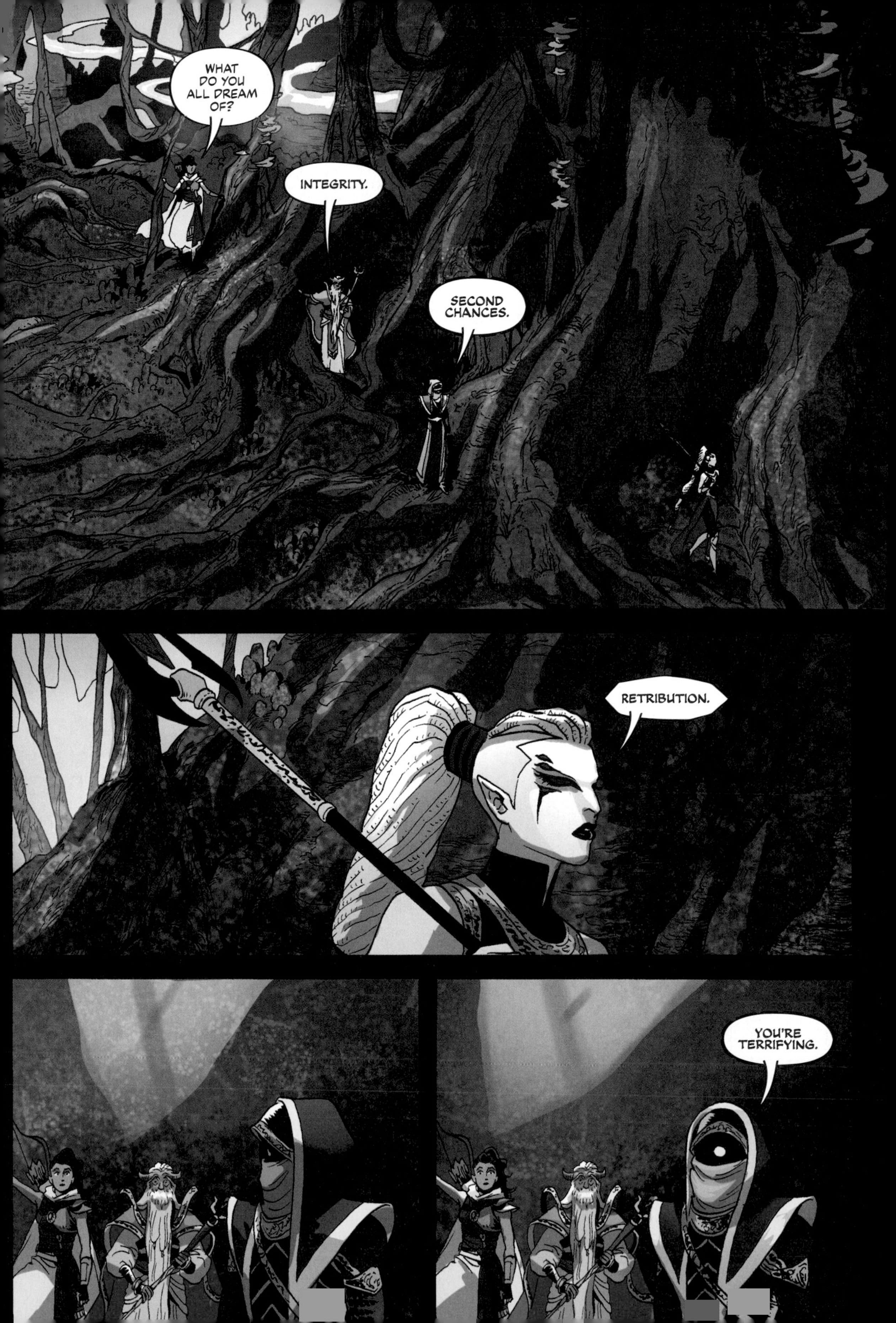
WHAT DO YOU ALL DREAM OF?
INTEGRITY.
SECOND CHANCES.
RETRIBUTION.
YOU'RE TERRIFYING.

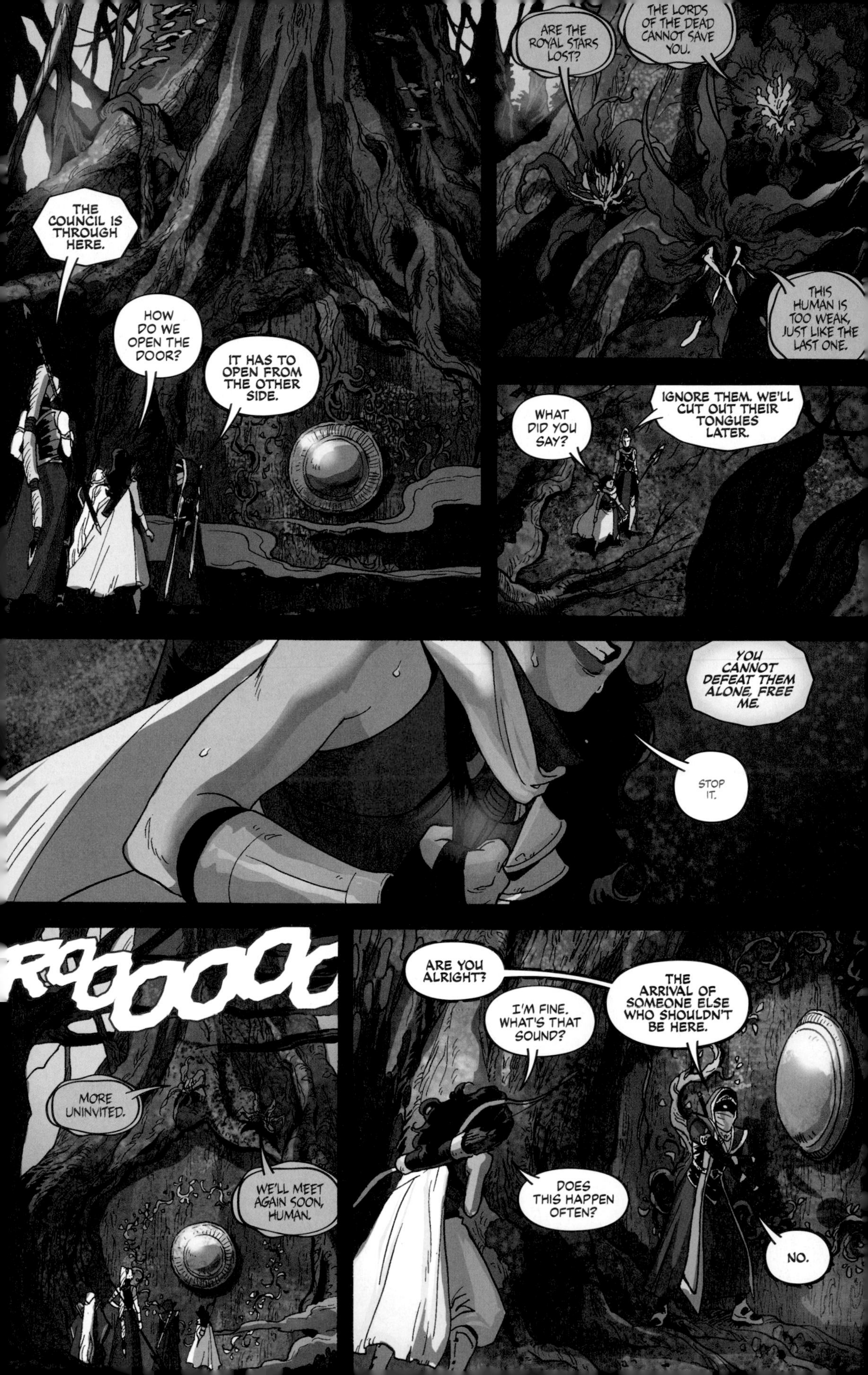
THE COUNCIL IS THROUGH HERE.
HOW DO WE OPEN THE DOOR?
IT HAS TO OPEN FROM THE OTHER SIDE.
ARE THE ROYAL STARS LOST?
THE LORDS OF THE DEAD CANNOT SAVE YOU.
THIS HUMAN IS TOO WEAK, JUST LIKE THE LAST ONE.
WHAT DID YOU SAY?
IGNORE THEM. WE'LL CUT OUT THEIR TONGUES LATER.
YOU CANNOT DEFEAT THEM ALONE, FREE ME.
STOP IT.
ROOOOOO
MORE UNINVITED.
WE'LL MEET AGAIN SOON, HUMAN.
ARE YOU ALRIGHT?
I'M FINE. WHAT'S THAT SOUND?
THE ARRIVAL OF SOMEONE ELSE WHO SHOULDN'T BE HERE.
DOES THIS HAPPEN OFTEN?
NO.

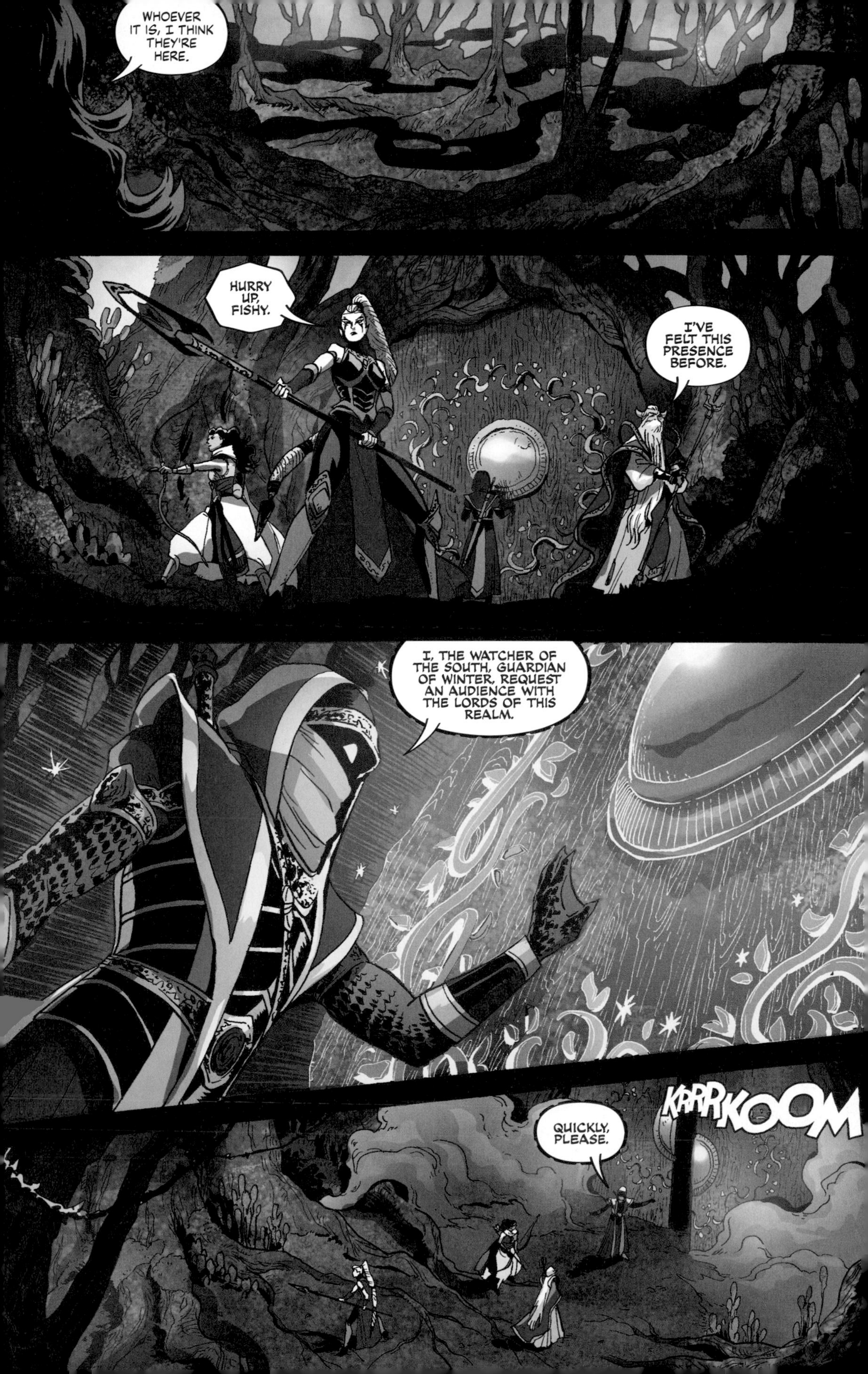
WHOEVER IT IS, I THINK THEY'RE HERE.
HURRY UP, FISHY.
I'VE FELT THIS PRESENCE BEFORE.
I, THE WATCHER OF THE SOUTH, GUARDIAN OF WINTER, REQUEST AN AUDIENCE WITH THE LORDS OF THIS REALM.
KRRRKOOM
QUICKLY, PLEASE.

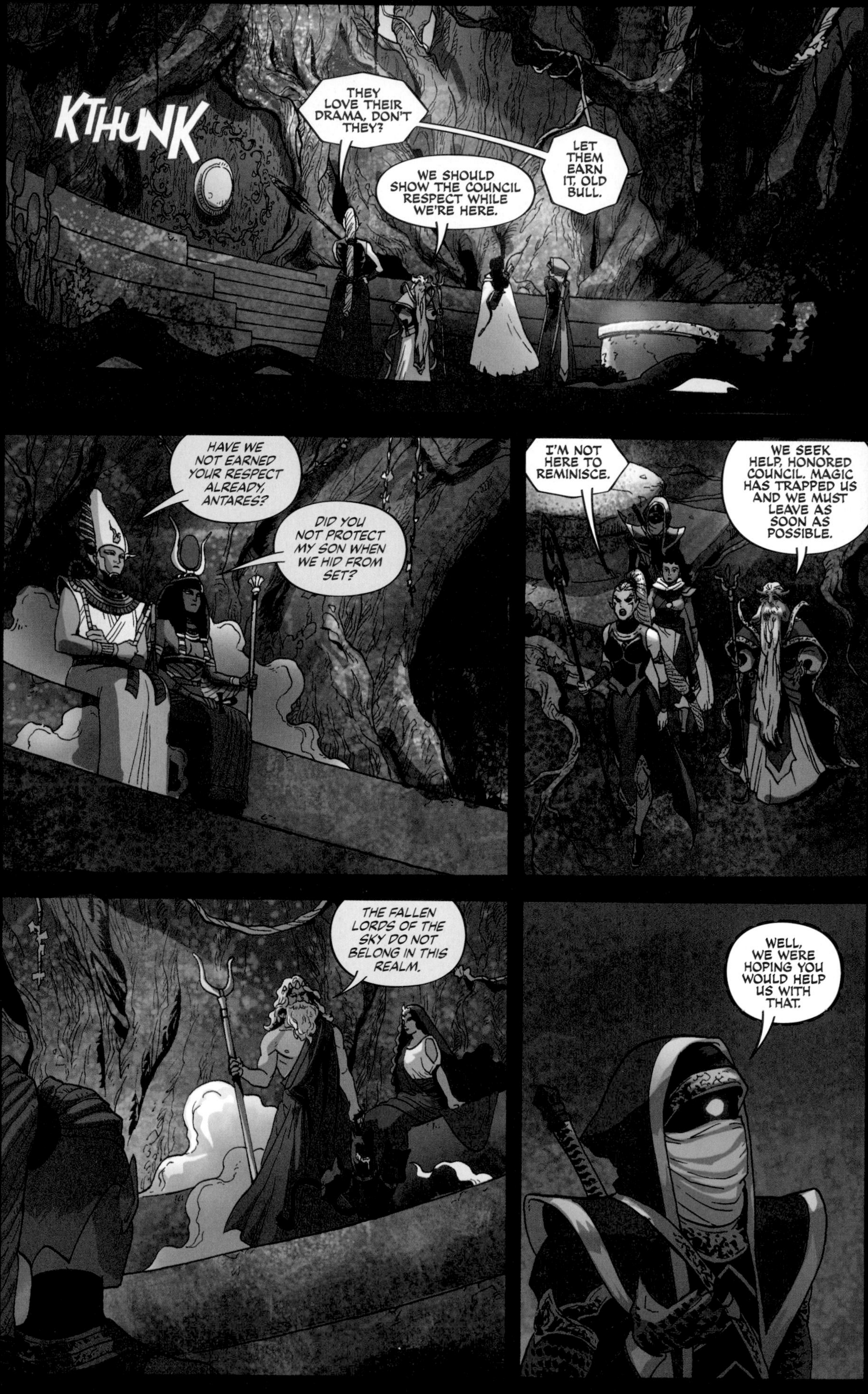
KTHUNK
THEY LOVE THEIR DRAMA, DON'T THEY?
LET THEM EARN IT, OLD BULL.
WE SHOULD SHOW THE COUNCIL RESPECT WHILE WE'RE HERE.
HAVE WE NOT EARNED YOUR RESPECT ALREADY, ANTARES?
DID YOU NOT PROTECT MY SON WHEN WE HID FROM SET?
I'M NOT HERE TO REMINISCE.
WE SEEK HELP, HONORED COUNCIL. MAGIC HAS TRAPPED US AND WE MUST LEAVE AS SOON AS POSSIBLE.
THE FALLEN LORDS OF THE SKY DO NOT BELONG IN THIS REALM.
WELL, WE WERE HOPING YOU WOULD HELP US WITH THAT.

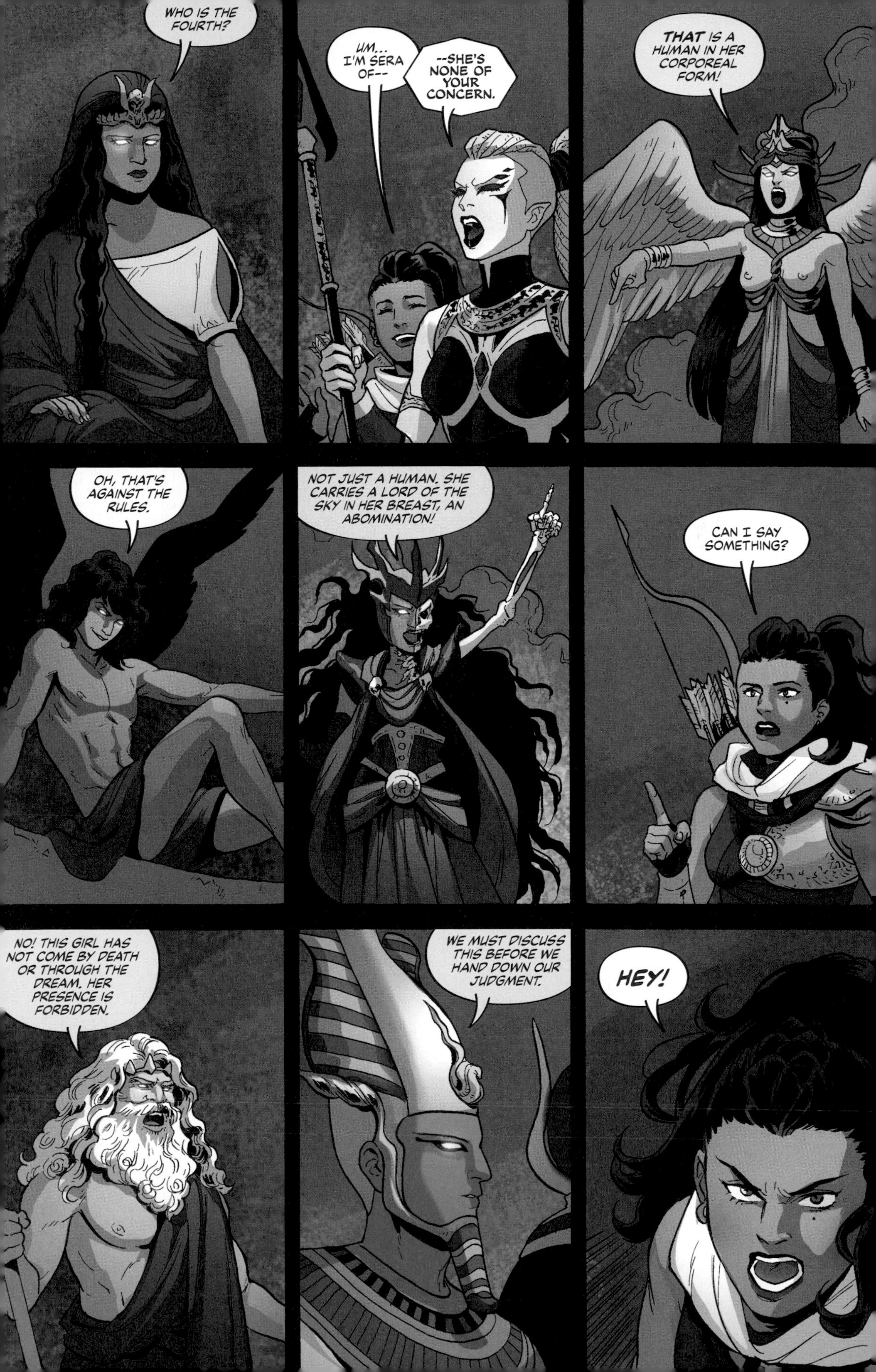
WHO IS THE FOURTH?
UM... I'M SERA OF--
--SHE'S NONE OF YOUR CONCERN.
THAT IS A HUMAN IN HER CORPOREAL FORM!
OH, THAT'S AGAINST THE RULES.
NOT JUST A HUMAN. SHE CARRIES A LORD OF THE SKY IN HER BREAST, AN ABOMINATION!
CAN I SAY SOMETHING?
NO! THIS GIRL HAS NOT COME BY DEATH OR THROUGH THE DREAM. HER PRESENCE IS FORBIDDEN.
WE MUST DISCUSS THIS BEFORE WE HAND DOWN OUR JUDGMENT.
HEY!

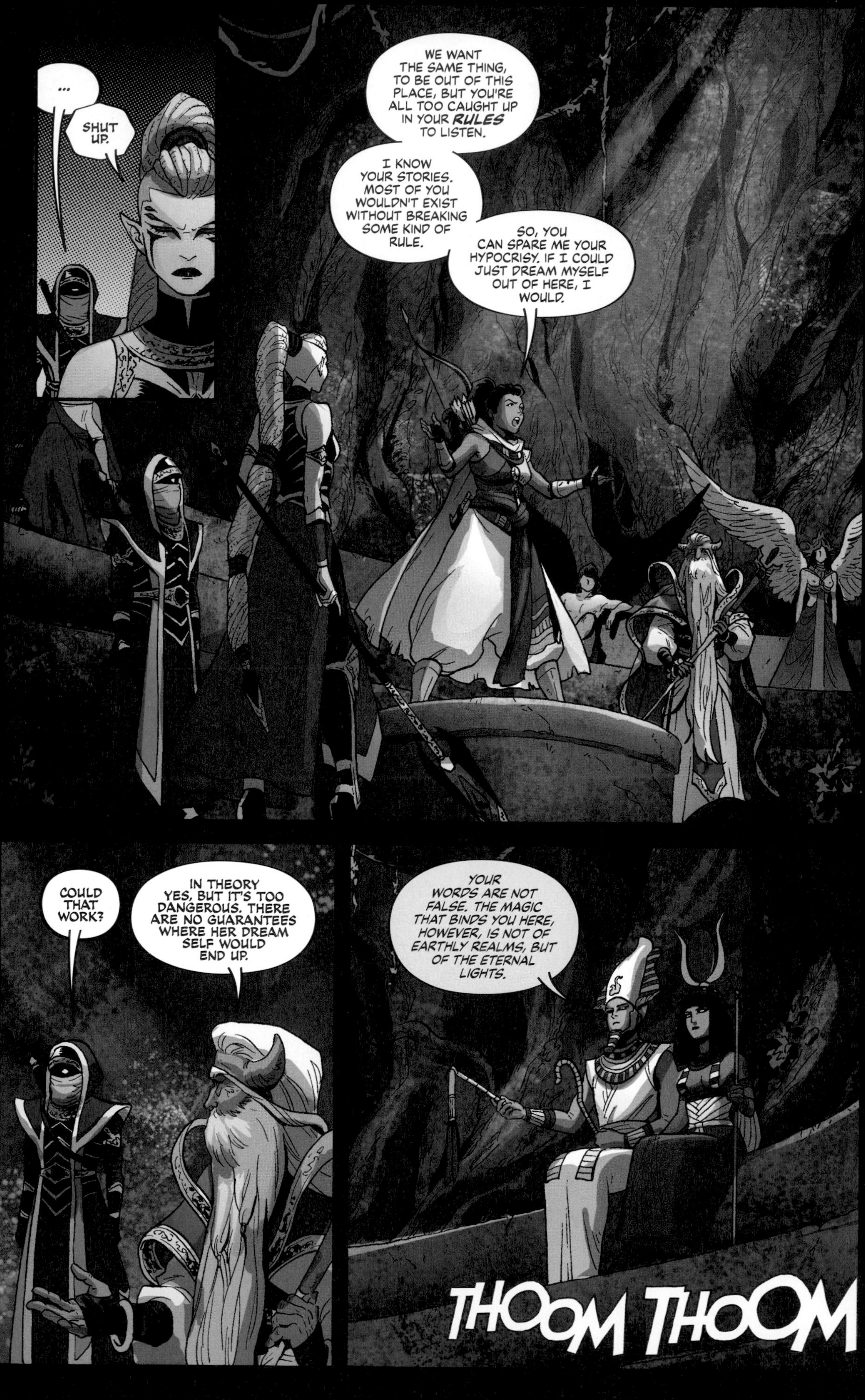
...
SHUT UP.
WE WANT THE SAME THING, TO BE OUT OF THIS PLACE, BUT YOU'RE ALL TOO CAUGHT UP IN YOUR RULES TO LISTEN.
I KNOW YOUR STORIES. MOST OF YOU WOULDN'T EXIST WITHOUT BREAKING SOME KIND OF RULE.
SO, YOU CAN SPARE ME YOUR HYPOCRISY. IF I COULD JUST DREAM MYSELF OUT OF HERE, I WOULD.
COULD THAT WORK?
IN THEORY YES, BUT IT'S TOO DANGEROUS. THERE ARE NO GUARANTEES WHERE HER DREAM SELF WOULD END UP.
YOUR WORDS ARE NOT FALSE. THE MAGIC THAT BINDS YOU HERE, HOWEVER, IS NOT OF EARTHLY REALMS, BUT OF THE ETERNAL LIGHTS.
THOOM THOOM

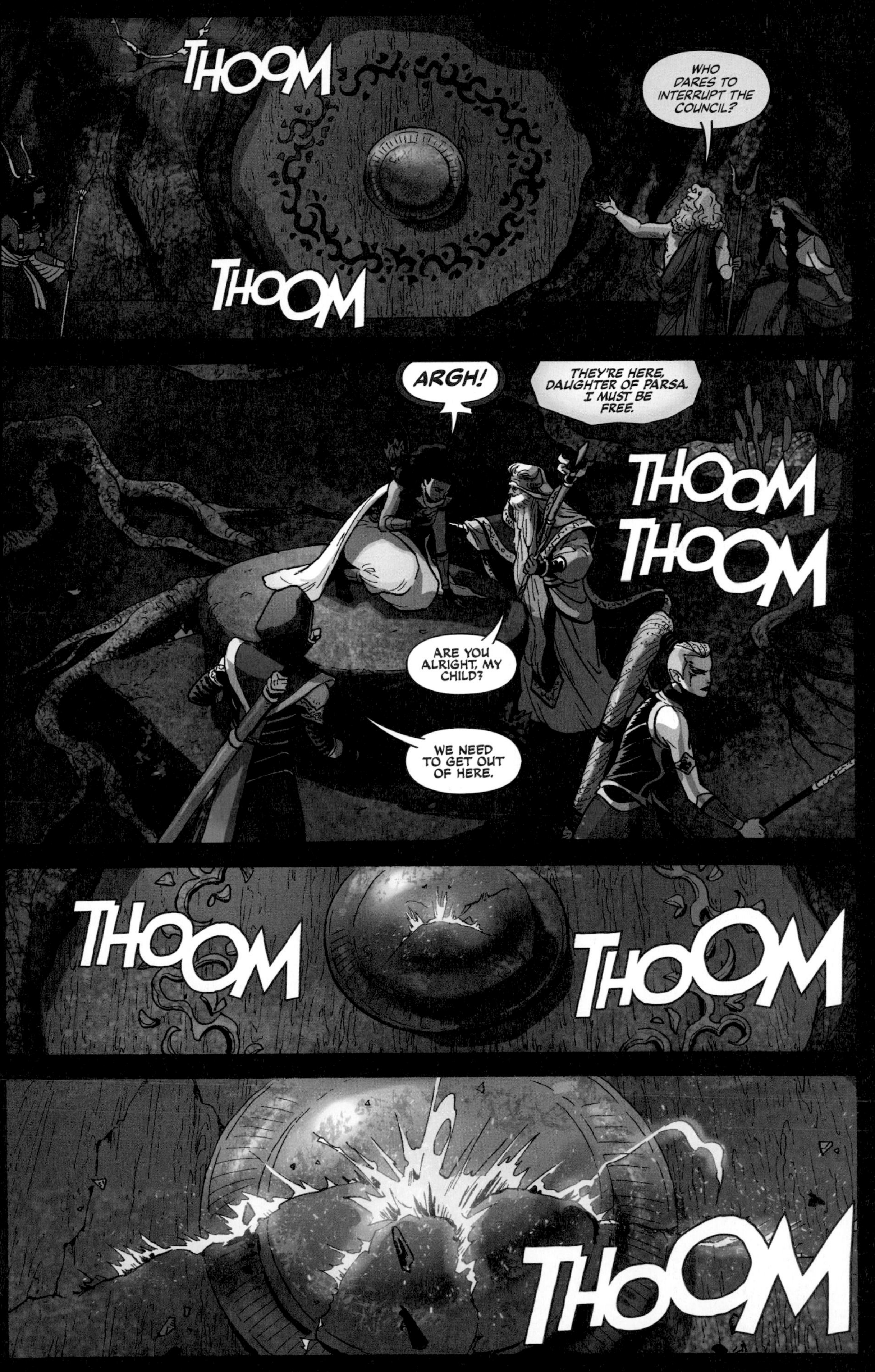
THOOM
THOOM
WHO DARES TO INTERRUPT THE COUNCIL?
ARGH!
THEY'RE HERE, DAUGHTER OF PARSA. I MUST BE FREE.
THOOM
THOOM
ARE YOU ALRIGHT, MY CHILD?
WE NEED TO GET OUT OF HERE.
THOOM
THOOM
THOOM

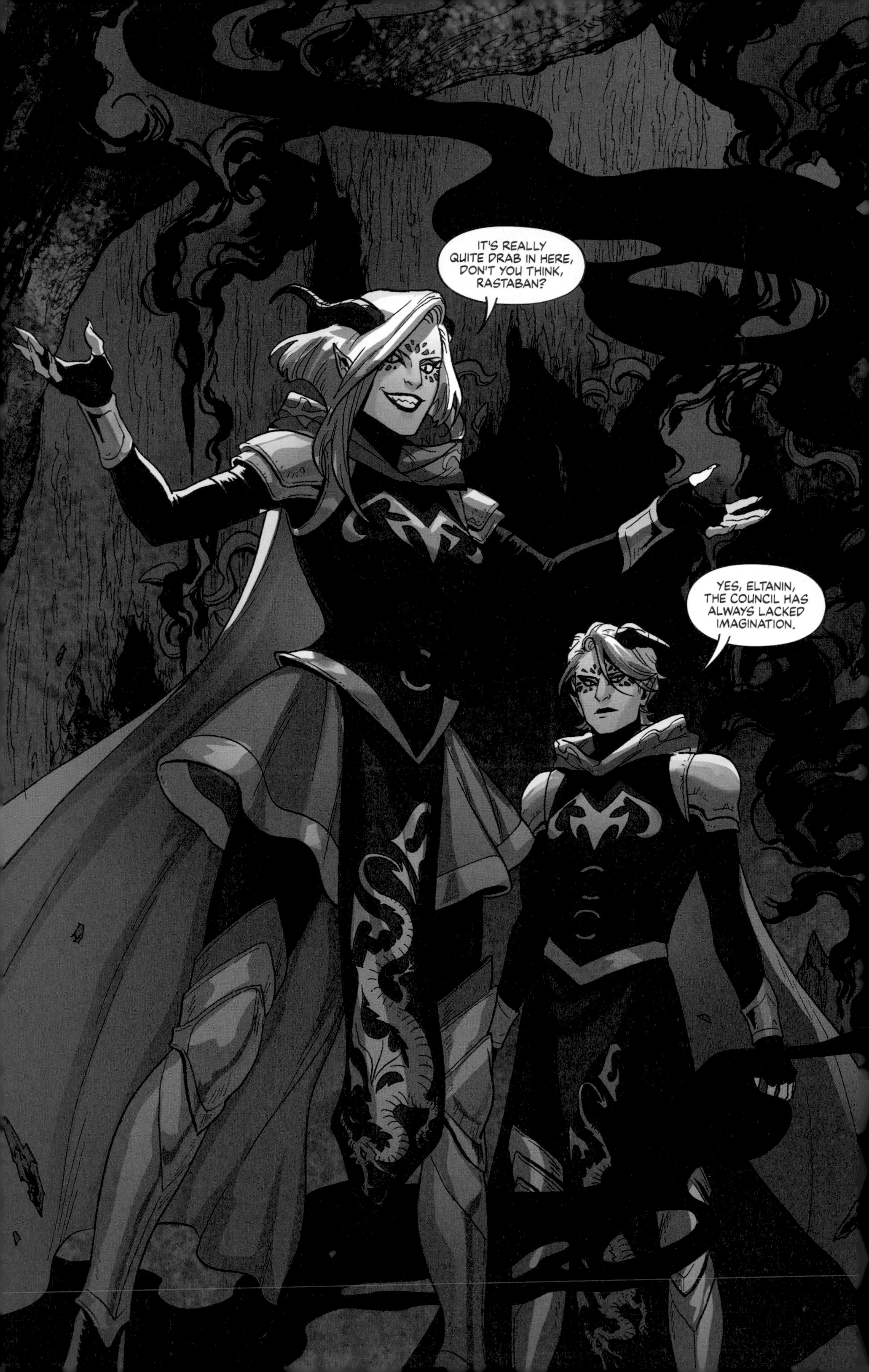
IT'S REALLY QUITE DRAB IN HERE, DON'T YOU THINK, RASTABAN?
YES, ELTANIN, THE COUNCIL HAS ALWAYS LACKED IMAGINATION.

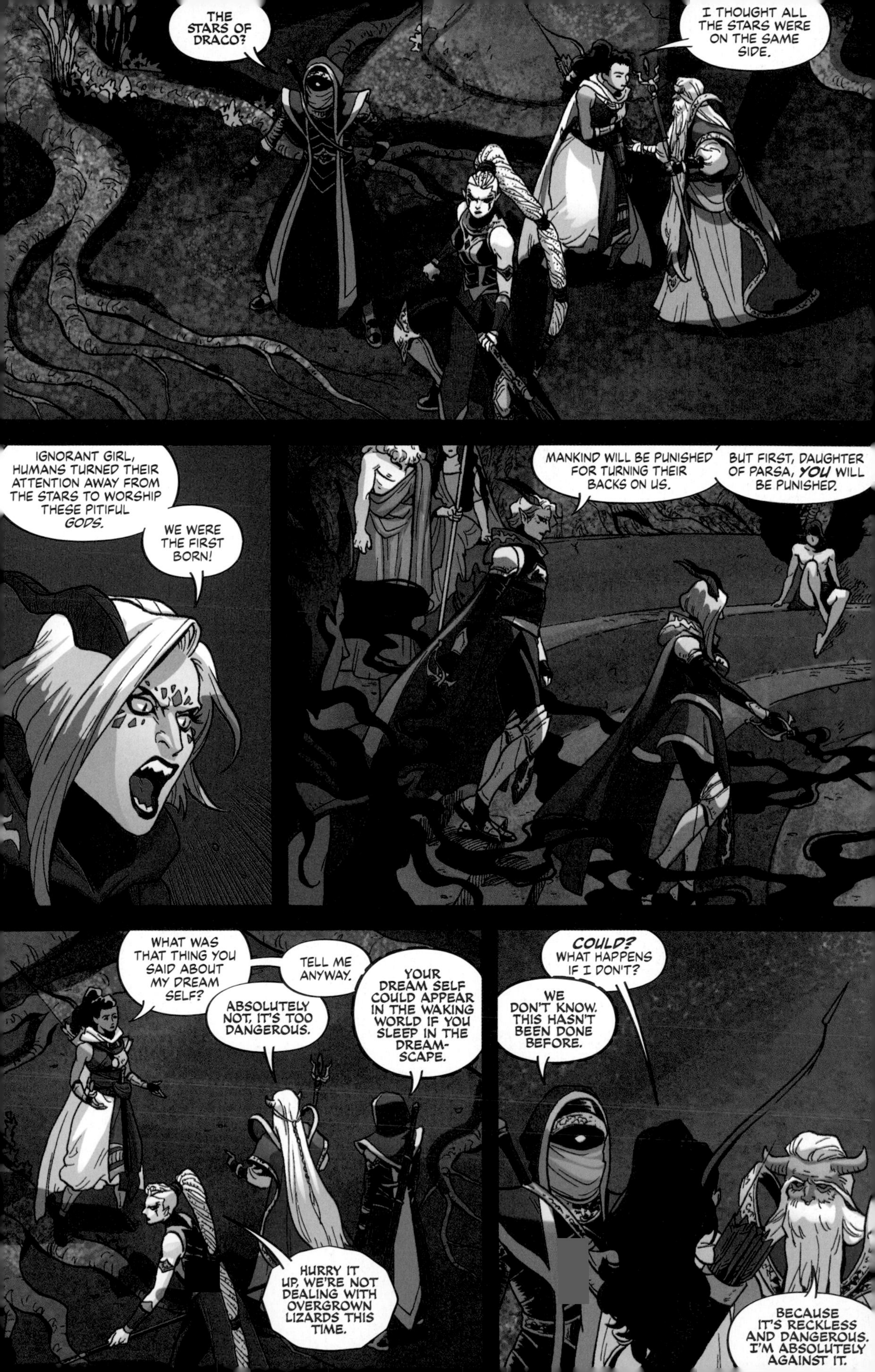
THE STARS OF DRACO?
I THOUGHT ALL THE STARS WERE ON THE SAME SIDE.
IGNORANT GIRL, HUMANS TURNED THEIR ATTENTION AWAY FROM THE STARS TO WORSHIP THESE PITIFUL GODS.
WE WERE THE FIRST BORN!
MANKIND WILL BE PUNISHED FOR TURNING THEIR BACKS ON US.
BUT FIRST, DAUGHTER OF PARSA, YOU WILL BE PUNISHED.
WHAT WAS THAT THING YOU SAID ABOUT MY DREAM SELF?
ABSOLUTELY NOT, IT'S TOO DANGEROUS.
TELL ME ANYWAY.
YOUR DREAM SELF COULD APPEAR IN THE WAKING WORLD IF YOU SLEEP IN THE DREAM-SCAPE.
HURRY IT UP, WE'RE NOT DEALING WITH OVERGROWN LIZARDS THIS TIME.
COULD? WHAT HAPPENS IF I DON'T?
WE DON'T KNOW. THIS HASN'T BEEN DONE BEFORE.
BECAUSE IT'S RECKLESS AND DANGEROUS. I'M ABSOLUTELY AGAINST IT.

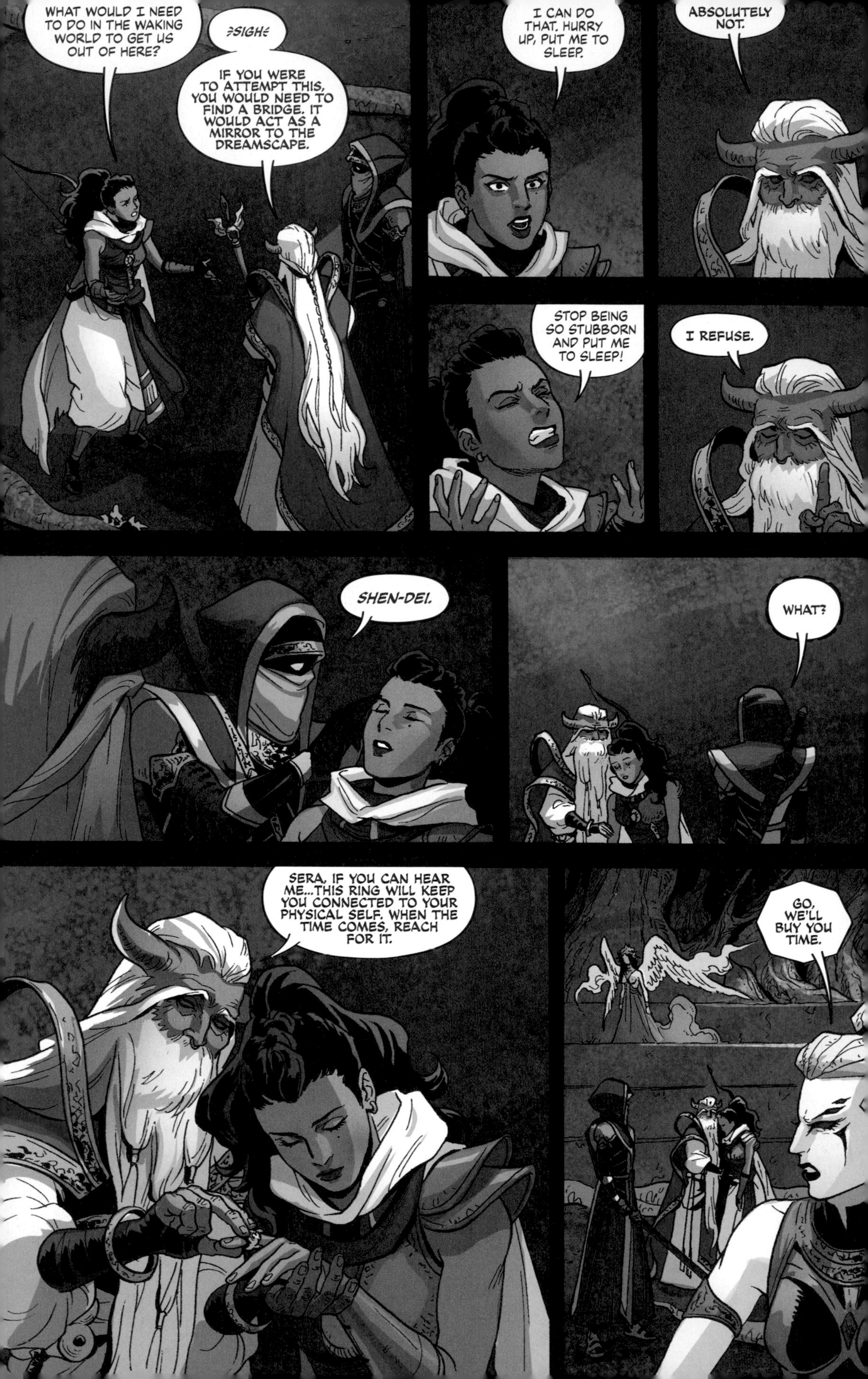
WHAT WOULD I NEED TO DO IN THE WAKING WORLD TO GET US OUT OF HERE?
⁂SIGH⁂
IF YOU WERE TO ATTEMPT THIS, YOU WOULD NEED TO FIND A BRIDGE. IT WOULD ACT AS A MIRROR TO THE DREAMSCAPE.
I CAN DO THAT. HURRY UP, PUT ME TO SLEEP.
ABSOLUTELY NOT.
STOP BEING SO STUBBORN AND PUT ME TO SLEEP!
I REFUSE.
SHEN-DEI.
WHAT?
SERA, IF YOU CAN HEAR ME...THIS RING WILL KEEP YOU CONNECTED TO YOUR PHYSICAL SELF. WHEN THE TIME COMES, REACH FOR IT.
GO, WE'LL BUY YOU TIME.

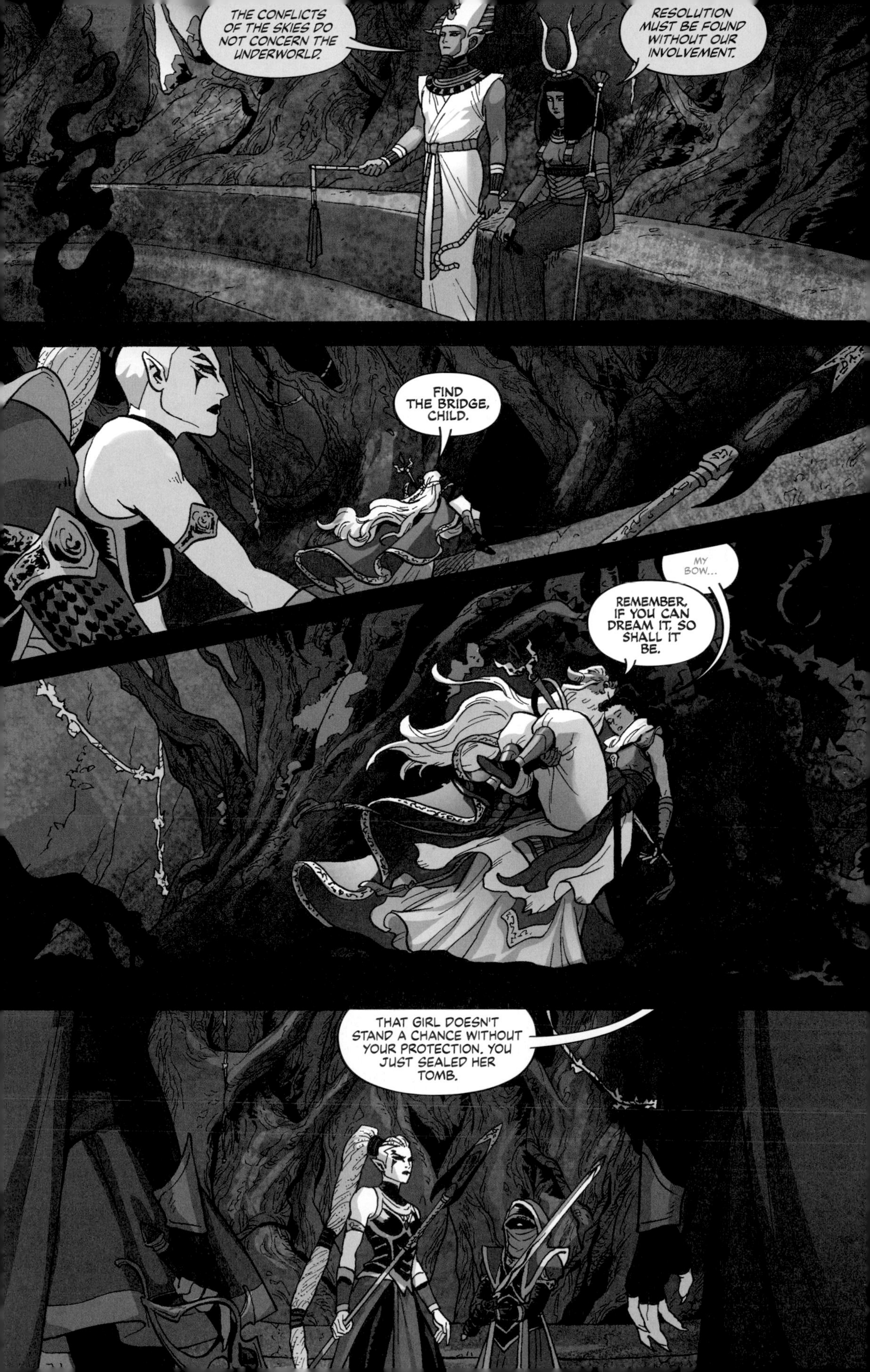
THE CONFLICTS OF THE SKIES DO NOT CONCERN THE UNDERWORLD.
RESOLUTION MUST BE FOUND WITHOUT OUR INVOLVEMENT.
FIND THE BRIDGE, CHILD.
MY BOW...
REMEMBER, IF YOU CAN DREAM IT, SO SHALL IT BE.
THAT GIRL DOESN'T STAND A CHANCE WITHOUT YOUR PROTECTION. YOU JUST SEALED HER TOMB.

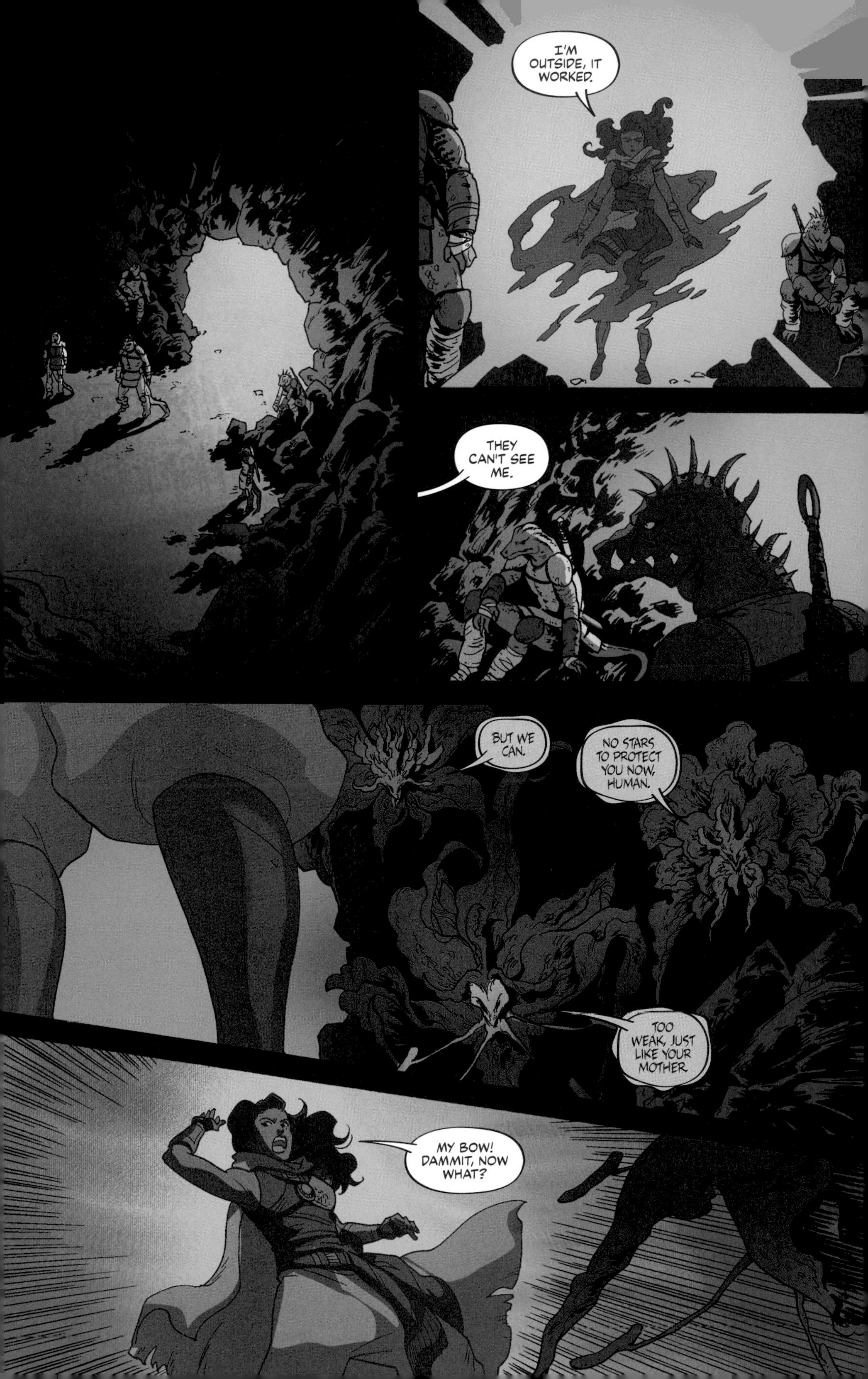
I'M OUTSIDE, IT WORKED.
THEY CAN'T SEE ME.
BUT WE CAN.
NO STARS TO PROTECT YOU NOW, HUMAN.
TOO WEAK, JUST LIKE YOUR MOTHER.
MY BOW! DAMMIT, NOW WHAT?

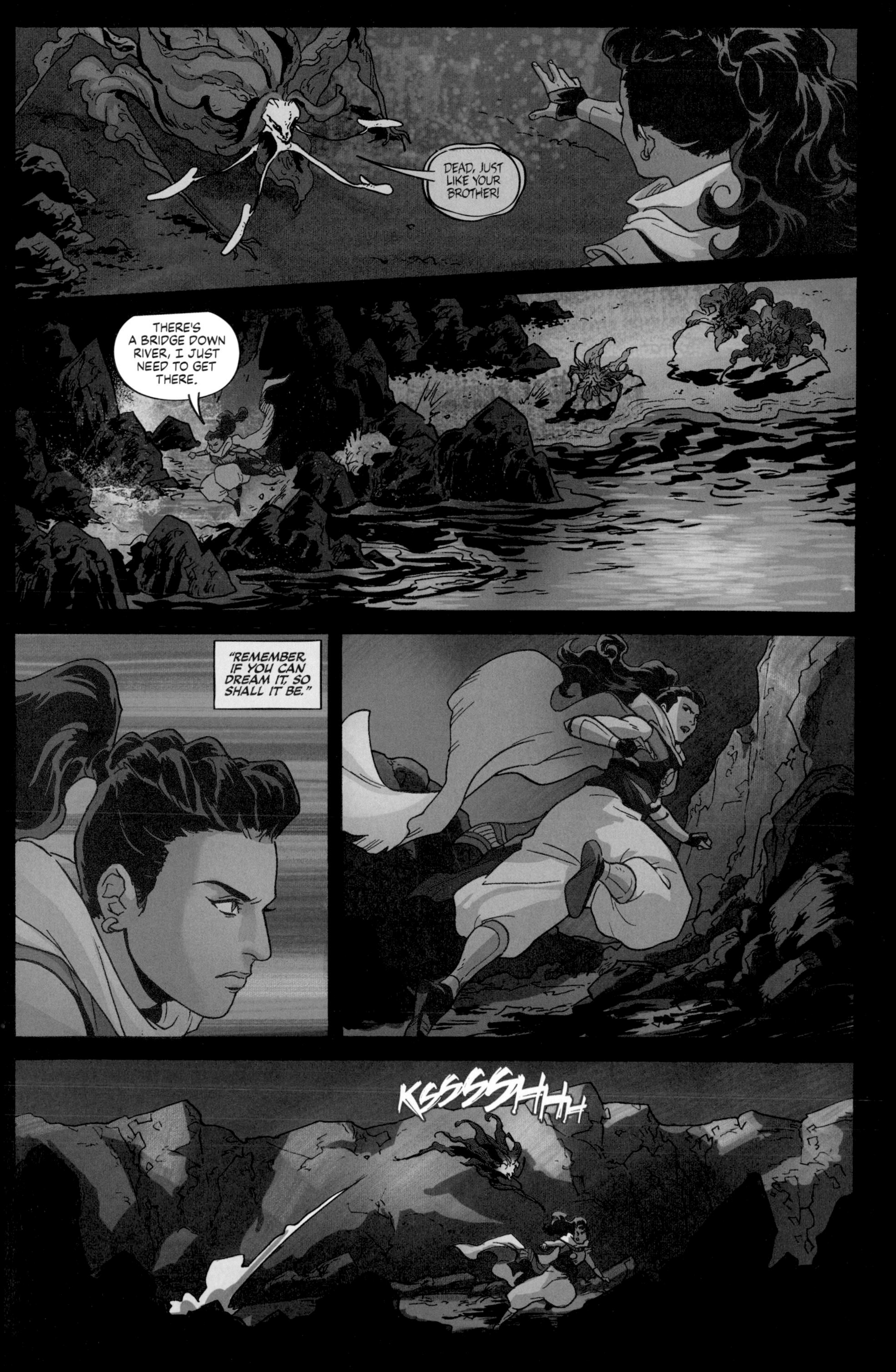

DEAD, JUST LIKE YOUR BROTHER!
THERE'S A BRIDGE DOWN RIVER, I JUST NEED TO GET THERE.
"REMEMBER, IF YOU CAN DREAM IT, SO SHALL IT BE."
KSSSSHHH

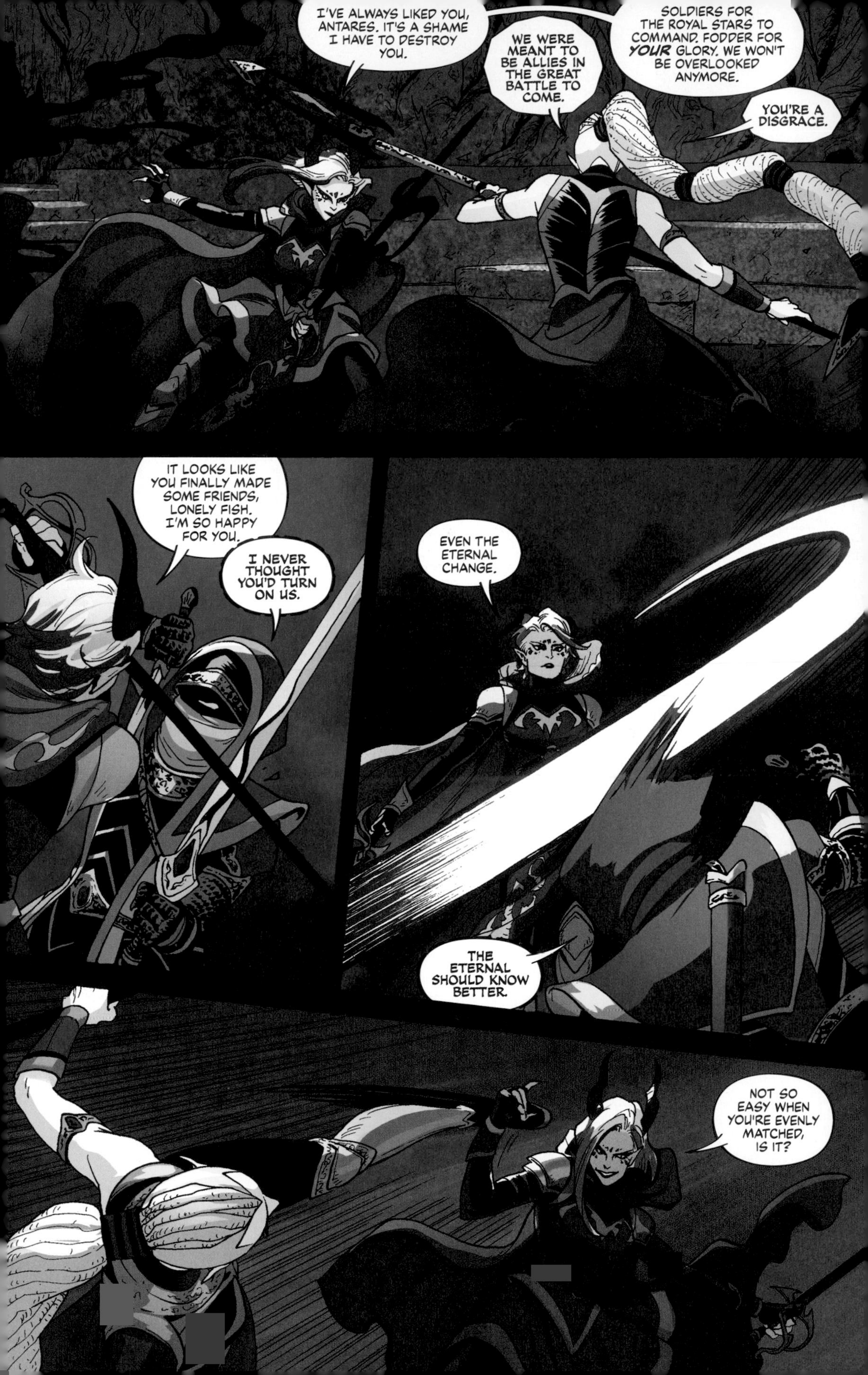
I'VE ALWAYS LIKED YOU, ANTARES. IT'S A SHAME I HAVE TO DESTROY YOU.
WE WERE MEANT TO BE ALLIES IN THE GREAT BATTLE TO COME.
SOLDIERS FOR THE ROYAL STARS TO COMMAND. FODDER FOR *YOUR* GLORY. WE WON'T BE OVERLOOKED ANYMORE.
YOU'RE A DISGRACE.
IT LOOKS LIKE YOU FINALLY MADE SOME FRIENDS, LONELY FISH. I'M SO HAPPY FOR YOU.
I NEVER THOUGHT YOU'D TURN ON US.
EVEN THE ETERNAL CHANGE.
THE ETERNAL SHOULD KNOW BETTER.
NOT SO EASY WHEN YOU'RE EVENLY MATCHED, IS IT?

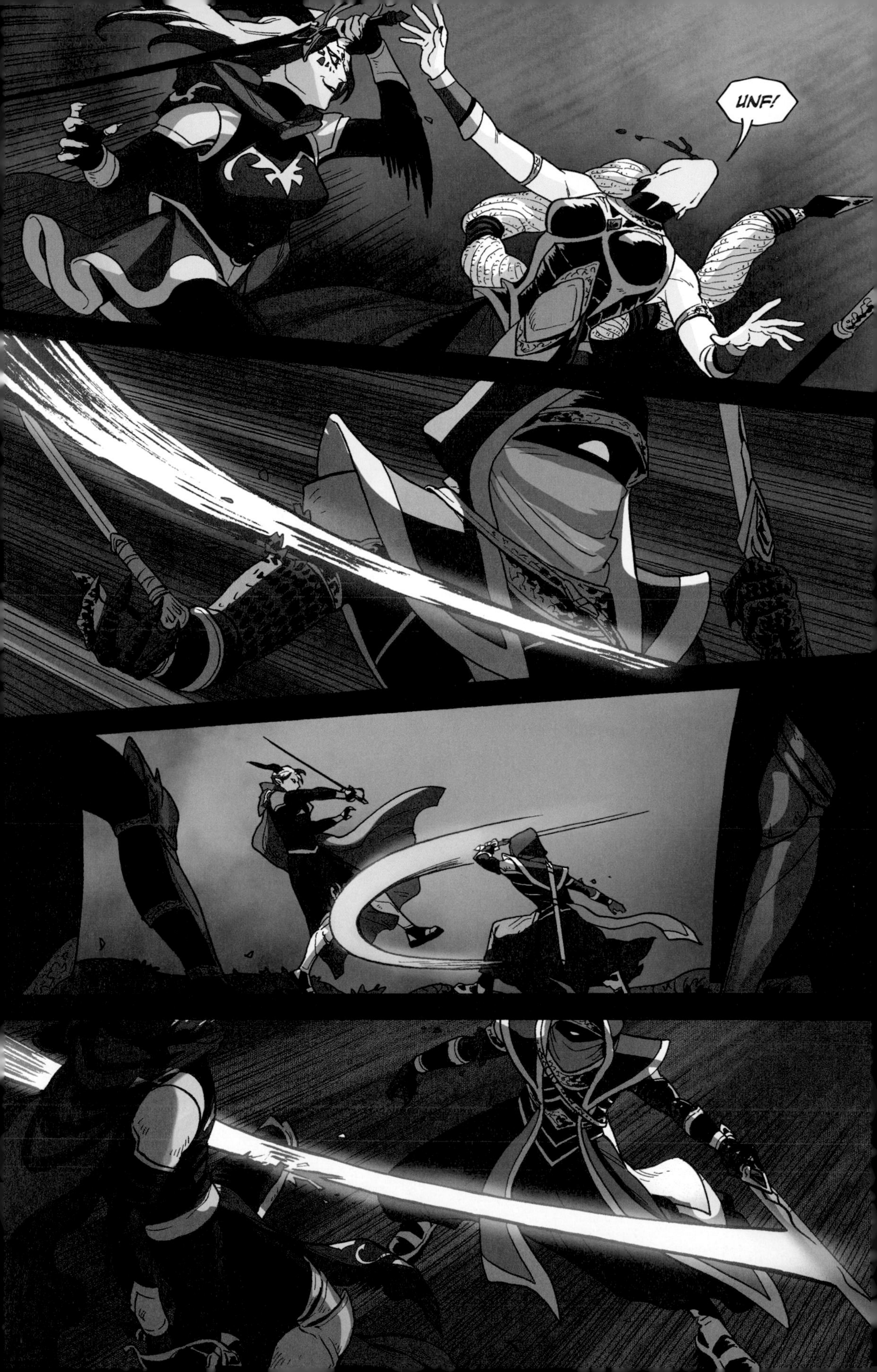
UNF!

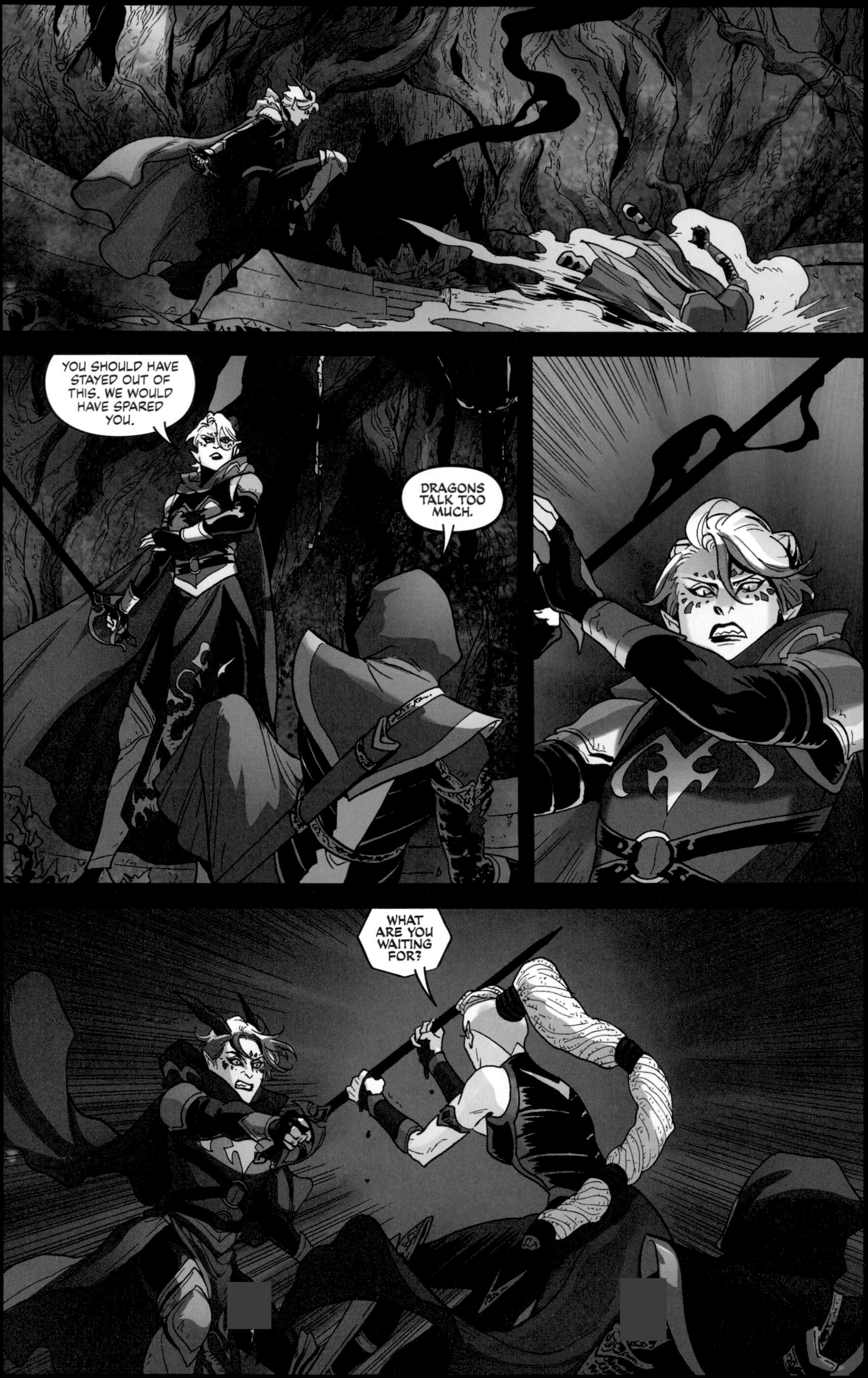
YOU SHOULD HAVE STAYED OUT OF THIS. WE WOULD HAVE SPARED YOU.
DRAGONS TALK TOO MUCH.
WHAT ARE YOU WAITING FOR?

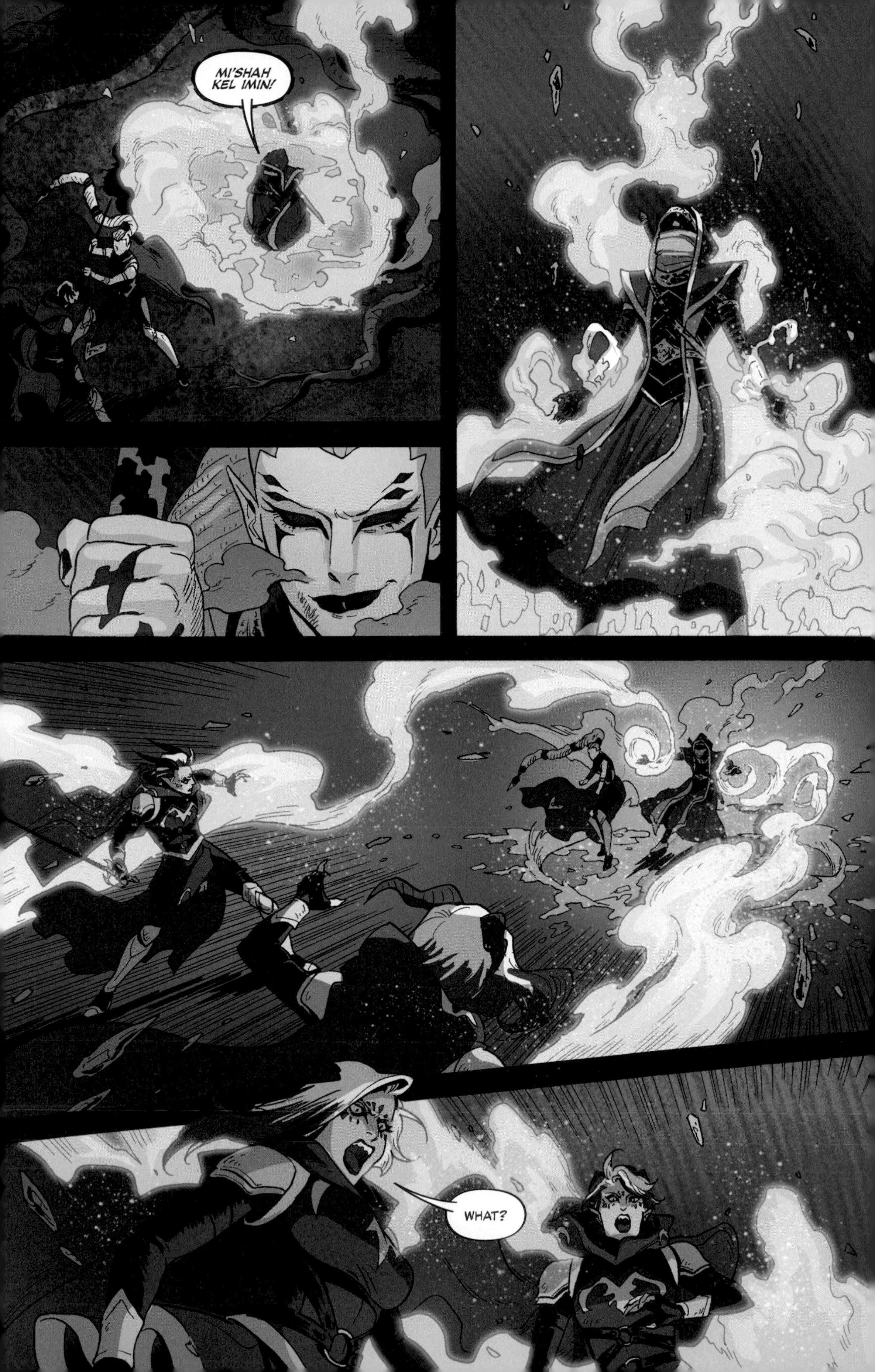
MI'SHAH KEL IMIN!
WHAT?

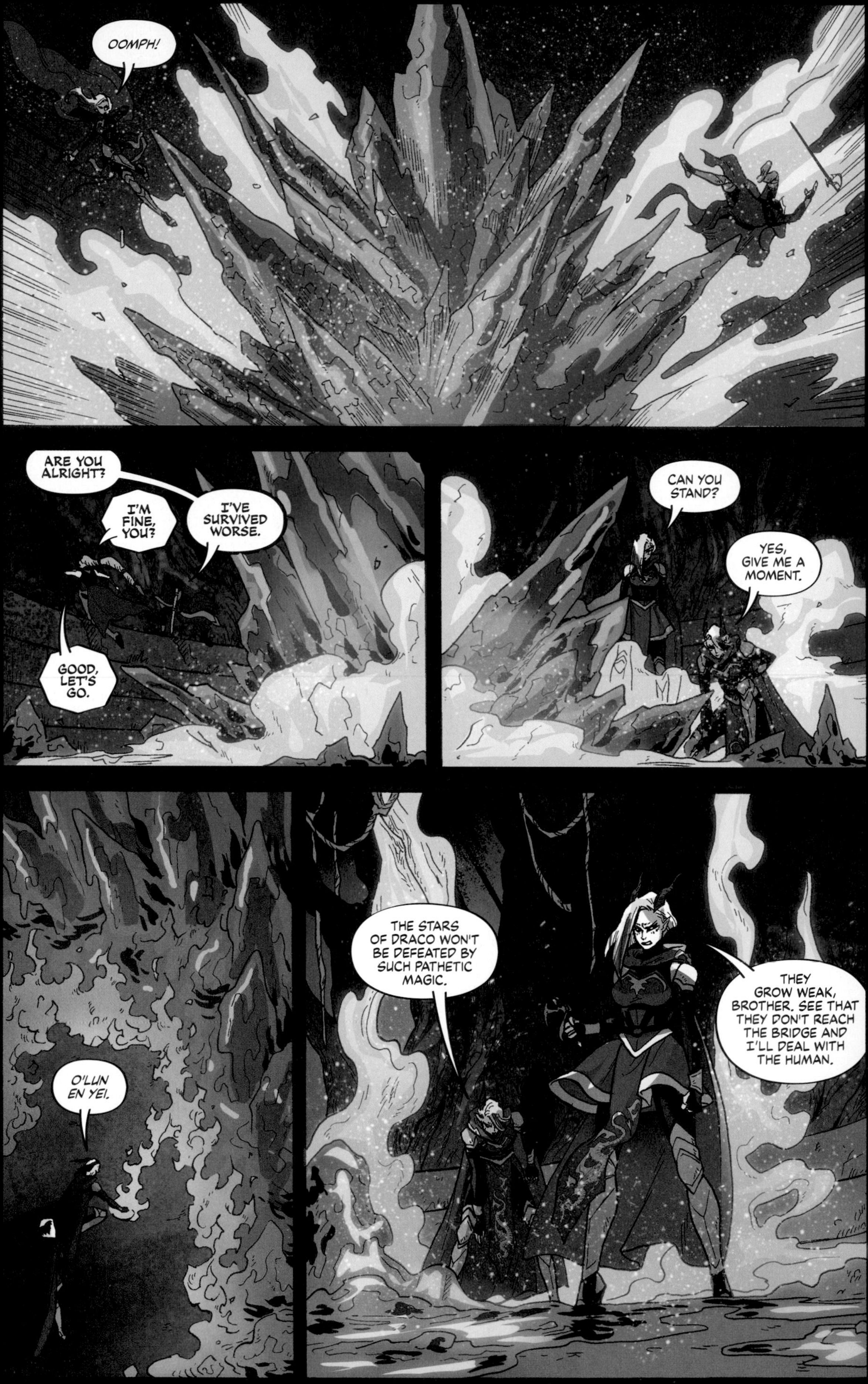
OOMPH!
ARE YOU ALRIGHT?
I'M FINE, YOU?
I'VE SURVIVED WORSE.
GOOD, LET'S GO.
CAN YOU STAND?
YES, GIVE ME A MOMENT.
O'LUN EN YEI.
THE STARS OF DRACO WON'T BE DEFEATED BY SUCH PATHETIC MAGIC.
THEY GROW WEAK, BROTHER. SEE THAT THEY DON'T REACH THE BRIDGE AND I'LL DEAL WITH THE HUMAN.

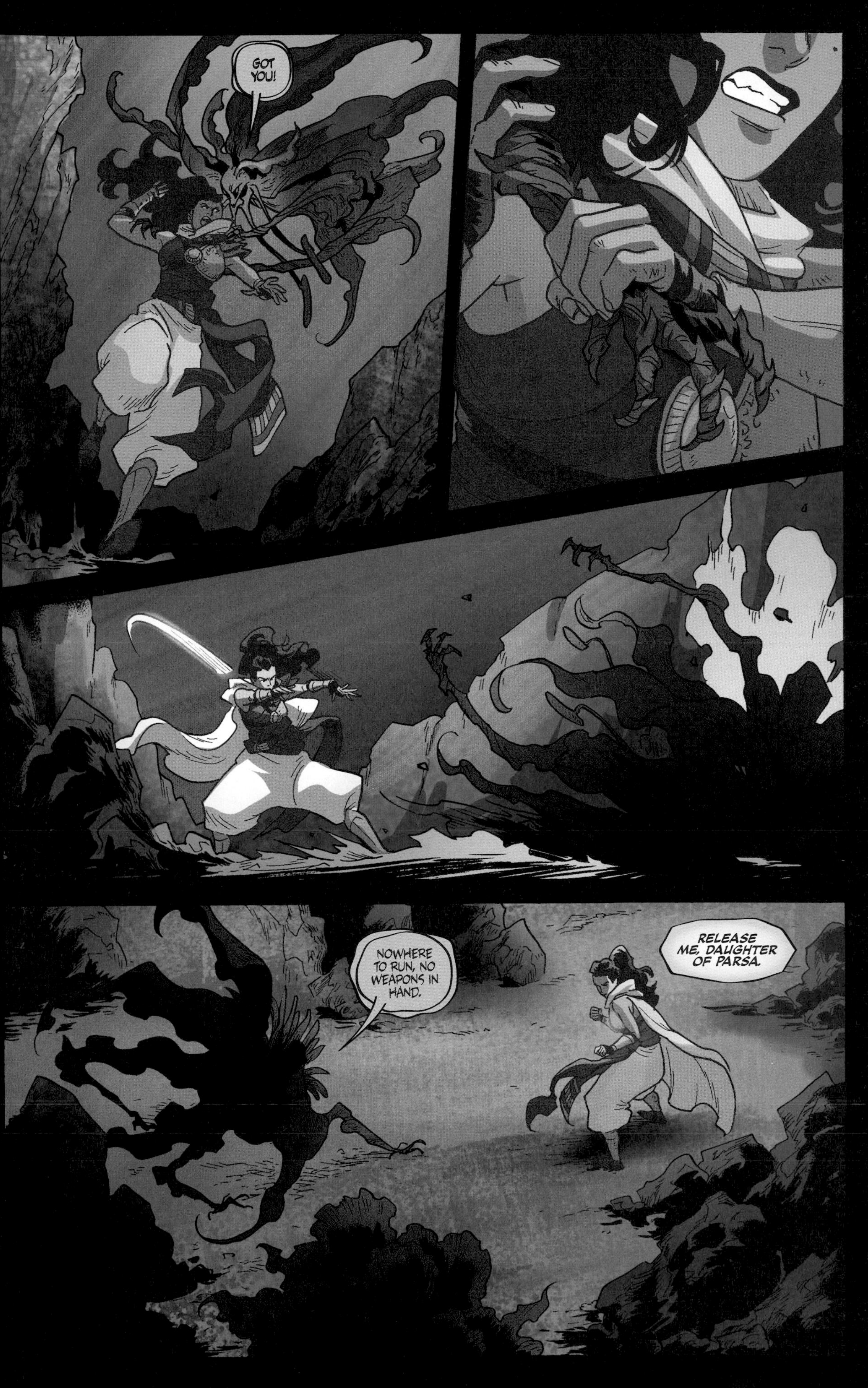
GOT YOU!
NOWHERE TO RUN, NO WEAPONS IN HAND.
RELEASE ME, DAUGHTER OF PARSA.

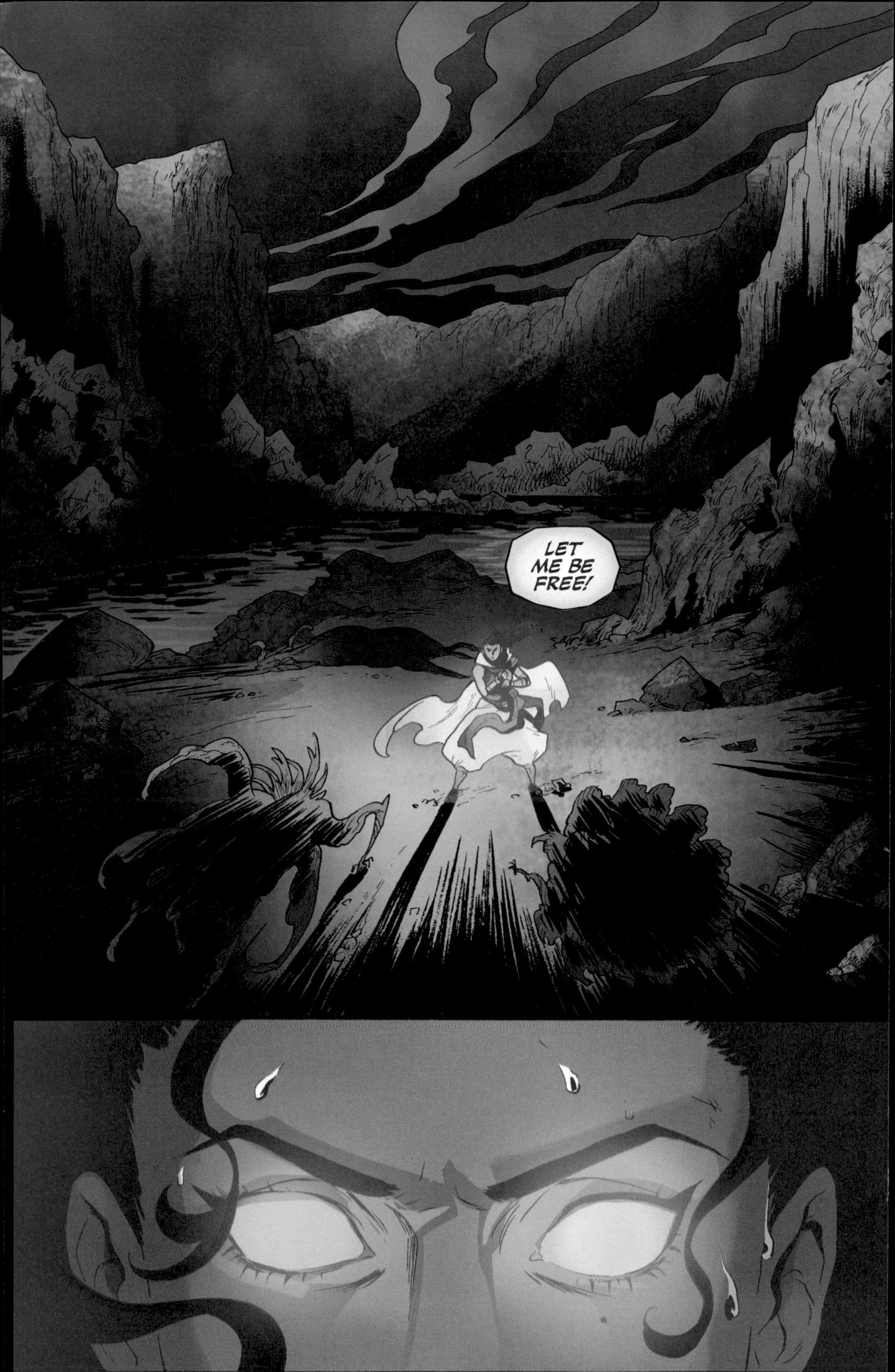
LET ME BE FREE!

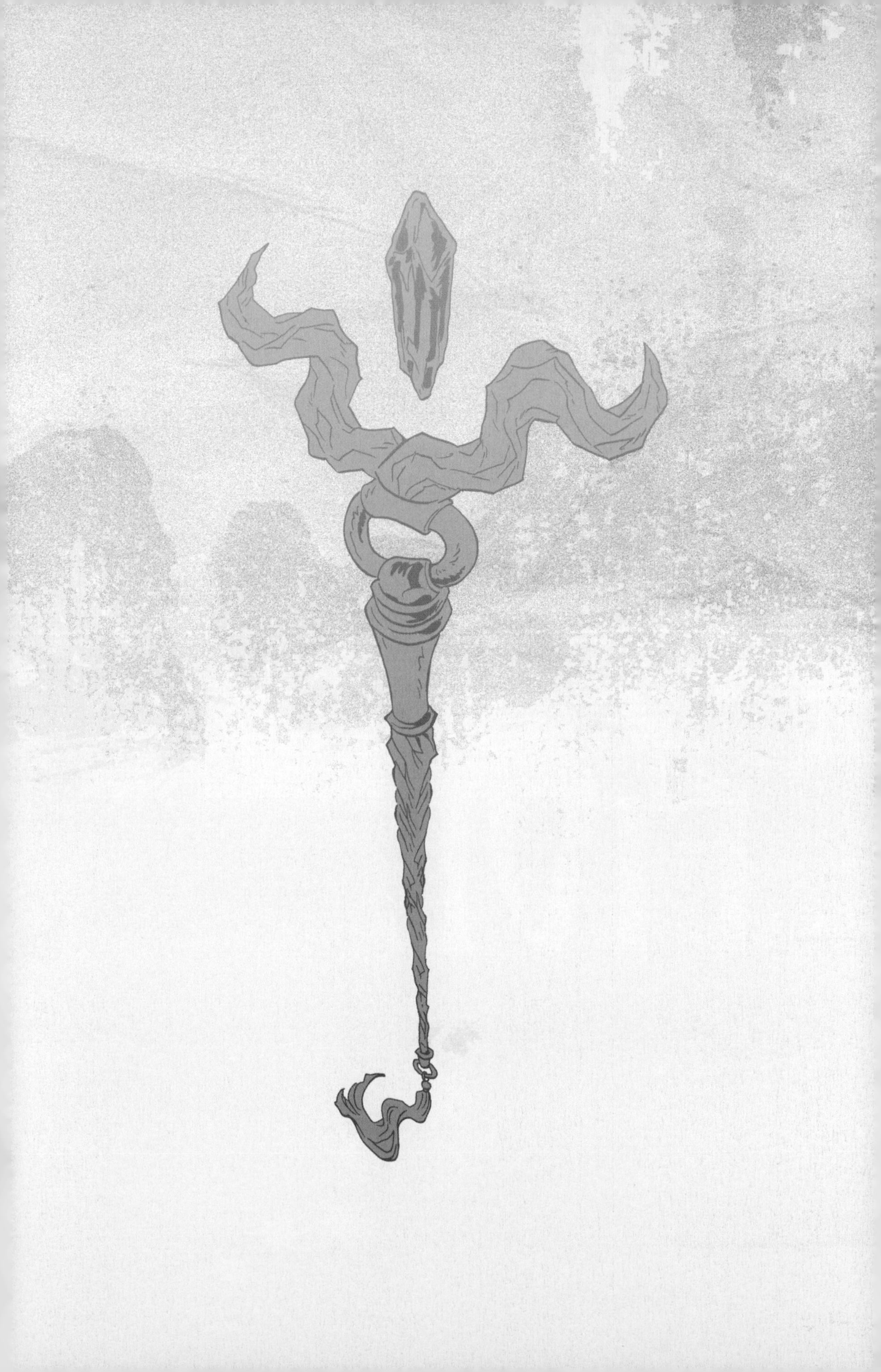

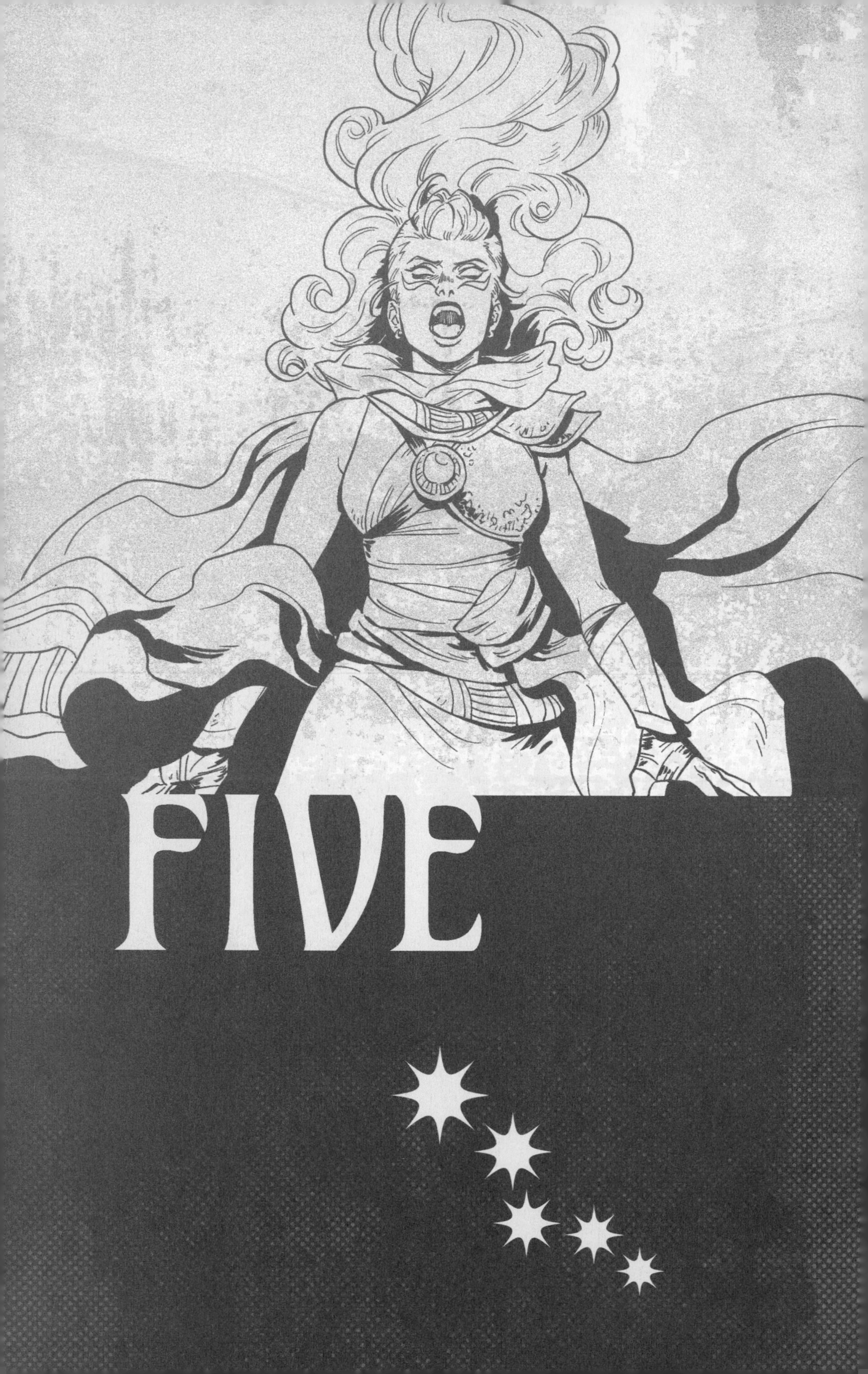

FIVE

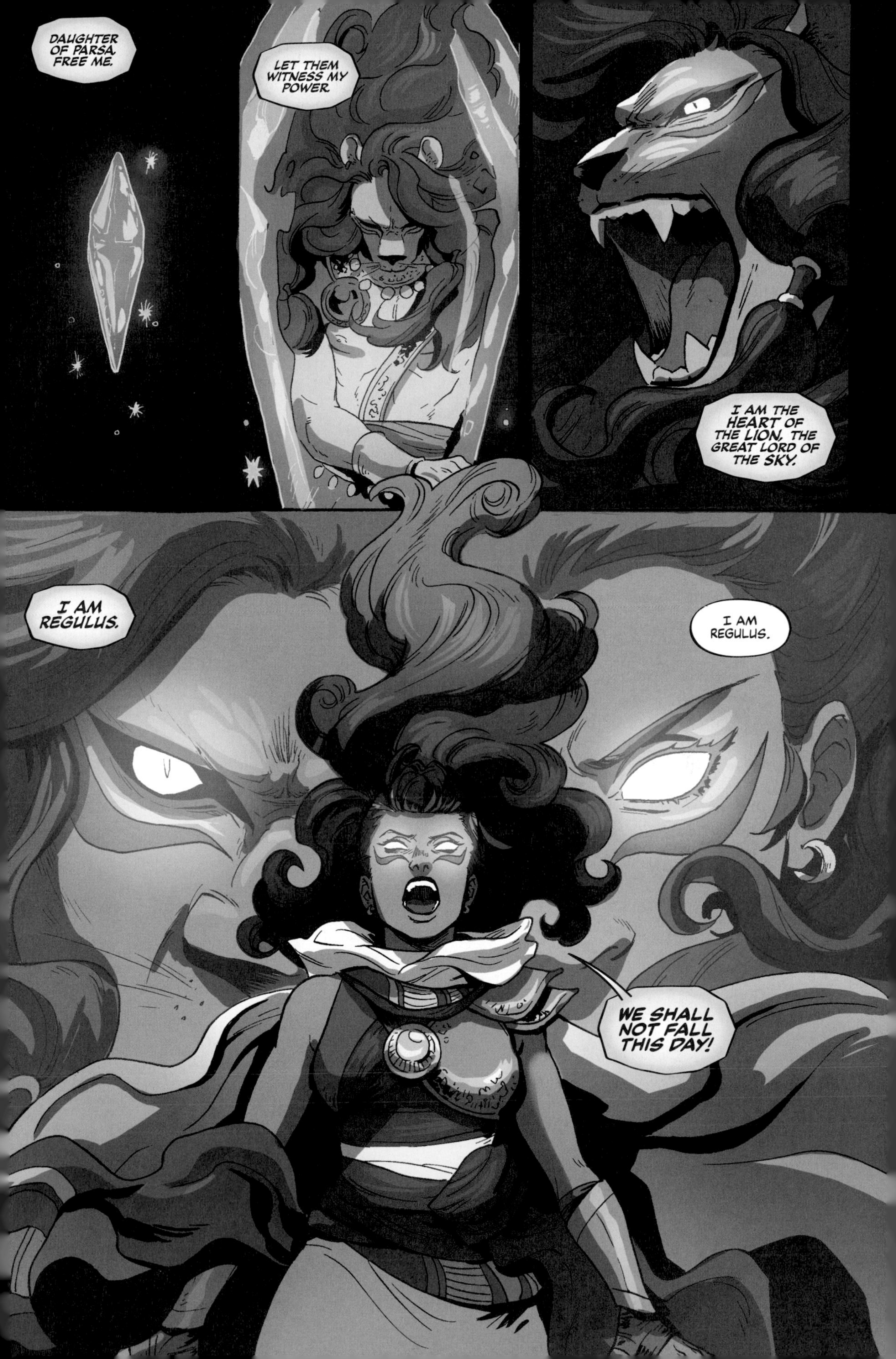
DAUGHTER OF PARSA. FREE ME.
LET THEM WITNESS MY POWER.
I AM THE HEART OF THE LION, THE GREAT LORD OF THE SKY.
I AM REGULUS.
I AM REGULUS.
WE SHALL NOT FALL THIS DAY!

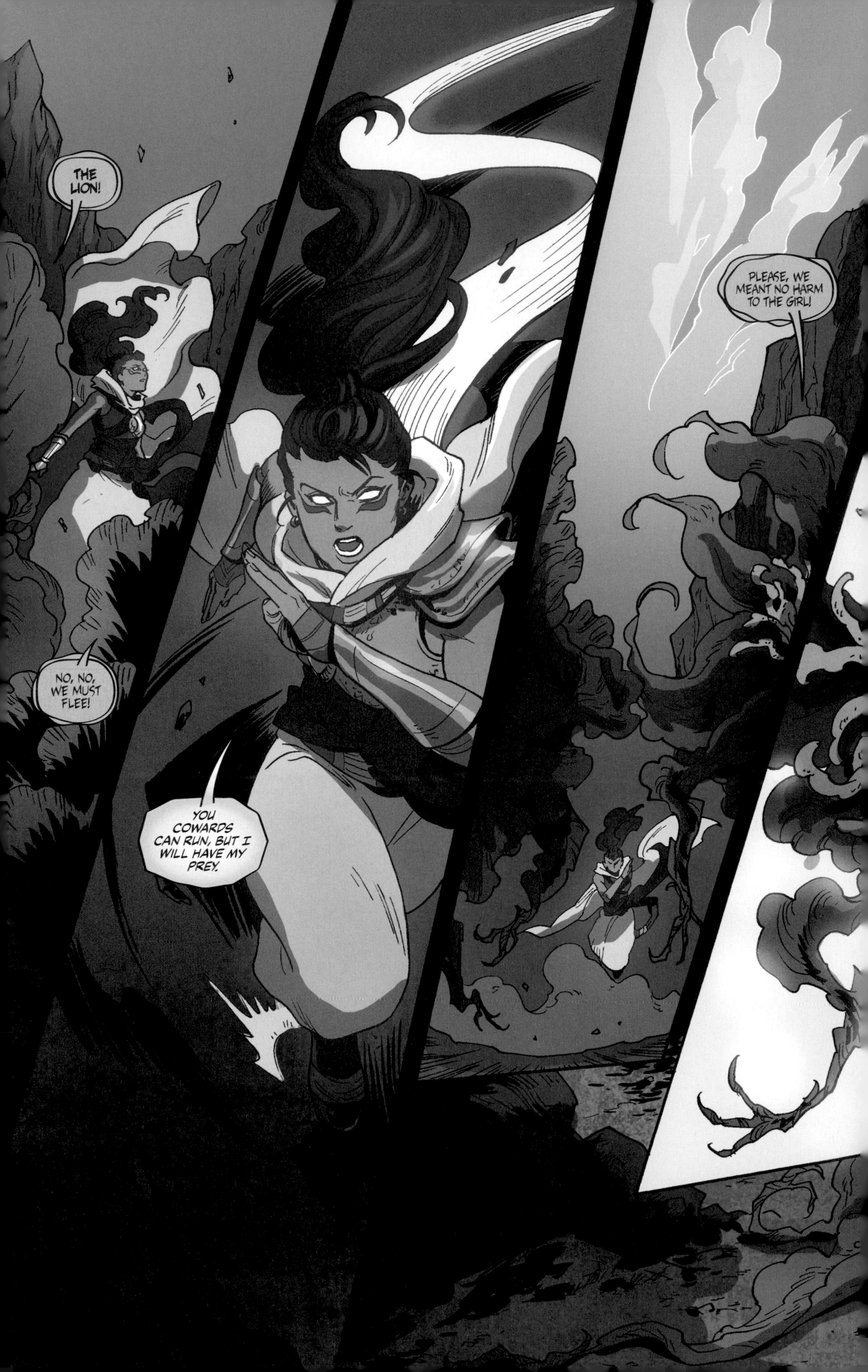
THE LION!
NO, NO, WE MUST FLEE!
YOU COWARDS CAN RUN, BUT I WILL HAVE MY PREY.
PLEASE, WE MEANT NO HARM TO THE GIRL!

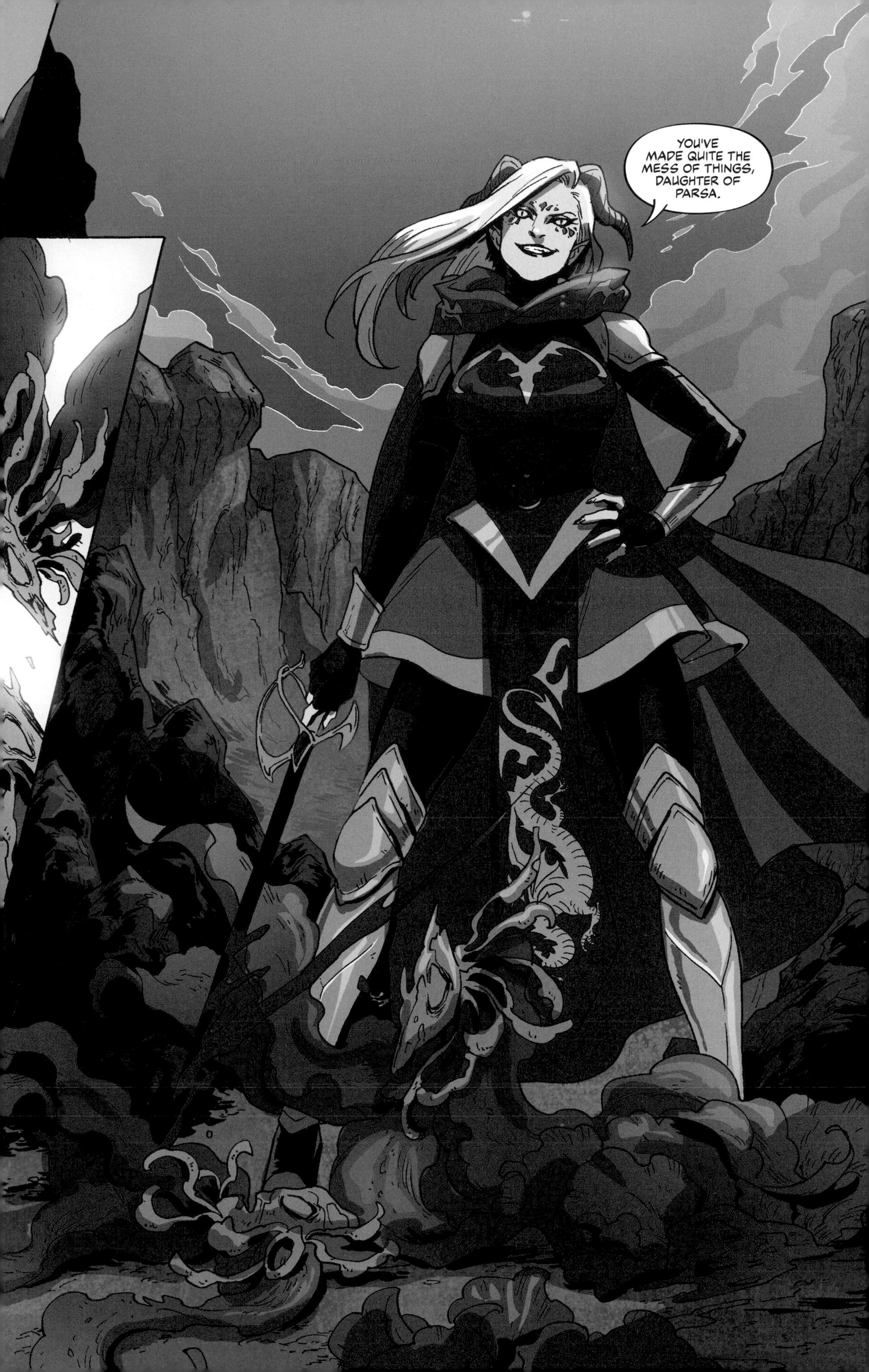
YOU'VE MADE QUITE THE MESS OF THINGS, DAUGHTER OF PARSA.

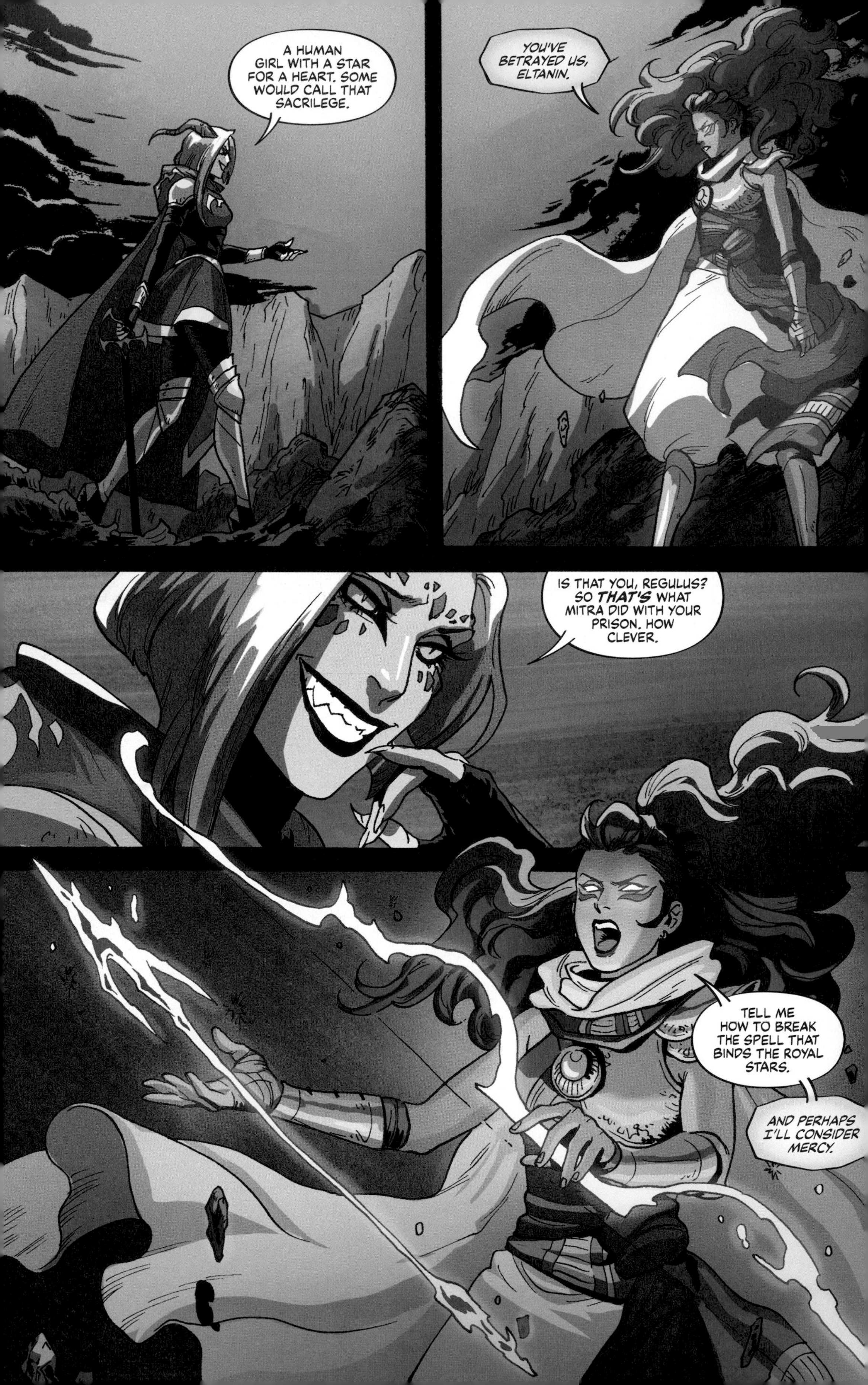
A HUMAN GIRL WITH A STAR FOR A HEART. SOME WOULD CALL THAT SACRILEGE.
YOU'VE BETRAYED US, ELTANIN.
IS THAT YOU, REGULUS? SO **THAT'S** WHAT MITRA DID WITH YOUR PRISON. HOW CLEVER.
TELL ME HOW TO BREAK THE SPELL THAT BINDS THE ROYAL STARS.
AND PERHAPS I'LL CONSIDER MERCY.

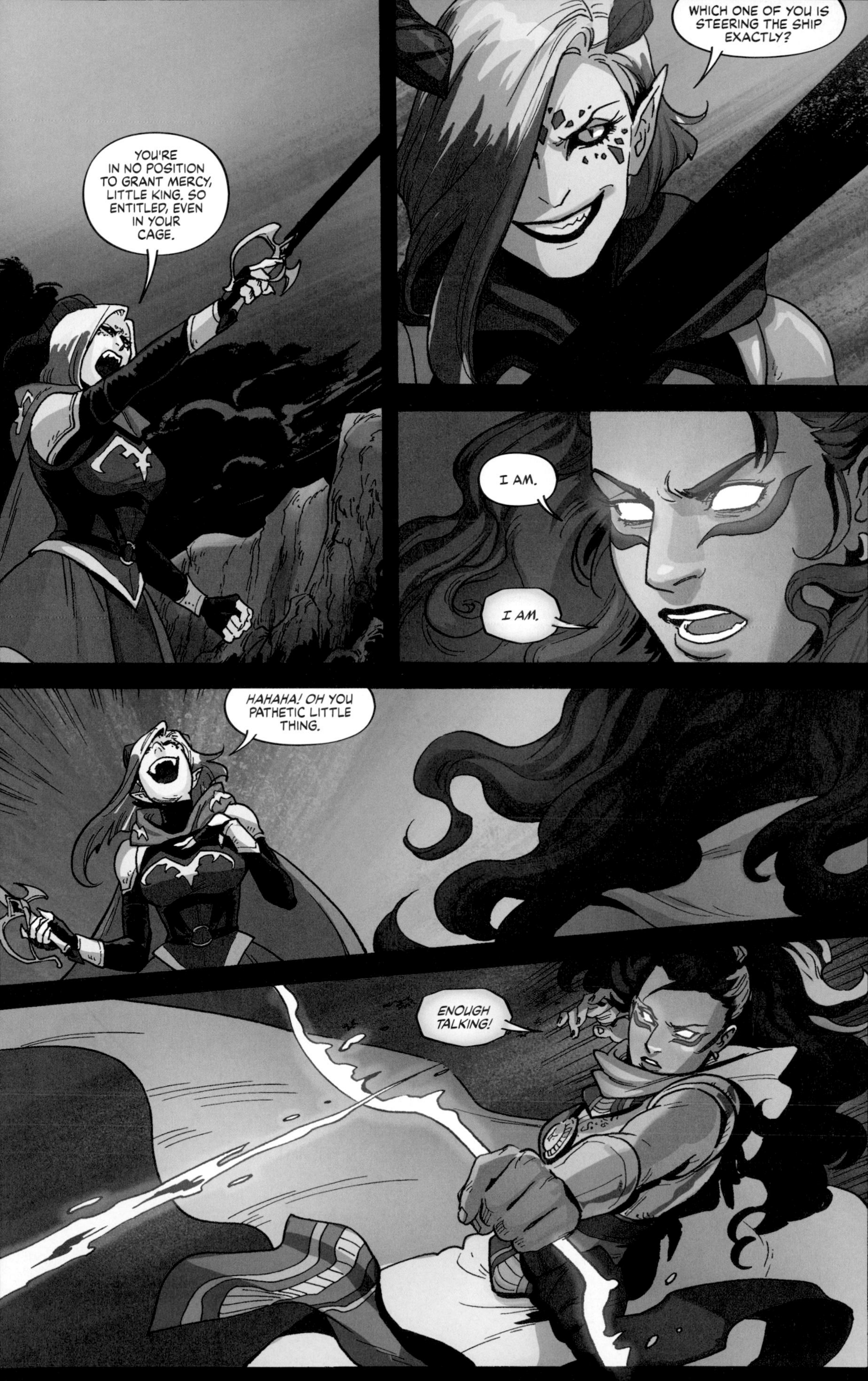
YOU'RE IN NO POSITION TO GRANT MERCY, LITTLE KING. SO ENTITLED, EVEN IN YOUR CAGE.
WHICH ONE OF YOU IS STEERING THE SHIP EXACTLY?
I AM.
I AM.
HAHAHA! OH YOU PATHETIC LITTLE THING.
ENOUGH TALKING!

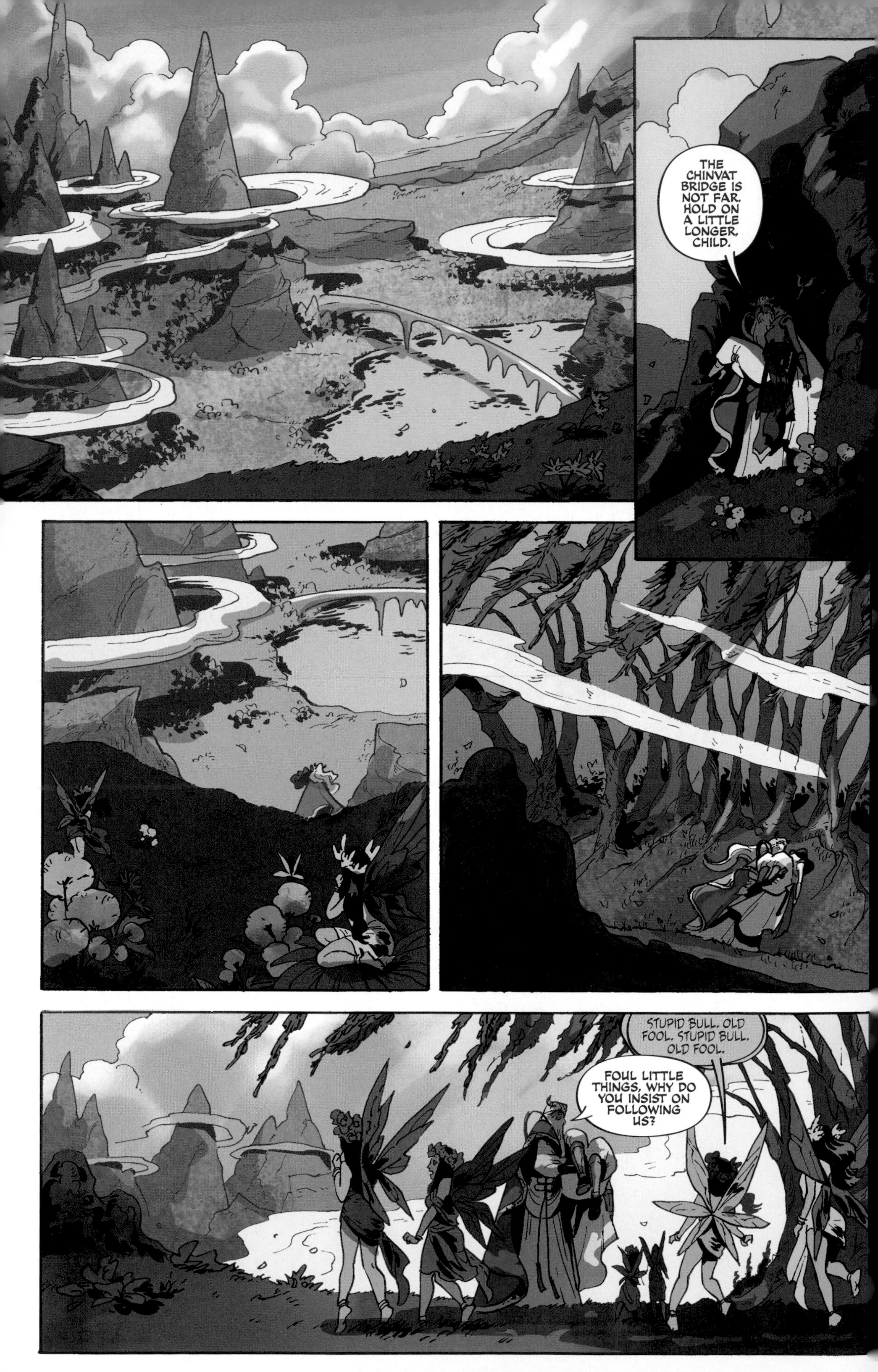
THE CHINVAT BRIDGE IS NOT FAR. HOLD ON A LITTLE LONGER, CHILD.
STUPID BULL. OLD FOOL. STUPID BULL. OLD FOOL.
FOUL LITTLE THINGS, WHY DO YOU INSIST ON FOLLOWING US?

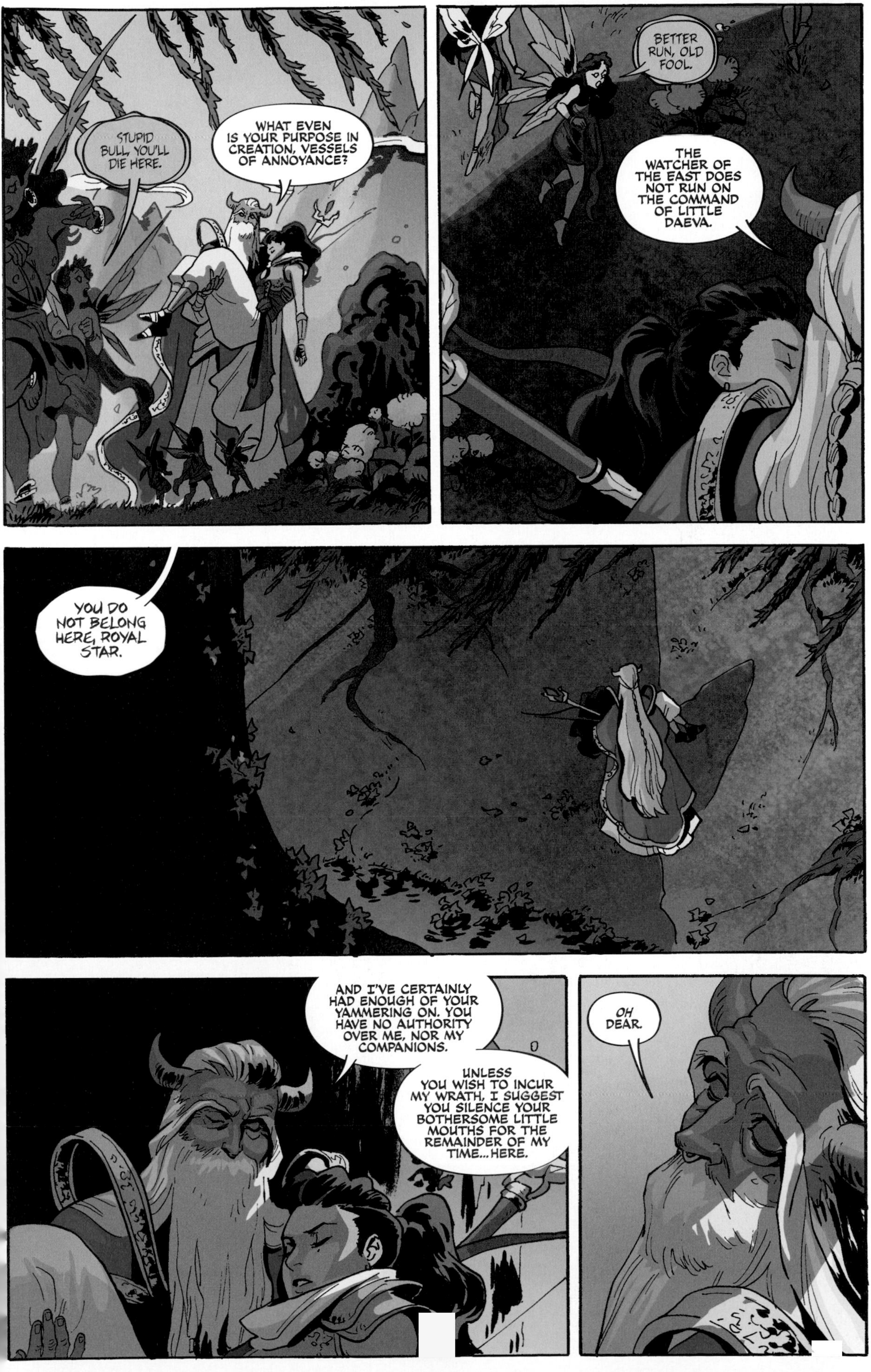
STUPID BULL, YOU'LL DIE HERE.
WHAT EVEN IS YOUR PURPOSE IN CREATION, VESSELS OF ANNOYANCE?
BETTER RUN, OLD FOOL.
THE WATCHER OF THE EAST DOES NOT RUN ON THE COMMAND OF LITTLE DAEVA.
YOU DO NOT BELONG HERE, ROYAL STAR.
AND I'VE CERTAINLY HAD ENOUGH OF YOUR YAMMERING ON. YOU HAVE NO AUTHORITY OVER ME, NOR MY COMPANIONS.
UNLESS YOU WISH TO INCUR MY WRATH, I SUGGEST YOU SILENCE YOUR BOTHERSOME LITTLE MOUTHS FOR THE REMAINDER OF MY TIME... HERE.
OH DEAR.

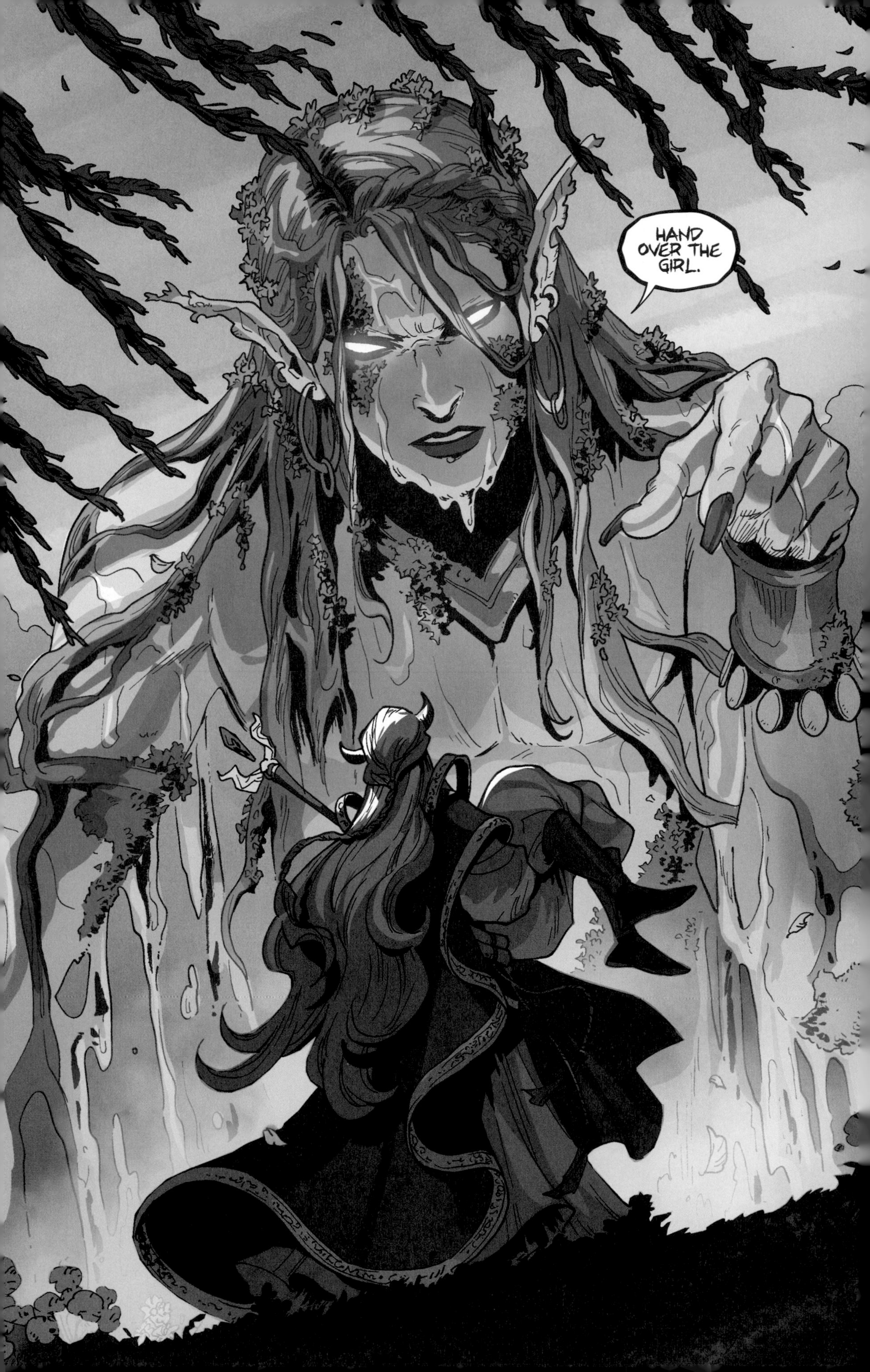
HAND OVER THE GIRL.

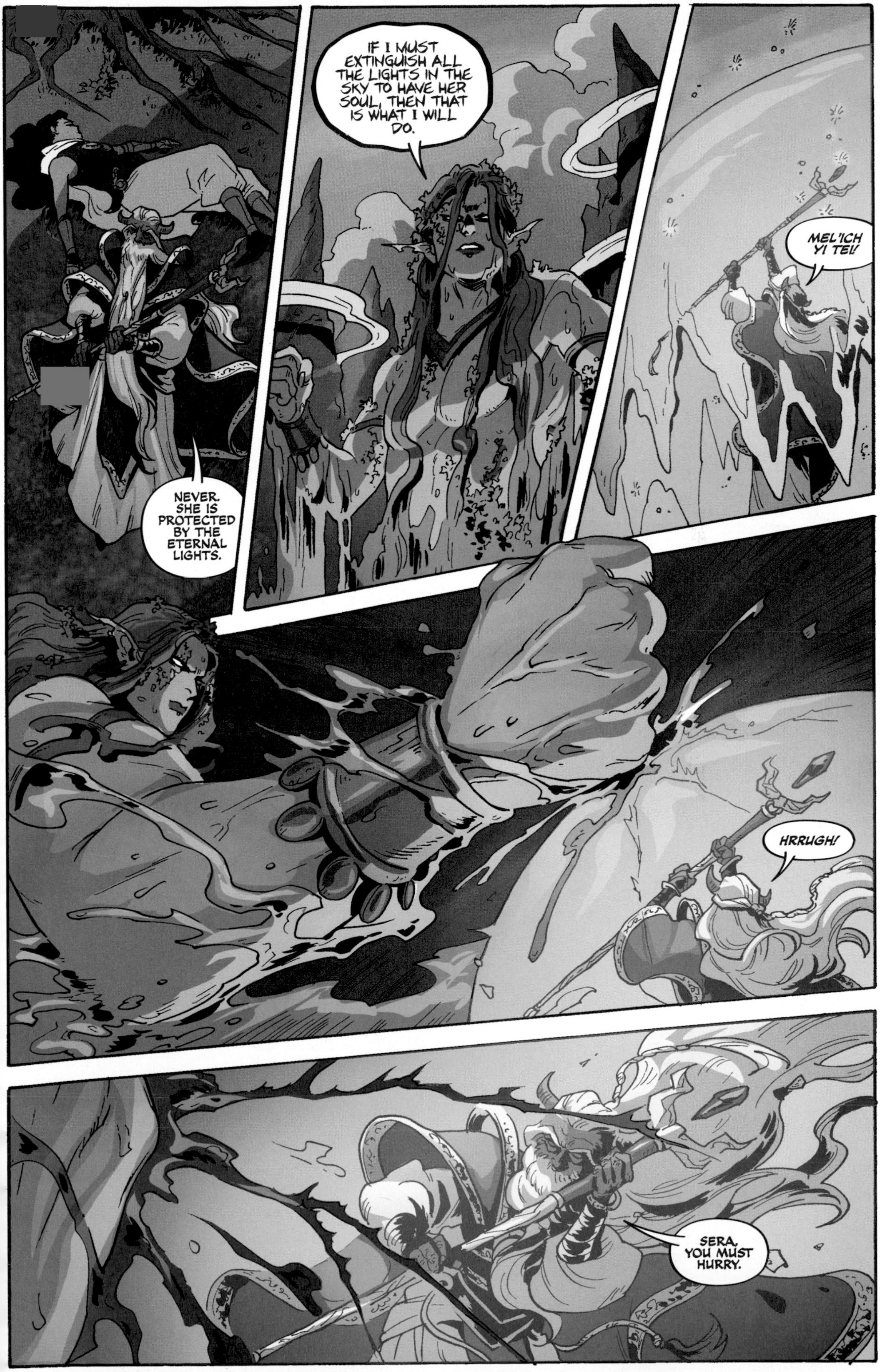
NEVER. SHE IS PROTECTED BY THE ETERNAL LIGHTS.
IF I MUST EXTINGUISH ALL THE LIGHTS IN THE SKY TO HAVE HER SOUL, THEN THAT IS WHAT I WILL DO.
MEL'ICH YI TEI!
HRRUGH!
SERA, YOU MUST HURRY.

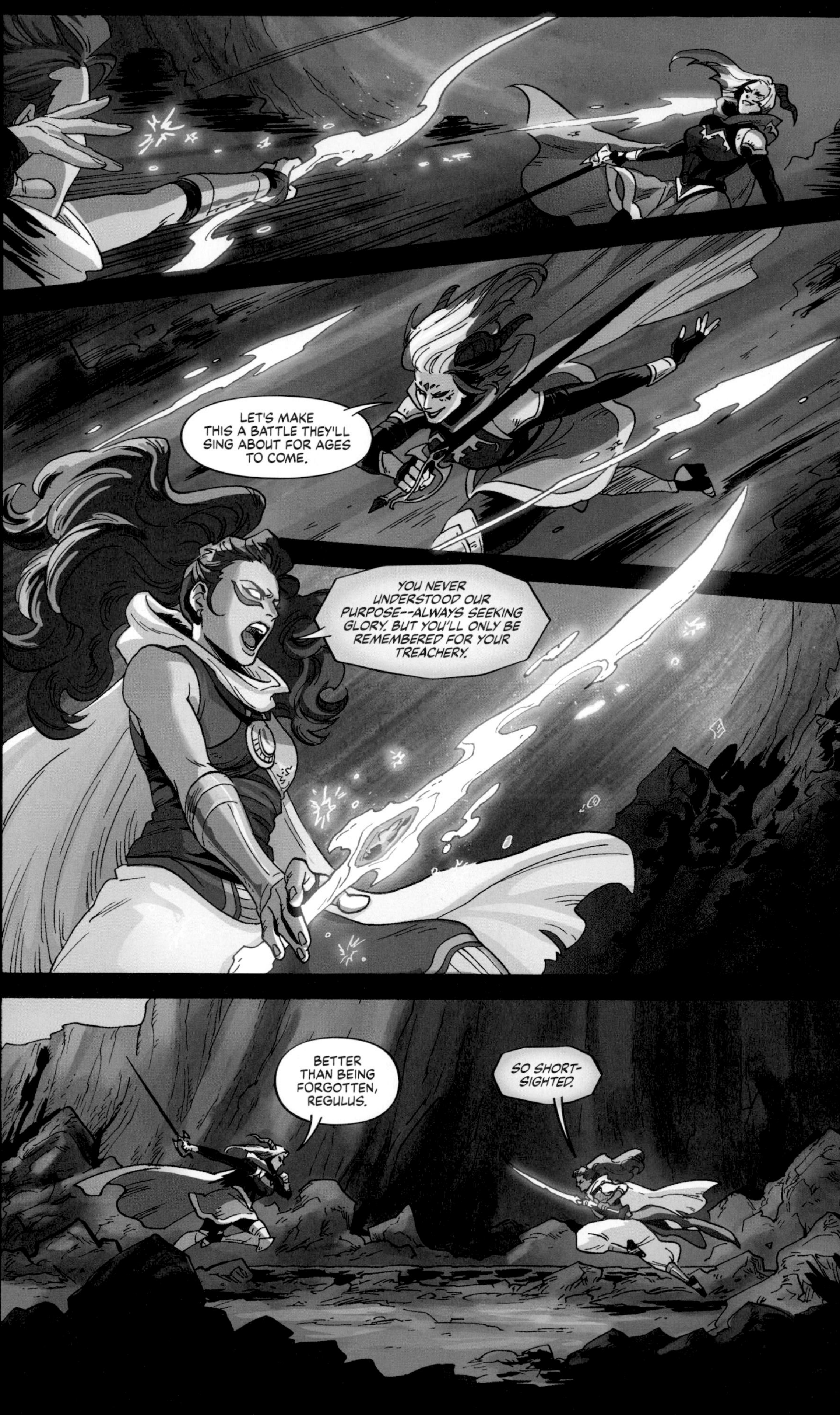
LET'S MAKE THIS A BATTLE THEY'LL SING ABOUT FOR AGES TO COME.
YOU NEVER UNDERSTOOD OUR PURPOSE--ALWAYS SEEKING GLORY. BUT YOU'LL ONLY BE REMEMBERED FOR YOUR TREACHERY.
BETTER THAN BEING FORGOTTEN, REGULUS.
SO SHORT-SIGHTED.

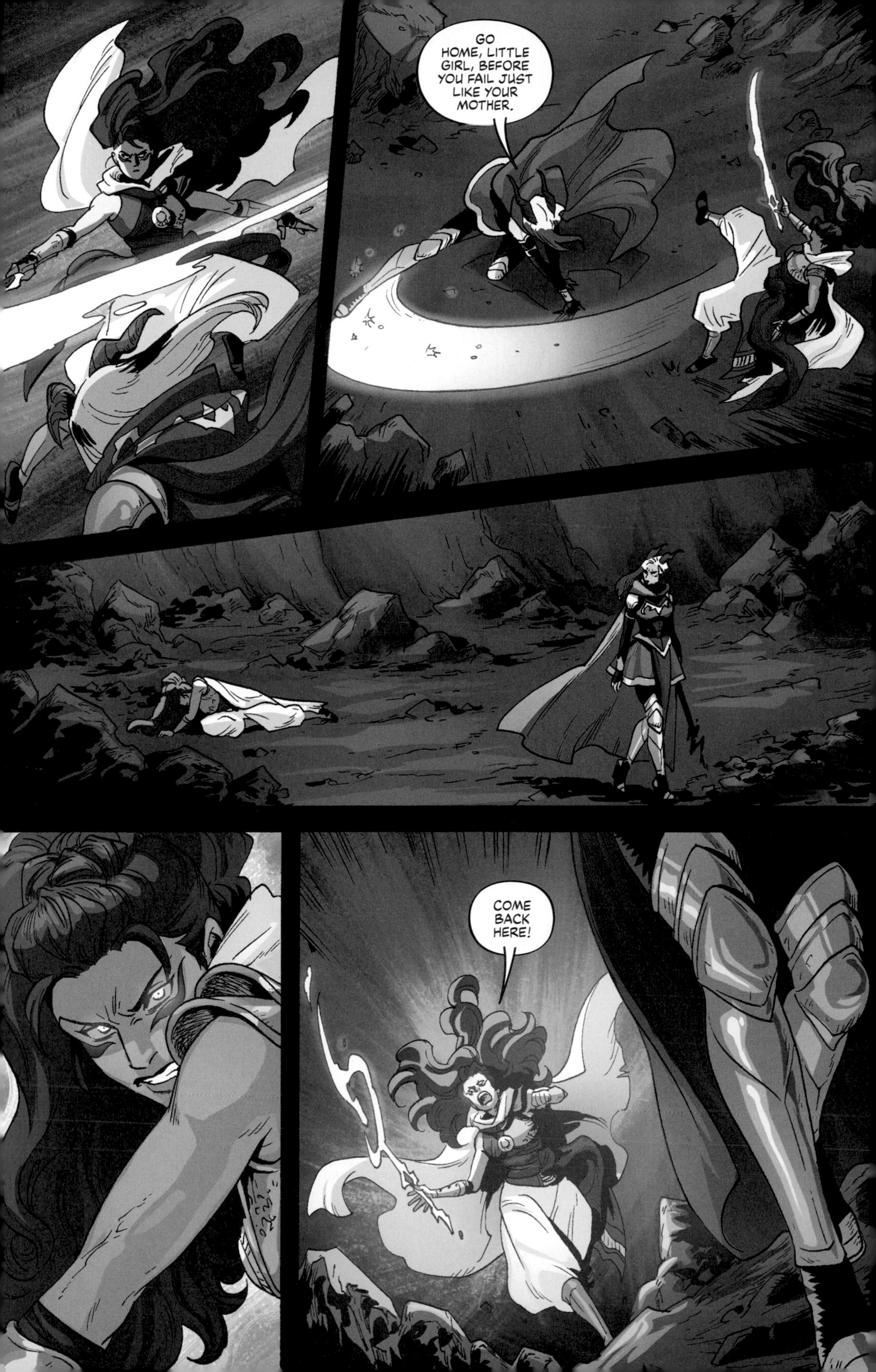
GO HOME, LITTLE GIRL, BEFORE YOU FAIL JUST LIKE YOUR MOTHER.
COME BACK HERE!

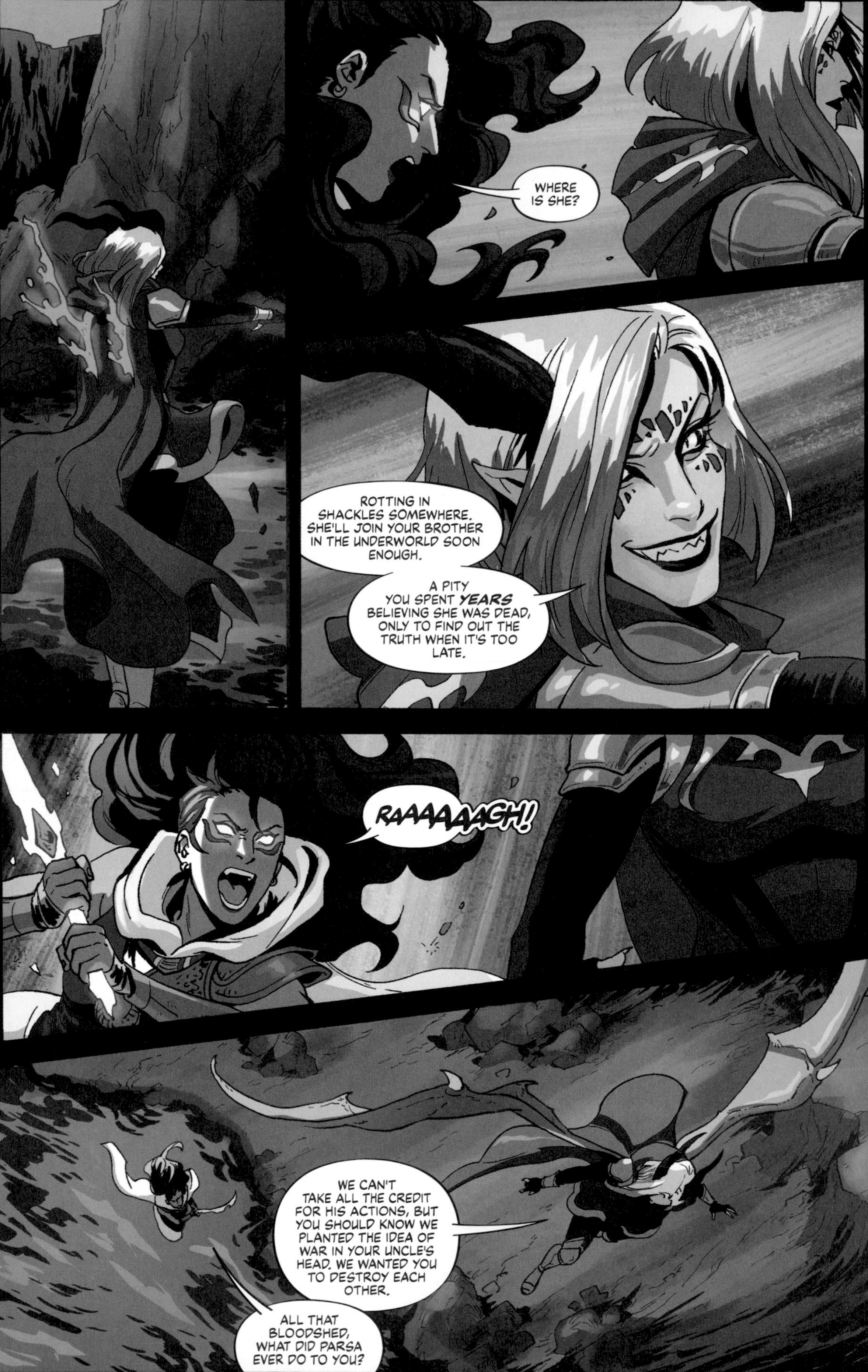
WHERE IS SHE?
ROTTING IN SHACKLES SOMEWHERE. SHE'LL JOIN YOUR BROTHER IN THE UNDERWORLD SOON ENOUGH.
A PITY YOU SPENT YEARS BELIEVING SHE WAS DEAD, ONLY TO FIND OUT THE TRUTH WHEN IT'S TOO LATE.
RAAAAAAGH!
WE CAN'T TAKE ALL THE CREDIT FOR HIS ACTIONS, BUT YOU SHOULD KNOW WE PLANTED THE IDEA OF WAR IN YOUR UNCLE'S HEAD. WE WANTED YOU TO DESTROY EACH OTHER.
ALL THAT BLOODSHED, WHAT DID PARSA EVER DO TO YOU?

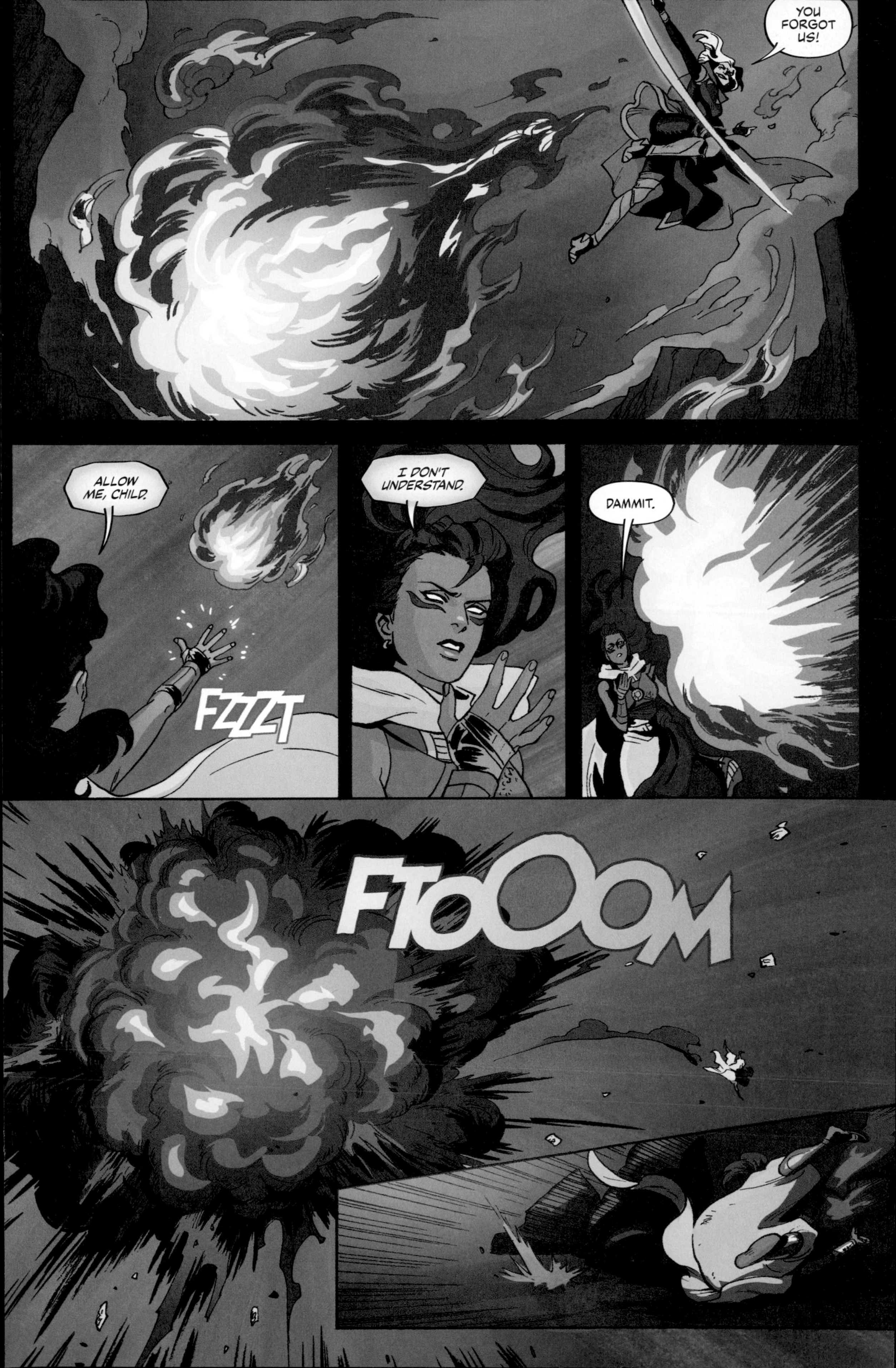
YOU FORGOT US!
ALLOW ME, CHILD.
FZZZT
I DON'T UNDERSTAND.
DAMMIT.
FTOOOM

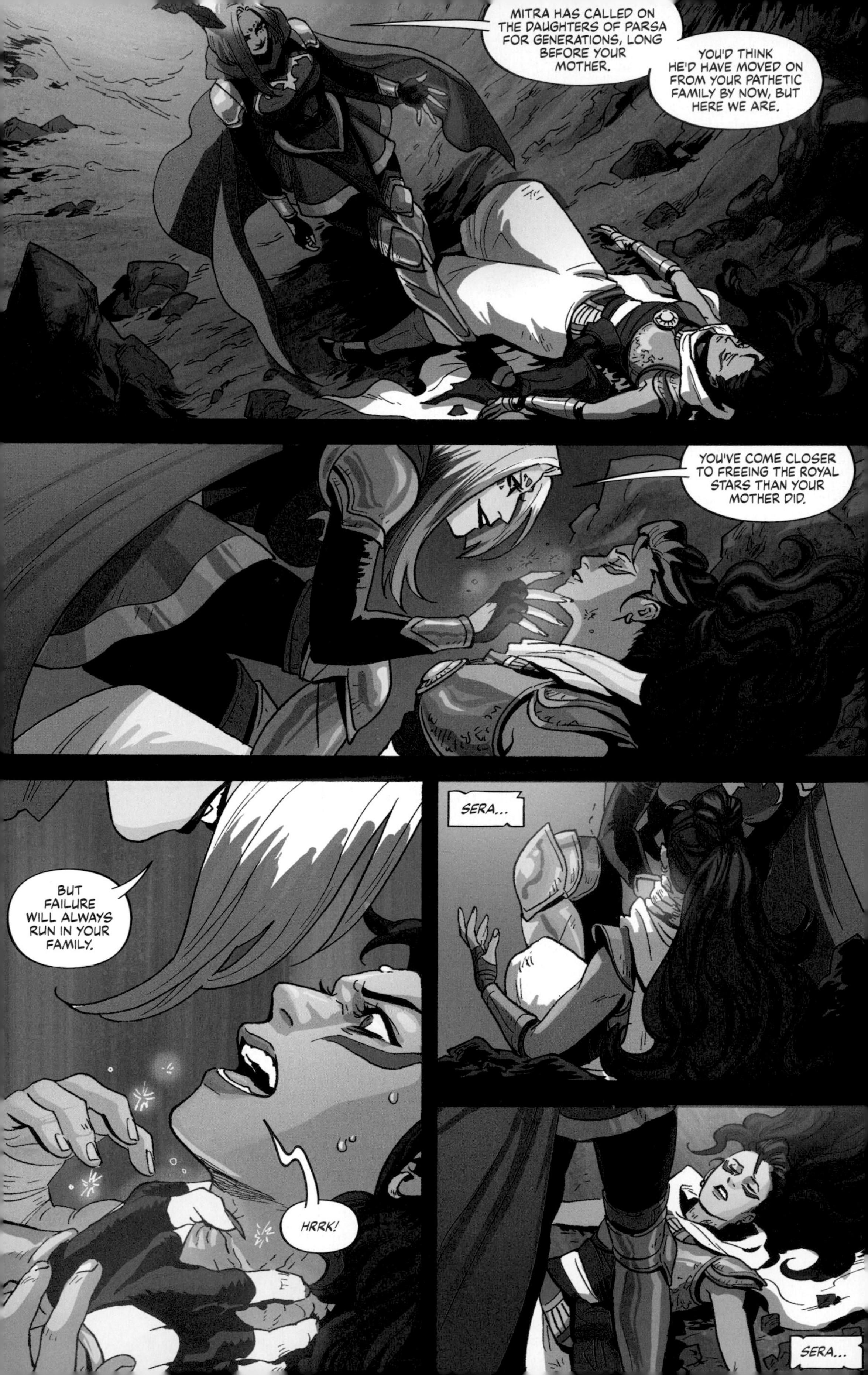
MITRA HAS CALLED ON THE DAUGHTERS OF PARSA FOR GENERATIONS, LONG BEFORE YOUR MOTHER.
YOU'D THINK HE'D HAVE MOVED ON FROM YOUR PATHETIC FAMILY BY NOW, BUT HERE WE ARE.
YOU'VE COME CLOSER TO FREEING THE ROYAL STARS THAN YOUR MOTHER DID.
BUT FAILURE WILL ALWAYS RUN IN YOUR FAMILY.
HRRK!
SERA...
SERA...

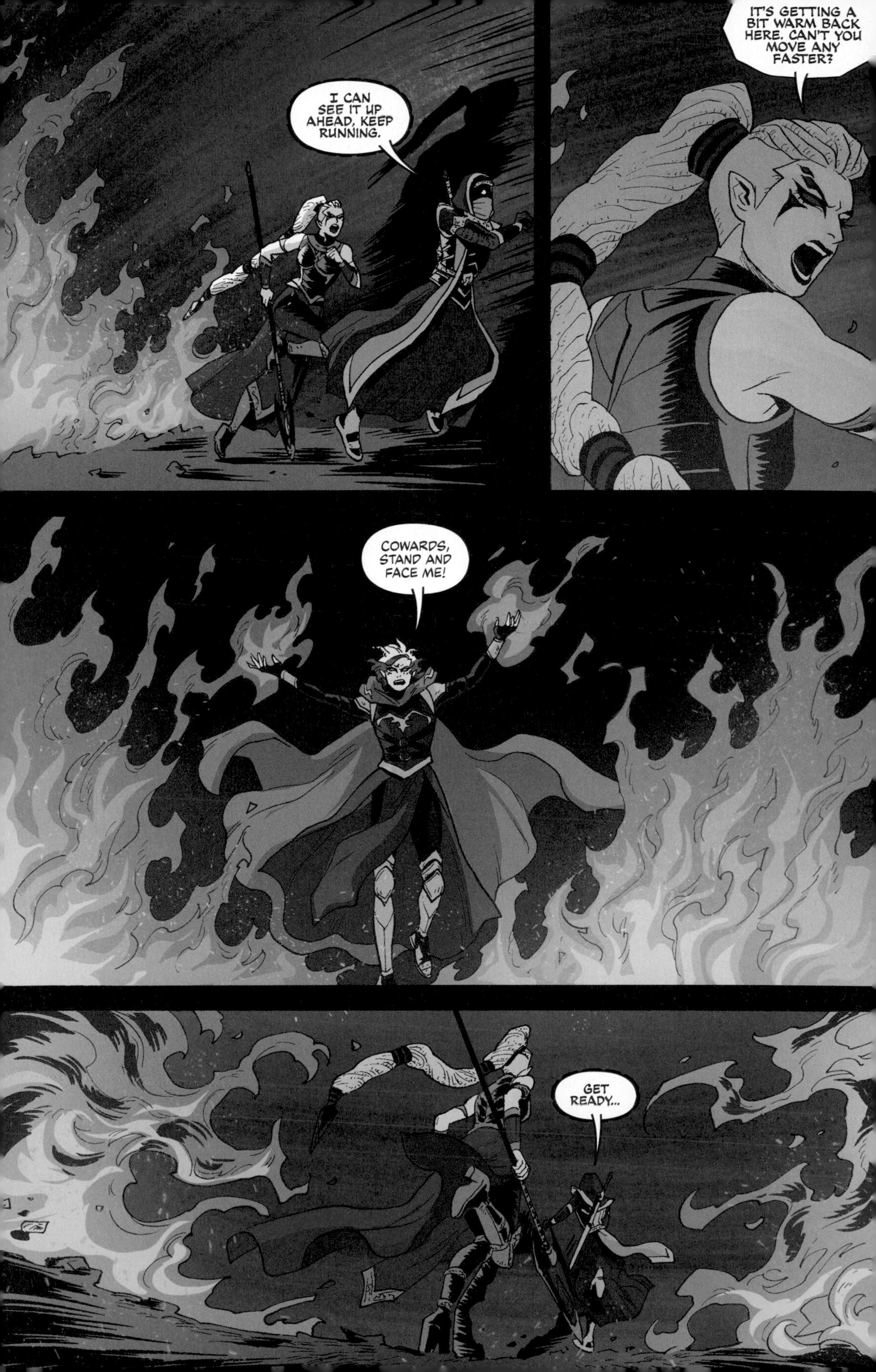
I CAN SEE IT UP AHEAD, KEEP RUNNING.
IT'S GETTING A BIT WARM BACK HERE. CAN'T YOU MOVE ANY FASTER?
COWARDS, STAND AND FACE ME!
GET READY...

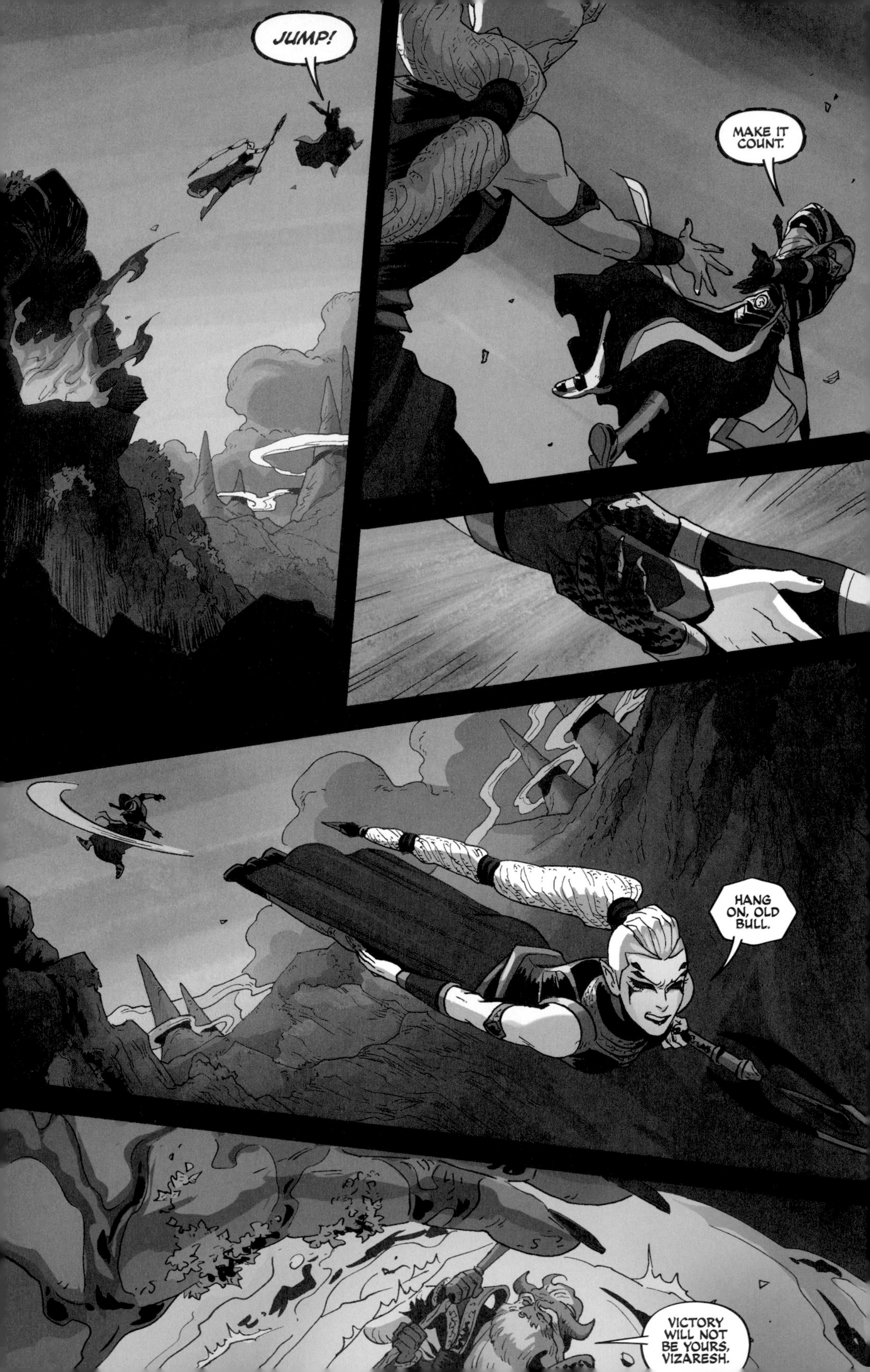
JUMP!
MAKE IT COUNT.
HANG ON, OLD BULL.
VICTORY WILL NOT BE YOURS, VIZARESH.

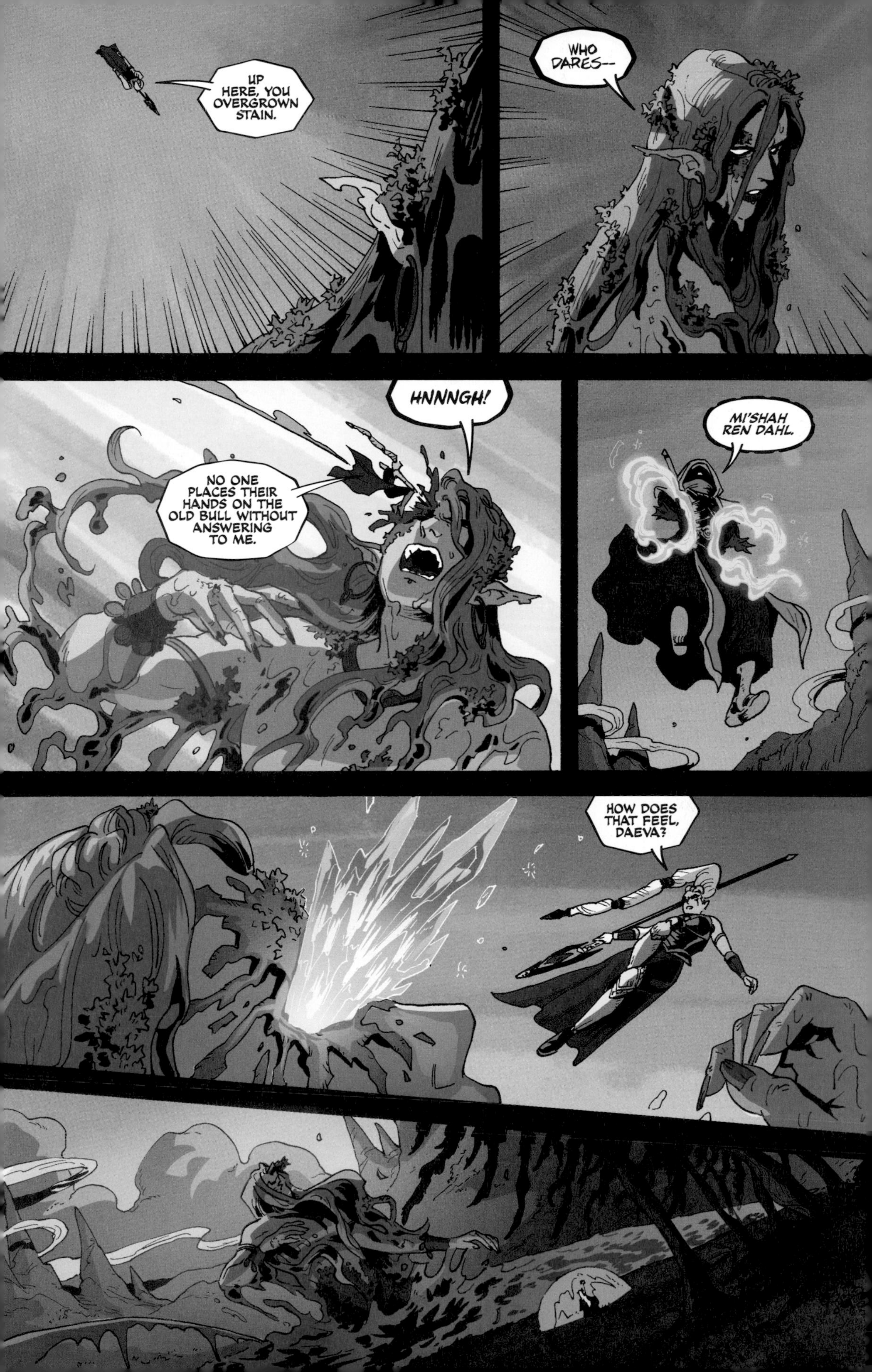
UP HERE, YOU OVERGROWN STAIN.
WHO DARES--
HNNNGH!
NO ONE PLACES THEIR HANDS ON THE OLD BULL WITHOUT ANSWERING TO ME.
MI'SHAH REN DAHL.
HOW DOES THAT FEEL, DAEVA?

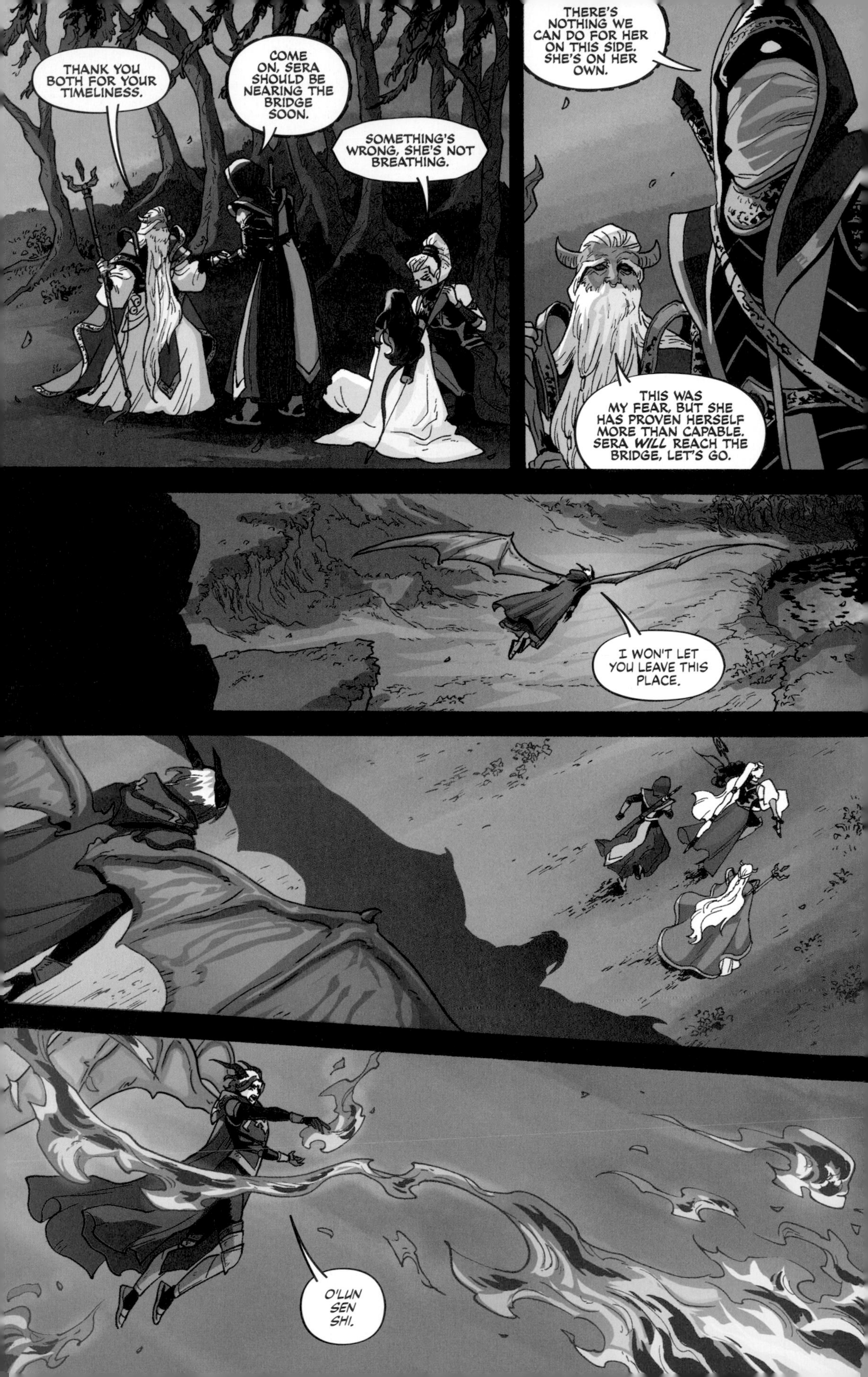
THANK YOU BOTH FOR YOUR TIMELINESS.
COME ON, SERA SHOULD BE NEARING THE BRIDGE SOON.
SOMETHING'S WRONG, SHE'S NOT BREATHING.
THERE'S NOTHING WE CAN DO FOR HER ON THIS SIDE. SHE'S ON HER OWN.
THIS WAS MY FEAR, BUT SHE HAS PROVEN HERSELF MORE THAN CAPABLE. SERA *WILL* REACH THE BRIDGE, LET'S GO.
I WON'T LET YOU LEAVE THIS PLACE.
O'LUN SEN SHI.

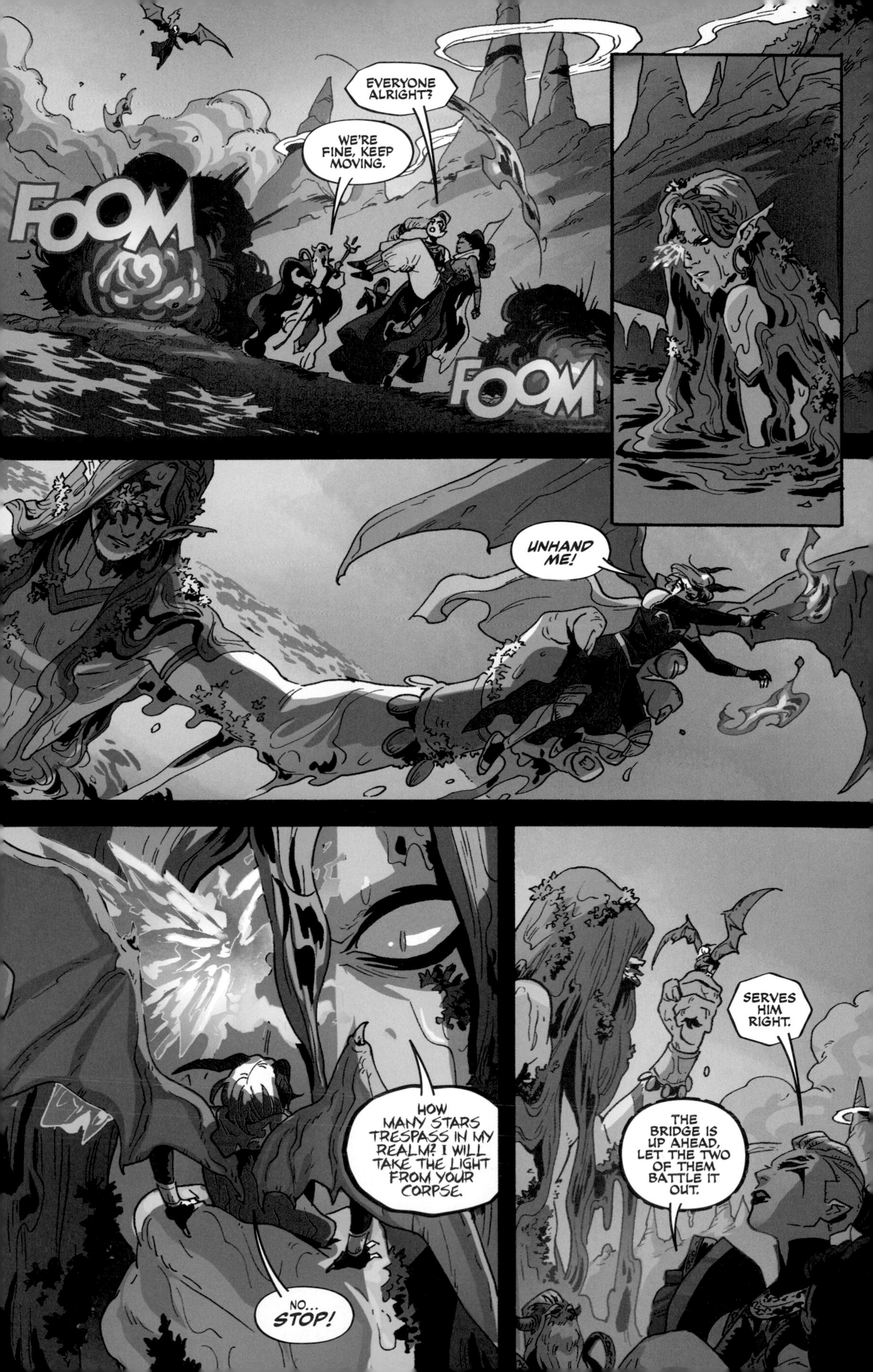
EVERYONE ALRIGHT?
WE'RE FINE, KEEP MOVING.
FOOM
FOOM
UNHAND ME!
HOW MANY STARS TRESPASS IN MY REALM? I WILL TAKE THE LIGHT FROM YOUR CORPSE.
NO... STOP!
SERVES HIM RIGHT.
THE BRIDGE IS UP AHEAD, LET THE TWO OF THEM BATTLE IT OUT.

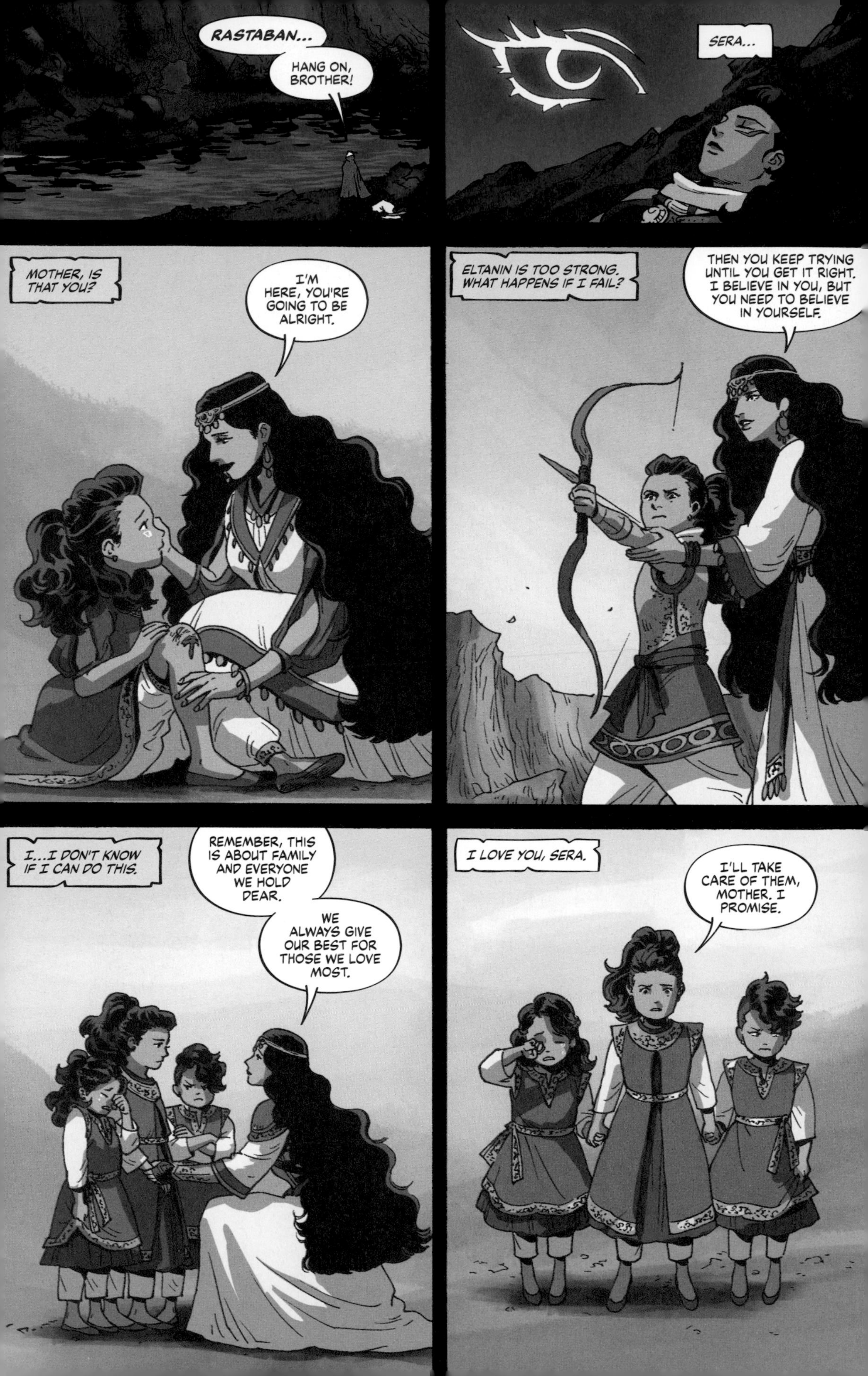
RASTABAN...
HANG ON, BROTHER!
SERA...
MOTHER, IS THAT YOU?
I'M HERE, YOU'RE GOING TO BE ALRIGHT.
ELTANIN IS TOO STRONG. WHAT HAPPENS IF I FAIL?
THEN YOU KEEP TRYING UNTIL YOU GET IT RIGHT. I BELIEVE IN YOU, BUT YOU NEED TO BELIEVE IN YOURSELF.
I...I DON'T KNOW IF I CAN DO THIS.
REMEMBER, THIS IS ABOUT FAMILY AND EVERYONE WE HOLD DEAR.
WE ALWAYS GIVE OUR BEST FOR THOSE WE LOVE MOST.
I LOVE YOU, SERA.
I'LL TAKE CARE OF THEM, MOTHER. I PROMISE.

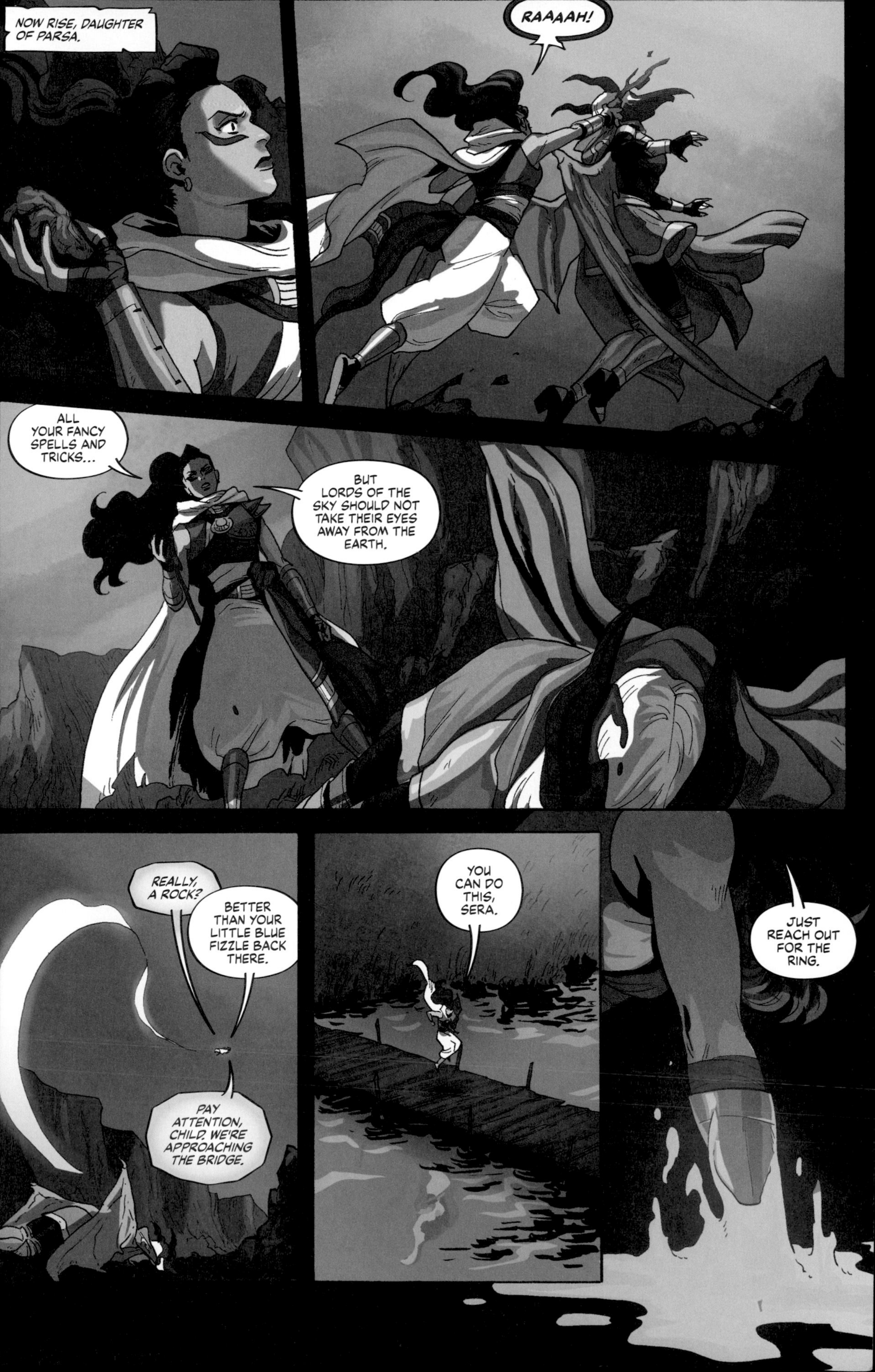
NOW RISE, DAUGHTER OF PARSA.
RAAAAH!
ALL YOUR FANCY SPELLS AND TRICKS...
BUT LORDS OF THE SKY SHOULD NOT TAKE THEIR EYES AWAY FROM THE EARTH.
REALLY, A ROCK?
BETTER THAN YOUR LITTLE BLUE FIZZLE BACK THERE.
PAY ATTENTION, CHILD. WE'RE APPROACHING THE BRIDGE.
YOU CAN DO THIS, SERA.
JUST REACH OUT FOR THE RING.

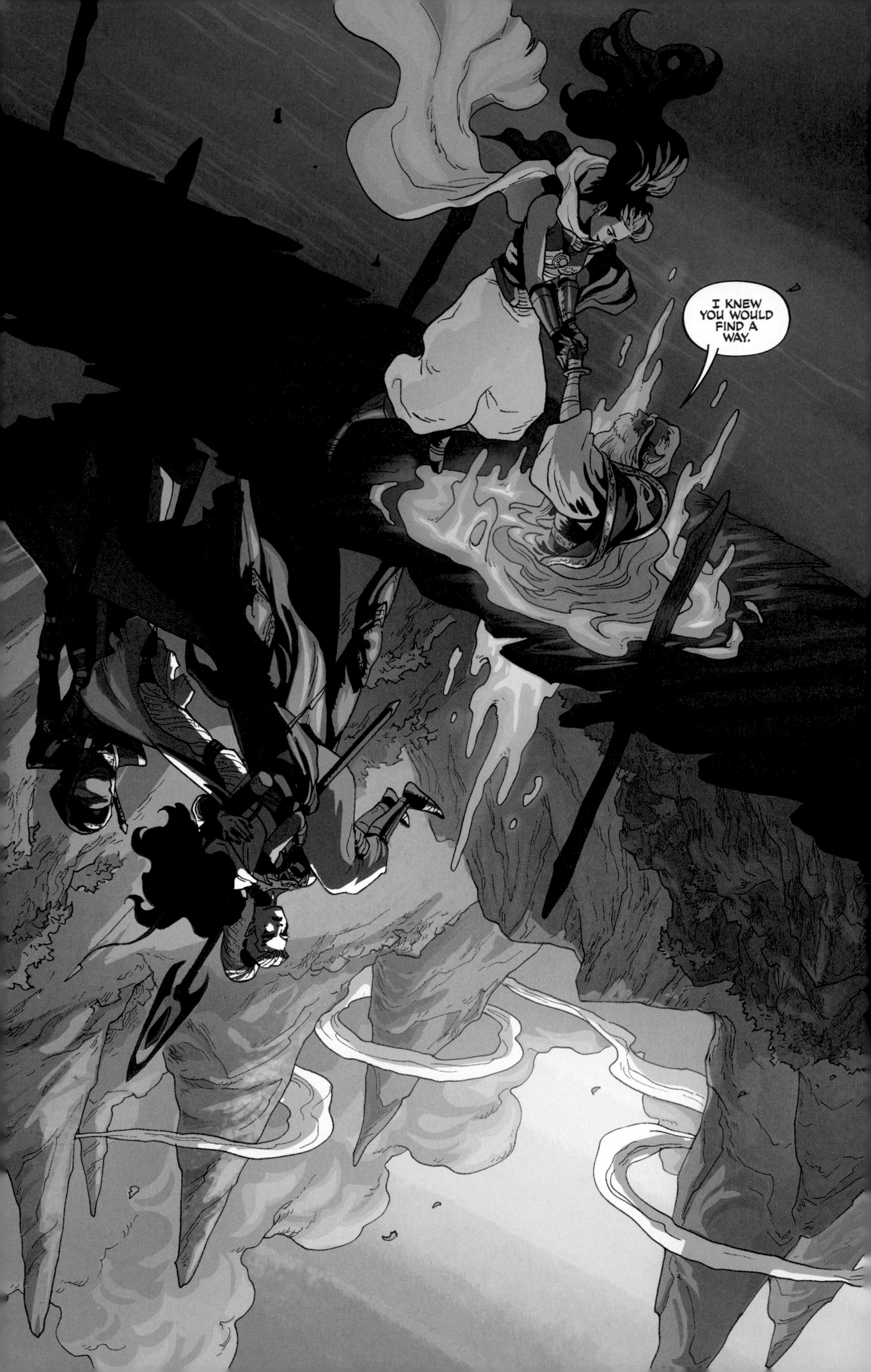
I KNEW YOU WOULD FIND A WAY.

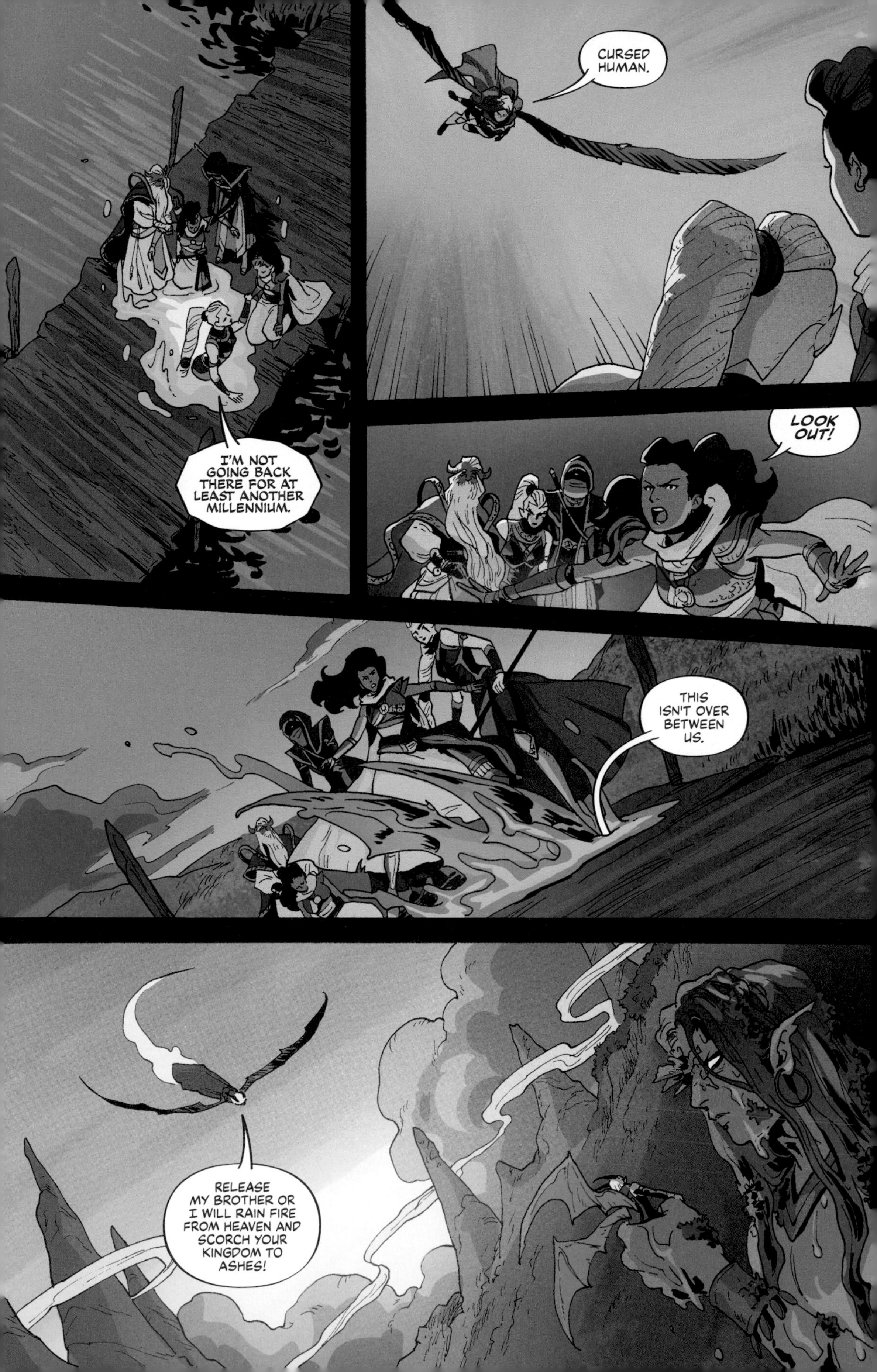
I'M NOT GOING BACK THERE FOR AT LEAST ANOTHER MILLENNIUM.
CURSED HUMAN.
LOOK OUT!
THIS ISN'T OVER BETWEEN US.
RELEASE MY BROTHER OR I WILL RAIN FIRE FROM HEAVEN AND SCORCH YOUR KINGDOM TO ASHES!

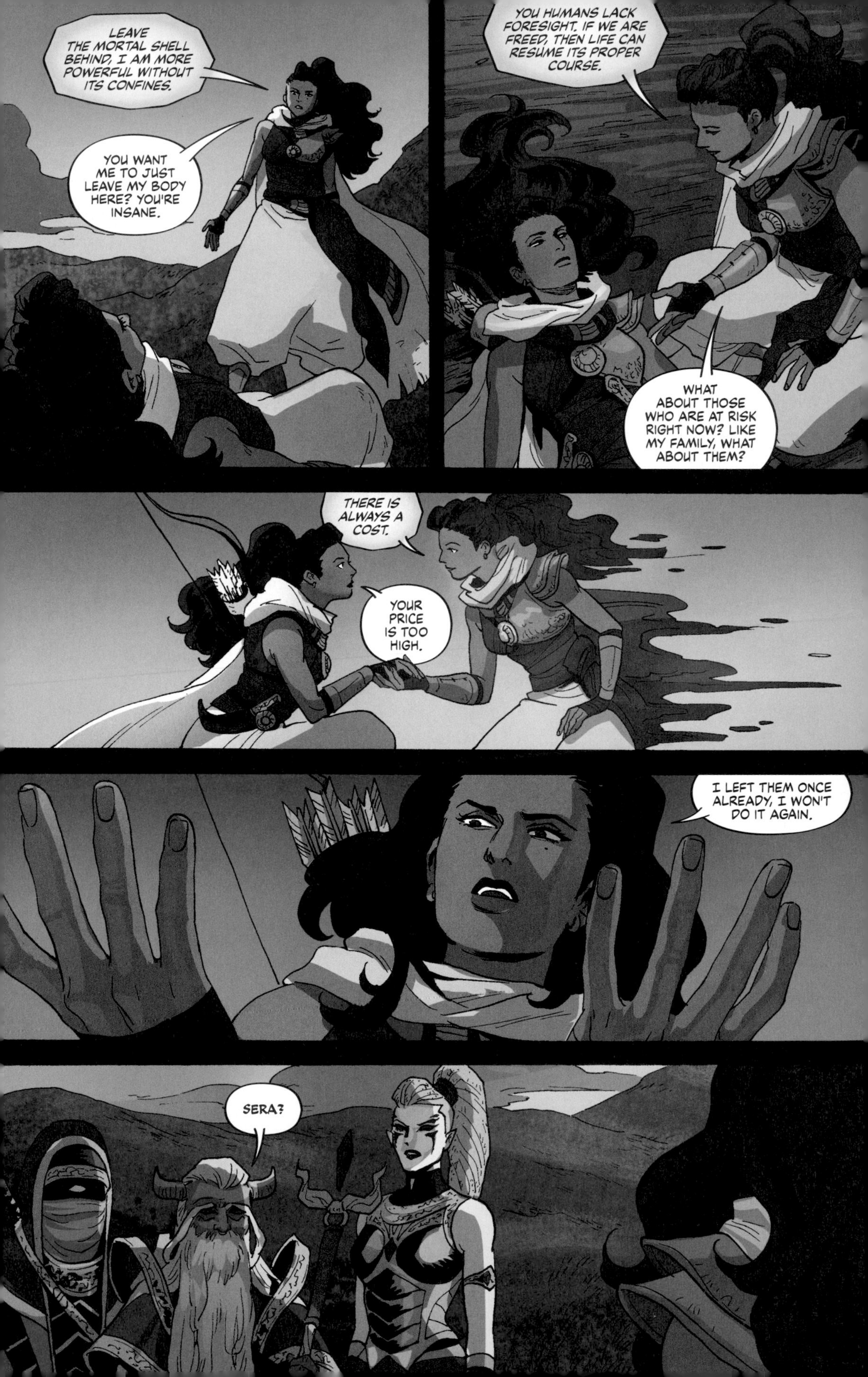

LEAVE THE MORTAL SHELL BEHIND, I AM MORE POWERFUL WITHOUT ITS CONFINES.
YOU WANT ME TO JUST LEAVE MY BODY HERE? YOU'RE INSANE.
YOU HUMANS LACK FORESIGHT. IF WE ARE FREED, THEN LIFE CAN RESUME ITS PROPER COURSE.
WHAT ABOUT THOSE WHO ARE AT RISK RIGHT NOW? LIKE MY FAMILY, WHAT ABOUT THEM?
THERE IS ALWAYS A COST.
YOUR PRICE IS TOO HIGH.
I LEFT THEM ONCE ALREADY, I WON'T DO IT AGAIN.
SERA?

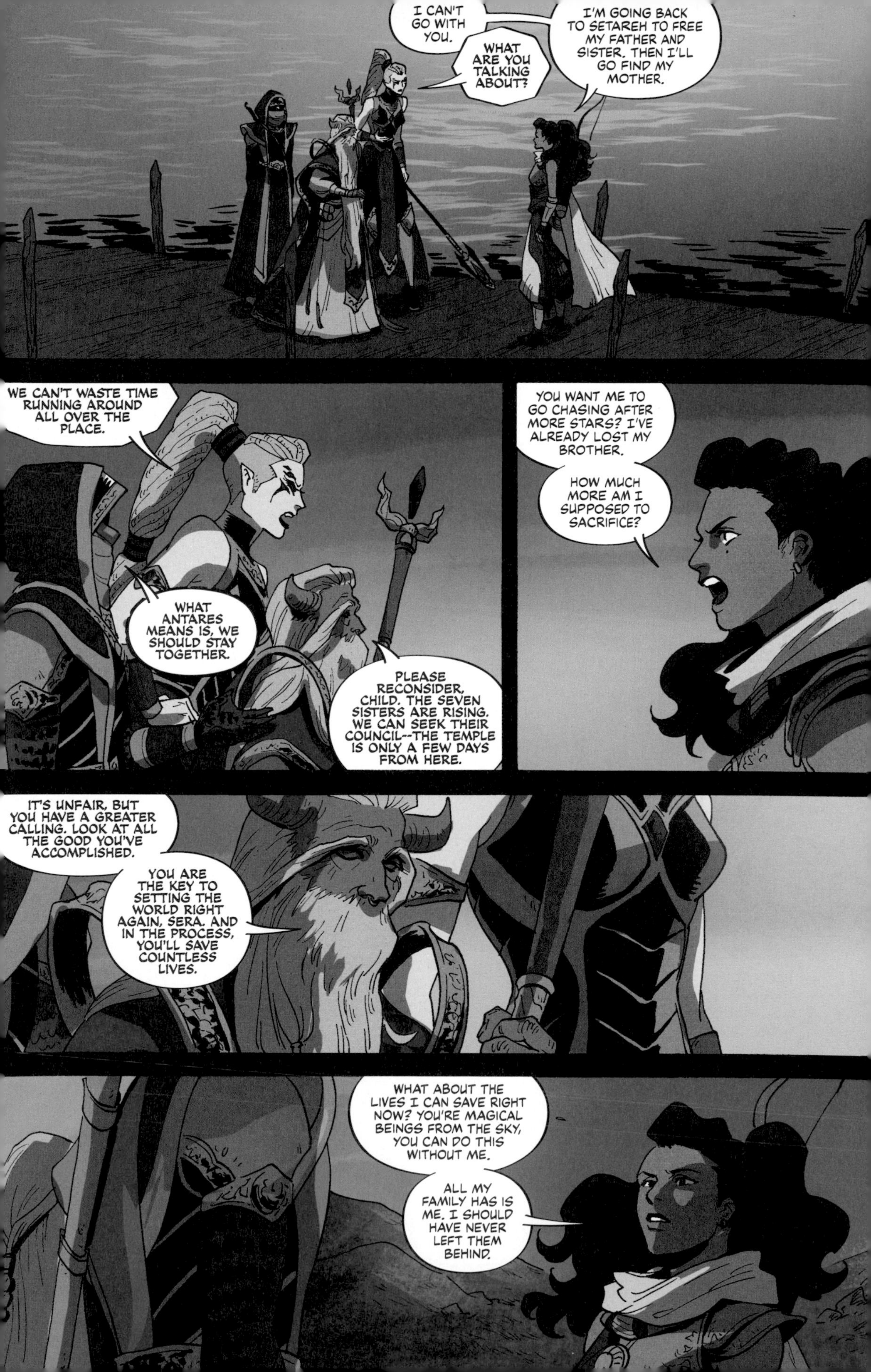
I CAN'T GO WITH YOU.
WHAT ARE YOU TALKING ABOUT?
I'M GOING BACK TO SETAREH TO FREE MY FATHER AND SISTER. THEN I'LL GO FIND MY MOTHER.
WE CAN'T WASTE TIME RUNNING AROUND ALL OVER THE PLACE.
WHAT ANTARES MEANS IS, WE SHOULD STAY TOGETHER.
PLEASE RECONSIDER, CHILD. THE SEVEN SISTERS ARE RISING. WE CAN SEEK THEIR COUNCIL--THE TEMPLE IS ONLY A FEW DAYS FROM HERE.
YOU WANT ME TO GO CHASING AFTER MORE STARS? I'VE ALREADY LOST MY BROTHER.
HOW MUCH MORE AM I SUPPOSED TO SACRIFICE?
IT'S UNFAIR, BUT YOU HAVE A GREATER CALLING. LOOK AT ALL THE GOOD YOU'VE ACCOMPLISHED.
YOU ARE THE KEY TO SETTING THE WORLD RIGHT AGAIN, SERA. AND IN THE PROCESS, YOU'LL SAVE COUNTLESS LIVES.
WHAT ABOUT THE LIVES I CAN SAVE RIGHT NOW? YOU'RE MAGICAL BEINGS FROM THE SKY, YOU CAN DO THIS WITHOUT ME.
ALL MY FAMILY HAS IS ME. I SHOULD HAVE NEVER LEFT THEM BEHIND.

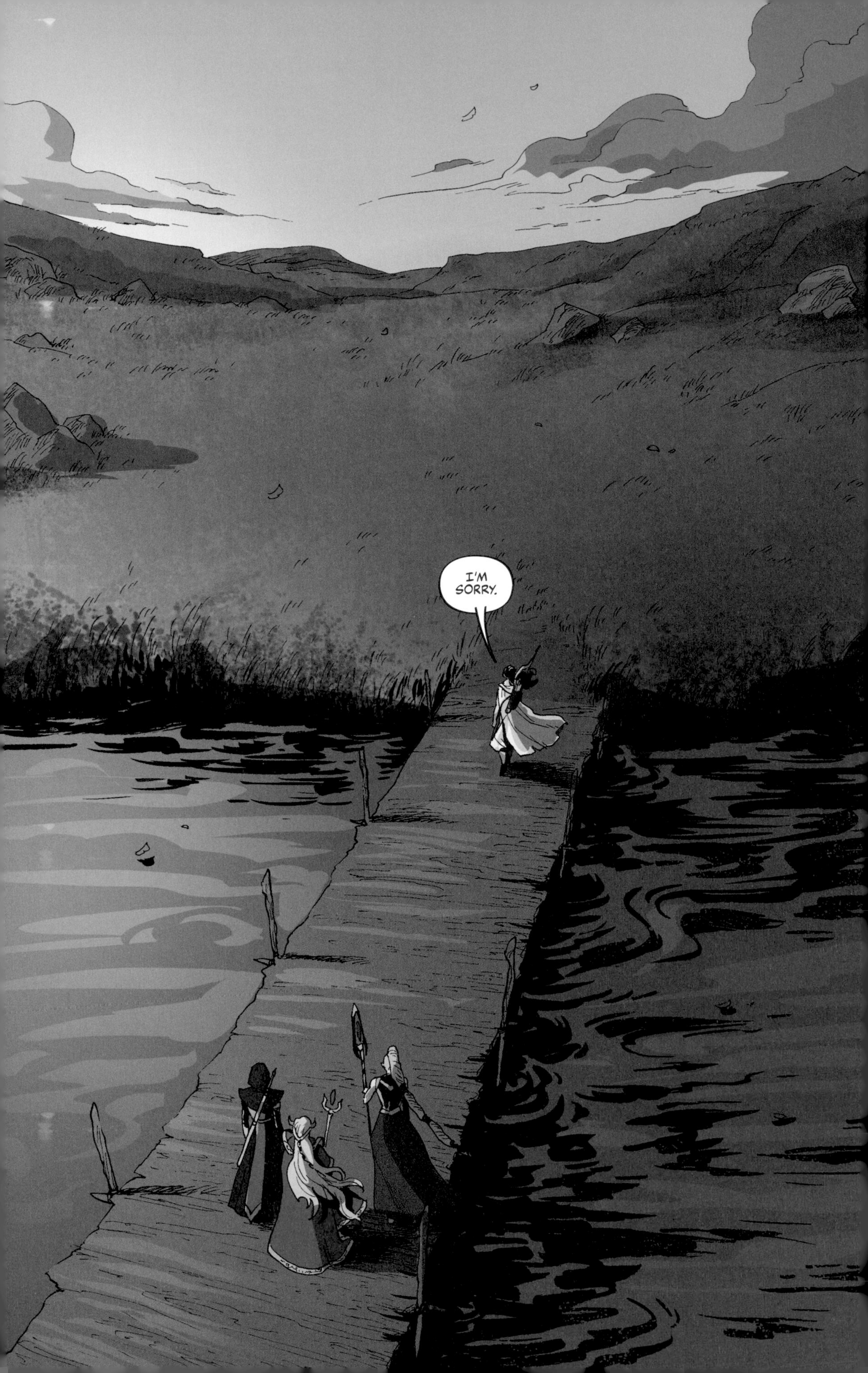
I'M SORRY.

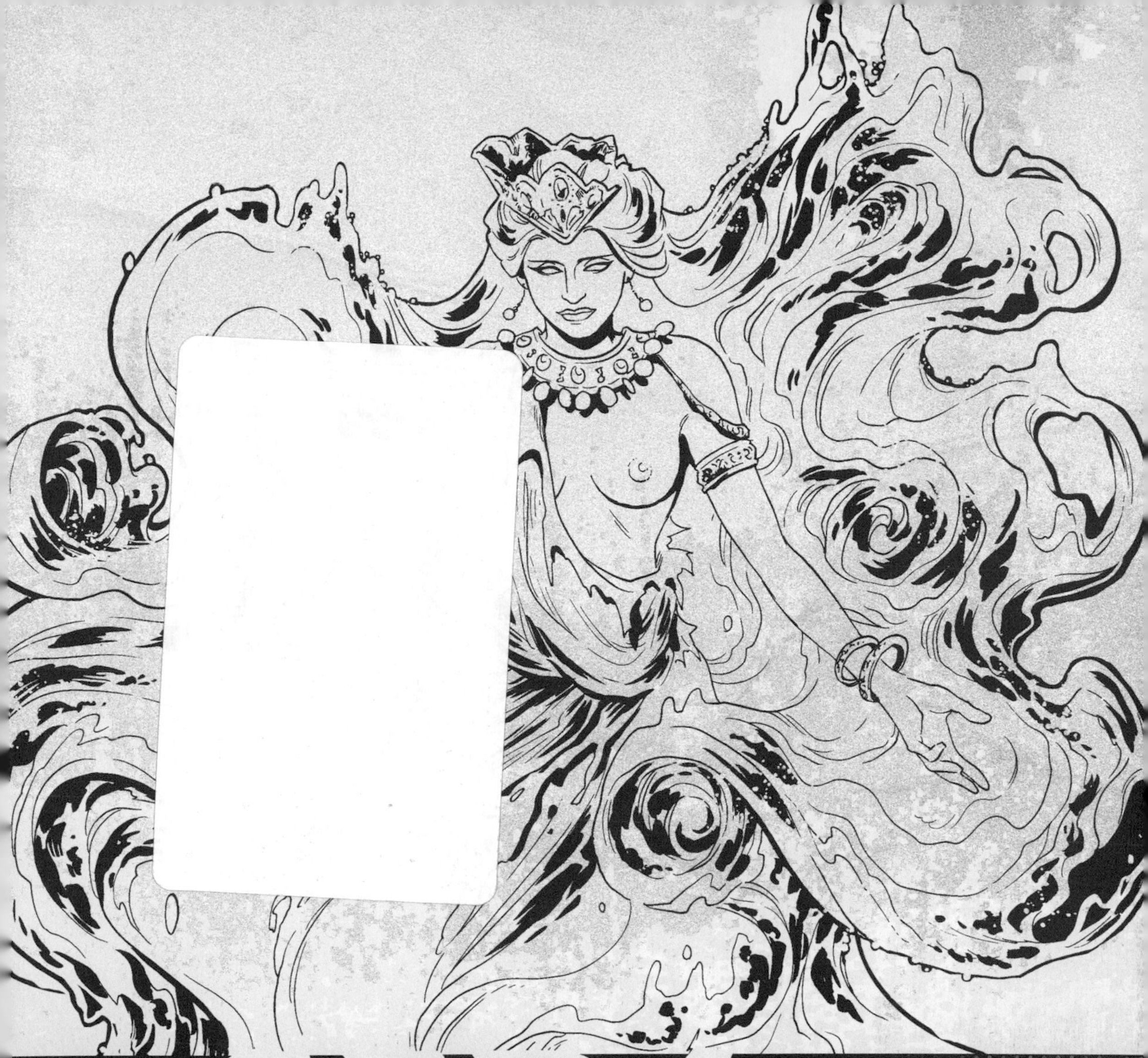

SERA & THE ART OF AUDREY MOK

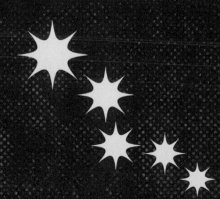

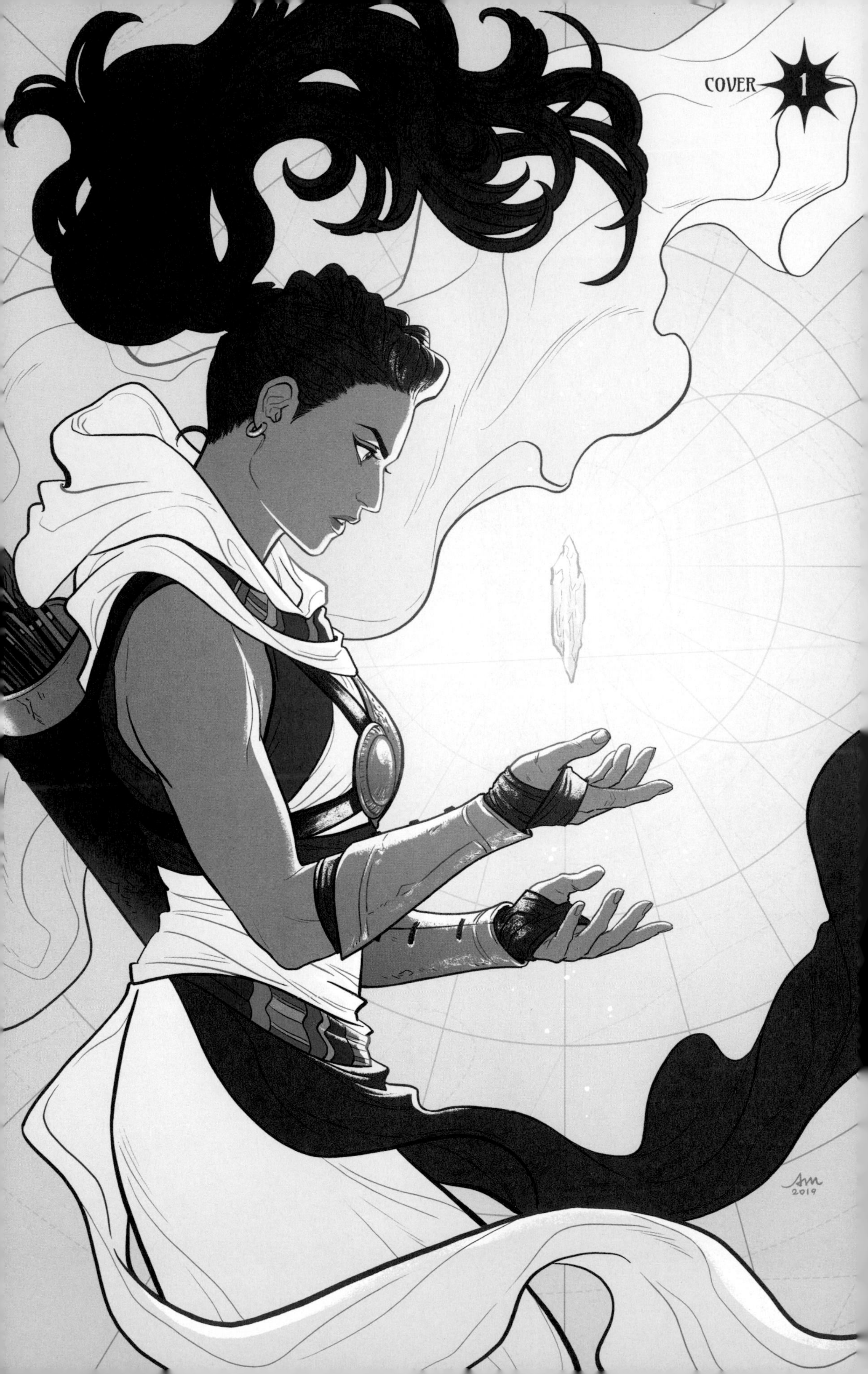
COVER 1
AM
2019

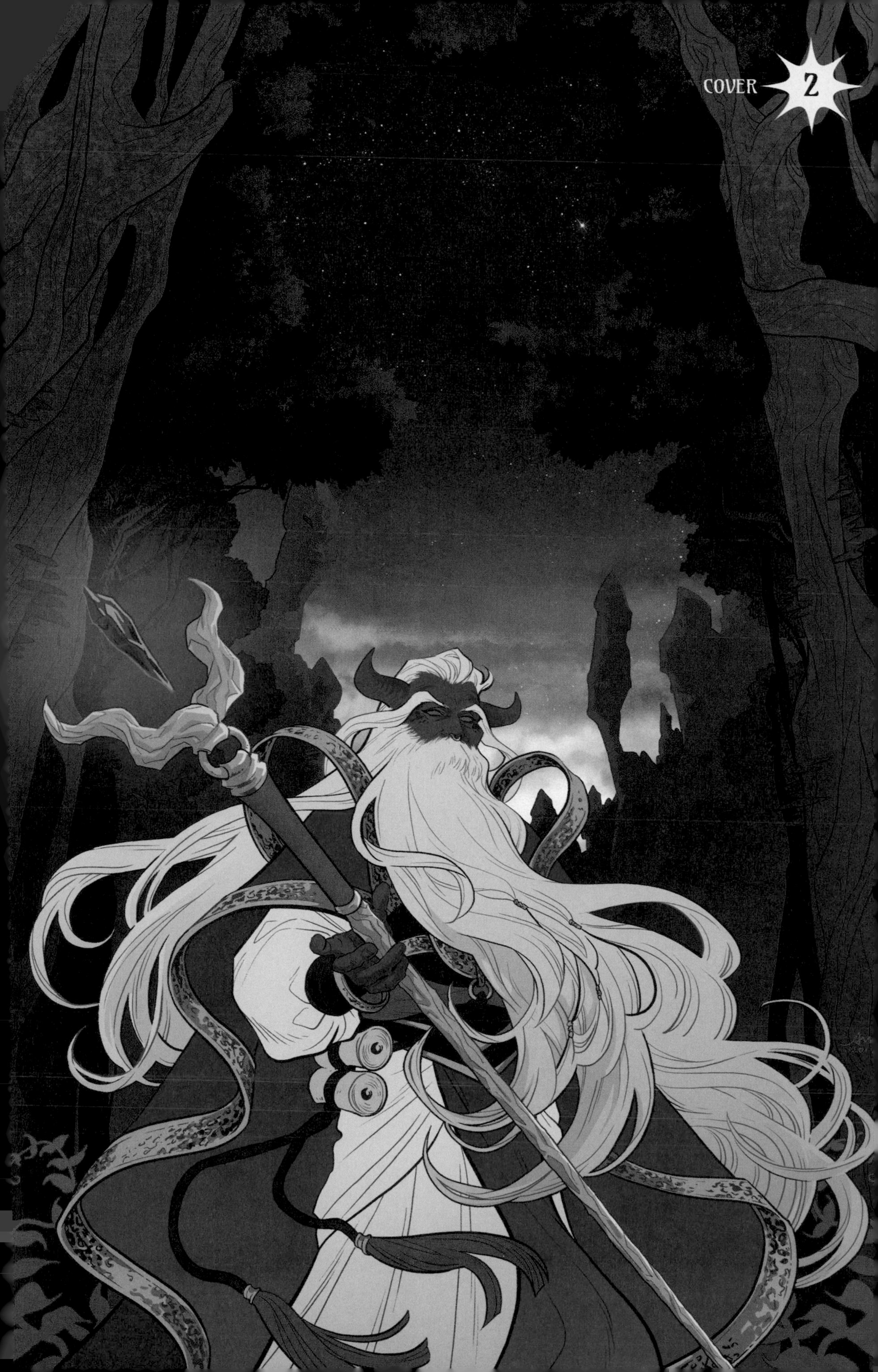
COVER
2

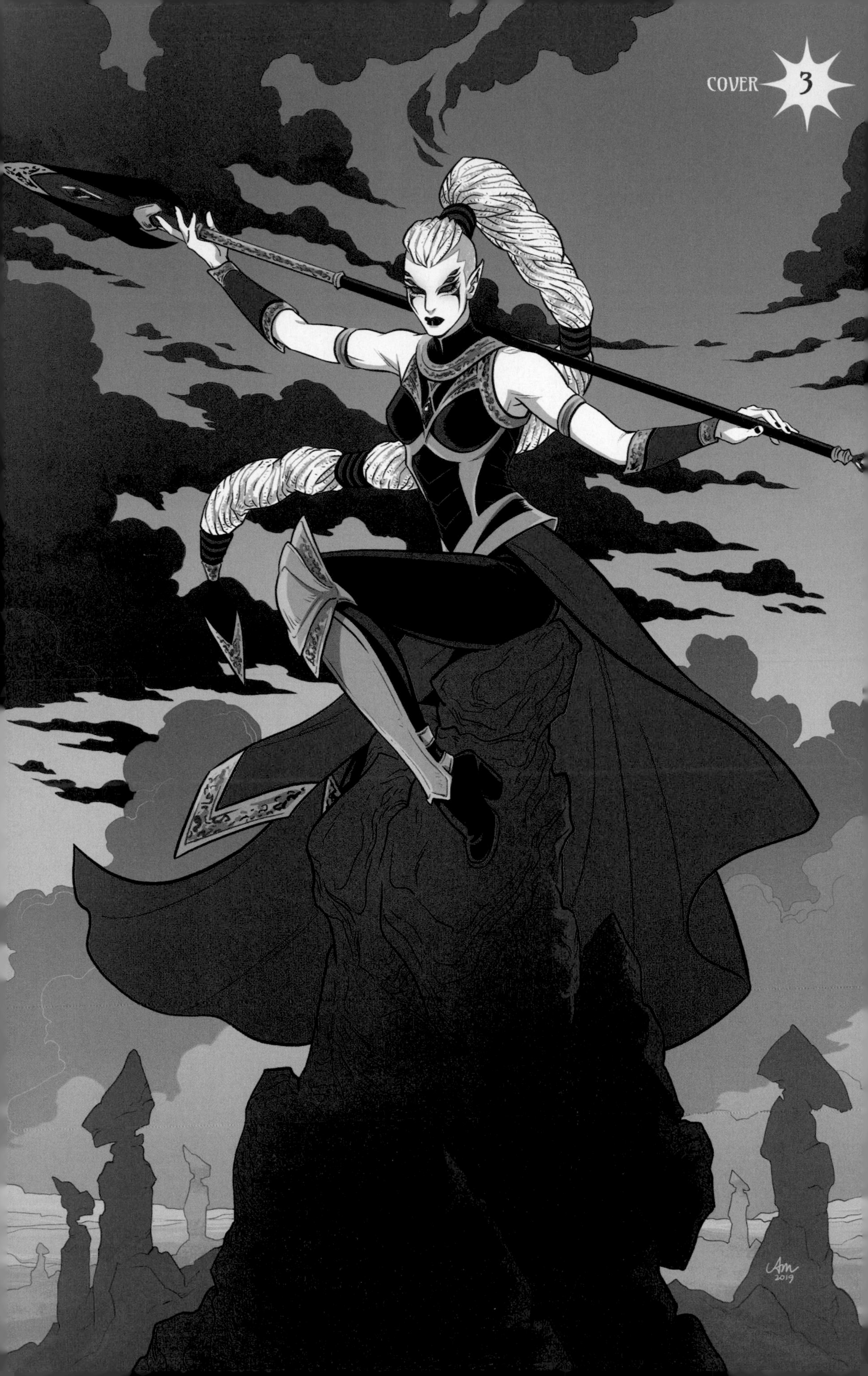
COVER 3

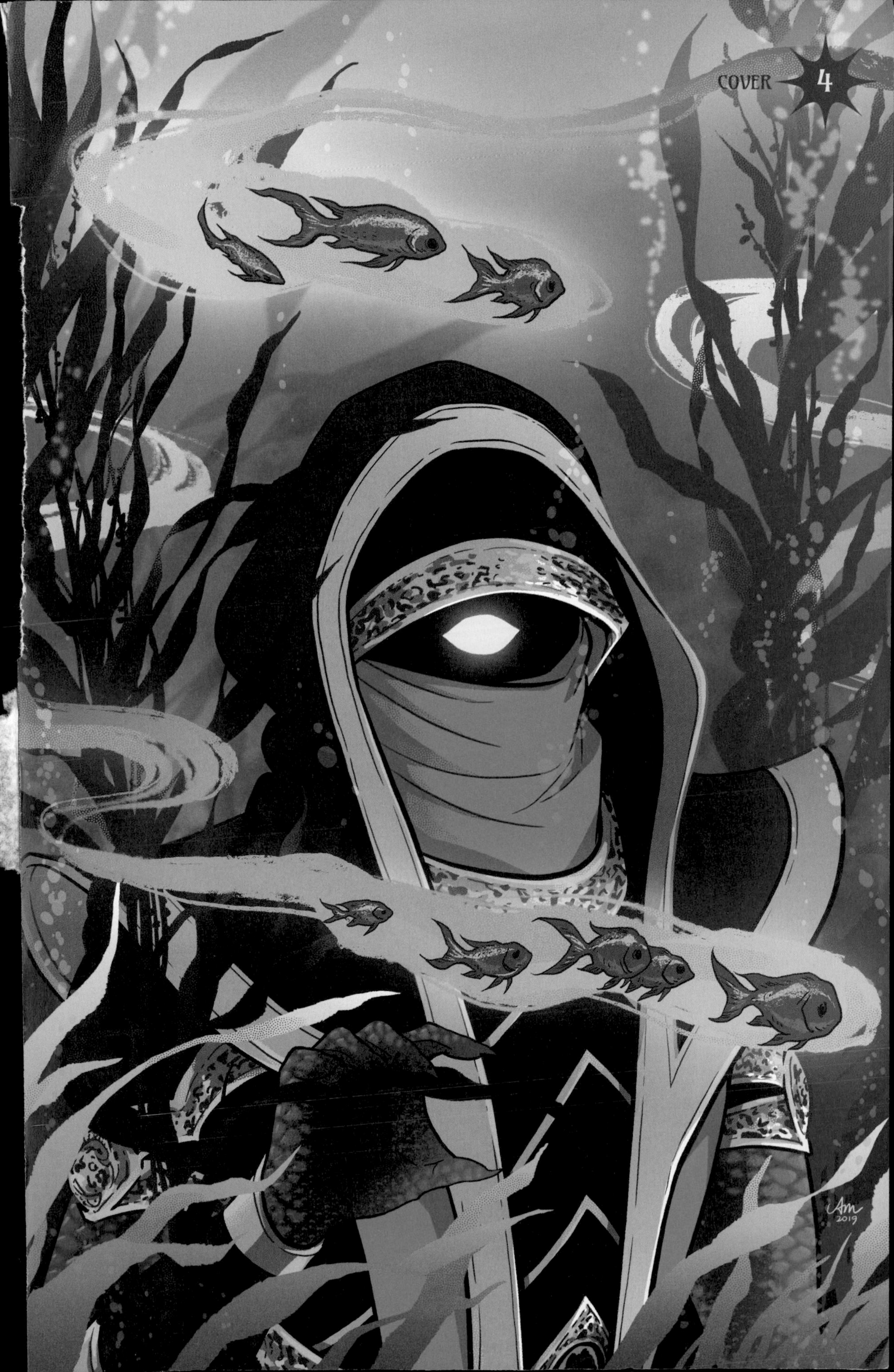
COVER
4
Am
2019

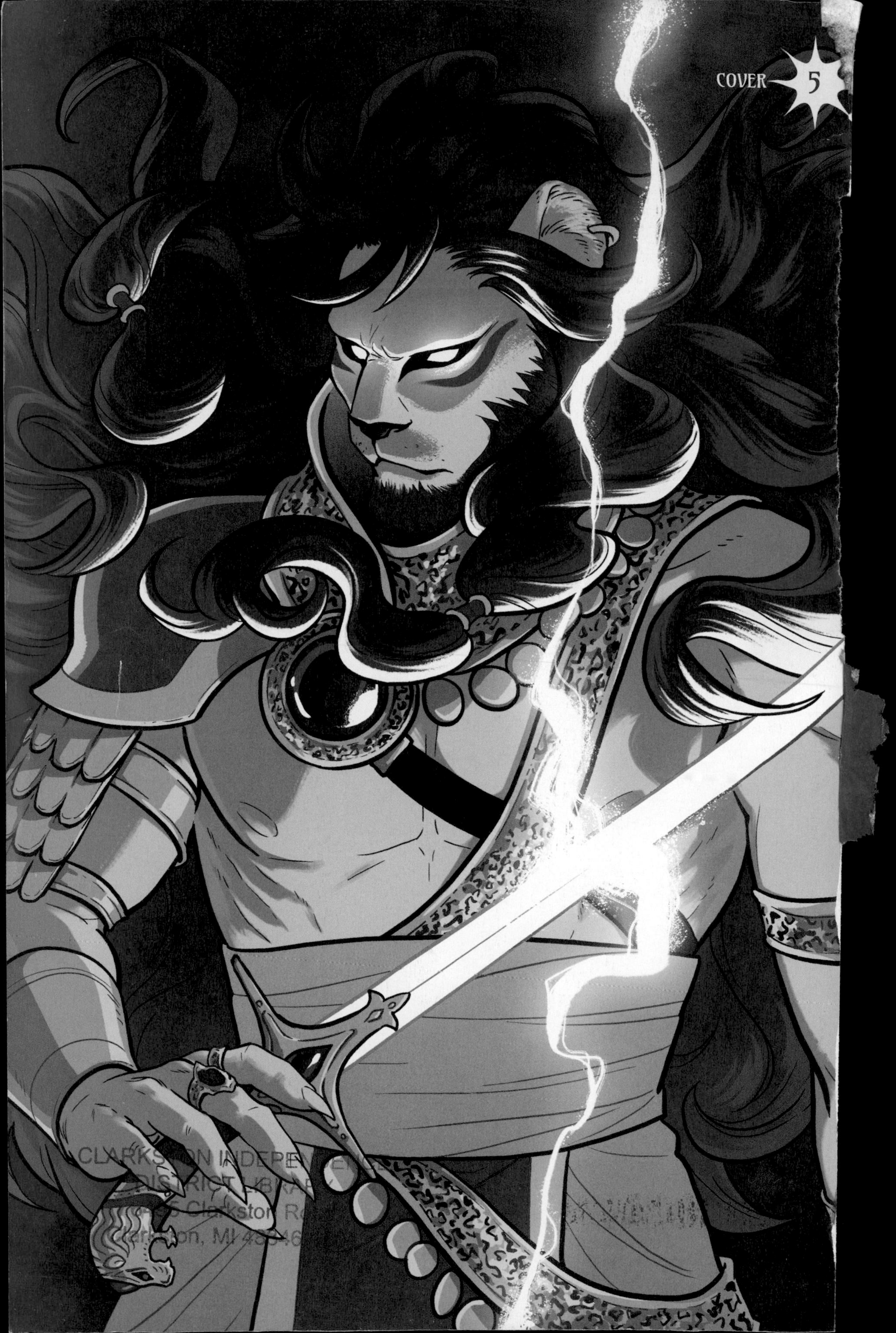
COVER
5